MERCHANTS OF MENACE

A Mystery Writers of America Classic Anthology

JOAN AIKEN   SUZANNE BLANC   ROBERT BLOCH

MICHAEL BUTTERWORTH

ROD AMATEAU AND DAVID DAVIS

MIRIAM ALLEN DEFORD   STANLEY ELLIN

ROBERT L. FISH   CELIA FREMLIN

ELSIN ANN GARDNER   RON GOULART

PATRICIA HIGHSMITH   ROSS MACDONALD

AL NUSSBAUM   ELLERY QUEEN   FRED S. TOBEY

LAWRENCE TREAT   DON VON ELSNER

DONALD E. WESTLAKE   CORNELL WOOLRICH

Edited by
HILLARY WAUGH

Mystery Writers of America
Presents

MERCHANTS OF MENACE

Copyright © 1969, 2018 by Mystery Writers of America.

A Mystery Writers of America Presents: MWA Classics Book published by arrangement with the authors

Cover art image by Alexander Kirch
Cover design by David Allan Kerber
Editorial and layout by Stonehenge Editorial

PRINTING HISTORY

Mystery Writers of America Presents: MWA Classics edition / October 2018

Mystery Writers of America gratefully acknowledges the permission granted to reproduce the copyrighted material in this book.

Every effort has been made to locate the copyright holders or their heirs and assigns and to obtain their permission for the use of copyrighted material, and MWA would be grateful if notified of any corrections that should be incorporated in future reprints or editions of this book.

For information contact: Mystery Writers of America, 1140 Broadway, Suite 1507, New York, NY 10001

Contents

A Message from Mystery Writers of America

The stories in this collection are products of their specific time and place, namely, the USA in 1969. Some of the writing contains dated attitudes and offensive ideas. That certain thoughtless slurs were commonplace—and among writers, whose prime task is to inhabit the skin of all their characters—can be both troubling and cause for thought.

We decided to publish these stories as they originally appeared, rather than sanitize the objectionable bits with a modern editorial pencil. These stories should be seen as historical mysteries, reflective of their age. If their lingering prejudices make us uncomfortable, well, perhaps history's mirror is accurate, and the attitudes are not so distant as we might have hoped.

Foreword

Ideally, it would be Hillary Waugh who'd be writing this foreword. It was, after all, he who edited this anthology and provided the original introduction—which you'll be able to read for yourself once I get out of the way. But Hillary, who was born in 1920, is no longer around to write it. He had a good long run before giving up the ghost in 2008.

When I think of Hillary I always picture him in a tuxedo, because I was most apt to run into him at MWA's annual Edgar Dinner and its after-party at Mary Higgins Clark's apartment. For all I know he spent the rest of his time in ripped jeans and a fisherman's sweater, but I somehow doubt it. I don't know that Hillary was born to wear a tux, but no one so attired ever looked more at ease. He was good company, with social grace that matched his clothes. I can't say I knew him well, but I liked him.

He wrote a good many books over a good many years, and has a definite claim on the title Father of the Police Procedural; his early novel, Last Seen Wearing, published in 1952, is at once a ground-breaker and a classic. MWA honored him as a Grand Master in 1989, and could as well have given him an award for faithful service, as he was always an ardent and devoted member.

And look at the stories he contrived to round up!

Larry Treat, for heaven's sake. Cornell Woolrich, Bob Bloch, Ross

Macdonald. Stan Ellin, Patricia Highsmith, Ellery Queen. Al Nussbaum. Bob Fish.

And Don Westlake. I read his story, "Domestic Intrigue," as soon as the PDF arrived, and was astonished that it was one I'd never read before. Alas, this tells me more than I care to know about my aging memory, as the Acknowledgments page makes it clear that the story appeared in The Saint (where I surely didn't read it) and Don's collection, The Curious Facts Preceding My Execution (where I unarguably did). Ah well. I read it again, and enjoyed every word of it, even the partial word with which it concludes.

The authors I listed above are all with Hillary at that big Edgar dinner in the sky. And so are most of the others. David Davis and Michael Butterworth would seem still to be with us, and Ron Goulart, God love him, is still writing, with four books published this century, the most recent in 2016.

But the rest are gone. And in all too many cases, we've lost not only them but their work, especially their short fiction. Books tend to endure, and the internet now makes it possible for almost anyone to find a copy of almost anything ever printed and bound. And not a few of these authors have a book or two still in print, and the novels of still more of them have been given a new life as ebooks.

Ah, but the short stories. Aside from a handful of scholars and collectors, nobody pays much attention to old magazines...

So I'll wrap this up with a bouquet of virtual flowers to everyone responsible for the program of reissuing these MWA anthologies. They give life to worthy short stories, and win readers for deserving writers.

Enough. Now you can read what Hillary has to say, and then you can read the stories. A good couple of hours is guaranteed.

—Lawrence Block

Introduction

It Is not for editors to sound off in print. By their authors *should* ye know them. This, therefore, will be as brief as Foreword requirements permit.

It is the annual custom of Mystery Writers of America to publish an anthology of crime short stories. It is a custom that has been going on for twenty-four years or virtually since the inception of MWA. In the beginning, the purpose of the anthology was to earn money for the infant organization's infant coffers. For that reason, the editors of the anthology donated their time, and the authors who appeared in it donated their stories.

The same is true today. It is still a gratis operation, but there is a difference. Appearance in the MWA anthology is no longer merely a benefit performance on the part of the author. It has become a mark of high prestige.

This fact makes life very easy for the editor, for authors not only donate everything willingly, they willingly donate everything. There is, in other words, no holding back of top stories for more profitable markets. The editor's task, then, is not that of trying to find enough good stories to make a book, it is that of deciding which of the galaxy of fine stories he should use to obtain the kind of balance and shape and effect he desires. This is anthologizing as it should be, and as it so rarely is.

The following collection represents the results of such an effort, and all of us who helped to produce it are pleased to let it serve as MWA's showcase of stories for 1969. Let it not be thought, however, that these are the only fine stories that came our way, or even that they represent the finest of the fine. Limitations of space do force a cut-off point and the ways of handling that space also affects the selection of stories. This, then, is not so much a collection of "Best Stories" as it is a collection of "Some of the Best Stories.'"

My thanks and appreciation go to Liz Lewis, the editor at Doubleday responsible for the real labor that goes into such an undertaking, and to Gloria Amoury, Executive Secretary and laborer-in-chief at MWA. They did the work and I had the fun.

My thanks and appreciation go also to those many people whose recommendations gave me guidance and to all the writers and their agents, who sent in submissions so willingly and generously.

It is their stories that made the job the fun it was and I hope the following sample of their work will bring to you, the reader, equal enjoyment.

—HILLARY WAUGH
APRIL 1, 1969

H as in Homicide

Lawrence Treat

Larry Treat says he wrote his first police story back in 1945. That was a long time before Dragnet, *and may make Larry the father of the procedural school of mystery writing. This story, for which he won an Edgar, is an example of that school at its best.*

SHE CAME through the door of the Homicide Squad's outer office as if it were disgrace to be there, as if she didn't like it, as if she hadn't done anything wrong—and never could or would.

Still, here she was. About twenty-two years old and under weight Wearing a pink, sleeveless dress. She had dark hair pulled back in a bun; her breasts were close together; and her eyes ate you up.

Mitch Taylor had just come back from lunch and was holding down the fort all alone. He nodded at her and said, "Anything I can do?"

"Yes. I—I—"

Mitch put her down as a nervous stutterer and waited for her to settle down.

"They told me to come here," she said. "I went to the neighborhood police station, and they said they couldn't do anything, that I had to come here."

"Yeah," Mitch said. It was the old run-around, and he was willing to bet this was Pulasky's doing, up in the Third Precinct. He never took a complaint unless the rule book said, *"You, Pulasky—you got to handle this, or you'll lose your pension."*

So Mitch said, "Sure. What's the trouble?"

"I don't like to bother you, and I hope you don't think me silly, but —well, my friend left me. And I don't know where, or why."

"Boyfriend?" Mitch said.

She blushed a deep crimson. "Oh, no! A real *friend.* We were traveling together and she took the car and went, without even leaving me a note. I can't understand it."

"Let's go inside and get the details," Mitch said.

He brought her into the Squad Room and sat her down at a desk. She looked up shyly, sort of impressed with him. He didn't know why, because he was only an average-looking guy, of medium height, on the cocky side, with stiff, wiry hair and a face nobody particularly remembered.

He sat down opposite her and took out a pad and pencil. "Your name?" he said.

"Prudence Gilford"

"Address?"

"New York City, but I gave up my apartment there."

"Where I come from, too. Quite a ways from home, aren't you?"

"I'm on my way to California—my sister lives out there. I answered an ad in the paper—just a moment, I think I still have it."

She fumbled in a big, canvas bag, and the strap broke off and the whole business dropped. She picked it up awkwardly, blushing again, but she kept on talking. "Bella Tansey advertised for somebody to share the driving to California. She said she'd pay all expenses. It was a wonderful chance for me... Here, I have it."

She took out the clipping and handed it to Mitch. It was the usual thing: woman companion to share the driving, and a phone number.

"So you got in touch?" Mitch prodded.

"Yes. We liked each other immediately, and arranged to go the following week."

She was fiddling with the strap, trying to fix it, and she finally fitted the tab over some kind of button. Mitch, watching, wondered how long *that* was going to last.

Meanwhile she was still telling him about Bella Tansey. 'We got along so well," Prudence said, "and last night we stopped at a motel— The Happy Inn, it's called—and we went to bed. When I woke up, she was gone."

"Why did you stop there?" Mitch asked sharply.

"We were tired and it had a *Vacancy* sign." She drew in her breath and asked anxiously, "Is there something wrong with it?"

"Not too good a reputation," Mitch said. "Did she take all her things with her? Her overnight stuff, I mean,"

"Yes, I think so. Or at least, she took her bag."

Mitch got a description of the car: a dark blue Buick; 1968 or 1969, she wasn't sure; New York plates, but she didn't know the number.

"Okay," Mitch said. "We'll check. We'll send out a flier and have her picked up and find out why she left in such a hurry."

Prudence Gilford's eyes got big. "Yes," she said. "And please, can you help me? I have only five dollars, and the motel is expensive. I can't stay there, and I don't know where to go."

"Leave it to me," Mitch said. "I'll fix it up at the motel and get you a place in town for a while. You can get some money, can't you?"

"Oh, yes. I'll write my sister for it."

"Better wire," Mitch said. "And will you wait here a couple of minutes? I'll be right back."

"Of course."

Lieutenant Decker had come in and was working on some thing in his tiny office which was jammed up with papers and stuff. Mitch reported on the Gilford business and the Lieutenant listened.

"Pulasky should have handled it," Mitch said, finishing up. "But what the hell—the kid's left high and dry, so maybe we could give her a little help."

"What do you think's behind this?" Decker asked.

"I don't know," Mitch said. "She's a clinger—scared of every thing and leans on people. Maybe the Tansey woman got sick and tired of her, or maybe this is lesbian stuff. Hard to tell."

"Well, go ahead with an S-4 for the Buick. It ought to be on a main highway and within a five-hundred-mile radius. Somebody'll spot it. We'll see what cooks."

MITCH DROVE Prudence out to the motel and told her to get her things. While she was busy, he went into the office and spoke to Ed Hiller, who ran the joint. Hiller, a tall, stoop shouldered guy who'd been in and out of jams most of his life, was interested in anything from a nickel up, but chiefly up. He rented cabins by the hour, day, or week, and you could get liquor if you paid the freight; but most of his trouble came from reports of cars that had been left unlocked and rifled. The police had never been able to pin anything on him.

He said, "Hello, Taylor. Anything wrong?"

"Just want to know about a couple of dames that stayed here last night—Bella Tansey and Prudence Gilford. Tansey pulled out during the night."

"Around midnight," Ed said. "She came into the office to make a phone call, and a little later I heard her car pull out."

Time for the missing girl to pack, Mitch decided. So far, everything checked out. "Who'd she call?" he asked. "What did she say?"

Hiller shrugged. "I don't listen in," he said. "I saw her open the door and then I heard her go into the phone booth. I mind my own business. You know that."

"Yeah," Mitch said flatly. "You heard the coins drop, didn't you? Local call, or long distance?"

Hiller leaned over the counter. "Local," he said softly. "I think."

"Got their registration?" Mitch asked. Hiller nodded and handed Mitch the sheet, which had a record of the New York license plates.

That was about all there was to it. Nobody picked up Bella Tansey and her Buick, Prudence Gilford was socked away in a rooming house in town, and Mitch never expected to see her again.

WHEN HE GOT HOME that night, Amy kissed him and asked him about things, and then after he'd horsed around with the kids a little, she showed him a letter from her sister. Her sister's husband was on strike, and what the union paid them took care of food and rent and that was about all; but they had to keep up their payments on the car and the new dishwasher, and the TV had broken down again, and could Mitch and Amy help out for a little while—they'd get it back soon.

So after the kids were in bed, Mitch and Amy sat down on the sofa to figure things out, which took about two seconds and came to fifty bucks out of his next paycheck. It was always like that with the two of them: they saw things the same way and never had any arguments. Not many guys were as lucky as Mitch.

THE NEXT MORNING, Decker had his usual conference with the Homicide Squad and went over all the cases they had in the shop. The only thing he said about the Gilford business was, the next time Pulasky tried to sucker them, figure it out so he had to come down here personally, and then make him sweat.

Mitch drew a couple of minor assault cases to investigate, and he'd finished up with one and was on his way to the other when the call came in on his radio. Go out to French Woods, on East Road. They had a homicide and it looked like the missing Tansey woman.

He found a couple of police cars and an oil truck and the usual bunch of snoopers who had stopped out of curiosity. There was a kind of rough trail going into the woods.

A couple of hundred yards in, the Lieutenant and a few of the boys and Jub Freeman, the lab technician, were grouped around a dark blue car. It didn't take any heavy brainwork to decide it was the Tansey Buick.

When Mitch got to the car, he saw Bella Tansey slumped in the front seat with her head resting against the window. The right hand door was open and so was the glove compartment, and Decker was looking at the stuff he'd found there.

He gave Mitch the main facts. "Truck driver spotted the car, went in to look, and then got in touch with us. We've been here about fifteen minutes, and the Medical Examiner ought to show up pretty soon. She was strangled—you can see the marks on her neck—and I'll bet a green hat that it happened the night before last, not long after she left the motel."

Mitch surveyed the position of the body with a practiced eye. "She wasn't driving, either. She was pushed in there, after she was dead."

"Check," Decker said. Very carefully, so that he wouldn't spoil any possible fingerprints, he slid the junk he'd been examining onto the front seat. He turned to Jub Freeman, who was delicately holding a handbag by the two ends and scrutinizing it for prints.

"Find anything?" the Lieutenant asked.

"Nothing," Jub said. "But the initials on it are B.T.W."

"Bella Tansey What?" the Lieutenant said. He didn't laugh, and neither did anybody else. He stooped to put his hands on the door sill, leaned forward, and stared at the body. Mitch, standing behind him, peered over his head.

Bella had been around thirty and she'd been made for men. She was wearing a blue dress with a thing that Amy called a bolero top, and, except where the skirt had pulled up maybe from moving the body, her clothes were not disturbed. The door of the glove compartment and parts of the dashboard were splotched with fingerprint powder.

Mitch pulled back and waited. After about a minute the Lieutenant stood up.

"Doesn't look as if there was a sex angle," Decker said. "And this stuff—" he kicked at the dry leaves that covered the earth, "—doesn't take footprints, If we're lucky, we'll find some body who saw the killer somewhere around here." He made a sound with his thin, elastic lips and watched Jub.

Jub had taken off his coat and dumped the contents of the pocket-book onto it. Mitch spotted nothing unusual—just the junk women usually carried; but he didn't see any money. Jub was holding the purse and rummaging inside it.

"Empty?" the Lieutenant asked sharply.

Jub nodded. "Except for one nickel. She must have had money, so whoever went through this missed out on five cents."

"Couldn't be Ed Hiller, then," Mitch said, and the gang laughed.

"Let's say the motive was robbery," Decker said. "We got something of a head start on this, but brother, it's a bad one. Why does a woman on her way to California make a phone call and then sneak off in the middle of the night? Leaving her girl friend in the lurch, too. Doesn't sound like robbery now, does it?"

"Sounds like a guy," Mitch said. "She had a late date, and the guy robbed her, instead of—"

"We'll talk to Ed Hiller about that later," the Lieutenant said. "Taylor, you better get going on this. Call New York and get a line on her. Her friends, her background. If she was married. How much money she might have had with her. Her bank might help on that."

"Right," Mitch said.

"And then get hold of the Gilford dame and pump her," Decker said.

Mitch nodded. He glanced into the back of the car and saw the small overnight bag. "That," he said, pointing. "She packed, so she didn't expect to go back to the motel. But she didn't put her bag in the trunk compartment, so she must have expected to check in somewhere else, and pretty soon."

"She'd want to sleep somewhere, wouldn't she?" Decker asked.

"That packing and unpacking doesn't make sense," Mitch said.

Decker grunted. "Homicides never do," he said grimly.

MITCH DROVE BACK to headquarters thinking about that overnight bag, and it kept bothering him. He didn't know exactly why, but it was the sort of thing you kept in the back of your mind until something happened or you found something else, and then everything clicked and you got a pattern.

But, what with organizing the questions to ask New York, he couldn't do much doping out right now. Besides, there was a lot more information to come in.

He got New York on the phone and they said they'd move on it right away; so he hung up and went to see Prudence. He was lucky to find her in.

She was shocked at the news, but had nothing much to contribute. "We didn't know each other very long," she said, "and I was asleep when she left. I was so tired. We'd been driving all day, and I'd done most of it."

"Did she mention knowing anybody around—anybody in town?"

Mitch asked. Prudence shook her head, but he put her through the wringer anyhow—it was easy for people to hear things and then forget them. You had to jog their memories a little. And besides, how could he be sure she was telling all she knew? He felt sorry for her, though—she looked kind of thin and played out, as if she hadn't been eating much. So he said, "That five bucks of yours isn't going to last too long, and if you need some dough—"

"Oh, thanks!" she said, sort of glowing and making him feel that Mitch Taylor, he was okay. "Oh, thanks! It's perfectly wonderful of you, but I have enough for a while, and I'm sure my sister will send me the money I wired her for."

By that afternoon most of the basic information was in. Locally, the Medical Examiner said that Bella Tansey had been strangled with a towel or a handkerchief; he placed the time as not long after she'd left the motel. The Lieutenant had questioned Ed Hiller without being able to get anything. Hiller insisted he hadn't left the motel, but his statement depended only on his own word.

Jub had used a vacuum cleaner on the car and examined the findings with a microscope, and he'd shot enough pictures to fill a couple of albums.

"They stopped at a United Motel the first night," he recapitulated, "and they had dinner at a Howard Johnson place. They ate sandwiches in the car, probably for lunch, and they bought gas in Pennsylvania and Indiana, and the car ate up oil. There was a gray kitten on the rear seat sometime or other. They both drove. Bella Tansey had ear trouble, and she bought her clothes at Saks Fifth Avenue. I can tell you a lot more about her, but I'm damned if I've uncovered anything that will help on the homicide. No trace in that car of anybody except the two women."

The New York police, however, came up with a bombshell. Bella Tansey had drawn $1,800.00 from her bank, in cash, and she'd been married to Clyde Warhouse, and they'd been divorced two years ago. She'd used her maiden name—Tansey.

"Warhouse!" the Lieutenant said.

Everybody knew that name. He ran a column in the local paper—he called it "Culture Corner"—and he covered art galleries, visiting orchestras, and egghead lecturers. Whenever he had nothing else to write about, he complained how archaic the civic architecture was.

"That's why she had the *W* on her bag," Mitch said. "Bella Tansey Warhouse. And Ed Hiller didn't lie about the phone call. She made it all right—to her ex-husband."

Decker nodded. "Let's say she hotfooted it out to see him. Let's say she still had a yen for him and they scrapped, that he got mad and lost his head and strangled her. But why would he take her dough? She must've had around seventeen hundred with her. Why would he rob her?"

"Why not?" Mitch said. "It was there, wasn't it?"

"Let's think about this," Decker said. "Prudence says Bella unpacked. Did Bella start to go to bed, or what?"

"Prudence doesn't know," Mitch said. "I went into that for all it was worth, and Prudence *assumes* Bella unpacked—she can't actually remember. Says she was bushed and went right to sleep. Didn't even wash her face."

"Well," Decker said, "I guess Warhouse is wondering when we'll get around to him. I'll check on him while you go up there." The Lieutenant's jaw set firmly. "Bring him in."

Mitch rolled his shoulders, tugged on the lapels of his jacket, and went out The first time you hit your suspect, it could make or break the case.

CLYDE WARHOUSE LIVED in a red brick house with tall white columns on the front. Mitch found him at home, in his study. He was a little guy with big teeth, and he didn't really smile; he just pulled his lips back, and you could take it any way you pleased.

Warhouse came right to the point. "You're here about my former wife," he said. "I just heard about it on the radio, and I wish I could give you some information, but I can't. It's certainly not the end I wished for her."

'What kind of end were you hoping for?" Mitch asked.

"None." The Warhouse lips curled back, telling you how smart he was. "And certainly not one in this town."

"Let's not kid around," Mitch said. "You're coming back with me. You know that, don't you?"

The guy almost went down with the first punch. "You mean—you mean I'm being arrested?"

"What do *you* think?" Mitch said. "We know she phoned you and you met her. We know you saw her."

"But I didn't see her," Warhouse said, "She never showed up."

Mitch didn't even blink. "How long did you wait?"

"Almost an hour. Maybe more."

"Where?"

"On the corner of Whitman and Cooper." Warhouse gasped, then put his head in his hands and said, "Oh, God!" And that was all Mitch could get out of him until they had him in the Squad Room, with Decker leading off on the interrogation.

The guy didn't back down from that first admission. He knew he'd been tricked, but he stuck to his guns and wouldn't give another inch. He said Bella had called him around midnight and said she must see him. He hadn't known she was in town, didn't want to see her, had no interest in her, but he couldn't turn her down. So he went, and be waited. And waited and waited. And then went home.

They kept hammering away at him. First, Mitch and Decker, then Bankhart and Balenky, then Mitch and Decker again.

In between, they consulted Jub. He'd been examining Warhouse's car for soil that might match samples from French Woods; for evidence of a struggle, of Bella's presence—of any thing at all. The examination drew a blank.

Warhouse just grinned his toothy grin and kept saying no. And late that evening they gave up on him, brought him across the court-yard to the city jail, and left him there for the night. He needed sleep —and so did the Homicide Squad.

AT THE CONFERENCE the next morning, Decker was grim. "We have an ex-wife calling her ex-husband at midnight and making an appointment; we have his statement that he went and she never showed up; and we have a homicide and that's all."

"The dough," Bankhart said.

Decker nodded "When we find that seventeen hundred, then we might have a case, We'll get warrants and we'll look for it, but let's assume we draw another blank. Then what?"

"Let's have another session with Ed Hiller," Mitch said.

They had it, and they had a longer one with Warhouse, and they were still nowhere. They'd gone into his background thoroughly. He earned good money, paid his bills promptly, and got along well with his second wife. He liked women, they went for him, and he was a humdinger with them, although he was not involved in any scandal. But in Mitch's book, he'd humdinged once too often. Still, you had to prove it.

For a while they concentrated on The Happy Inn. But the motel guests either couldn't be found—because they'd registered under fake names with fake license numbers—or else they said they'd been asleep and had no idea what was going on outside.

The usual tips came in—crank stuff that had to be followed up. The killer bad been seen, somebody had heard Bella scream for help, somebody else had had a vision. Warhouse had been spotted waiting on the corner, which proved nothing except he'd arrived there first. Every tip checked out either as useless or a phony.

The missing $1,700.00 didn't show up. Decker ran out of jokes, and Mitch came home tired and irritable. The case was at a full stop.

THEN DECKER HAD this wild idea, and he told it to Jub and Mitch the next day. "My wife says I woke up last night and asked for a drink of water, and I don't even remember it."

"So you were thirsty," Mitch remarked.

"Don't you get it?" Decker exclaimed. "People wake up, then go back to sleep, and in the morning they don't even know they were awake. Well, we know Bella packed her bag, and she was in that motel room with Prudence and must have made some noise and possibly even talked. I'll bet a pair of pink panties that Prudence woke up, and then forgot all about it. She has a clue buried deep in her mind."

"Granted," Jub said, "but how are you going to dig it up?"

"I'll hypnotize her," Decker said with fire in his eyes. "I'll ask a psychiatrist to get her to free-associate. Taylor, ask her to come in tomorrow morning, when my mind is fresh. And hers, too."

Mitch dropped in on Prudence and gave her the message, but the way he saw things, the Lieutenant was sure reaching for it—far out. Mitch told Amy about this screwy idea of Decker's, but all she said was that tomorrow was payday and not to forget to send the fifty dollars to her sister.

THAT WAS why Mitch wasn't around when Prudence showed up. He took his money over to the Post Office and there, on account he liked to jaw a little, make friends, set up contacts you never knew when you might need them—he got to gabbing with the postal clerk.

His name was Cornell and he was tired. Mitch figured the guy was born that way. Besides, there was something about a Post Office that dragged at you. No fun in it, nothing ever happened. All the stamps were the same (or looked the same) and all the clerks were the same (or looked the same) and if anything unusual came up, you checked it in the regulations and did what the rules said, exactly. And if the rules didn't tell you, then the thing couldn't be done, so you sent the customer away and went back to selling stamps. Which people either wanted, or they didn't, There were no sales, no bargains. A damaged stamp was never marked down—it was worth what it said on its face, or nothing. There was nothing in between.

Still, the Post Office was a hell of a lot better than what Decker was doing over at the Homicide Squad, so Mitch handed in his fifty bucks for the money order and said, "It's not much dough, I guess. What's the most you ever handled?"

The clerk came alive. "Ten thousand dollars. Six years ago."

"The hell with six years ago. Say this week."

"Oh. That dame with seventeen hundred dollars. Seventeen money orders. That was the biggest."

Click.

Mitch said cautiously, "You mean Prudence Gilford?"

"No. Patsy Grant."

"P.G.—same thing," Mitch said with certainty. "Same girl. And I'll bet she sent the dough to herself care of General Delivery, somewhere in California."

Cornell looked as if he thought Mitch were some kind of magician. "That's right," he said. "How did you know?"

"Me?" Mitch said, seeing that it all fitted like a glove. Prudence— or whatever her name was—had strangled Bella for the dough, then packed Bella's bag, dragged her out to the car, driven it to the woods, and left it there. And probably walked all the way back. That's why Prudence had been so tired.

"Me?" Mitch said again, riding on a cloud. "I know those things. That's what makes me a cop. Ideas—I got bushels of 'em." He thought of how the Lieutenant would go bug-eyed. Mitch Taylor, Homicide Expert.

He walked over to the phone booth, gave his shield number to the operator so he could make the call free and save himself a dime, and got through to the Homicide Squad.

Decker answered. "Taylor?" he said. "Come on back. The Gilford dame just confessed."

"She—*what?*"

"Yeah, yeah, confessed. While she was in here, the strap on her bag broke and she dropped it. Everything fell out—including seventeen money orders for a hundred bucks each. We had her cold, and she confessed. She knew all about Warhouse, and planned it so we'd nail him."

There was a buzz on the wire and Lieutenant Decker's voice went fuzzy. "Taylor," he said after a couple of seconds. "Can you hear me? Are you listening?"

"Sure," Mitch said. "But what for?"

And he hung up.

Yeah, Mitch Taylor, Homicide Expert.

Domestic Intrigue

Donald E. Westlake

When Mike Avallone recommended this story, he wrote, "Donald Cutesy Again." I would say, "Donald very cutesy indeed."

"MRS. CARROLL," said the nasty man, "I happen to know that your husband is insanely jealous."

I happened to know the same thing myself, and so there was nothing for me to do but agree. Robert *was* insanely jealous. "However," I added, "I fail to see where that is any of your business."

The nasty man smiled at me, nastily. "I'll come to that," he said.

"You entered this house," I reminded him, "under the guise of taking some sort of survey. Yet you ask me no questions at all about my television viewing habits. On the contrary, you promptly begin to make comments about my personal life. I think it more than likely that you are a fraud."

"Ah, madam," he said, with that nasty smile of his, under that nasty little mustache, "of course I'm a fraud. Aren't we all frauds, each in his—or *her*—own way?"

"I think," I said, as icily as possible, "it would be best if you were to leave. At once."

He made no move to get up from the sofa. In fact, he even spread out a bit more than before, acting as though at any instant he might kick off his shoes and take a nap. "If your husband," he said lazily, "were to discover another man making love to you, there's no doubt in my mind that Mr. Carroll would shoot the other man on the spot."

Once again I had no choice but to agree, since Robert had more than once said the same thing to me, waving that great big pistol of his around and shouting, "If I ever see another man so much as *kiss* you, I'll blow his brains out, I swear I will!"

Still, that was my cross to bear, and hardly a subject for idle chatter with perfect strangers who had sailed into my living room under false colors, and I said as much. "I don't know where you got your information," I went on, "and I don't care. Nor do I care to discuss my private life with you. If you do not leave, I shall telephone the police at once."

The nasty man smiled his nasty smile and said, "I don't think you'll call the police, Mrs. Carroll. You aren't a stupid woman. I think you realize by now I'm here for a reason, and I think you'd like to know what that reason is. Am I right?"

He was right to an extent, to the extent that I had the uneasy feeling he knew even more about my private life than he'd already mentioned, possibly even more than Robert knew, but I was hardly anxious to hear him say the words that would confirm my suspicions, so I told him, "I find it unlikely that you could have anything to say to me that would interest me in the slightest."

"I haven't bored you so far," he said, with a sudden crispness in his tone, and I saw that the indolent way he had of lounging on my sofa was pure pretense, that underneath he was sharp and hard and very self-aware. But this glimpse of his interior was as brief as it was startling; he slouched at once back into that infuriating pose of idleness and said, "Your husband carries that revolver of his everywhere, doesn't he? A Colt Cobra, isn't it? Thirty-eight caliber. Quite a fierce little gun."

"My husband is in the jewelry business," I said. "He very frequently carries on his person valuable gems or large amounts of money. He has a permit for the gun, because of the business he's in."

"Yes, indeed, I know all that." He looked around admiringly and said, "And he does very well at it, too, doesn't he?"

"You *are* beginning to bore me," I said, and half-turned away. "I believe I'll call the police now."

Quietly, the nasty man said, "Poor William."

I stopped. I turned around. I said, "What was that?"

"No longer bored?" Under the miserable mustache, he smiled once again his nasty smile.

I said, "Explain yourself!"

"You mean, why did I say, 'Poor William'? I was merely thinking about what would happen to William if a Colt Cobra were pointed at him, and the trigger pulled, and a thirty-eight caliber bullet were to crash through his body."

I suddenly felt faint. I took three steps to the left and rested my hands on the back of a chair. "What's his last name?" I demanded, though the demand was somewhat nullified by the tremor in my voice. "William who?"

He looked at me, and again he gave me a glimpse of the steel within. He said, "Shall I really say the name, Mrs. Carroll? Is there more than one William in your life?"

"There are no Williams in my life,'" I said, but despairingly, knowing now that this nasty man knew everything. But how? How?

"Then I must say the name," he said. "William Car—"

"*Stop!*"

He smiled. His teeth were very even and very white and very sparkly. I hated them. He said softly, "Won't you sit down, Mrs. Carroll? You seem a bit pale."

I moved around the chair I'd been holding for support, and settled into it, rather heavily and gracelessly. I said, "I don't know when my husband will be home, he could be—"

"I do," he said briskly. "Not before one-fifteen. He has appointments till one, and it's at least a fifteen minute drive here from his last appointment." He flickered back to indolence, saying lazily, "I come well prepared, you see, Mrs. Carroll."

"So I see."

"You are beginning," he said, "to wonder what on Earth it is that I want. I seem to know so very much about you, and so far I have shown no interest in doing anything but talk. Isn't that odd?"

From the alert and mocking expression on his face, I knew he required an answer, and so I said, "I suppose you can do what you want. It's your party."

"So it is. Mrs. Carroll, would you like to see your good friend William dead? Murdered? Shot down in cold blood?"

My own blood ran cold at the thought of it. William! My love! In all this bleak and brutal world, only one touch of tenderness, of beauty, of hope do I see, and that is William. If it weren't for those stolen moments with William, how could I go on another minute with Robert?

If only it were William who was rich, rather than Robert. But William was poor, pitifully poor, and as he was a poet, it was unlikely he would ever be anything but poor. And as for me, I admit that I was spoiled, that the thought of giving up the comforts and luxuries which Robert's money could bring me made me blanch just as much as the thought of giving up William. I needed them both in equal urgency; William's love and Robert's money.

The nasty man, having waited in vain for me to answer his rhetorical question, at last said, "I can see you would not like it. William is important to you."

"Yes," I said, or whispered, unable to keep from confessing it. "Oh, yes, he is."

Until William, I had thought that all men were beasts. My mother —bless her soul—had said constantly that all men were beasts, all through my adolescence, after my father disappeared, and I had come to maturity firmly believing that she was right. I had married Robert even though I'd known he was a beast, but simply because I had believed there was no choice in the matter, that one married a beast or one didn't marry at all. And Robert did have the advantage of being rich.

But now I had found William, and I had found true love, and I had learned what my mother never knew; that not *all* men are beasts. Almost all, yes, but not entirely all. Here and there one can find the beautiful exception. Like William. But not, obviously, like this nasty man in front of me. I would have needed none of my mother's training to know that *this* man was a beast. Perhaps, in his own cunning way, an even worse beast than brutal and blustering Robert. Perhaps, in his own way, even more dangerous.

I said, "What is it you want from me?"

"Oh, my dear lady," he protested, "*I* want from *you?* Not a thing, I assure you. It is what *you* want from *me.*"

I stared at him. I said, "I don't understand. What could I possibly want from you?"

As quickly as a striking snake, his hand slid within his jacket, slid out again with a long blank white envelope, and flipped it through the air to land in my lap. "These," he said. "Take a look at them."

I opened the envelope. I took out the pictures. I looked at them, and I began to feel my face go flaming red.

I recognized the room in the pictures, remembered that motel. The faces were clear in every one of the photographs.

"What you'll want," said the nasty man, smiling triumphantly, "is the negatives."

I whispered, "You mean, you'll show these to my husband?"

"Oh, I would much rather not. Wouldn't you like to have them for yourself? The prints *and* the negatives?"

"How much?"

'Well, I really hadn't thought," he said, smiling and smiling. "I'd rather leave that up to you. How much would you say they are worth to *you,* Mrs. Carroll?"

I looked at the photos again, and something seemed to go *click* in my mind. I said, "I believe I'm going to faint," Then my eyes closed, and I fell off the chair onto the floor.

He had a great deal of difficulty awaking me, patting my cheeks and chafing my hands, and when at last I opened my eyes, I saw that he was no longer smiling, but was looking very worried.

"Mrs. Carroll," he said. "Are you all right?"

"My heart," I whispered. "I have a weak heart." It was untrue, but it seemed a lie that might prove useful.

It did already. He looked more worried than ever, and backed away from me, looking down at me lying on the floor and saying, "Don't excite yourself, Mrs. Carroll. Don't get yourself all upset. We can work this out."

"Not now," I whispered. "Please." I passed a hand across my eyes. "I must rest. Call me. Telephone me, I'll meet you somewhere."

"Yes, of course. Of course."

"Call me this evening. At six."

"Yes."

"Say your name is Boris."

"Boris," he repeated. "Yes, I will." Hastily he retrieved the fallen photos. "Call at six," he said, and dashed out of the house.

I got to my feet, brushed off my toreadors, and went to phone William. "Darling," I said.

"Darling!" he cried.

"My love."

"Oh, my heart, my sweet, my rapture!"

"Darling, I must—"

"Darling! Darling! Darling!"

"Yes, sweetheart, thank you, that's all very—"

"My life, my love, my all!"

"William!"

There was a stunned silence, and then his voice said, faintly, "Yes, Mona?"

There were advantages to having a poet for a lover, but there were also disadvantages, such as a certain difficulty in attracting his attention sometimes.

But I had his attention now. I said, "William, I won't be able to see you tonight."

"Ob, *sweet*heart!"

"I'm sorry, William, believe me I am, but something just came up."

"Is it—" his voice lowered to a whisper, "—is it *him?*"

He meant Robert. I said, "No, dear, not exactly. I'll tell you all about it tomorrow."

"Shall I see you tomorrow?"

"Of course. At the Museum. At noon."

"Ah, my love, the hours shall have broken wings."

"Yes, dear."

With some difficulty I managed to end the conversation. I then took the other car, the Thunderbird, and drove to the shopping center. In the drugstore there I purchased a large and foul-looking cigar, and in the Mister-Master Men's Wear Shoppe I bought a rather loud and crude necktie.

I returned to the house, lit the cigar, and found that it tasted even worse than I had anticipated. Still, it was all in a good cause. I went upstairs, puffing away at the cigar, and draped the necktie over the doorknob of the closet door in my bedroom. I then went back to the first floor, left a conspicuous gray cone of cigar ash in the ashtray beside Robert's favorite chair, puffed away until the room was full of cigar smoke and I felt my flesh beginning to turn green, and then tottered out to the kitchen. I doused the cigar under cold water at the kitchen sink, stuffed it down out of sight in the rubbish bag, and went away to take two Alka-Seltzer and lie down.

BY ONE-FIFTEEN, when Robert came bounding home, I was recovered and was in the kitchen thawing lunch. *"My* love!" roared Robert, and crushed me in his arms.

That was the difference right there. William would have put the accent on the other word.

I suffered his attentions, as I always did, and then he went away to read the morning paper in the living room while I finished preparing lunch.

When he came to the table he seemed somewhat more subdued than usual. He ate lunch in silence, with the exception of one question, asked with an apparent attempt at casualness: "Umm, darling, did you have any visitors today?"

I dropped my spoon into my soup. "Oh! Wasn't that clumsy! What did you say, dear?"

His eyes narrowed. "I asked you, did you have any visitors today?"

"Visitors? Why—why, no, dear." I gave a guilty sort of little laugh. "What makes you ask, sweetheart?"

"Nothing," he said, and ate his soup.

After lunch he said, "I have time for a nap today. Wake me at three, will you?"

"Of course, dear."

I woke him at three. He said he'd be home by five-thirty, and left. I checked, and the crude necktie was no longer hanging on the doorknob in my bedroom.

WHEN ROBERT CAME HOME at five-thirty he was even quieter than before. I caught him watching me several times, and each time I gave a nervous start and a guilty little laugh and went into some other room.

I was in the kitchen at six o'clock, when the phone rang.

"I'll get it, dear!" I shouted. "It's all right, dear! I'll get it! I'll get it!"

I picked up the phone and said hello and the nasty man's voice said, "This is Boris."

"Yes, of course," I said, keeping my voice low.

"Can we talk?"

"Yes."

"Isn't your husband home?"

"It's all right, he's in the living room, he can't hear me. I want to meet you tonight, to *discuss* things." I gave a heavy emphasis to that word, and put just a touch of throatiness into my voice.

He gave his nasty laugh and said, "Whenever you say, dear lady. I take it you're recovered from this afternoon?"

"Oh, yes. It was just tremors. But listen, here's how we'll meet. You take a room at the Flyaway Motel, under the name of Clark. I'll—"

"Take a room?"

"We'll have a lot to—*talk* about. Don't worry, I'll pay for the room."

"Well," he said, "in that case..."

"I'll try to be there," I said, "as soon after nine as possible. Wait for me."

"All right, M—"

"I must hang up," I said hastily, before he could call me Mrs. Carroll. I broke the connection, went into the living room, and found Robert standing near the extension phone in there. I said, "Dinner will be ready soon, dear."

"Any time, darling," he said. His voice seemed somewhat strangled. He seemed to be under something of a strain.

Dinner was a silent affair, though I tried to make small talk without much success. Afterward, Robert sat in the living room and read the evening paper.

I walked into the living room at five minutes to nine, wearing my suede jacket. "I have to go out for a while, dear."

He seemed to control himself with difficulty. "Where to, dear?"

"The drugstore. I need nail polish remover."

"Oh, yes," he said.

I went out and got into the Thunderbird. As I drove away I saw the lights go on in my bedroom.

If it was nail polish remover Robert was looking for, he'd have little trouble finding it. There was a nearly full bottle with my other cosmetics on the vanity table.

I drove at moderate speeds, arriving at the Flyaway Motel at ten minutes past nine. "I'm Mrs. Clark," I told the man at the desk "Could you tell me which unit my husband is in?"

"Yes, ma'am." He checked his register and said, "Six."

"Thank you."

Walking across the gravel toward unit 6, I thought it all out again, as it had come to me in a flash of inspiration this afternoon just before I had had my 'faint.' The idea that I could have Robert's money without necessarily having to have Robert along with it had never occurred to me before. But now it had, and I liked it. To have Robert's money without having Robert meant I could have William!

What a combination! William *and* Robert's money! My step was light as I approached unit 6.

The nasty man opened the door to my knock. He seemed somewhat nervous. "Come on in, Mrs. Carroll."

As I went in, I glanced back and saw an automobile just turning into the motel driveway. Was that a Lincoln? A *blue* Lincoln?

The nasty man shut and locked the door, but I said, "None of that. Unlock that door."

"Don't worry about me, lady," he said, grinning nastily. "All I want from you is your money." Nevertheless, he unlocked the door again.

"Fine," I said. I took off my suede jacket.

"Now," he said, coming across the room, rubbing his hands together, "to get to business."

"Of course," I said. I took off my blouse.

He blinked at me. He said, "Hey! What are you doing?"

"Don't worry about a thing," I told him, and unzipped my toreadors.

His eyes widened and he waved his hands at me, shouting, "Don't *do* that! You got it all wrong, don't *do* that!"

"I don't believe I have it wrong," I said, and stepped out of the toreadors.

With utter panic and bewilderment, the nasty man said, "But William said you'd—" And stopped.

We both stopped. I stared at the nasty man in sudden comprehension. All at once I understood how it was he had known so much about me, how it had been possible for him to take those pictures.

So William couldn't live on the amount I gave him willingly. Mother was right, all men *are* beasts.

As I stood there, trying to get used to this new realization, the door burst open and Robert came bellowing in, waving that huge and ugly pistol of his.

I still wasn't recovered from my shock. To think, to think I'd been trying to save William from being killed, to think I'd been willing to sacrifice both Robert and the nasty man for William's sake. And all the time, all the time, William had betrayed me.

But then I *did* recover from the shock, and fast, because I saw that Robert had stopped his enraged bellowing and was glaring at me. At *me.* And pointing that filthy pistol at me.

At *me.*

"Not me!" I cried, and pointed at the nasty man. "Him! *Him!*"

The first shot buzzed past my ear and smashed the glass over the woodland painting above the bed.

I ran left, I ran right. The nasty man cowered behind the dresser. Robert's second shot chunked into the wall behind me.

"You lied!" I screamed. "You *lied!*"

All men are bea—

The Front Room

Michael Butterworth

You know the English and their front rooms. Here is a front room that will outdo them all.

ON THE LAST Saturday of that hot September, the brown bus put down Naomi and Bevis in the sun-faded holiday hamlet at the end of the naked stretch of new concrete road that ran parallel to the sand dunes, because this was as far as it went.

Top End, the bus driver told them, was at the far end of the new road and a little way on. You couldn't miss it; there was a pub and a shop, and the chalets and bungalows were up on the sand hills off the narrow road. Anyone would tell them where their place was, he said.

There was a little clump of people at the bus stop; flowered print dresses and baggy shorts, peeled noses and pale varicosed legs. It was mostly the older folk who came to this unfashionable coast. Before the war it had teemed, and it was still cheap.

The people got into the bus, and it rattled off round the semi-circle of wooden-fronted buildings: the chemist's shop with the hand-written ticket about printing and developing snapshots, the picture postcard stand and the dusty piles of children's buckets and spades, the amusement arcade with the pin tables and the pop music: past all these and back the way it came—to where the sky met the flat, raw sweep of fenland behind the sea, and crazy lanes zig-zagged the great dyked fields.

Naomi felt suddenly forsaken. "Wouldn't there be any chance of getting a taxi, darling?" she said, and wished she hadn't, because it always annoyed Bevis when she seemed to take the initiative in things. Yes, the suggestion had prickled him; he breathed heavily through his nose when he looked about them. There was no sign of a garage; apart from an old red sports car parked at the end of the buildings, where the road gave way to sand, at the deep cutting through the sand hills leading to the beach, there was nothing on wheels.

"Well, what do *you* think?" he snapped, and stooped to pick up their cases. "Come on, let's get on with it." He set off up the straight, hot road—and Naomi followed him.

The blare of the pop music faded behind them, and they were walking in tandem in the middle of the empty road to a point up ahead, with whispering hay in the fields at either side; on their right the high dunes shielding the sea, and the endless fens on their left. And all the while she watched this man she had married that spring.

It will be all right, she told herself. *We haven't made a good start, but it hasn't been easy, what with both of us having to go out to work to scrape together the money for the mortgage on the house. This fortnight's going to make all the difference. Two inexpensive weeks by the sea with just the basic joys of sunshine and idleness. Time to find ourselves again. Next year, maybe, we'll start a family...*

Strange how thin and frail Bevis looked with his arms tautened by the weight of the cases. They had met and courted in the winter, and he had looked almost burly in winter clothes. Quite different now. She would have to fatten him up during the holiday. Only trouble was he had an appetite like a little bird, and smoked far too much. The strain of carrying the heavy cases was telling on him already; he was breathing heavily, and tendrils of his wispy, fair hair were sticking to his pale brow.

No use offering to carry one of them, though they both knew she was basically the stronger. And that was another thing he detested.

He dumped down the cases in the sandy grass at the road verge and lit a cigarette, avoiding her gaze. There was a frosting of sweat

around his mouth, and his fingers holding the match trembled with
fatigue.

Naomi said: "That's right, darling. Have a bit of a rest, there isn't
much further to go." And she crossed to the fence and looked across a
narrow field to the sand hills, where the wind from the sea was
ruffling the spiky crests of the grass up there, and some of it reached
her because she felt its languorous breath mold her dress, lightly, to
her body. She wondered if Bevis was watching her.

She stretched herself lazily, and suddenly felt very alive. "It really
is a most wonderful September," she said. But he didn't reply, and
when she turned he was already hefting the cases and setting off
again down the middle of the road.

Top End was how they had been told it would be, and the pub was
closed, so they enquired at the shop, which was really only a glass
lean-to on the end of a weatherboard bungalow, and the woman had
to call her husband in from the garden, and after some thought he
remembered that the Leevis place was the last house along the sand
hills. How far? Perhaps half a mile or a bit more.

In the end, the man offered to deliver their cases in his van later
on in the afternoon, so they set off again unencumbered, and Bevis's
spirits rose; he took Naomi's hand, and they swung along gaily, specu-
lating on what the place was going to be like, not to mention Mrs.
Leevis, who was no more to them than a semi-illiterate, pencilled
note telling them that in reply to their advertisement she could offer
her bungalow, et cetera.

"Well, at any rate, however awful the place is, we're right on the
beach," said Naomi.

The narrow road hugged the foot of the sand hills, and the
bungalows were set on the crests, among the dry grass and the straggling gorse, each plot bounded by a wire fence. They were spaced at
haphazard intervals, and none of them were close together. Weatherboard, concrete, and flaking paint with the silvery wood showing
through. Bijou verandahs of fretted wood peering over the crests to
the grey, crawling sea below, where the seagulls swooped. Seedy,

small monuments of insularity, and not a soul in sight; everywhere seemed deserted. But then it was nearly October.

"It can't be much further," cried Naomi, and she slipped off her shoes and ran barefoot to the top of the next rise in the narrow road. "Yes, there it is!" calling back to him as he strode up to join her.

The last roof lay half-hidden by a copse of tall gorse, and beyond that the road wound on to an infinity of solitude.

"It's terribly isolated out here," she said, and suddenly wished she hadn't.

The bungalow, when they came to it, was a crouching block of salt-bleached concrete in a sand declivity, with a low-pitched roof of grey slate. Naked-looking iron pipes; eyeless, curtained windows; an uncompromising back door with an empty milk bottle on the step.

Quelling a sudden stab of disappointment, Naomi said: "Come on, darling. This is really the back of the house. The front of it will be facing the sea, and that might be quite nice." And they walked together through the warm, yielding sand round the small building. "Yes, it's not too bad at all. There's a verandah and a French window looking right out to sea."

They were standing together, in the open space of sand in front of the verandah, when the woman came out of the gate in the wire fence from the gorse copse.

"Are you the people?" she called to them. "Yes, I can see you must be. I'll get Ned to carry your cases indoors. Where's your cases?"

Bevis was no good with strangers, so Naomi walked the few paces to meet her, smiling.

"The man from the village shop's going to deliver them later," she said, adding interrogatively: "Mrs. Leevis?"

She was about fifty-five, and wore a gillyflower-colored dress and beads to match, and a large hat of shiny black straw under which the straggly tendrils of white hair were scraped back into a bun that pushed out the hat at the back. Broken veins crazed her cheeks pinkly under a heavy tan, and her eyes were palest blue and disconcertingly watchful. She was tall, and moved with a memory of straightness and strength.

"Yes, that's right dear," she said. Her teeth were white, and her own. "Well, I expect you'd like to go inside and get settled in." And she led them round to the back door and unlocked it standing aside to let them pass, her eyes flickering over the slender girl and the pale young man. "I think you and your husband will find everything quite comfortable."

There was a narrow, dark-wallpapered passage with four doors leading off. First, a kitchen. "It's not big, but very convenient, you'll find," said Mrs. Leevis. And Naomi looked at her doubtfully: cramped as a ship's galley, with painted whitewood table and two chairs; a dresser with plates and a row of dusty, hanging cups; a food cupboard. There was no fridge, and the cooker worked with bottled gas.

"There's plenty of gas for your fortnight," said Mrs. Leevis, opening the cupboard, "and you're welcome to the bits and pieces in here." These comprised half empty packets of rice and sugar, some condiments and preserves, and a bottle with dried sauce lacquered around the stopper. Naomi made a mental resolve to consign the lot to the waste bin and wipe out the shelves as soon as the woman's back was turned.

"Well, it's a lovely bright kitchen," she made herself say. And indeed the afternoon sun came full into the narrow room, mellowing its dusty rawness.

Mrs. Leevis nodded dismissively; she seemed to want to hurry on with the tour of the bungalow; eager, like a child, to reach the best part which lay just around the next corner, through another door.

She showed them the bedroom opposite the kitchen, with the double bed, and drew back the blinds to show the tangled thicket of gorse beyond the fence.

"You're not overlooked here," she said.

The second bedroom was only a windowed cupboard with an iron cot covered by an army blanket. There was a musky smell of maleness in the room, and Naomi winced to see a spider scurry across the bare floorboards and disappear in the wainscoting.

"Well, that just leaves the front room," said Mrs. Leevis, and there was no mistaking the edge of pride in her tone. "I'll go first, 'cos I keep it locked always."

It lay at the end of the passage; the last remaining door, and Mrs.

Leevis unlocked it, casting them a sidelong glance as if to say: *"This is what you've been waiting for, and you won't be disappointed."*

Naomi tried to catch Bevis's eye, but he was watching the woman gravely, and she was able to quench a wayward impulse to giggle.

"There!" exclaimed Mrs. Leevis, moving aside to let them pass. "This is where you're going to spend many a happy evening, I shouldn't wonder."

It's hideous, thought Naomi. *Hideous in every possible way, and I hate it!* She looked to Bevis for a confirming glance, but he was still regarding the woman, and nodding as she spoke. "All my treasures. And you'll live amongst them, and they'll become part of you also..."

It was dark, to begin with. The French window at the end was shaded by the verandah roof, which cut off the view of sea and sky, so that there were only the sand hills to be seen, and they were in deep shadow from the wall of the building. There were no other windows in the room.

And it was shaped like a cube. Five paces to the window and five paces across (heaven knows, it might have been five paces up the maroon-papered walls to the high, dark ceiling). Mrs. Leevis pressed a switch, and a single bulb burned starkly inside a raw glass cone, picking out the hotchpotch of heavy furniture that crammed the space beneath it: boggle-tasselled Victoriana and tubular steel side by side; spindly small tables loaded with domed, wax fruit, pale photographs in silver frames and passepartout. They followed Mrs. Leevis across to the fireplace, turning and weaving through the maze of objects that lay between.

"This is a pretty thing," said Mrs. Leevis, taking an object from the cluttered mantelpiece. "I had it since I was a girl like you, dear, and I often pick it up and turn it over in my hands to remind me..."

What she was holding was small and brightly colored, but it remained a glazed blur on the edge of Naomi's vision. Her whole shocked attention was on the thing she could see under the woman's arm, among the jumble of knickknacks, between the swelling base of a lustre vase and a brass bell shaped like a crinolined lady.

In a sealed, liquid-filled cylinder of glass lay slackly turned coils of ochre and brown, ending in a tiny, v-marked head, and the dead eyes were opaque like drowned seed pearls.

She screamed as she tripped and fell back over something, and Bevis steadied her; shocked at first, then irritated to see the cause of her sudden terror.

Mrs. Leevis stooped to right the footstool that Naomi had overturned. "Well, I never saw such a fuss," she said disapprovingly. "It's only a little adder our Ned killed up in the sand hills when he was a lad. He put it in pickle. I'm sure it couldn't harm a soul, and it always looks so pretty in the light. All those soft colors."

"I can't bear—such things," faltered Naomi, looking to Bevis for support, but he only pursed his lips and fumbled for his cigarette packet.

There was not much else to say after that. Mrs. Leevis was last out of the room. She looked back adoringly before she turned off the light and relocked the door. They went outside with her, and stood to watch her go.

"Anything you want, just call," she said, pointedly addressing Bevis. "We're not far away, and Ned is always very willing." She went out through the gate in the wire fence and into the dappled sunlight of the gorse. And now they could see it: half-hidden there a stone's throw away: an old railway carriage with a green-painted roof and steps leading up to a door with a rustic arch. And then they heard the heavy rasp of a big saw biting into wood. It came from somewhere behind the strange building.

"That must be her son," said Bevis, and then he growled: "What did you have to go and make that ridiculous scene for? The old girl thought you'd gone crazy."

Naomi didn't answer. Still grumbling, he followed her into the kitchen and watched her fill a kettle and put it on the stove for tea.

She shut her mind to him, telling herself that it would be all right soon, and that she had to make this holiday work for both their sakes —and it would be she who would have to make all the allowances.

Only—one thing—she would never be able to use that awful front room. It wasn't just the thing in the glass cylinder, but something about the whole room that was infinitely disturbing.

Later, when the man from the shop had delivered their cases, she suggested a swim—their first that year—but he had found a deck chair in the toolshed and was reading a paperback, sulkily, in the sunlight at the back of the bungalow. "All right, then, I'll go on my own," she said.

It was while she was changing in the bedroom that she had the sensation of being watched. The curtains were still open, and she rushed to close them. Before the folds shut her in secretly, she peered along the blank mass of gorse hedge ten feet away from the window; no sign of anyone.

But later, when she glissaded down the far side of the sand hills, and walked alone across the empty shore to the distant, murmuring sea—and even when the sea's coolness closed about her and greenly bid her—there was still the sensation that she was being watched.

IN THE DAYS THAT FOLLOWED, the unsubstantial relationship between the young couple faltered and broke under the strain of their nearness to each other. Five months of married life in a mortgaged semidetached suburban house, where they had met over breakfast and the radio weather forecast, and parted outside the insurance office where Naomi worked, to meet again in the evening for supper and television, had been the only background they had known together before; three days and nights of the small bungalow on the sand hills sundered them.

Naomi quickened to the sun and the sea, and came alive. She lived in her bikini, her rounded limbs browned and free. Bevis, fair and pale-skinned, kept out of the sun; sat reading all day on the verandah, outside the open French window. And on the third night he went to sleep alone in the small bedroom.

On the morning of the fourth day, the mares' tails came in from the west. By mid-afternoon, the sky was tumbled grey ness, and the rain slanted down, pockmarking the sand. He sat alone in the front room—where she had never set foot since that first time—and Naomi was hunched at the kitchen table, tapping a fingernail nervously on the rim of an empty teacup and staring out through the window across the inland fens.

Around five o'clock, the downpour slackened and retreated in a line across the sand hills. A thin fan of sunlight burst through a widening patch of cerulean blue, and Naomi scraped back the chair and went out into the passage.

"I'm going to walk down to the shop," she called, taking down her mackintosh. "Coming?"

No reply. She went out, slamming the door behind her; across the damp sand to the narrow road that wound back to the village.

Free. She felt free again, with the tangy wind plastering her hair to her cheek, and her hands thrust deep into the secret warmth of her coat pockets. Free from Bevis and his sulky tantrums, his half-hearted desires and his self-doubting. But what was going to happen now; what was going to happen when they went home after next week? She'd hoped that the holiday would have given them a fresh start, but would they ever—now—be able to pick up even the flat, untrammeled, undemanding routine of the house and their jobs...?

What was that?

She stopped and stared up at the swaying spikes of grass fringing the crest of the sand hills on her left.

Something had moved up there: a dark shape had bobbed up from behind the dunes, in a flickering instant, caught in the corner of her eye!

Something—someone—watching her? Following her along the far side of the sand hills?

She waited a few moments, then set off again, quickening her pace. And then the rain came down again.

Whatever—whoever—it was must now be behind me at the speed I was walking, she thought. And in any event, she was now more than halfway to Top End. Up the next rise in the road, and around the next bend, she would be able to see the pub and the shop; to see and be seen. There was no comfort for her in the straggling line of bungalows on the dunes, with their dead-eyed windows. And to go toward them meant approaching whoever was following her. Better anything than that. Keep going. Keep whatever it was behind her. She broke into a run.

On the next rise she could see her goal, and there she dared to pause and force herself to turn slowly and look back along the line of dunes, silhouetted against a pinky-grey band of sky below the black overcast

Of course, there was no one there. But she went on even faster, breaking into a run, and not just because the rain was now sluicing down, soaking her under the sodden mackintosh, but because she sensed, again, the watching eyes. And they were fingering her back.

Naomi didn't dare turn again—and above all she didn't dare to turn quickly—because then she would surprise her watcher *and then she would see him!*

At length, soaked and sobbing with relief, she opened the door of the lean-to shop, and the tiny clang of the bell made the woman look up from behind the counter, slack-mouthed.

"Why! You're wet through. And you look as if you've seen a ghost!"

Naomi found a smile to put on, and bought a few things she had no need of, inconsequential things: a pot of chocolate spread, which she detested; some matches; a packet of sweet biscuits; salt. Then she found that she had brought no money with her.

The woman had been joined by her husband, now, and Naomi could feel them staring at her as she stood with her head bowed in the middle of the tiny shop, clutching her purchases, while the rain roared down on the sloping glass roof above.

"You don't look well to me, love," said the woman; and to her husband: "She don't look well, and it isn't fit to turn a dog out. Get the van and drive the young lady back to her place. You know where it is."

It was a blessed relief to go back in the van. The man didn't say much, and Naomi avoided looking toward the sand hills. He put her off at the gate, and said she could drop the money in at the shop next time she was by. Naomi thanked him, and ran through the rain to the door.

Dusk was closing in above the overcast, and she nearly trod on the thing that lay on the step.

It was a wild bouquet of daisies, rose hips, and hawthorn, mixed with waxy leaves of laurel, all neatly tied together with a strip of bass. It signified nothing to her, so she pushed it aside with her foot.

As soon as she had closed the door behind her, Naomi sensed that something was wrong. She heard Bevis moving about in the small bedroom; he dropped something on the floor and swore savagely so that she should hear.

"Bevis—what are you doing, darling?"

No answer. And he came out before she could reach the bedroom door, brushing past her, sullen-faced, and into the kitchen.

Oh, God, she thought. *He's off in one of his tantrums again. What have I said? What have I done?*

She followed him. He was filling a kettle of water at the sink, and, with a sick, numbed feeling, she saw that his hands were shaking. He was going through the motions of making a cup of tea, but she knew it was a meaningless performance, put on for her sake.

But why...?

Go carefully. Ease the bitterness from him gently. Don't tempt the flood that could engulf us both in more acrimony.

She took off her coat. "It wasn't a very successful trip to the shop," she said. "I forgot the things we really need, and got myself soaked."

He slammed the kettle on the stove and lit the burner with the third match, cursing the two that broke in his hasty fingers. Then he took up his stand with his back to her, arms akimbo, waiting for it to boil.

Wearily, she sat down at the table. It was nearly dark out side, and the rain had settled down to a steady drizzle that promised to last all night. She shivered in her damp dress.

"What's the matter, Bevis?" she asked dully.

No reply.

When the kettle gave a tinny whistle he slopped hot water into the teapot and poured himself a cup. She watched him carry it to the door and pause there. Then she looked down at her fingers and waited for it; when he was in this kind of mood, he could never resist an exit line.

"You must think I'm a complete cretin!" he snarled, and without waiting for her to answer, walked down the corridor. The door of the front room slammed behind him.

Hold on, that was it. Hold on with both hands and let some time go past. She sat for a while, making a blank in her mind against the hurt and the emptiness; then she changed her clothes and began to prepare their supper, standing at the sink, where she could see her face in the streaming, dark window pane, and it seemed to her that the rain made tears down her reflected cheeks.

When it was done, she went out into the passage. "Bevis—supper's ready!" Her voice was as calm and matter-of-fact as she could make it; and when he didn't reply or come out, she walked slowly down the passage, though she had no intention of going into that dreadful room.

"Bevis—can't you hear me?"

The door of the small bedroom was open, and she knew that he had staged it this way—for her to see.

His suitcase lay on the bed, bulging and strapped.

Then he was standing there, watching her. He must have been waiting behind the door of the front room with his hand poised to open it at the sound of her footsteps hesitating and stopping.

"Tomorrow," he growled. "Tomorrow, we're getting out of here. And we'd go tonight, if there was a bus."

"Why...why?" Naomi shook her head in dazed bewilderment.

"*Why?*...you innocent-faced little..." She saw him coming at her, and she shrank away against the wall. He reached her in two strides, and then his hand was cupping her chin, forcing her head back hard against the wall. His face was close to hers, so that she could smell the stale tobacco on his breath.

"Bevis...please...you're hurting me!"

"*Hurt?*" His spittle splashed her face. And then the rambling abuse: the torrent of reproaches mouthed with all the fury of an inadequate personality exploding under the stress of a massive obsession. She cowered back against the wall, eyes closed, willing herself away from there.

Suddenly, shockingly, the burden of his complaint came through to her.

It concerned—unbelievingly—a man. A lover. *Her* lover!

"Bevis, you must be crazy!"

"Don't lie. I've seen you together!"

A great calm settled over her, She stared at him and shook her head. "No, Bevis."

"Down there on the beach!" he shouted. "You weren't alone all those times. While I was up here on my own, you were with your fancy boy!"

Dully, she raised her hand and dragged his from her face. "No, you're not mad, Bevis," she said bitterly. "You're just a child who's never grown up. Your imagination—"

And then all her strength was cut away from under her; destroyed in the instant by his next spluttering words:

"I saw you together today! He followed you to the village!"

NO DEFENSE NOW; no protesting. She was face-to-face again with the horror of the afternoon; her secret imaginings dragged out and dressed before her eyes; a ghoul with a turnip head and scarecrow rags brought to life. She saw again the thing on the sand hills, and felt the watching eyes that probed her back.

"Yes, I saw him. The big, handsome boy from next door. You like them like that, don't you?"

Unresisting, as his hand slashed her face. Uncaring of the hurt. Falling down the wall with the taste of blood in her mouth when he struck her with his clenched fist And, through it all, his voice screaming at her:

"You like them big and tough, don't you?"

Lying with her cheek against the cold floorboards with his feet inches from her eyes. Watching as they turned and went into the small bedroom. And when he came out he was carrying his case.

He walked past her, and out of the front door, slamming it behind him. A few moments later, she thought she heard him cry out to her, but surely it must have been her imagining.

SHE LAY in the dark passage while an age went past, listening to the million tiny creaks of the woodwork, the wayward sound pattern of the rain, the bass roll of the breakers on the shore below the sand hills.

He wasn't coming back.

Naomi got up and switched on the passage light. The door of the front room was still open; lowering her eyes so that she wouldn't have to see inside, she pulled it close.

Alone. She was alone.

Outside, the sand and the desolation of fen, the silent bungalows on the dunes, and the winding road that she would never find the courage to tread. Not now.

"Bevis!...come back!"

She ran to the back door and dragged it open, hoping that he might be standing there in the loom of light, in the rain, with his suitcase in his hand; pale, defenseless, and frightened of what he had done to her; waiting for her to come to him and tell him that it was all right, that it didn't matter; waiting for her greater strength to reassure him.

There was nothing but the sweep of rain-splattered sand, and the forlorn bunch of wild foliage lying just where she had left it.

And something else. Something sprawled by the gate.

Sprawled and shapeless, like...

She ran across the wet sand. It was Bevis's suitcase. The handle had been wrenched from its fastenings, and the thick strap broken, the lid burst open, and the contents scattered in heaps like a trampled man. She fingered his leather shaving case—her wedding present to him—it had been twisted and riven apart like a rotten apple. His thick paperback book lay in two pieces, ripped across the spine.

She forced the knuckles of her hand into her mouth to choke the cry of horror, and stumbled back to the door, locked and bolted it behind her, and turned out the light.

As she leaned back, wild-eyed, she seemed to hear it again: Bevis's cry for help, the cry she had disregarded.

If he called again, she would answer. But in her heart she knew that he was beyond the compass of her voice; that his frail body and peevish spirit had ended out there in the night.

To LIVE THROUGH THE NIGHT; to survive. She forced herself to come to grips with it.

Adding it up: the windows were all shut against the rain, and the door was locked and bolted behind her.

Nothing—no one—could reach her in here without her hearing the noise of his coming in. And, if that happened, she would run out the door and down the road, screaming all the while.

Calm. Be calm. All you have to do is crouch very still. And just exist.

And then—with a choked intake of breath—she remembered!

The French window!

The window in that awful room. Bevis had been out on the veranda all the morning, before the rain came. And she knew he would never have thought to lock it when he came in.

Her frail house of cards, her only defense, was yawning open not twenty paces from where she stood.

She had to go in there and lock that door; cross that obscene room, under the eyes of the thing in the glass cylinder. Now, before it was too late.

Ten dread-filled steps down the corridor, and the handle squeaked to her touch. The light was still on, as Bevis had left it.

Deliberately fixing her gaze on the French window, she crossed the room, swaying past the cluttered furniture. The wave of relief was a physical, tangible thing, and she almost smiled to herself to find the door locked and the key there.

And so, she never saw them till she turned round...

They were sitting very still, side by side, on a Victorian sofa near the fireplace. And, before her stupefied gaze, they got up together.

Mrs. Leevis wore a dress of beige lace with a corsage of artificial pansies, and a picture hat trimmed with a velvet cabbage rose, She had the air of a proud mother at a country wedding.

"It's nice we all meet in my lovely room," she said. "Now we can all be happy together—" turning fondly to the looming figure at her side, "—just you and me and our Ned."

Brown boots and a lumpy suit reeking of mothballs. A spray of ferns in his buttonhole. Great red hands hanging limply. And his eyes were quite mad.

"He'll be kind and gentle to you," said Mrs. Leevis. "Not like the other."

Then he was coming toward her, and, through her own screams, Naomi heard the woman tut-tutting with mild disfavor as she moved behind her to block the way to the door.

The Real Bad Friend

Robert Bloch

This story, Bob tells me, first appeared in Mike Shayne magazine back in 1956 and hasn't reappeared since 1957 so it probably isn't known to many readers. "Yet," he says, "I think it might interest buffs—since in it, I can now discover the germ of what later became Psycho.*"*

IT WAS REALLY all Roderick's idea in the first place.

George Foster Pendleton would never have thought of it. He couldn't have; he was much too dull and respectable. George Foster Pendleton, vacuum-cleaner salesman, aged forty-three, just wasn't the type. He had been married to the same wife for fourteen years, lived in the same white house for an equal length of time, wore glasses when he wrote up orders, and was completely complacent about his receding hairline and advancing waistline.

Consequently, when his wife's uncle died and left her an estate of some eighty-five thousand dollars after taxes, George didn't make any real plans.

Oh, he was delighted, of course—any ten-thousand-a-year salesman would be—but that's as far as it went. He and Ella decided to put in another bathroom on the first floor and buy a new Buick, keeping the old car for her to drive. The rest of the money could go into something safe, like a savings and loan, and the interest would take care of a few little luxuries now and then. After all, they had no children or close relatives to look after. George was out in the territory a few days every month, and often called on local sales prospects at night, so they'd never developed much of a social life. There was no reason to expand their style of living, and the money wasn't quite enough to make him think of retiring.

So they figured things out, and after the first flurry of excitement and congratulations from the gang down at George's office, people gradually forgot about the inheritance. After all, they weren't really living any differently than before. George Foster Pendleton was a quiet man, not given to talking about his private affairs. In fact, he didn't have any private affairs to talk about.

Then Roderick came up with his idea.

"Why not drive Ella crazy?"

George couldn't believe his ears. "You're the one who's crazy," George told him. "Why, I never heard of anything so ridiculous in all my life!"

Roderick just smiled at him and shook his head in that slow, funny way of his, as if he felt sorry for George. Of course, he *did* feel sorry for George, and maybe that's why George thought of him as his best friend. Nobody seemed to have any use for Roderick, and Roderick didn't give a damn about anyone else, apparently. But he liked George, and it was obvious he had been doing a lot of thinking about the future.

"You're a fine one to talk about being ridiculous," Roderick said. That quiet, almost inaudible way he had of speaking always carried a lot of conviction. George was handicapped as a salesman by his high, shrill voice, but Roderick seldom spoke above a whisper. He had the actor's trick of deliberately underplaying his lines. And what he said usually made sense.

Now George sat in his five-dollar room at the Hotel LeMoyne and listened to his friend. Roderick had come to the office today just before George left on his monthly road trip, and decided to go along. As he'd fallen into the habit of doing this every once in a while, George thought nothing of it. But this time, apparently, he had a purpose in mind.

"If anyone is being ridiculous," Roderick said, "it's you. You've been selling those lousy cleaners since nineteen forty-six. Do you like your job? Are you ever going to get any higher in the company? Do you want to keep on in this crummy rut for an other twenty years?"

George opened his mouth to answer, but it was Roderick who spoke. "Don't tell me," he said. "I know the answers. And while we're on the subject, here's something else to think about. Do you really love Ella?"

George had been staring at the cracked mirror over the bureau. Now he turned on the bed and gazed at the wall. He didn't want to look at himself, or Roderick, either.

"Why, she's been a good wife to me. More than a wife—like a mother, almost."

"Sure. You've told me all about that. That's the real reason you married her, wasn't it? Because she reminded you of your mother, and your mother had just died, and you were afraid of girls in the first place, but you had to have someone to take care of you."

Damn that Roderick! George realized he never should have told him so much in the first place. He probably wouldn't, except that Roderick had been his best—maybe his only—friend. He'd come along back in '44, in the service, when George had been ready to go to pieces completely.

Even today, after all those years, George hated to remember the way he'd met Roderick. He didn't like to think about the service, or going haywire there on the island and trying to strangle the sergeant, and ending up in the stockade. Even so, it might have been much worse, particularly after they stuck him in solitary, if he hadn't met Roderick. Funny part of it was, Roderick had become his intimate friend, and heard everything about him long before George ever set eyes on him. Roderick had been down in solitary, too, and for the first month he was just a voice that George could talk to in the dark. It wasn't what you'd call the best way in the world to develop a close friendship, but at the time it kept George from cracking up. He had someone to confide in at last, and pretty soon he was spilling his guts, his heart, his soul; telling things he hadn't even known about himself until the words came out.

Oh, Roderick knew, at right. He knew the things George had carefully concealed from everyone—the kids back in school, the guys in the army, the gang at the office, the card-playing friends and neighbors, even Ella. Most especially Ella. There were lots of things George wouldn't dream of telling Ella, any more than he would have told his mother, years ago.

Roderick was right about that. Ella did remind George of his mother. And when his mother died, he'd married Ella because she was big and took care of him, and the way it worked out it was she who made most of the decisions. As a child he'd been taught to be a good little boy. Now he was a good little salesman, a good little potbellied householder, a fetcher-home of Kleenex, a mower of lawns, a wiper of dishes, a wrapper of garbage. Twelve years of it since the war. And if it hadn't been for Roderick, he never could have stood it.

Could he stand another twelve years of it? Or twenty, or thirty, or even more?

"You don't have to put up with it, you know," Roderick murmured, reading his thoughts. "You don't have to be mommy's boy any longer. This is your big chance, George. If you got rid of the house, you'd have over ninety thousand in cash. Suppose you settled down on one of those little islands in the Caribbean. There's dozens of them, according to the travel guide I saw on your desk in the office today."

"But Ella wouldn't like that," George protested. "She hates hot climates. That's why we've never traveled south on vacations. Besides, what on earth could she do down there?"

"She wouldn't be going," Roderick answered patiently. "She'd stay here. That's the whole point of it, George. You could live like a king there for a few hundred a month. Have a big house, all the servants you want. Plenty to drink. And the *girls,* George! You've heard about the girls. Every color under the sun. Why, you can even buy them down there, the way those old Southern planters used to buy slaves. Quadroons and octoroons and mulattoes—probably can't even speak a word of English. But you wouldn't have to worry about that. All you'd want is obedience, and you could have a whip to take care of that They'd have to do anything you wanted, because you'd be their master. You could even kill them if you liked. The way you'd like to kill Ella."

"But I don't want to kill Ella," George said very quickly, and his voice was quite loud and shrill.

Roderick's answering laugh was soft. "Don't kid me," he said. "I know you. You'd like to kill her, the same way you'd have liked to kill that sergeant back on the island, but you can't because you're chicken. And besides, it isn't practical. Murder is no solution to this problem, George, but my way is. Drive Ella crazy."

"Preposterous."

"What's preposterous about it? You want to get rid of her, don't you? Get rid of your job, get rid of taking orders from a wife and a boss and every stinking customer with ninety bucks for a cleaner who thinks he can make you jump. And here's your chance. The chance of a lifetime, George, sitting right in your lap."

"But I can't drive Ella insane."

"Why not? Take a look around you, man. It's being done every day. Ask the lawyers about the sons and daughters and in-laws of people who have money, and how they get the old folks put away in the asylum. Getting power of attorney from grandpa and grandma— things like that, Don't you think a lot of them help the deal along a little? You can drive anyone crazy, George, if you plan."

"Ella isn't the type," George insisted. "Besides, anything I did— don't you think she'd know about it and see through it? Even if I tried, it wouldn't work."

"Who said anything about you trying?" Roderick drawled. He seemed very sure of himself, now. "That's my department, George. Let me do it."

"You? But—"

"I wouldn't fool you. It's not merely a beautiful gesture of friend-ship. I want those West Indies, too. We can go there together. You'd like that, wouldn't you, George? The two of us down there, I mean, where we wouldn't have to be afraid of what we did, what people would say or think? I could help you, George. I could help you get hold of some of those girls. Do you remember that book you read once, about the Roman Emperor, Tiberius—the one who had the villa on the island, and the orgies? You told me about some of those orgies, George. We could do it, you and I."

George felt sweat oozing down the insides of his wrists. He sat up.

"I don't even want to think of such things," he said. "Besides, what if you got caught?"

"I won't get caught," Roderick calmly assured him. "Don't forget, Ella doesn't even know me. I've steered clear of your friends all these years. I'm a free agent, George, and that's our ace in the hole. You've always treated me like a poor relation, never introducing me or even mentioning my name. Oh, I'm not complaining. I understand. But now that little situation is going to come in handy. Let me think things out, work up a plan."

George bit his upper lip. "Ella's too sensible," he said. "You'd never get her upset."

Roderick laughed without making a sound. "Nobody is really 'sensible,' George. It's just a false front, that's all. Like the one you've built up." He was suddenly quite serious again. "Think about it. How many people would believe you were capable of even talking to me the way you have just now, let alone of carrying out any such ideas? Would your boss believe it? Or Ella, even? Of course not! To the world, you're just another middle-aged salesman, a Willy Loman type, only worse. A spineless, gutless, chicken-hearted, yellow-bellied coward. *A* weak-kneed sissy, a little panty-waist, a mommy's boy, a—"

"*Shut up!*" George almost screamed the words, and then he was on his feet with his sweat-soaked hands balled into fists, ready to smash at the voice and the face, ready to kill...

And then he was back on the bed, breathing hoarsely, and Roderick was laughing at him without making a sound.

"You see? I knew the words to use, all right. In one minute I turned you into a potential murderer, didn't I? You, the respectable suburban type who's never gotten out of line since they shoved you into the stockade.

"Well, there are words for everyone, George. Words and phrases and ideas that can churn rage, trigger emotion, fill a person with incoherent, hysterical fear. Ella is no different. She's a woman; there's a lot of things she must be afraid of. We'll find those things, George. We'll press the right buttons until the bells ring. The bells in the belfry, George. The bats in the belfry—"

George made a noise in his throat. "Get out of here."

"All right. But you think over what I've said. This is your big opportunity—our big opportunity. I'm not going to stand by and see you toss it away." Then he was gone.

Alone in his room, George turned out the light and got ready for bed. He wondered if there was a threat hidden in Roderick's last words, and that startled him. All his life George had been afraid of other people because they were violent, aggressive, cruel. At times he could sense the same tendencies in himself, but he always suppressed them. His mother had made him behave like a little gentleman. And except for that one terrible interlude in the service, he had always been a little gentleman. He'd kept out of trouble, kept away from people that could harm him.

And Roderick had helped. He'd gotten out of the army at the same time George did, settled down in the same city. Of course, he didn't really settle down, inasmuch as he had no wife or family and never kept a regular job. Still, he seemed to get by all right. In spite of his hand-to-mouth existence, he dressed as well as George did. And he was taller and leaner and darker and looked a good ten years younger. It often occurred to George that Roderick lived off women— he seemed to be that type, always hinting of sexual conquests. But be never volunteered any information about himself. "What you don't know won't hurt you," he'd say.

And George was satisfied with the arrangement, because as a result he could talk about himself. Roderick was the sounding board, the confessional booth, the one person who could really understand.

He'd drop in at the office from time to time when George was free, and sometimes he'd ride along with him for a day when George went out of town, or in the evenings when he called on prospects. After a few perfunctory overtures, George stopped trying to get Roderick to meet his wife. And he'd never mentioned Roderick to her—mainly because of the circumstances of their having been in the stockade together, and George had never dared tell Ella about *that.* So Ella didn't know about Roderick, and somehow this made everything quite exciting. Once, when Ella had gone down to Memphis for her mother's funeral, Roderick consented to move in with George at the house for two days. They got violently and disastrously drunk together, but on the third morning Roderick left.

It was all very clandestine, almost like having a mistress. Only without the messy part. The messy part was no good, though it might be different if you were on one of those islands and nobody could see you or stop you and you owned those girls body and soul; then you could have a whip, a long black whip with little pointed silver spikes at the end, and the spikes would tear the soft flesh and you would make the girls dance and little red ribbons would twine around the naked bodies and then—

But that was Roderick's doing, putting such thoughts into his head! And suddenly George knew he was afraid of Roderick. Roderick, always so soft-voiced and calm and understanding; always ready to listen and offer advice and ask nothing in return. George had never realized until now that Roderick was as cruel as all the rest.

Now he had to face the fact. And he wondered how he could have escaped the truth all these years. Roderick had been in the stockade for a crime of violence, too. But the difference was that Roderick wasn't repentant. Repentance wasn't in him—only defiance and hatred, and the terrible strength that comes of being untouched and untouchable. It seemed as though nothing could move him or hurt him. He bowed to no conventions. He went where he pleased, did what he pleased. And apparently there was a streak of perversity in him; obviously he hated Ella and wanted George to get rid of her. If George had listened to him tonight...

The little vacuum-cleaner salesman fell asleep in his sagging bed, his mind firmly made up. He was finished with Roderick. He wouldn't see him any more, wouldn't listen to any of his wild schemes. He wanted no part of such plans. From now on he'd go his way alone. He and Ella would be safe and happy together...

DURING THE NEXT FEW DAYS, George often thought of what he'd say to Roderick when he turned up, but Roderick left him alone. Maybe he'd figured out the situation for himself and realized he'd gone too far.

Anyway, George completed his trip, returned home, kissed Ella, helped supervise the installation of the second bathroom, and finished up his paperwork at the office.

Being on the road had left him feeling pretty tired, but there came a time when he just had to catch up with his prospect list here in town, so he finally spent an evening making calls. Since he was just plain fagged out, he violated one of his rules and stopped for a quick drink before he began his rounds. After the first call he had another, as a reward for making a sale, and from then on things went easier. George knew he had no head for alcohol, but just this once a few drinks helped. He got through his customer list in a sort of pleasant fog, and when he was done he had several more fast shots in a tavern near the house. By the time he put the car in the garage, he was feeling no pain.

He wondered vaguely if Ella would be waiting up to bawl him out She didn't like him to drink. Well, perhaps she'd be asleep by now. He hoped so, as he went up the walk and started to unlock the door.

Before he could tum the key the door opened and Ella was in his arms. "Thank goodness you're here!" she cried. She *was* crying, George realized, and then he noticed that all the lights in the house were on.

"Hey, what's the matter? What's all this about?"

She began to gurgle. "The face, in the window—"

Alcohol plays funny tricks, and for a moment George wanted to laugh. Something about the melodramatic phrase, and the way Ella's jowls quivered when she uttered it, was almost painfully amusing. But Ella wasn't joking. She was frightened. She quivered against him like a big blob of Jell-o.

"I had this awful headache—you know the kind I get—and I was just sitting in the front room watching TV with the lights off. I guess I must have been dozing a little, when all of a sudden I got this feeling, like somebody was watching me. So I looked up, and there in the window was this awful face. It was like one of those terrible rubber masks the kids wear for Halloween—all green and grinning. And I could see hands clawing at the window, trying to open it and get in!"

"Take it easy now," George soothed, holding her. "Then what happened?"

Gradually he got it out of her. She had screamed and turned on the big overhead light, and the face had disappeared. So she'd turned on all the lights and gone around locking the doors and windows After that she'd just waited.

"Maybe we ought to call the police," she said. "I thought I'd tell you about it first."

George nodded. "Sensible idea. Probably was just what you thought—some kid playing a trick." He was quite sober now, and thoughtful. "Which window did you see this through, the big one? Here, let me get a flashlight from the garage. I'm going to look for footprints."

He got the flashlight, and when Ella refused to accompany him, walked across the lawn himself. The flower bed beneath the window was damp from a recent rain, but there were no footprints.

When George told Ella about it, she seemed puzzled. "I can't understand it," she said.

"Neither can I," George answered. "If it was a kid, he'd probably have run off when you spotted him, instead of waiting to smooth out his tracks. On the other hand, if it was a prowler, he'd cover up his traces. But a prowler wouldn't have let you see him in the first place." He paused. "You're sure about what you saw?"

Ella frowned. "Well...it was only for a second, you know, and the room was so dark. But there was this big green face, like a mask, and it had those long teeth..." Her voice trailed away.

"Nobody tried the doors or windows? You didn't hear any sounds?"

"No. There was just this face." She blinked. "I told you about my headache, and how I was dozing off, watching that late movie. It was all sort of like a nightmare."

"I see." George nodded. "Did you ever stop to think that maybe it was a nightmare?"

Ella didn't answer.

"How's the head? Still aching? Better take a couple of aspirins and go up to bed. You just had a bad dream, dear. Come on, let's go to bed and forget about it, shall we?"

So they went to bed.

Maybe Ella forgot about it and maybe she didn't, but George wasn't forgetting. He knew. Roderick must be starting to carry out his plan. And this would only be the beginning...

It was only the beginning, and after that things moved fast. The next afternoon, George was sitting in the office all alone when Ella called him from the house. She sounded very excited.

"George, did you tell the plumbers to come back?"

"Why no, dear, of course not."

"Well, Mr. Thornton is here, and he said they got a call to come over and rip everything out again. I don't understand it, and I've been trying to explain that it's some kind of mistake and—"

Ella sounded very upset now, and George tried to calm her down. "Better put him on, dear. I'll talk to him."

So Ella put Mr. Thornton on and George told him not to bother, there was a mixup somewhere. And when Mr. Thornton got mad and said there was no mixup, he'd taken the call himself, George just cut him off and got Ella back on the wire.

"It's all taken care of now," he assured her. "Don't worry about a thing. I'll be home early."

"Maybe you'd better get something to eat downtown," Ella said. "I've got such an awful headache, and I want to lie down for a while."

"You go ahead," George said. "I'll manage."

So George managed, but if Ella lay down, she didn't get very much rest.

George found that out when he got home. She was quivering, her voice and body trembling.

"Somebody's trying to play a trick on us," she told him. "The doorbell's been ringing all afternoon. First it was Gimbel's delivery truck. With *refrigerators.*"

"I didn't order a refrigerator," George said.

"I know you didn't, and neither did I." Ella was trying to hold back the tears. "But somebody did. And not just one. They had four of them."

"Four?"

"That's not the worst of it. Some man from Kelly's called and asked when I was going to move. They'd gotten an order for a van..."

"Let me get this straight." George paced the floor. "How did they get the order?"

"Over the phone," Ella said. "Just the way Mr. Thornton did. That's why I thought at first you might have called." She was sniffling now, and George made her sit down.

"So you said," George told her. "But I asked Mr. Thornton about that. He happened to take that particular call himself. And he was quite positive the caller was a woman."

"A woman?"

"Yes." George sat down next to Ella and took her band. "He claimed he recognized your voice."

"But George, that's impossible! Why, I never even used the phone once today. I was lying down with my headache and—"

George shook his head. "I believe you, dear. But who else could it be? What other woman would know that Thornton was the plumber who put in our bathroom? Did you mention his name to anyone?"

"No, of course not. At least, I don't remember." Ella was pale. "Oh, I'm so upset I can't think straight." She put her hands up to her forehead. "My head feels like its splitting wide open. I can't stand it..." She stared at George. "Where are you going?"

"I'm calling Dr. Vinson."

"But I'm not sick. I don't need a doctor."

"He'll give you a sedative, something for that head of yours. Now just calm down and relax."

So Dr. Vinson came over, and he did give Ella a sedative. She didn't mention anything about the calls, so he only went through a routine examination.

But afterward, when she was asleep upstairs, George took Dr. Vinson aside and told him the story—including the part about the face in the window.

"What do you think, Doc?" he asked. "I've heard about such things happening when women start going through change of life. Maybe—"

Dr. Vinson nodded. "Better have her call my office for an appointment later in the week," he said. "We'll see that she gets a complete checkup. Meanwhile, don't let yourself get upset. It could be somebody's idea of a practical joke, you know."

George nodded, but he wasn't reassured.

The part that really bothered him was the business about Ella's voice being recognized over the phone.

NEXT MORNING HE LEFT EARLY, and Ella was still asleep. Down at the office he called Gimbel's and then Kelly's. After much confusion, he was able to locate the clerks who had taken the orders. Both insisted they had talked to a woman.

So George called Dr. Vinson and told him so.

No sooner had he hung up than Ella was on the phone. She could scarcely speak.

A man had come from the Humane Society with a Great Dane. A West Side furrier, somebody Ella had never heard of, drove up with samples of mink coats—mink coats in July! A travel agency had kept calling, insisting that she had asked for information about a flight around the world. Her head was killing her; she didn't know what to do; she wanted George to phone the police and—

She broke off in the middle of her hysterical account, and George quickly asked what was happening. A moment later he realized he could have spared himself the question. The sound of what was happening was clearly audible over the wire: he recognized the hideous wailing.

"Fire engines!" Ella gasped. "Somebody called the Fire Department!"

"I'll be right home," George said, hanging up quickly.

And he went right home. The trucks were gone by the time he arrived, but a lieutenant was still there, and a detective from the Police Department. Ella was trying to explain the situation to them, and it was a lucky thing George was on hand to straighten things out. He had Ella go upstairs, and then he told the men the story.

"Please," he said. "Don't press any charges. If there's any expense, anything like a fine, I'll be glad to pay it. My wife is under doctor's care—she's going to have a complete examination later in the week This is all very embarrassing, but I'm sure we can straighten things out..."

The men were quite sympathetic. They promised to let him know what the costs would be, and the detective gave George his card and told him to keep in touch in case there was anything he could do.

Then George got on the phone and squared things with the Humane Society, the furrier, and the travel agency. After that he went up to Ella's bedroom, where he found her lying on the bed with all the shades pulled down. He offered to fix her something to eat, but she said she wasn't hungry.

"Something's happening," she told him. "Somebody's trying to harm us. I'm frightened."

"Nonsense." George forced a smile, "Besides, we've got protection now." And then, to cheer her up, he told her that the detective had promised to put a watch on the house and tap the telephone.

"If there's anybody pulling any funny business, we'll catch him," George reassured her. "All you have to do is rest. By the way, Dr. Vinson said it would be a good idea if you stopped in for a checkup towards the end of the week. Why not call him for an appointment?"

Ella sat up. "You told him?"

"I had to, dear. After all, he's your doctor. He's in a position to help if—"

"If *what?*"

"Nothing."

"George. Look at me." He didn't, but she went on. "Do you think I made those calls? Do you?"

"I never said so. It's just that Thornton claims he recognized your voice. Why would he want to lie about a thing like that?"

"I don't know. But he's lying. He *must* be! I never called him, George. I swear it! And I didn't call anyone this morning. Why, I was in bed until almost noon. That sedative made me so dopey I couldn't think straight."

George was silent.

"Well, aren't you going to say something?"

"I believe you, dear. Now, try and get some rest."

"But I can't rest now. I'm not tired. I want to talk to you."

"Sorry, I've got to get back to the office and clean up my desk. Don't forget, I'm leaving town again tomorrow."

"But you can't go now. You can't leave me alone like this!"

"Only for three days. You know, Pittsville and Bakerton. I'll be back by Saturday." George tried to sound cheerful. "Anyway, the police will keep an eye on the house, so you needn't worry about prowlers."

"George, I—"

"We'll talk about it again tonight. Right now, I've got a job to attend to, remember?"

So George left her weeping softly on the bed and went back to his office. But he didn't pay much attention to his job.

Roderick was waiting for him when he came in.

THE OTHER SALESMEN were out that afternoon, and there was no one else near the hot, stuffy little back-room cubicle George used for an office. He and Roderick were all alone, and Roderick spoke very softly. George was glad of that, at least, because he wouldn't have wanted anyone to hear the things Roderick told him. Nor, for that matter, would he have cared to have been overheard himself.

The moment he saw Roderick he almost shouted, "So it was you, after all!"

Roderick shrugged. "Who else?"

"But I told you I didn't want any part of it, and I meant it!"

"Nonsense, George. You don't know what you mean, or what you really want." Roderick smiled and leaned forward. "You talked to this Dr. Vinson and to the detective. Did you mention my name?"

"No, I didn't, but—"

"You see? That proves it. You must have realized who was responsible, but you kept silent. You *wanted* the scheme to work. And it is working, isn't it? I have everything all planned."

In spite of himself, George had to ask the question. "How did you manage to imitate her voice?"

"Simple. I've called her on the phone several times—wrong number, you know, or pretending to be a telephone solicitor. I heard enough to be able to fake it. She's got one of those whiney voices, George. Like this. *"I think I'll lie down for a while. My head is killing me."* It was uncanny to hear Ella's voice issuing from those sardonically curled lips.

George's heart began to pound. "You—you said you had plans," he murmured.

Roderick nodded. "That's right. You're going out of town for a few days, I believe?"

"Yes. Tomorrow."

"Good. Everything will be arranged."

"What do you intend to do?"

"Maybe you'd better not ask that question, George. Maybe you ought to keep out of this completely. Just leave everything to me." Roderick cocked his head to one side. "Remember, what you don't know won't hurt you."

George sat down, then stood up again hastily. "Roderick, I want you to stop this! Lay off, do you hear me?"

Roderick smiled.

"Do you hear me?" George repeated. He was trembling now.

"I heard you," Roderick said. "But you're upset now, George. You aren't thinking straight. Stop worrying about Ella. She won't really come to any harm. They'll take quite good care of her where she's going. And you and I will take good care of ourselves where we're going. That's what you want to concentrate on, George. The Caribbean. The Caribbean, with ninety thousand dollars in our pockets. A little boat, maybe, and those long, moonlit tropical nights. Think about the girls, George—those nice, slim young girls. They aren't fat and blubbery, always whining and complaining about headaches and telling you not to touch them. They like to be touched, George. They like to be touched, and held, and caressed, and—"

"Stop it! It's no use. I've changed my mind."

"Too late, George. You can't stop it now." Roderick was very casual, but very firm. "Besides, you don't really want to stop. It's only that you're afraid. Well, don't be. I promise you won't be involved in this at all. Just give me three days. Three days, while you're gone—that's all I need."

"I won't go!" George shouted. "I won't leave her! I'll go to the police!"

"And just what will you tell them?" Roderick paused to let the question sink in. "Oh, that would be a fine idea, wouldn't it, going to the police? Not on your life, George. You're going out of town like a good little boy. Because this is a job for a bad little boy—like me."

He was laughing at George now, and George knew it. Any further protest on his part would be useless, Still, he might have tried to do something about it if the boss hadn't come in through the side entrance at that very moment Roderick stood up, crossed the room, slipped out the door and was gone.

And George, staring after him, realized that his last chance had gone with him.

THINGS SEEMED a little bit better that evening. Ella had had no further disturbances during the rest of the day, and as a result she was considerably calmer. By the time they had finished a makeshift supper and got ready for bed, both of them felt a trifle more reconciled to the coming separation.

Ella said she had phoned Dr. Vinson and made an appointment for Friday afternoon, two days hence. George, for his part, promised to call her faithfully every evening he was away.

"And if you need me, I'll drive right back," he told her. "I won't be much more than a hundred miles away any time during the trip. Come on now, I'll finish packing and we can get some sleep."

So they left it at that. And the next morning, George was up and on the road long before Ella awakened.

He had a fairly easy day of it in Pittsville and finished his calls long before he had anticipated. Perhaps that's why he started to worry; he had nothing else to occupy his mind.

What was it Roderick had said? *What you don't know won't hurt you?*

Well, that wasn't true. Not knowing was the worst part of it. Not knowing and suspecting. Roderick had told him he had everything planned. George believed that, all right. And Roderick had told him he wouldn't actually harm Ella. This part George wasn't certain about; he didn't know whether he could believe it or not. Roderick couldn't be trusted. He'd proved it by the way he'd gone ahead with the scheme despite George's protests. There was no telling what he might be capable of doing. After all, what did George know about the man? He might already be guilty of far greater crimes than the one he proposed.

George thought of Roderick with a knife, a gun, or even his bare hands... And then he thought of those same bare hands ripping away a dress, fastening themselves like hungry mouths on naked flesh. And he saw his face, like the face of one of those fiends in that old copy of *Paradise Lost* with the Doré etchings, the one his mother had owned.

The thought made his hands tremble, made his voice quaver. But he forced himself to be calm as he dialed the long-distance operator from his hotel room, put through the call to the house. And then he heard Ella's voice, and everything was all right.

Everything was fine.

Yes, she could hear him. And no, nothing had happened. Nothing at all. Apparently, whoever had been playing those tricks had decided to stop. She'd been cleaning house all day. And how did he feel?

"Fine, just fine," George said. And meant it. His relief was tremendously exhilarating. He hung up, suddenly jubilant. Ella was undisturbed, and that meant Roderick had been scared off after all.

George went down to the bar for a few drinks. It was still early, and he felt like celebrating. He struck up a conversation with a leather-goods salesman from Des Moines, and they hit a few of the local spots. Eventually his companion picked up a girl and wandered off. George continued on alone for quite a time, blacking out pleasantly every now and then, but always remaining under control; he liked the good feeling that came with knowing he was under control and would always behave like a little gentleman. He had the right to celebrate because he had won a victory.

Roderick had told the truth in a way; for a while George had been tempted to let the scheme go through. But he had changed his mind in time, and Roderick must have known he meant it. Now Ella was safe, and he was safe, and they'd be happy together. Ninety thousand dollars and an island in the West Indies—what a pipe dream! George Foster Pendleton wasn't that kind of a person. And now it was time to find the hotel, find his room, find the keyhole, find the bed, find the whirling darkness and the deep peace that waited within it.

THE NEXT MORNING George had a hangover, and he was feeling pretty rocky as he drove to Bakerton. He made a few calls around noon, but just couldn't seem to hit the ball. So in the afternoon he decided to call it quits, because he still had Friday to finish up there.

He went back to his room intending to take a late afternoon nap, but he slept right straight through. He didn't wake up to eat supper or call Ella or anything.

When he woke up the next morning, he was surprised to find that Ella had apparently called him several times; he had slept right through the rings. But he felt good, and he was out making the rounds by nine.

He called Ella immediately after supper. Her voice was relaxed and reassuring.

"Did you go to the doctor today?" he asked.

She had seen Dr. Vinson, she told him, and everything was fine. He had checked her over thoroughly—cardiograph, blood tests, even head x-rays. There was nothing wrong. He'd given her a few pills for her headaches, that was all.

"Any other disturbances?" George asked.

"No. It's been very quiet here." Ella sounded quite calm. "When are you coming in tomorrow?"

"Around noon, I hope. Right after lunch."

"Right after lunch," Ella repeated. "I'll see you then."

"Good night," George said, and hung up.

He felt very happy, and yet there was something bothering him. He didn't quite know what it was, but there was an uneasy feeling, a feeling of having forgotten an important message. Like when he was a boy and his mother sent him to the store for groceries, and he couldn't remember one of the items on the list

George sat there, holding the phone in his hand, and then he jumped when he heard the tapping on the door.

He got up and opened it and Roderick came into the room. He was smiling gaily.

"Always stay at the best hotel in town, don't you?" he said. "Knew I'd find you here."

"But what—"

"Just thought I ought to take a run over," Roderick said "You're coming back tomorrow, and I figured you'd better be prepared."

"Prepared for what?"

Roderick stood in front of the mirror and cocked his head. "I've been working hard," he told George. "But it's paid off. Like I told you, all I needed was three days."

George opened his mouth, but Roderick wasn't to be interrupted.

"While you've been snoozing away here, I've been up and doing." He chuckled. "No rest for the wicked, you know. Let me give you a quick rundown. Wednesday, the day you left I made a few calls in the evening. The first one was to the savings and loan people—they're open Wednesday nights until nine, you know. I did the Ella impersonation and told them I wanted my money out as soon as I could get it. Talked to old Higgins himself. When he asked why, I told him I was planning on getting a divorce and going to Cuba."

Roderick nodded to himself and continued, "Then I went around to the house and did the mask routine again. Ella was in the kitchen, drinking a glass of milk before she got ready for bed. When she saw me I thought she was going to jump right out of her skin. She ran for the telephone, and I guess she called the police. I didn't wait around to find out.

"Yesterday I figured it might be best to keep away from the house, so I went through the telephone gag again. I talked to Higgins once more and told him I needed the money at once, because you were deathly ill and had to have an operation on your brain. That was a neat touch, wasn't it?

"Then I talked to the bank, and after that I phoned a few stores and had them promise to make deliveries this morning. Just a few odds and ends—a piano, and two trombones from the Music Mart, and seventy-five dozen roses from the florist. Oh yes, as a final touch, I called Phelps Brothers and told them I wanted to stop in and look at a casket because I anticipated a death in the family."

Roderick giggled over that one, almost like a naughty little boy. But his eyes were serious as he continued.

"Finally, I called that old goat, Dr. Vinson, and told him I wanted to cancel my appointment. He couldn't quite figure out why until I told him I was leaving for Europe on a midnight flight. He wanted to know if you were going and I said no, it was a big surprise because I was going to have a baby over there, and you weren't the father.

"After that, I went out to the house—but I was very careful, you understand, in case any cops should happen to be around. Lucky for me I'd anticipated them, because not only was there a prowl car parked down the street, but when I sneaked back through the alley and looked in the kitchen window, I could see this detective talking to Ella in the hall. So I got out of there. But it wasn't necessary to do any more. I could see that. Ella looked like the wrath of God. I don't imagine she'd had any sleep for two nights. And by today, word must have gotten around. Old Higgins in saving and loan will do his share of talking. So will Doc Vinson, and some of the others. And your wife will keep insisting to the police that she saw this face. Now all you have to do is go back and wrap everything up in one neat package."

"What do you mean?" George asked.

"I imagine they'll all be calling you. Your only job is to give the right answers. Tell them that Ella *has* talked about taking a lot of crazy trips. Tell them she wants to hide her money in the house. Tell Doc Vinson she's afraid he wants to poison her, or attack her, or something. You ever hear about paranoid delusions? That's when people get the idea that everybody's persecuting them. Built up a yarn like that. You know what to tell Ella; she's so confused now that she'll go for anything you say. Mix her up a little more. Ask her about things she's told you, like trading in the Buick for a Cadillac. She'll deny she ever said anything like that, and then you drop the subject and bring up something else. A day or two—with a few more looks through the window at the mask—and you'll have *her* convinced she's screwy. That's the most important thing. Then you go to Vinson with a sob story, have her examined while she's scared and woozy, and you've got it made." Roderick laughed. "If you could have seen her face..."

George shook his head in bewilderment. Why was Roderick lying to him? He'd talked to Ella Wednesday night and tonight, and she'd been quite normal. Nothing had happened, nothing at all. And yet here was Roderick, coming a hundred miles and boasting about all kinds of crazy stuff—

Crazy stuff.

Suddenly George knew.

Crazy stuff. A crazy scheme to drive someone crazy. It added up.

Roderick was the crazy one.

That was the answer, the real answer. He was more than cruel, more than childish, more than antisocial. The man was psychotic, criminally insane. And it was all a fantasy; he'd started to carry out his delusions, then halted. The rest of it took place only in his disordered imagination.

George didn't want to look at him, didn't want to hear his voice. He wanted to tell him to go away, wanted to tell him be had just talked to Ella and she was okay, nothing had happened.

But he knew that he mustn't. He couldn't. Roderick would never accept such an answer. He was crazy, and he was dangerous. There had to be some other way of handling him.

All at once, George found the obvious solution.

"I'm all through here," he said. "Thought I might drive back tonight. Want to ride along?"

Roderick nodded. "Why not?" Again the childish giggle. "I get it. You can't wait, isn't that it? Can't wait to see the look on her fat foolish face. Well, go ahead. One good thing, you won't have to look at it very much longer. They're going to put her on ice. And we'll have the sunshine. The sunshine, and the moonlight, and all the rest of it. The tropics are great stuff, George. You're going to be happy there. I know you don't like insects, but even they can come in handy. Take ants, for instance. Suppose one of these girls disobeys us, George. Well, we can tie her to a tree, see? Spread-eagle, sort of. Strip her naked and rub honey all over her. Then the ants come and…"

Roderick talked like that all during the drive back home. Sometimes he whispered and sometimes he giggled, and George got a splitting headache worse than anything Ella could ever have had. But still Roderick kept on talking. He was going to have Ella locked up. He was going to take George to the islands. Sometimes it even sounded as if he meant *the* island, the one where they'd been in the stockade. And he was going to do things to the girls the way the guards used to do things to the prisoners. It was crazy talk, crazy.

The only thing that kept George going was the knowledge that it *was* crazy talk, and if anyone else heard it they'd realize the truth right away. All he had to do was get Roderick into town, stall him on some pretext or other, and call in the police. Of course Roderick would try to implicate George in the scheme, but bow could he? Looking back, George couldn't remember any slip-up on his part; *he* hadn't actually said or done anything out of line. No, it was all Roderick. And that was his salvation.

Still, cold sweat was trickling down his forehead by the time he pulled up in front of the house. It must have been close to midnight, but the front room lights were still burning. That meant Ella was up. Good.

"Wait here," George told Roderick. "I'm just going in to tell her I'm home. Then I'll put the car away."

Roderick seemed to sense that something was phony. "I shouldn't hang around," he said. "What if the cops have a stake out?"

"Let me check on that," George said. "I've got an idea. If the cops aren't here, you could give her one more taste of the rubber mask. Then I can deny seeing it. Get the pitch?"

"Yes." Roderick smiled. "Now you're cooperating, George. Now you're with it. Go ahead."

So George got out of the car and walked up to the front door and opened it.

Ella was waiting for him. She *did* look tired, and she jumped when she saw him, but she was all right. Thank God for that, she was all right! And now he could tell her.

"Don't say a word," George whispered, closing the door. "I've got a lunatic out in the car there."

"Would you mind repeating that?"

George looked around, and sure enough he recognized him. It was the detective he'd talked to after the fire alarm was turned in.

"What are you doing here this time of night?" George asked.

"Just checking up," said the detective. "Now what's all this you were saying about a lunatic?"

So George told him. George told him and he told Ella, and they both listened very quietly and calmly. George had to talk fast, because he didn't want Roderick to get suspicious, and he stumbled over some of his words. Then he asked the detective to sneak out to the car with him before Roderick could get away, and the detective said he would. George warned him that Roderick was dangerous and asked him if he had a gun. The detective had a gun, all right, and George felt better.

They walked right out to the car together, and George yanked open the door.

But Roderick wasn't there.

George couldn't figure it out, and then he realized that Roderick might have been just crazy enough to pull his rubber mask trick without waiting, and he told the detective about that and made him look around under the front windows. The detective wasn't very bright; he didn't seem to understand about the mask part, so George showed him what he meant—how you could stand under the window on this board from the car and look in without leaving any footprints. The detective wanted to know what the mask looked like, but George couldn't quite describe it, and then they were back at the car and the detective opened the glove compartment and pulled something out and asked George if this was the mask he meant.

Of course it was, and George explained that Roderick must have left it there. Then they were back inside the house and Ella was crying, and George didn't want her to cry so he said there was nothing to be frightened about because Roderick was gone. And she didn't have to be afraid if somebody played tricks on her like imitating her voice, because anyone could do that.

The detective asked him if he could, and of course he could do it perfectly. He was almost as good as Roderick, only he had such a splitting headache...

Maybe that's why the doctor came, not Dr. Vinson, but a police doctor, and he made George tell everything all over again. Until George got mad and asked why were they talking to him, the man they should be looking for was Roderick.

It was crazy, that's what it was. They were even crazier than Roderick, the way they carried on. There were more police now, and the detective was trying to tell him that he was the one who had made the calls and worn the mask. He, George! It was utterly ridiculous, and George explained how he had met Roderick on the island in solitary and how he looked like the fiend in the Doré book and everything, and how he was a bad boy.

But the detective said that George's boss had heard him talking to himself in the office the other afternoon and called Ella to tell her, and that she had talked to the police. Then when George went on his trip they'd checked up on him and found he drove back to town the night he got drunk and also the night he said he was sleeping in his hotel room, and that he was the one who had done it all.

Of course they didn't tell him this all at once—there was this trip to the station, and all those doctors who talked to him, and the lawyers and the judge. After a while, George stopped paying attention to them and to that nonsense about schizophrenia and split personalities. His head was splitting, and all he wanted to do was get them to find Roderick. Roderick was the one to blame. Roderick was the crazy one. They had to understand that.

But they didn't understand that, and it was George whom they locked up. George Foster Pendleton, not George Roderick the naughty boy.

Still, George was smarter than they were, in the end. Because he found Roderick again. Even though he was locked up, he found Roderick. Or rather, Roderick found him, and came to visit.

He comes quite often, these days, moving in that quiet way of his and sneaking in when nobody's around to see him. And he talks to George in that soft, almost inaudible voice of his when George sits in front of the mirror. George isn't mad at him any more. He realizes now that Roderick is his best friend, and wants to help him.

Roderick still dreams about getting his hands on all that money and going away with George to the Caribbean. And he has a plan. This time there won't be any slip-ups. He'll get George out of here, even if he has to kill a guard to do it. And he'll kill Ella, too, before he goes.

And then they'll travel on down to the islands, just the two of them. And there'll be girls, and whips gleaming in the moonlight...

Oh, George trusts Roderick now. He's his only friend. And he often wonders just where he'd be without him.

Wide O–

Elsin Ann Gardner

This is Mrs. Gardner's first published story. With it she gives us a fresh talent and a nice soporific for the suburban housewife.

MAYBE I'LL PUT my head under the pillow—no, that's no good at all. I can imagine him, whoever he is, sneaking up on me.

Okay, that does it! I'm going to get up and stay up, put the lights on in the living room, turn on the television. Oh, I hate going into the dark...there! Overhead light on floor lamp on, TV on nice and loud. Now I'll just sit down and relax and watch the—

Hey, what was that? Oh. Old houses creak, remember? If it creaked when Russell was here, it'll creak when he's away, and it's just —just something in the house. It's only your imagination, old girl, that's what it is. And the more sleepy you get, the more vivid your imagination will get.

All the doors are locked, right? And all the windows, ditto. Okay then. So I feel like an idiot, trying to stay up all night. Well, sitting here in the living room is a lot better than doing what I did the *last* time Russ was away overnight! Locking myself in the bathroom and staying there all night, for heaven's sake—

Oh! Oh, the furnace clicked on, that's all *that* was. Calm down, girl, calm down! The trouble with you is, you read the papers. You should read the comics and stop there. No, I have to read *Mother of Three Attacked by Intruder* and *Woman Found Beaten to Death in Home.* But, oooh, they were so close to us! That old lady lived—what was it, only three-four blocks away?

But she lived alone, and nobody knows I'm alone tonight. I hope.

What *is* the matter with me, anyway? I'm acting like a child. Other women live alone—for years, even—and here I have to stay by myself for just one measly little night, and I go all to pieces.

Oh, it sure seems cold in here. The furnace was on—still is on, in fact. Must be my nerves. I'll go into the kitchen and make myself a nice hot cup of tea. Good idea! Maybe that'll warm me up.

Now where is that light switch...there...well, no *wonder* I'm cold, with the back door standing wide o—

Death on Christmas Eve

Stanley Ellin

I read this story years ago when helping on an earlier MWA anthology and it haunted me long after I'd forgotten the title and author. Now it's been rediscovered, and you can see if it haunts you too.

As a child, I had been vastly impressed by the Boerum house. It was fairly new then, and glossy; a gigantic pile of Victorian rickrack, fretwork, and stained glass, flung together in such chaotic profusion that it was hard to encompass in one glance.

Standing before it this early Christmas Eve, however, I could find no echo of that youthful impression. The gloss was long since gone; woodwork, glass, metal, all were merged to a dreary gray, and the shades behind the windows were drawn completely, so that the house seemed to present a dozen blindly staring eyes to the passerby.

When I rapped my stick sharply on the door, Celia opened it.

"There is a doorbell right at hand," she said. She was still wearing the long outmoded and badly wrinkled black dress she must have dragged from her mother's trunk, and she looked, more than ever, the image of old Katrin in her later years: the scrawny body, the tightly compressed lips, the colorless hair drawn back hard enough to pull every wrinkle out of her forehead. She reminded me of a steel trap ready to snap down on anyone who touched her incautiously.

I said, "I am aware that the doorbell has been disconnected, Celia," and walked past her into the hallway. Without turning my head, I knew that she was glaring at me; then she sniffed once, hard and dry, and flung the door shut. Instantly we were in a murky dimness that made the smell of dry rot about me stick in my throat.

I fumbled for the wall switch, but Celia said sharply, "No! This is not the time for lights."

I turned to the white blur of her face, which was all I could see of her. "Celia," I said, "spare me the dramatics."

"There has been a death in this house. You know that."

"I have good reason to," I said, "but your performance now does not impress me."

"She was my own brother's wife. She was very dear to me."

I took a step toward her in the murk and rested my stick on her shoulder. "Celia," I said, "as your family's lawyer, let me give you a word of advice. The inquest is over and done with, and you've been cleared. But nobody believed a word of your precious sentiments then, and nobody ever will. Keep that in mind."

She jerked away so sharply that the stick almost fell from my hand. "Is that what you have come to tell me?"

I said, "I came because I knew your brother would want to see me today. And if you don't mind my saying so, I suggest that you keep to yourself while I talk to him. I don't want any scenes."

"Then keep away from him yourself!" she cried. "He was at the inquest. He saw them clear my name. In a little while he will forget the evil he thinks of me. Keep away from him so that he can forget."

She was at her infuriating worst, and to break the spell I started up the dark stairway, one hand warily on the balustrade. But I heard her follow eagerly behind, and in some eerie way it seemed as if she were not addressing me, but answering the groaning of the stairs under our feet.

"When he comes to me," she said, "I will forgive him. At first I was not sure, but now I know. I prayed for guidance, and I was told that life is too short for hatred. So when he comes to me, I will forgive him."

I reached the head of the stairway and almost went sprawling. I swore in annoyance as I righted myself. "If you're not going to use lights, Celia, you should at least keep the way clear. Why don't you get that stuff out of here?"

"Ah," she said, "those are all poor Jessie's belongings. It hurts Charlie so to see anything of hers, I knew this would be the best thing to do—to throw all her things out."

Then a note of alarm entered her voice. "But you won't tell Charlie, will you? You won't tell him?" she said, and kept repeating it on a higher and higher note as I moved away from her, so that when I entered Charlie's room and closed the door behind me it almost sounded as if I had left a bat chittering behind me.

As in the rest of the house, the shades in Charlie's room were drawn to their full length. But a single bulb in the chandelier overhead dazzled me momentarily, and I had to look twice before I saw Charlie sprawled out on his bed with an arm flung over his eyes. Then he slowly came to his feet and peered at me.

"Well," he said at last, nodding toward the door, "she didn't give you any light to come up, did she?"

"No," I said, "but I know the way."

"She's like a mole," he said. "Gets around better in the dark than I do in the light. She'd rather have it that way, too. Otherwise she might look into a mirror and be scared of what she sees there."

"Yes," I said, "she seems to be taking it very hard."

He laughed, short and sharp as a sea-lion barking. "That's because she's still got the fear in her. All you get out of her now is how she loved Jessie, and how sorry she is. Maybe she figures if she says it enough, people might get to believe it. But give her a little time, and she'll be the same old Celia again."

I dropped my hat and stick on the bed and laid my overcoat beside them. Then I drew out a cigar and waited until he fumbled for a match and helped me to a light. His hand shook so violently that he had hard going for a moment and muttered angrily at himself. Then I slowly exhaled a cloud of smoke toward the ceiling, and waited.

Charlie was Celia's junior by five years, but seeing him then it struck me that he looked a dozen years older. His hair was the same pale blond, almost colorless so that it was hard to tell if it was graying or not. But his cheeks wore a fine, silvery stubble, and there were huge blue-black pouches under his eyes. And where Celia was braced against a rigid and uncompromising backbone, Charlie sagged, standing or sitting, as if he were on the verge of falling forward. He stared at me and tugged uncertainly at the limp mustache that dropped past the corners of his mouth.

"You know what I wanted to see you about, don't you?" he said.

"I can imagine," I said, "but I'd rather have you tell me."

"I'll put it to you straight," he said. "It's Celia. I want to see her get what's coming to her. Not jail. I want the law to take her and kill her, and I want to be there to watch it."

A large ash dropped to the floor, and I ground it carefully into the rug with my foot. I said, "You were at the inquest, Charlie; you saw what happened. Celia's cleared, and unless additional evidence can be produced, she stays cleared."

"Evidence! My God, what more evidence does anyone need! They were arguing hammer and tongs at the top of the stairs. Celia just grabbed Jessie and threw her down to the bottom and killed her. That's murder, isn't it? Just the same as if she used a gun or poison or whatever she would have used if the stairs weren't handy?"

I sat down wearily in the old leather-bound armchair there and studied the new ash forming on my cigar. "Let me show it to you from the legal angle," I said, and the monotone of my voice must have made it sound like a well-memorized formula. "First, there were no witnesses."

"I heard Jessie scream and I heard her fall," he said doggedly, "and when I ran out and found her there, I heard Celia slam her door shut right then. She pushed Jessie and then scuttered like a rat to be out of the way."

"But you didn't *see* anything. And since Celia claims that she wasn't on the scene, there were no witnesses. In other words, Celia's story cancels out your story, and since you weren't an eyewitness, you can't very well make a murder out of what might have been an accident."

He slowly shook his head.

"You don't believe that," he said. "You don't really believe that. Because if you do, you can get out now and never come near me again."

"It doesn't matter what I believe; I'm showing you the legal aspects of the case. What about motivation? What did Celia have to gain from Jessie's death? Certainly there's no money or property involved; she's as financially independent as you are."

Charlie sat down on the edge of his bed and leaned toward me with his hands resting on his knees. "No," he whispered, "there's no money or property in it."

I spread my arms helplessly. "You see?"

"But you know what it is," he said. "It's me. First, it was the old lady with her heart trouble any time I tried to call my soul my own. Then, when she died and I thought I was free, it was Celia. From the time I got up in the morning until I went to bed at night, it was Celia every step of the way. She never had a husband or a baby—but she had me!"

I said quietly, "She's your sister, Charlie. She loves you," and he laughed that same unpleasant, short laugh.

"She loves me like ivy loves a tree. When I think back now, I still can't see how she did it, but she would just look at me a certain way and all the strength would go out of me. And it was like that until I met Jessie... I remember the day I brought Jessie home, and told Celia we were married. She swallowed it, but that look was in her eyes the same as it must have been when she pushed Jessie down those stairs."

I said, "But you admitted at the inquest that you never saw her threaten Jessie or do anything to hurt her."

"Of course I never *saw!* But when Jessie would go around sick to her heart every day and not say a word, or cry in bed every night and not tell me why, I knew damn well what was going on. You know what Jessie was like. She wasn't so smart or pretty, but she was good-hearted as the day was long, and she was crazy about me. And when she started losing all that sparkle after only a month, I knew why. I talked to her and I talked to Celia, and both of them just shook their heads. All I could do was go around in circles, but when it happened, when I saw Jessie lying there, it didn't surprise me. Maybe that sounds queer, but it didn't surprise me at all."

"I don't think it surprised anyone who knows Celia," I said, "but you can't make a case out of that."

He beat his fist against his knee and rocked from side to side. "What can I do?" he said. "That's what I need you for—to tell me what to do. All my life I never got around to doing anything because of her. That's what she's banking on now—that I won't do anything, and that she'll get away with it. Then after a while, things'll settle down, and we'll be right back where we started from."

I said, "Charlie, you're getting yourself all worked up to no end."

He stood up and stared at the door, and then at me. "But I can do something," he whispered. "Do you know what?"

He waited with the bright expectancy of one who has asked a clever riddle that he knows will stump the listener. I stood up facing him, and shook my head slowly. "No," I said. "Whatever you're thinking, put it out of your mind."

"Don't mix me up," he said. "You know you can get away with murder if you're as smart as Celia. Don't you think I'm as smart as Celia?"

I caught his shoulders tightly. "For God's sake, Charlie," I said, "don't start talking like that."

He pulled out of my hands and went staggering back against the wall. His eyes were bright, and his teeth showed behind his drawn lips. "What should I do?" he cried. "Forget everything now that Jessie is dead and buried? Sit here until Celia gets tired of being afraid of me and kills me, too?"

My years and girth had betrayed me in that little tussle with him, and I found myself short of dignity and breath. "I'll tell you one thing," I said. "You haven't been out of this house since the inquest. It's about time you got out, if only to walk the streets and look around you."

"And have everybody laugh at me as I go!"

"Try it," I said, "and see. Al Sharp said that some of your friends would be at his bar and grill tonight, and he'd like to see you there. That's my advice—for whatever it's worth."

"It's not worth anything," said Celia. The door had been opened, and she stood there rigid, her eyes narrowed against the light in the room.

Charlie turned toward her, the muscles of his jaw knotting and unknotting. "Celia," he said, "I told you never to come into this room!"

Her face remained impassive. "I'm not *in* it. I came to tell you that your dinner is ready."

He took a menacing step toward her. "Did you have your ear at that door long enough to hear everything I said? Or should I repeat it for you?"

"I heard an ungodly and filthy thing," she said quietly, "an invitation to drink and roister while this house is in mourning. I think I have every right to object to that."

He looked at her incredulously and had to struggle for words. "Celia," he said, "tell me you don't mean that! Only the blackest hypocrite alive or someone insane could say what you've just said, and mean it."

That struck a spark in her. "Insane!" she cried. "*You* dare use that word? Locked in your room, talking to yourself, thinking heaven knows what!" She turned to me suddenly. "You've talked to him. You ought to know. Is it possible that—"

"He is as sane as you, Celia," I said heavily.

"Then he should know that one doesn't drink in saloons at a time like this. How could you ask him to do it?"

She flung the question at me with such an air of malicious triumph that I completely forgot myself. "If you weren't preparing to throw out Jessie's belongings, Celia, I would take that question seriously!"

It was a reckless thing to say, and I had instant cause to regret it. Before I could move, Charlie was past me and had Celia's arms pinned in a paralyzing grip.

"Did you dare go into her room?" he raged, shaking her savagely. "Tell me!" And then, getting an immediate answer from the panic in her face, he dropped her arms as if they were red hot, and stood there sagging with his head bowed.

Celia reached out a placating hand toward him. "Charlie," she whimpered, "don't you see? Having her things around bothers you. I only wanted to help you."

"Where are her things?"

"By the stairs, Charlie. Everything is there."

He started down the hallway, and with the sound of his uncertain footsteps moving away I could feel my heartbeat slowing down to its normal tempo. Celia turned to look at me, and there was such a raging hatred in her face that I knew only a desperate need to get out of that house at once. I took my things from the bed and started past her, but she barred the door.

"Do you see what you've done?" she whispered hoarsely. "Now I will have to pack them all over again. It tires me, but I will have to pack them all over again—just because of you."

"That is entirely up to you, Celia," I said coldly.

"You," she said. "You old fool. It should have been you along with her when I—"

I dropped my stick sharply on her shoulder and could feel her wince under it. "As your lawyer, Celia," I said, "I advise you to exercise your tongue only during your sleep, when you can't be held accountable for what you say."

She said no more, but I made sure she stayed safely in front of me until I was out in the street again.

FROM THE BOERUM house to Al Sharp's Bar and Grill was only a few minutes' walk, and I made it in good time, grateful for the sting of the clear winter air in my face.

Al was alone behind the bar, busily polishing glasses, and when he saw me enter he greeted me cheerfully. "Merry Christmas, counsellor."

"Same to you," I said, and watched him place a comfortable-looking bottle and a pair of glasses on the bar.

"You're regular as the seasons, counsellor," said Al, pouring out two stiff ones. "I was expecting you along right about now."

We drank to each other, and Al leaned confidingly on the bar. "Just come from there?"

"Yes," I said.

"See Charlie?"

"And Celia," I said.

"Well," said Al, "that's nothing exceptional. I've seen her too when she comes by to do some shopping. Runs along with her head down and that black shawl over it like she was being chased by something. I guess she is at that."

"I guess she is," I said.

"But Charlie, he's the one. Never see him around at all. Did you tell him I'd like to see him some time?"

"Yes," I said. "I told him."

"What did he say?"

"Nothing. Celia said it was wrong for him to come here while he was in mourning."

Al whistled softly and expressively, and twirled a forefinger at his forehead. "Tell me," be said, "do you think it's safe for them to be alone together like they are? I mean, the way things stand, and the way Charlie feels, there could be another case of trouble there."

"It looked like it for a while tonight," I said. "But it blew over."

"Until next time," said Al.

"I'll be there," I said.

Al looked at me and shook his head. "Nothing changes in that house," he said. "Nothing at all. That's why you can figure out all the answers in advance. That's how I knew you'd be standing here right about now talking to me about it."

I could still smell the dry rot of the house in my nostrils, and knew it would take days before I could get it out of my clothes.

"This is one day I'd like to cut out of the calendar permanently," I said.

"And leave them alone to their troubles. It would serve them right."

"They're not alone," I said. "Jessie is with them. Jessie will always be with them until that house and everything in it is gone."

Al frowned. "It's the queerest thing that ever happened in this town, all right. The house all black, her running through the streets like something hunted, him lying there in that room with only the walls to look at, for—when was it Jessie took that fall, counsellor?"

By shifting my eyes a little I could see in the mirror behind Al the reflection of my own face: ruddy, deep jowled, a little incredulous.

"Twenty years ago," I heard myself saying. "Just twenty years ago tonight."

Gone Girl

Ross Macdonald

Carpers like to claim that Ross MacDonald copies Raymond Chandler. Don't kid yourself. He sets his stories in the same hunk of real estate, but Ross Macdonald is Ross Macdonald. And that's about as good as you can get.

IT WAS A FRIDAY NIGHT. I was tooling home from the Mexican border in a light blue convertible and a dark blue mood. I had followed a man from Fresno to San Diego and lost him in the maze of streets in Old Town. When I picked up his trail again, it was cold. He had crossed the border, and my instructions went no further than the United States.

Halfway home, just above Emerald Bay, I overtook the worst driver in the world. He was driving a black fishtail Cadillac as if he were tacking a sailboat. The heavy car wove back and forth across the freeway, using two of its four lanes, and sometimes three. It was late, and I was in a hurry to get some sleep. I started to pass it on the right, at a time when it was riding the double line. The Cadillac drifted towards me like an unguided missile, and forced me off the road in a screeching skid.

I speeded up to pass on the left. Simultaneously, the driver of the Cadillac accelerated. My acceleration couldn't match his. We raced neck and neck down the middle of the road. I wondered if he was drunk or crazy or afraid of me. Then the freeway ended. I was doing eighty on the wrong side of a two-lane highway, and a truck came over a rise ahead like a blazing double comet. I floorboarded the gas pedal and cut over sharply to the right, threatening the Cadillac's fenders and its driver's life. In the approaching headlights, his face was as blank and white as a piece of paper, with charred black holes for eyes. His shoulders were naked.

At the last possible second, he slowed enough to let me get by. The truck went off onto the shoulder, honking angrily. I braked gradually, hoping to force the Cadillac to stop. It looped past me in an insane arc, tires skittering, and was sucked away into darkness.

When I finally came to a full stop, I had to pry my fingers off the wheel. My knees were remote and watery. After smoking part of a cigarette, I U-turned and drove very cautiously back to Emerald Bay. I was long past the hot-rod age, and I needed rest.

The first motel I came to, the Siesta, was decorated with a *Vacancy* sign and a neon Mexican sleeping luminously under a sombrero. Envying him, I parked on the gravel apron in front of the motel office. There was a light inside. The glass-paned door was standing open, and I went in. The little room was pleasantly furnished with rattan and chintz. I jangled the bell on the desk a few times. No one appeared, so I sat down to wait and lit a cigarette. An electric clock on the wall said a quarter to one.

I must have dozed for a few minutes. A dream rushed by the threshold of my consciousness, making a gentle noise. Death was in the dream. He drove a black Cadillac loaded with flowers. When I woke up, the cigarette was starting to burn my fingers. A thin man in a gray flannel shirt was standing over me with a doubtful look on his face.

He was big-nosed and small-chinned, and he wasn't as young as he gave the impression of being. His teeth were bad, the sandy hair was thinning and receding. He was the typical old youth who scrounged and wheedled his living around motor courts and restaurants and hotels, and hung on desperately to the frayed edge of other people's lives.

"What do you want?" he said. "Who are you? What do you want?" His voice was reedy and changeable like an adolescent's.

"A room."

"Is that all you want?"

From where I sat, it sounded like an accusation. I let it pass. "What else is there? Circassian dancing girls? Free popcorn?"

He tried to smile without showing his bad teeth. The smile was a dismal failure, like my joke. "I'm sorry, sir," he said. "You woke me up. I never make much sense right after I just wake up."

"Have a nightmare?"

His vague eyes expanded like blue bubblegum bubbles. "Why did you ask me that?"

"Because I just had one. But skip it. Do you have a vacancy or don't you?"

"Yes, sir. Sorry, sir." He swallowed whatever bitter taste he had in his mouth, and assumed an impersonal obsequious manner. "You got any luggage, sir?"

"No luggage."

Moving silently in tennis sneakers like a frail ghost of the boy he once had been, he went behind the counter, and took my name, address, license number, and five dollars. In return, he gave me a key numbered fourteen and told me where to use it. Apparently he despaired of a tip.

Room fourteen was like any other middle-class motel room touched with the California-Spanish mania. Artificially roughened plaster painted adobe color, poinsettia-red curtains, imitation parchment lampshade on a twisted black iron stand. A Rivera reproduction of a sleeping Mexican hung on the wall over the bed. I succumbed to its suggestion right away, and dreamed about Circassian dancing girls.

Along toward morning one of them got frightened, through no fault of mine, and began to scream her little Circassian lungs out. I sat up in bed, making soothing noises, and woke up. It was nearly nine by my wristwatch. The screaming ceased and began again, spoiling the morning like a fire siren outside the window. I pulled on my trousers over the underwear I'd been sleeping in, and went outside.

A young woman was standing on the walk outside the next room.

She had a key in one hand and a handful of blood in the other. She wore a wide multi-colored skirt and a low-cut gypsy sort of blouse. The blouse was distended and her mouth was open, and she was yelling her head off. It was a fine dark head, but I hated her for spoiling my morning sleep.

I took her by the shoulders and said, "Stop it."

The screaming stopped. She looked down sleepily at the blood on her hand. It was as thick as axle grease, and almost as dark in color.

"Where did you get that?"

"I slipped and fell in it. I didn't see it."

Dropping the key on the walk, she pulled her skirt to one side with her clean hand. Her legs were bare and brown. Her skirt was stained at the back with the same thick fluid.

"Where? In this room?"

She faltered, "Yes."

Doors were opening up and down the drive. Half a dozen people began to converge on us. A dark-faced man about four and a half feet high came scampering from the direction of the office, his little pointed shoes dancing in the gravel.

"Come inside and show me," I said to the girl.

"I can't. I won't." Her eyes were very heavy, and surrounded by the bluish pallor of shock.

The little man slid to a stop between us, reached up and gripped the upper part of her arm. "What is the matter, Ella? Are you crazy, disturbing the guests?"

She said, "Blood," and leaned against me with her eyes closed.

His sharp glance probed the situation. He turned to the other guests, who had formed a murmuring semicircle around us. "It is perfectly hokay. Do not be concerned, ladies and gentlemen. My daughter cut herself a little bit. It is perfectly all right."

Circling her waist with one long arm, he hustled her through the open door and slammed it behind him. I caught it on my foot and followed them in.

The room was a duplicate of mine, including the reproduction over the unmade bed, but everything was reversed as in a mirror image. The girl took a few weak steps by herself and sat on the edge of the bed. Then she noticed the blood spots on the sheets. She stood up quickly. Her mouth opened, rimmed with white teeth.

"Don't do it," I said. "We know you have a very fine pair of lungs."

The little man turned on me. "Who do you think you are?"

"The name is Archer. I have the next room."

"Get out of this one, please."

"I don't think I will."

He lowered his greased black head as if he were going to butt me. Under his sharkskin jacket, a hunch protruded from his back like a displaced elbow. He seemed to reconsider the butting gambit, and decided in favor of diplomacy.

"You are jumping to conclusions, mister. It is not so serious as it looks. We had a little accident here last night."

"Sure, your daughter cut herself. She heals remarkably fast."

"Nothing like that." He fluttered one long hand. "I said to the people outside the first thing that came to my mind. Actually, it was a little scuffle. One of the guests suffered a nosebleed."

The girl moved like a sleepwalker to the bathroom door and switched on the light. There was a pool of blood coagulating on the black and white checkerboard linoleum, streaked where she had slipped and fallen in it.

"Some nosebleed," I said to the little man. "Do you run this joint?"

"I am the proprietor of the Siesta motor hotel, yes. My name is Salanda. The gentleman is susceptible to nosebleed. He told me so himself."

"Where is he now?"

"He checked out early this morning."

"In good health?"

"Certainly in good health."

I looked around the room. Apart from the unmade bed with the brown spots on the sheets, it contained no signs of occupancy. Someone had spilled a pint of blood and vanished.

The little man opened the door wide and invited me with a sweep of his arm to leave. "If you will excuse me, sir, I wish to have this cleaned up as quickly as possible. Ella, will you tell Lorraine to get to work on it right away pronto? Then maybe you better lie down for a little while, eh?"

"I'm all right now, father. Don't worry about me."

WHEN I CHECKED out a few minutes later, she was sitting behind the desk in the front office, looking pale but composed.

I dropped my key on the desk in front of her. "Feeling better, Ella?"

"Oh. I didn't recognize you with all your clothes on."

"That's a good line. May I use it?"

She lowered her eyes and blushed. "You're making fun of me. I know I acted foolishly this morning."

"I'm not so sure. What do *you* think happened in thirteen last night?"

"My father told you, didn't he?"

"He gave me a version, two of them, in fact. I doubt that they're the final shooting script."

Her hand went to the central hollow in her blouse. Her arms and shoulders were slender and brown, the tips of her fingers carmine. "Shooting?"

"A cinema term," I said. "But there might have been a real shooting at that. Don't you think so?"

Her front teeth pinched her lower lip. She looked like somebody's pet rabbit. I restrained an impulse to pat her sleek brown head.

"That's ridiculous. This is a respectable motel. Anyway, father asked me not to discuss it with anybody."

"Why would he do that?"

"He loves this place, that's why. He doesn't want any scandal made out of nothing. If we lost our good reputation here, it would break my father's heart."

"He doesn't strike me as the sentimental type."

She stood up, smoothing her skirt. I saw that she'd changed it. "You leave him alone. He's a dear little man. I don't know what you think you're doing, trying to stir up trouble where there isn't any."

I backed away from her righteous indignation—female indignation is always righteous—and went out to my car. The early spring sun was dazzling. Beyond the freeway and the drifted sugary dunes, the bay was Prussian blue. The road cut inland across the base of the peninsula and returned to the sea a few miles north of the town. Here a wide blacktop parking space shelved off to the left of the highway, overlook ing the white beach and whiter breakers. Signs at each end of the turnout stated that this was a *County Park, No Beach Fires.*

The beach and the blacktop expanse above it were deserted except for a single car, which looked very lonely. It was a long black Cadillac nosed into the cable fence at the edge of the beach. I braked and turned off the highway and got out. The man in the driver's seat of the Cadillac didn't turn his head as I approached him. His chin was propped on the steering wheel, and he was gazing out across the endless blue sea.

I opened the door and looked into his face. It was paper white. The dark brown eyes were sightless. The body was unclothed except for the thick hair matted on the chest, and a clumsy bandage tied around the waist. The bandage was composed of several blood-stained towels, held in place by a knotted piece of nylon fabric whose nature I didn't recognize immediately. Examining it more closely, I saw that it was a woman's slip. The left breast of the garment was embroidered in purple with a heart, containing the name, *"Fern,"* in slanting script. I wondered who Fern was.

The man who was wearing her purple heart had dark curly hair, heavy black eyebrows, a heavy chin sprouting black beard. He was rough-looking in spite of his anemia and the lipstick smudged on his mouth.

There was no registration on the steering post, and nothing in the glove compartment but a half-empty box of shells for a .38 automatic. The ignition was still turned on. So were the dash and headlights, but they were dim. The gas gauge registered empty. Curlyhead must have pulled off the highway soon after he passed me, and driven all the rest of the night in one place.

I untied the slip, which didn't look as if it would take fingerprints, and went over it for a label. It had one: *Gretchen, Palm Springs.* It occurred to me that it was Saturday morning, and that I'd gone all winter without a weekend in the desert. I retied the slip the way I'd found it, and drove back to the Siesta Motel.

Ella's welcome was a few degrees colder than absolute zero. "Well!" She glared down her pretty rabbit nose at me. "I thought we were rid of you."

"So did I. But I just couldn't tear myself away."

She gave me a peculiar look, neither hard nor soft. but mixed. Her hand went to her hair, then reached for a registration card. "I suppose if you want to rent a room, I can't stop you. Only please don't imagine you're making an impression on me. You're not. You leave me cold, mister."

"Archer," I said. "Lew Archer. Don't bother with the card. I came back to use your phone."

"Aren't there any other phones?" She pushed the telephone across the desk. "I guess it's all right, long as it isn't a toll call."

"I'm calling the Highway Patrol. Do you know their local number?"

"I don't remember." She handed me the telephone directory.

"There's been an accident," I said as I dialed.

"A highway accident? Where did it happen?"

"Right here, sister. Right here in room thirteen."

But I didn't tell that to the Highway Patrol. I told them I had found a dead man in a car on the parking lot above the county beach. The girl listened with widening eyes and nostrils. Before I finished, she rose in a flurry and left the office by the rear door.

She came back with the proprietor. His eyes were black and bright, like nailheads in leather, and the scampering dance of his feet was almost frenzied. "What is this?"

"I came across a dead man up the road a piece."

"So why do you come back here to telephone?" His head was in butting position, his hands outspread and gripping the corners of the desk. "Has it got anything to do with us?"

"He's wearing a couple of your towels."

"What?"

"And he was bleeding heavily before he died. I think somebody shot him in the stomach. Maybe you did."

"You're *loco*," he said, but not very emphatically. "Crazy accusations like that, they will get you into trouble. What is your business?"

"I'm a private detective."

"You followed him here, is that it? You were going to arrest him, so he shot himself?"

"Wrong on both accounts," I said. "I came here to sleep. And they don't shoot themselves in the stomach. It's too uncertain, and slow. No suicide wants to die of peritonitis."

"So what are you doing now, trying to make scandal for my business?"

"If your business includes trying to cover for murder."

"He shot himself," the little man insisted.

"How do you know?"

"Donny. I spoke to him just now."

"And how does Donny know?"

"The man told him."

"Is Donny your night keyboy?"

"He was. I think I will fire him, for stupidity. He didn't even tell me about this mess. I had to find it out for myself. The hard way."

"Donny means well," the girl said at his shoulder. "I'm sure he didn't realize what happened."

"Who does?" I said. "I want to talk to Donny. But first let's have a look at the register."

He took a pile of cards from a drawer and riffled through them. His large hands, hairy-backed, were calm and expert, like animals that lived a serene life of their own, independent of their emotional owner. They dealt me one of the cards across the desk. It was inscribed in block capitals: Richard Rowe, Detroit, Mich.

I said: "There was a woman with him."

"Impossible."

"Or he was a transvestite."

He surveyed me blankly, thinking of something else. "The HP, did you tell them to come here? They know it happened here?"

"Not yet. But they'll find your towels. He used them for a bandage."

"I see. Yes. Of course." He struck himself with a clenched fist on the temple. It made a noise like someone maltreating a pumpkin.

"You are a private detective, you say. Now if you informed the police that you were on the trail of a fugitive , a fugitive from justice... He shot himself rather than face arrest... For five hundred dollars?"

"I'm not that private," I said. "I have some public responsibility. Besides, the cops would do a little checking and catch me out."

"Not necessarily. He *was* a fugitive from justice, you know."

"I hear you telling me."

"Give me a little time, and I can even present you with his record."

The girl was leaning back away from her father, her eyes starred with broken illusions. "Daddy," she said weakly.

He didn't hear her. All of his bright black attention was fixed on me. "Seven hundred dollars?"

"No sale. The higher you raise it, the guiltier you look. Were you here last night?"

"You are being absurd," he said. "I spent the entire evening with my wife. We drove up to Los Angeles to attend the ballet." By way of supporting evidence, he hummed a couple of bars from Tchaikovsky. "We didn't arrive back here in Emerald Bay until nearly two o'clock."

"Alibis can be fixed."

"By criminals, yes," he said. "I am not a criminal."

The girl put a hand on his shoulder. He cringed away, his face creased by monkey fury, but his face was hidden from her.

"Daddy," she said. "Was he murdered, do you think?"

"How do I know?" His voice was wild and high, as if she had touched the spring of his emotion. "I wasn't here. I only know what Donny told me."

The girl was examining me with narrowed eyes, as if I were a new kind of animal she had discovered and was trying to think of a use for.

"This gentleman is a detective," she said, "or claims to be."

I pulled out my photostat and slapped it down on the desk. The little man picked it up and looked from it to my face. "Will you go to work for me?"

"Doing what, telling little white lies?"

The girl answered for him: "See what you can find out about this —this death. On my word of honor, Father had nothing to do with it."

I made a snap decision, the kind you live to regret. "All right. I'll take a fifty-dollar advance. Which is a good deal less than five hundred. My first advice to you is to tell the police everything you know. Provided that you're innocent."

"You insult me," he said.

But he flicked a fifty-dollar bill from the cash drawer and pressed it into my hand fervently, like a love token. I had a queasy feeling that I had been conned into taking his money, not much of it, but enough. The feeling deepened when he still refused to talk. I had to use all the arts of persuasion even to get Donny's address out of him.

The keyboy lived in a shack on the edge of a desolate stretch of dunes. I guessed that it had once been somebody's beach house before sand had drifted like unthawing snow in the angles of the walls and winter storms had broken the tiles and cracked the concrete foundations. Huge chunks of concrete were piled haphazardly on what had once been a terrace overlooking the sea.

On one of the tilted slabs, Donny was stretched like a long albino lizard in the sun. The onshore wind carried the sound of my motor to his ears. He sat up blinking, recognized me when I stopped the car, and ran into the house.

I descended flagstone steps and knocked on the warped door. "Open up, Donny."

"Go away," he answered huskily. His eye gleamed like a snail through a crack in the wood.

"I'm working for Mr. Salanda. He wants us to have a talk."

"You can go and take a running jump at yourself, you and Mr. Salanda both."

"Open it or I'll break it down."

I waited for a while. He shot back the bolt. The door creaked reluctantly open. He leaned against the doorpost, searching my face with his eyes, his hairless body shivering from an internal chill.

I pushed past him, through a kitchenette that was indescribably filthy, littered with the remnants of old meals, and gaseous with their odors. He followed me silently on bare soles into a larger room whose sprung floorboards undulated under my feet. The picture window had been broken and patched with cardboard. The stone fireplace was choked with garbage. The only furniture was an army cot in one corner where Donny apparently slept.

"Nice homey place you have here. It has that lived-in quality."

He seemed to take it as a compliment, and I wondered if I was dealing with a moron. "It suits me. I never was much of a one for fancy quarters. I like it here, where I can hear the ocean at night."

"What else do you hear at night, Donny?"

He missed the point of the question, or pretended to. "All different things. Big trucks going past on the highway. I like to hear those night sounds. Now I guess I can't go on living here. Mr. Salanda owns it, he lets me live here for nothing. Now he'll be kicking me out of here, I guess."

"On account of what happened last night?"

"Uh-huh." He subsided onto the cot, his doleful head supported by his hands.

I stood over him. "Just what did happen last night, Donny?"

"A bad thing," he said. "This fella checked in about ten o'clock—"

"The man with the dark curly hair?"

"That's the one. He checked in about ten, and I gave him room thirteen. Around about midnight I thought I heard a gun go off from there. It took me a little while to get my nerve up, then I went back to see what was going on. This fella came out of the room, without no clothes on. Just some kind of bandage around his waist. He looked like some kind of a crazy Indian or something. He had a gun in his hand, and he was staggering, and I could see that he was bleeding some. He come right up to me and pushed the gun in my gut and told me to keep my trap shut. He said I wasn't to tell anybody I saw him, now or later. He said if I opened my mouth about it to anybody, that he would come back and kill me. But now he's dead, isn't he?"

"He's dead."

I could smell the fear on Donny: there's an unexplained trace of canine in my chromosomes. The hairs were prickling on the back of my neck, and I wondered if Donny's fear was of the past or for the future. The pimples stood out in bas-relief against his pale, lugubrious face.

"I think he was murdered, Donny. You're lying, aren't you?"

"Me lying?" But his reaction was slow and feeble.

"The dead man didn't check in alone. He had a woman with him."

"What woman?" he said in elaborate surprise.

"You tell me. Her name was Fern. I think she did the shooting, and you caught her red-handed. The wounded man got out of the room and into his car and away. The woman stayed behind to talk to you. She probably paid you to dispose of his clothes and fake a new registration card for the room. But you both overlooked the blood on the floor of the bathroom. Am I right?"

"You couldn't be wronger, mister. Are you a cop?"

"A private detective. You're in deep trouble, Donny. You'd better talk yourself out of it if you can, before the cops start on you."

"I didn't do anything." His voice broke like a boy's. It went strangely with the glints of gray in his hair.

"Faking the register is a serious rap, even if they don't hang accessory to murder on you."

He began to expostulate in formless sentences that ran together. At the same time his hand was moving across the dirty gray blanket. It burrowed under the pillow and came out holding a crumpled card. He tried to stuff it into his mouth and chew it. I tore it away from between his discolored teeth.

It was a registration card from the motel, signed in a boyish scrawl: *Mr. and Mrs. Richard Rowe, Detroit, Mich.*

Donny was trembling violently. Below his cheap cotton shorts, his bony knees vibrated like tuning forks. "It wasn't my fault," he cried. "She held a gun on me."

"What did you do with the man's clothes?"

"Nothing. She didn't even let me into the room. She bundled them up and took them away herself."

'Where did she go?"

"Down the highway toward town. She walked away on the shoulder of the road and that was the last I saw of her."

"How much did she pay you, Donny?"

"Nothing, not a cent. I already told you, she held a gun on me."

"And you were so scared you kept quiet until this morning?"

"That's right. I was scared. Who wouldn't be scared?"

"She's gone now," I said. "You can give me a description of her."

"Yeah." He made a visible effort to pull his vague thoughts together. One of his eyes was a little off center, lending his face a stunned, amorphous appearance. "She was a big tall dame with blondey hair."

"Dyed?"

"I guess so, I dunno. She wore it in a braid like, on top of her head She was kind of fat, built like a lady wrestler, great big watermelons on her. Big legs,"

"How was she dressed?"

"I didn't hardly notice, I was so scared. I think she had some kind of a purple coat on, with black fur around the neck. Plenty of rings on her fingers and stuff."

"How old?"

"Pretty old, I'd say. Older than me, and I'm going on thirty-nine."

"And she did the shooting?"

"I guess so. She told me to say if anybody asked me, I was to say that Mr. Rowe shot himself."

"You're very suggestible, aren't you, Donny? It's a dangerous way to be, with people pushing each other around the way they do."

"I didn't get that, mister. Come again?" He batted his pale blue eyes at me, smiling expectantly.

"Skip it," I said and left him.

A few hundred yards up the highway, I passed an HP car with two uniformed men in the front seat looking grim. Donny was in for it now. I pushed him out of my mind and drove across country to Palm Springs.

Palm Springs is still a one-horse town, but the horse is a Palomino with silver trappings. Most of the girls were Palominos, too. The main street was a cross-section of Hollywood and Vine transported across the desert by some unnatural force and disguised in western costumes which fooled nobody. Not even me.

I found Gretchen's lingerie shop in an expensive-looking arcade built around an imitation flagstone patio. In the patio's center a little fountain gurgled pleasantly, flinging small lariats of spray against the heat. It was late in March, and the season was ending. Most of the shops, including the one I entered, were deserted except for the hired help.

It was a small shop, faintly perfumed by a legion of vanished dolls. Stocking and robes and other garments were coiled on the glass counters or hung like brilliant tree snakes on display stands along the narrow walls. A henna-headed woman emerged from rustling recesses at the rear and came tripping towards me on her toes.

"You are looking for a gift, sir?" she cried with a wilted kind of gaiety. Behind her painted mask, she was tired and aging, and it was Saturday afternoon and the lucky ones were dunking themselves in kidney-shaped swimming pools behind walls she couldn't climb.

"Not exactly. In fact, not at all. A peculiar thing happened to me last night. I'd like to tell you about it, but it's kind of a complicated story."

She looked me over quizzically and decided that I worked for a living, too. The phony smile faded away. Another smile took its place, which I liked better. "You look as if you'd had a fairly rough night And you could do with a shave."

"I met a girl," I said. "Actually she was a mature woman, a statuesque blond to be exact. I picked her up on the beach at Laguna, if you want me to be brutally frank."

"I couldn't bear it if you weren't. What kind of a pitch is this, brother?"

"Wait. You're spoiling my story. Something clicked when we met, in that sunset light, on the edge of the warm summer sea."

"It's always bloody cold when I go in."

"It wasn't last night. We swam in the moonlight and had a gay time and all. Then she went away. I didn't realize until she was gone that I didn't know her telephone number, or even her last name."

"Married woman, eh? What do you think I am, a lonely hearts club?" Still, she was interested, though she probably didn't believe me. "She mentioned me, is that it? What was her first name?"

"Fern."

"Unusual name. You say she was a big blonde?"

"Magnificently proportioned," I said. "If I had a classical education I'd call her Junoesque.'"

"You're kidding me, aren't you?"

"A little."

"I thought so. Personally I don't mind a little kidding. What did she say about me?"

"Nothing but good. As a matter of fact, I was complimenting her on her—er—garments."

"I see." She was long past blushing. "We had a customer last fall some time, by the name of Fern. Fern Dee. She had some kind of a job at the Joshua Club, I think. But she doesn't fit the description at all. This one was a brunette, a middle-sized brunette, quite young. I remember the name Fern because she wanted it embroidered on all the things she bought. A corny idea if you ask me, but that was her girlish desire, and who am I to argue with girlish desires?"

"Is she still in town?"

"I haven't see her lately, not for months. But it couldn't be the woman you're looking for. Or could it?"

"How long ago was she in here?"

She pondered. "Early last fall, around the start of the season. She only came in that once, and made a big purchase, stockings and nightwear and underthings. The works. I remember thinking at the time, here was a girlie who suddenly hit the chips but heavily."

"She might have put on weight since then, and dyed her hair. Strange things can happen to the female form."

"You're telling me," she said. "How old was—your friend?"

"About forty, I'd say, give or take a little."

"It couldn't be the same one then. The girl I'm talking about was twenty-five at the outside, and I don't make mistakes about women's ages. I've seen too many of them in all stages, from Quentin quail to hags, and I certainly do mean hags."

"I bet you have."

She studied me with eyes shadowed by mascara and experience. "You a policeman?"

"I have been."

"You want to tell mother what it's all about?"

"Another time. Where's the Joshua Club?"

"It won't be open yet."

"I'll try it anyway."

She shrugged her thin shoulders and gave me directions. I thanked her.

THE JOSHUA CLUB occupied a plain-faced one-story building half a block off the main street. The padded leather door swung inward when I pushed it. I passed through a lobby with a retractable roof, which contained a jungle growth of banana trees.

The big main room was decorated with tinted desert photomurals. Behind a rattan bar with a fishnet canopy, a white-coated Caribbean type was drying shot glasses with a dirty towel. His face looked uncommunicative.

On the orchestra dais beyond the piled chairs in the dining area, a young man in shirt sleeves was playing bop piano. His fingers shadowed the tune, ran circles around it, played leapfrog with it, and managed never to hit it on the nose. I stood beside him for a while and listened to him work. He looked up finally, still strumming with his left hand in the bass. He had soft-centered eyes and frozen-looking nostrils and a whistling mouth.

"Nice piano," I said.

"I think so."

"Fifty-second Street?"

"It's the street with the beat and I'm not effete." His left hand struck the same chord three times and dropped away from the keys. "Looking for somebody, friend?"

"Fern Dee. She asked me to drop by some time."

"Too bad. Another wasted trip. She left here end of last year, the dear. She wasn't a bad little nightingale, but she was no pro, Joe, you know? She had it, but she couldn't project it. When she warbled the evening died, no matter how hard she tried, I don't wanna be snide."

"Where did she lam, Sam, or don't you give a damn?"

He smiled like a corpse in a deft mortician's hands. "I heard the boss retired her to private life. Took her home to live with him. That is what I heard. But I don't mix with the big boy socially, so I couldn't say for sure that she's impure. Is it anything to you?"

"Something, but she's over twenty-one."

"Not more than a couple of years over twenty-one." His eyes darkened, and his thin mouth twisted sideways angrily. "I hate to see it happen to a pretty little twist like Fern. Not that I yearn—"

I broke in on his nonsense rhymes: "Who's the big boss you mentioned, the one Fern went to live with?"

"Angel. Who else?"

"What heaven does he inhabit?"

"You must be new in these parts—" His eyes swiveled and focused on something over my shoulder. His mouth opened and closed.

A grating tenor was behind me: "Got a question you want answered, bud?"

The pianist went back to the piano as if the ugly tenor had wiped me out, annulled my very existence. I turned to its source. He was standing in a narrow doorway behind the drums, a man in his thirties with thick black curly hair and a heavy jaw blue-shadowed by a closely shaven beard. He was almost the living image of the dead man in the Cadillac. The likeness gave me a jolt. The heavy black gun in his hand gave me another.

He came around the drums and approached me, bull-shouldered in a fuzzy tweed jacket, holding the gun in front of him like a dangerous gift. The pianist was doing wry things in quickened tempo with the dead march from *Saul*. A wit.

The dead man's almost-double waved his cruel chin and the crueler gun in unison. "Come inside, unless you're a government man. If you are, I'll have a look at your credentials."

"I'm a freelance."

"Inside then."

The muzzle of the automatic came into my solar plexus like a pointing iron finger. Obeying its injunction, I made my way between empty music stands and through the narrow door behind the drums. The iron finger, probing my back, directed me down a lightless corridor to a small square office containing a metal desk, a safe, a filing cabinet. It was windowless, lit by fluorescent tubes in the ceiling. Under their pitiless glare, the face above the gun looked more than ever like the dead man's face. I wondered if I had been mistaken about his deadness, or if the desert heat had addled my brain.

"I'm the manager here," he said, standing so close that I could smell the piney stuff he used on his crisp, dark hair. "You got anything to ask about the members of the staff, you ask me."

"Will I get an answer?"

"Try me, bud."

"The name is Archer," I said. "I'm a private detective."

"Working for who?"

"You wouldn't be interested."

"I am, though, very much interested." The gun hopped forward like a toad into my stomach again, with the weight of his shoulder behind it. "Working for who did you say?"

I swallowed anger and nausea, estimating my chances of knocking the gun to one side and taking him bare-handed. The chances seemed pretty slim. He was heavier than I was, and held the automatic as if it had grown out of the end of his arm. *You've seen too many movies,* I told myself.

I told him: "A motel owner on the coast. A man was shot in one of his rooms last night. I happened to check in there a few minutes later. The old boy hired me to look into the shooting."

"Who was it got himself ventilated?"

"He could be your brother," I said. "Do you have a brother?"

He lost his color. The center of his attention shifted from the gun to my face. The gun nodded. I knocked it up and sideways with a hard left uppercut. Its discharge burned the side of my face and drilled a hole in the wall. My right sank into his neck. The gun thumped the cork floor.

He went down but not out, his spread hand scrabbling for the gun, then closing on it. I kicked his wrist. He grunted, but wouldn't let go of it. I threw a punch at the short hairs on the back of his neck. He took it and came up under it with the gun, shaking his head from side to side.

"Up with the hands now," he murmured. He was one of those men whose voices go soft and mild when they are in killing mood. He had the glassy impervious eyes of a killer. "Is Bart dead? My brother?"

"Very dead. He was shot in the belly."

"Who shot him?"

"That's the question."

"Who shot him?" he said in a quite white-faced rage. The single eye of the gun stared emptily at my midriff. "It could happen to you, bud, here and now."

"A woman was with him. She took a quick powder after it happened."

"I heard you say a name to Alfie, the piano-player. Was it Fern?"

"It could have been."

"What do you mean, it could have been?"

"She was there in the room, apparently. If you can give me a description of her?"

His hard brown eyes looked past me. "I can do better than that. There's a picture of her on the wall behind you. Take a look at it. Keep those hands up high."

I shifted my feet and turned uneasily. The wall was blank. I heard him draw a breath and move, and tried to evade his blow. No use. It caught the back of my head. I pitched forward against the blank wall and slid down it into three dimensions of blankness.

THE BLANKNESS COAGULATED into colored shapes. The shapes were half-human and half-beast and they dissolved and reformed. A dead man with a hairy breast climbed out of a hole and doubled and quadrupled. I ran away from them through a twisting tunnel which led to an echo chamber. Under the roaring surge of the nightmare music, a rasping tenor was saying:

"—I figure it like this. Vario's tip was good. Bart found her in Acapulco, and he was bringing her back from there. She conned him into stopping off at this motel for the night. Bart always went for her."

"I didn't know that," a dry, old voice put in. "This is very interesting news about Bart and Fern. You should have told me before about this. Then I would not have sent him for her and this would not have happened. Would it, Gino?"

My mind was still. partly absent, wandering underground in the echoing caves. I couldn't recall the voices, or who they were talking about.. I had barely sense enough to keep my eyes closed and go on listening. I was lying on my back on a hard surface. The voices were above me.

The tenor said: "You can't blame Bartolomeo. She's the one, the dirty treacherous lying little bitch."

"Calm yourself, Gino. I blame nobody. But more than ever now, we want her back, isn't that right?"

"I'll kill her," he said softly, almost wistfully.

"Perhaps. It may not be necessary now. I dislike promiscuous killing—"

"Since when, Angel?"

"Don't interrupt, it's not polite. I learned to put first things first. Now what is the most important thing? Why did we want her back in the first place? I will tell you: to shut her mouth. The government heard she left me, they wanted her to testify about my income. We wanted to find her first and shut her mouth, isn't that right?"

"I know how to shut her mouth," the younger man said very quietly.

"First we try a better way, my way. You learn when you're as old as I am there is a use for everything, and not to be wasteful. Not even wasteful with somebody else's blood. She shot your brother, right? So now we have something on her, strong enough to keep her mouth shut for good. She'd get off with second degree, with what she's got, but even that is five to ten in Tehachapi. I think all I need to do is tell her that. First we have to find her, eh?"

"I'll find her. Bart didn't have any trouble finding her."

"With Vario's tip to help him, no. But I think I'll keep you here with me, Gino. You're too hot-blooded, you and your brother both. I want her alive. Then I can talk to her, and then we'll see."

"You're going soft in your old age, Angel."

"Am I?" There was a light slapping sound of a blow on flesh. "I have killed many men, for good reasons. So I think you will take that back."

"I take it back."

"And call me Mr. Funk. If I am so old, you will treat my gray hairs with respect. Call me Mr. Funk."

"Mr. Funk."

"All right, your friend here, does he know where Fern is?"

"I don't think so."

"Mr. Funk."

"Mr. Funk." Gino's voice was a whining snarl. "I think he's coming to. His eyelids fluttered."

The toe of a shoe prodded my side. Somebody slapped my face a number of times. I opened my eyes and sat up. The back of my head was throbbing like an engine fueled by pain. Gino rose from a squatting position and stood over me.

"Stand up."

I rose shakily to my feet. I was in a stone-walled room with a high beamed ceiling, sparsely furnished with stiff old black oak chairs and tables. The room and the furniture seemed to have been built for a race of giants.

The man behind Gino was small and old and weary. He might have been an unsuccessful grocer or a superannuated barkeep who had come to California for his health. Clearly his health was poor. Even in the stifling heat he looked pale and chilly, as if he had caught chronic death from one of his victims. He moved closer to me, his legs shuffling feebly in wrinkled blue trousers that bagged at the knees. His shrunken torso was swathed in a heavy blue turtleneck sweater. He had two days' beard on his chin, like moth-eaten gray plush.

"Gino informs me that you are investigating a shooting." His accent was Middle-European and very faint, as if he had forgotten his origins. "Where did this happen, exactly?"

"I don't think I'll tell you that. You can read it in the papers tomorrow night if you're interested."

"I am not prepared to wait. I am impatient. Do you know where Fern is?"

"I wouldn't be here if I did."

"But you know where she was last night."

"I couldn't be sure."

"Tell me anyway, to the best of your knowledge."

"I don't think I will."

"He doesn't think he will," the old man said to Gino.

"I think you better let me out of here. Kidnapping is a tough rap. You don't want to die in the pen."

He smiled at me, with a tolerance more terrible than anger. His eyes were like thin stab-wounds filled with watery blood. Shuffling unhurriedly to the head of the mahogany table behind him, he pressed a spot in the rug with the toe of one felt slipper.

Two men in blue serge suits entered the room and stepped toward me briskly. They belonged to the race of giants it had been built for.

Gino moved behind me and reached to pin my arms. I pivoted, landed one short punch, and took a very hard counter below the belt. Something behind me slammed my kidneys with the heft of a trailer truck bumper. I turned on weakening legs and caught a chin with my elbow. Gino's fist, or one of the beams from the ceiling, landed on my neck. My head rang like a gong. Under its clangor, Angel was saying pleasantly:

"Where was Fem last night?"

I didn't say.

The men in blue serge held me upright by the arms while Gino used my head as a punching bag. I rolled with his lefts and rights as well as I could, but his timing improved and mine deteriorated. His face wavered and receded. At intervals, Angel inquired politely if I was willing to assist him now. I asked myself confusedly in the hail of fists what I was holding out for or who I was protecting. Probably I was holding out for myself. It seemed important to me not to give in to violence. But my identity was dissolving and receding like the face in front of me.

I concentrated on hating Gino's face. That kept it clear and steady for a while: a stupid, square-jawed face barred by a single black brow, two close-set brown eyes staring glassily. His fists continued to rock me like an air-hammer.

Finally Angel placed a clawed hand on his shoulder, and nodded to my handlers. They deposited me in a chair. It swung on an invisible wire from the ceiling in great circles. It swung out wide over the desert, across a bleak horizon, into darkness.

I CAME TO, cursing. Gino was standing over me again. There was an empty water glass in his hand, and my face was dripping. Angel spoke up beside him, with a trace of irritation in his voice:

"You stand up good under punishment. Why go to all the trouble, though? I want a little information, that is all. My friend, my little girl-friend, ran away. I'm impatient to get her back."

"You're going about it the wrong way."

Gino leaned close, and laughed harshly. He shattered the glass on the arm of my chair, held the jagged base up to my eyes. Fear ran through me, cold and light in my veins. My eyes were my connection with everything. Blindness would be the end of me. I closed my eyes, shutting out the cruel edges of the broken thing in his hand.

"Nix, Gino," the old man said. "I have a better idea, as usual. There is heat on, remember."

They retreated to the far side of the table and conferred there in low voices. The young man left the room. The old man came back to me. His storm troopers stood one on each side of me, looking down at him in ignorant awe.

"What is your name, young fellow?"

I told him. My mouth was puffed and lisping, tongue tangled in ropes of blood.

"I like a young fellow who can take it, Mr. Archer. You say that you're a detective. You find people for a living, is that right?"

"I have a client," I said.

"Now you have another. Whoever he is, I can buy and sell him, believe me. Fifty times over." His thin, blue hands scoured each other. They made a sound like two dry sticks rubbing together on a dead tree.

"Narcotics?" I said. "Are you the wheel in the heroin racket? I've heard of you."

His watery eyes veiled themselves like a bird's. "Now don't ask foolish questions, or I will lose my respect for you entirely."

"That would break my heart."

"Then comfort yourself with this." He brought an old-fashioned purse out of his hip pocket, abstracted a crumpled bill and smoothed it out on my knee. It was a five-hundred-dollar bill.

"This girl of mine you are going to find for me, she is young and foolish. I am old and foolish, to have trusted her. No matter. Find her for me and bring her back, and I will give you another bill like this one. Take it."

"Take it," one of my guards repeated. "Mr. Funk said for you to take it."

I took it. "You're wasting your money. I don't even know what she looks like. I don't know anything about her."

"Gino is bringing a picture. He came across her last fall at a recording studio in Hollywood where Alfie had a date. He gave her an audition and took her on at the club, more for her looks than for the talent she had. As a singer she flopped. But she is a pretty little thing, about five foot four, nice figure, dark brown hair, big hazel eyes. I found a use for her." Lechery flickered briefly in his eyes and went out.

"You find a use for everything."

"That is good economics. I often think if I wasn't what I am, I would make a good economist. Nothing would go to waste." He paused and dragged his dying old mind back to the subject: "She was here for a couple of months, then she ran out on me, silly girl. I heard last week that she was in Acapulco, and the federal grand jury was going to subpoena her. I have tax troubles, Mr. Archer, all my life I have tax troubles. Unfortunately I let Fern help with my books a little bit. She could do me great harm. So I sent Bart to Mexico to bring her back. But I meant no harm to her. I still intend her no harm, even now. A little talk, a little realistic discussion with Fem, that is all that will be necessary. So even the shooting of my good friend Bart serves its purpose. Where did it happen, by the way?"

The question flicked out like a hook on the end of a long line.

"In San Diego," I said, "at a place near the airport: the Mission Motel."

He smiled paternally. "Now you are showing good sense."

Gino came back with a silver-framed photograph in his hand. He handed it to Angel, who passed it on to me.

It was a studio portrait, of the kind intended for publicity cheesecake. On a black velvet divan, against an artificial night sky, a young woman reclined in a gossamer robe that was split to show one bent leg. Shadows accentuated the lines of her body and the fine bones in her face. Under the heavy makeup which widened the mouth and darkened the half-closed eyes, I recognized Ella Salanda. The picture was signed in white, in the lower right-hand corner: "*To my Angel, with all my love, Fern.*"

A sickness assailed me, worse than the sickness induced by Gino's fists. Angel breathed into my face: "Fern Dee is a stage name. Her real name I never learned. She told me one time that if her family knew where she was, they would die of shame." He chuckled drily. "She will not want them to know that she killed a man."

I drew away from his charnel-house breath. My guards escorted me out. Gino started to follow, but Angel called him back.

"Don't wait to hear from me," the old man said after me. "I expect to hear from you."

The building we walked out of stood on a rise in the open desert. It was huge and turreted, like somebody's idea of a castle in Spain. The last rays of the sun washed its wall in purple light and cast long shadows across its barren acreage. It was surrounded by a ten-foot hurricane fence topped with three strands of barbed wire.

Palm Springs was a clutter of white stones in the distance, diamonded by an occasional light. The dull red sun was balanced like a glowing cigar-butt on the rim of the hills above the town. *A* man with a bulky shoulder harness under his brown suede windbreaker drove me toward it. The sun fell out of sight, and darkness gathered like an impalpable ash on the desert, like a column of blue-gray smoke towering into the sky.

THE SKY WAS blue-black and swarming with stars when I got back to Emerald Bay. A black Cadillac had followed me out of Palm Springs. I lost it in the winding streets of Pasadena. So far as I could see, I had lost it for good.

The neon Mexican lay peaceful under the stars. *A* smaller sign at his feet asserted that there was *No Vacancy*. The lights in the long low stucco buildings behind him shone brightly. The office door was open behind a screen, throwing a barred rectangle of light on the gravel. I stepped into it, and froze.

Behind the registration desk in the office, a woman was avidly reading a magazine. Her shoulders and bosom were massive. Her hair was blond, piled on her head in coroneted braids. There were rings on her fingers, a triple strand of cultured pearls around her thick white throat. She was the woman Donny had described to me.

I pulled the screen door open and said rudely, "Who are you?"

She glanced up, twisting her mouth in a sour grimace. "Well! I'll thank you to keep a civil tongue in your head."

"Sorry. I thought I'd seen you before somewhere."

"Well, you haven't." She looked me over coldly. "What happened to your face, anyway?"

"I had a little plastic surgery done. By an amateur surgeon."

She clucked disapprovingly. "Ii you're looking for a room, we're full up for the night. I don't believe I'd rent you a room even *if* we weren't. Look at your clothes."

"Uh-huh. Where's Mr. Salanda?"

"Is it any business of yours?"

"He wants to see me. I'm doing a job for him."

"What kind of a job?"

I mimicked her: "Is it any business of yours?" I was irritated. Under her mounds of flesh she had a personality as thin and hard and abrasive as a rasp.

"Watch who you're getting flip with, sonny boy." She rose, and her shadow loomed immense across the back door of the room. The magazine fell closed on the desk: it was *Teen-age Confessions.* "I am Mrs. Salanda. Are you a handyman?"

"A sort of one," I said. "I'm a garbage collector in the moral field. You look as if you could use me."

The crack went over her head. "Well, you're wrong. And I don't think my husband hired you, either. This is a respectable motel."

"Uh-huh. Are you Ella's mother?"

"I should say not. That little snip is no daughter of mine."

"Her stepmother?"

"Mind your own business. You better get out of here. The police are keeping a close watch on this place tonight, if you're planning any tricks."

"Where's Ella now?"

"I don't know and I don't care. She's probably gallivanting off around the countryside. It's all she's good for. One day at home in the last six months, that's a fine record for a young unmarried girl." Her face was thick and bloated with anger against her stepdaughter. She went on talking blindly, as if she had forgotten me entirely. "I told her father he was an old fool to take her back. How does he know what she's been up to? I say let the ungrateful filly go and fend for herself."

"Is that what you say, Mabel?" Salanda had softly opened the door behind her. He came forward into the room, doubly dwarfed by her blond magnitude. "I say if it wasn't for you, my dear, Ella wouldn't have been driven away from home in the first place."

She turned on him in a blubbering rage. He drew himself up tall and reached to snap his fingers under her nose. "Go back into the house. You are a disgrace to women, a disgrace to motherhood."

"I'm not *her* mother, thank God."

"Thank God," he echoed, shaking his fist at her. She retreated like a schooner under full sail, menaced by a gunboat. The door closed on her.

Salanda turned to me. "I'm sorry, Mr. Archer. I have difficulties with my wife, I am ashamed to say it. I was an imbecile to marry again. I gained a senseless hulk of flesh and lost my daughter. Old imbecile!" he denounced himself, wagging his great head sadly. "I married in hot blood. Sexual passion has always been my downfall. It runs in my family, this insane hunger for blondeness and stupidity and size." He spread his arms in a wide and futile embrace on emptiness.

"Forget it."

"If I could." He came closer to examine my face. "You are injured, Mr. Archer. Your mouth is damaged. There is blood on your chin."

"I was in a slight brawl."

"On my account?"

"On my own. But I think it's time you leveled with me."

"Leveled with you?"

"Told me the truth. You knew who was shot last night, and who shot him, and why."

He touched my arm, with a quick, tentative grace. "I have only one daughter, Mr. Archer, only the one child. It was my duty to defend her, as best as I could."

"Defend her from what?"

"From shame, from the police, from prison." He hung one arm out, indicating the whole range of human disaster. "I am a man of honor, Mr. Archer. But private honor stands higher with me than public honor. The man was abducting my daughter. She brought him here in the hope of being rescued. Her last hope."

"I think that's true. You should have told me this before."

"I was alarmed, upset. I feared your intentions. Any minute the police were due to arrive."

"But you had a right to shoot him. It wasn't even a crime. The crime was his."

"I didn't know that then. The truth came out to me gradually. I feared that Ella was involved with him." His flat black gaze sought my face and rested on it. "However, I did not shoot him, Mr. Archer. I was not even here at the time. I told you that this morning, and you may take my word for it."

"Was Mrs. Salanda here?"

"No sir, she was not. Why should you ask me that?"

"Donny described the woman who checked in with the dead man. The description fits your wife."

"Donny was lying. I told him to give a false description of the woman. Apparently he was unequal to the task of inventing one."

"Can you prove that she was with you?"

"Certainly I can. We had reserved seats at the theatre. Those who sat around us can testify that the seats were not empty. Mrs. Salanda and I, we are not an inconspicuous couple." He smiled wryly.

"Ella killed him then."

He neither assented, nor denied it. "I was hoping that you were on my side, my side and Ella's. Am I wrong?"

"I'll have to talk to her, before I know myself. Where is she?"

"I do not know, Mr. Archer, sincerely I do not know. She went away this afternoon, after the policemen questioned her. They were suspicious, but we managed to soothe their suspicions. They did not know that she had just come home, from another life, and I did not tell them. Mable wanted to tell them. I silenced her." His white teeth clicked together.

"What about Donny?"

"They took him down to the station for questioning. He told them nothing damaging. Donny can appear very stupid when he wishes. He has the reputation of an idiot, but he is not so dumb. Donny has been with me for many years. He has a deep devotion for my daughter. I got him released tonight."

"You should have taken my advice," I said, "taken the police into your confidence. Nothing would have happened to you. The dead man was a mobster, and what he was doing amounts to kidnapping. Your daughter was a witness against his boss."

"She told me that. I am glad that it is true. Ella has not always told me the truth. She has been a hard girl to bring up, without a good mother to set her an example. Where has she been these last six months, Mr. Archer?"

"Singing in a night club in Palm Springs. Her boss was a racketeer."

"A racketeer?" His mouth and nose screwed up, as if he sniffed the odor of corruption.

"Where she was isn't important, compared with where she is now. The boss is still after her. He hired me to look for her."

Salanda regarded me with fear and dislike, as if the odor originated in me. "You let him hire you?"

"It was my best chance of getting out of his place alive. I'm not his boy, if that's what you mean."

"You ask me to believe you?"

"I'm telling you. Ella is in danger. As a matter of fact, we all are." I didn't tell him about the second black Cadillac. Gino would be driving it, wandering the night roads with a ready gun in his armpit and revenge corroding his heart.

"My daughter is aware of the danger," he said. "She warned me of it."

"She must have told you where she was going."

"No. But she may be at the beach house. The house where Donny lives. I will come with you."

"You stay here. Keep your doors locked. If any strangers show and start prowling the place, call the police."

He bolted the door behind me as I went out. Yellow traffic lights cast wan reflections on the asphalt. Streams of cars went by to the north, to the south. To the west, where the sea lay, a great black emptiness opened under the stars.

THE BEACH HOUSE sat on its white margin, a little over a mile from the motel. For the second time that day, I knocked on the warped kitchen door. There was light behind it, shining through the cracks. A shadow obscured the light.

"Who is it?" Donny said. Fear or some other emotion had filled his mouth with pebbles.

"You know me, Donny."

The door groaned on its hinges. He gestured dumbly to me to come in, his face a white blur. When he turned his head, and the light from the living room caught his face, I saw that grief was the emotion that marked it. His eyes were swollen, as if he had been crying. More than ever he resembled a dilapidated boy whose growing pains had never paid off in manhood.

"Anybody with you?"

Sounds of movement in the living room answered my question. I brushed him aside and went in. Ella Salanda was bent over an open suitcase on the camp cot. She straightened, her mouth thin, eyes wide and dark. The .38 automatic in her hand gleamed dully under the naked bulb suspended from the ceiling.

"I'm getting out of here," she said, "and you're not going to stop me."

"I'm not sure I want to try. Where are you going, Fern?"

Donny spoke behind me, in his grief-thickened voice: "She's going away from me. She promised to stay here if I did what she told me. She promised to be my girl—"

"Shut up, stupid." Her voice cut like a lash, and Donny gasped as if the lash had been laid across his back

"What did she tell you to do, Donny? Tell me just what you did."

"When she checked in last night with the fella from Detroit, she made a sign I wasn't to let on I knew her. Later on, she left me a note. She wrote it with a lipstick on a piece of paper towel. I still got it hidden, in the kitchen."

"What did she write in the note?"

He lingered behind me, fearful of the gun in the girl's hand, more fearful of her anger.

She said: "Don't be crazy, Donny. He doesn't know a thing, not a thing. He can't do anything to either of us."

"I don't care what happens, to me or anybody else," the anguished voice said behind me. "You're running out on me, breaking your promise to me. I always knew it was too good to be true. Now I just don't care any more."

"I care," she said. "I care what happens to me." Her eyes shifted to me, above the unwavering gun. "I won't stay here. I'll shoot you if I have to."

"It shouldn't be necessary. Put it down, Fern. It's Bartolomeo's gun, isn't it? I found the shells to fit it in his glove compartment."

"How do you know so much?"

"I talked to Angel."

"Is he here?" Panic whined in her voice.

"No. I came alone."

"You better leave the same way then, while you can go under your own power."

"I'm staying. You need protection, whether you know it or not. And I need information. Donny, go in the kitchen and bring me that note."

"Don't do it, Donny. I'm warning you."

His sneakered feet made soft, indecisive sounds. I advanced on the girl, talking quietly and steadily: "You conspired to kill a man, but you don't have to be afraid. He had it coming. Tell the whole story to the cops, and my guess is they won't even book you. Hell, you can even become famous. The government wants you as a witness in a tax case."

"What kind of a case?"

"A tax case against Angel. It's probably the only kind of rap they can pin on him. You can send him up for the rest of his life like Capone. You'll be a heroine, Fern."

"Don't call me Fern. I hate that name," There were sudden tears in her eyes. "I hate everything connected with that name. I hate myself."

"You'll hate yourself more if you don't put down that gun. Shoot me and it all starts over again. The cops will be on your trail, Angel's troopers will be gunning for you."

Now only the cot was between us, the cot and the unsteady gun facing me above it.

"This is the turning point," I said. "You've made a lot of bum decisions and almost ruined yourself, playing footsie with the evilest men there are. You can go on the way you have been, getting in deeper until you end up in a refrigerated drawer, or you can come back out of it now, into a decent life."

"A decent life? Here? With my father married to Mabel?"

"I don't think Mabel will last much longer. Anyway, I'm not Mabel. I'm on your side."

I waited. She dropped the gun on the blanket. I scooped it up and turned to Donny: "Let me see that note."

He disappeared through the kitchen door, head and shoulders drooping on the long stalk of his body.

"What could I do?" the girl said. "I was caught. It was Bart or me. All the way up from Acapulco I planned how I could get away. He held a gun in my side when we crossed the border; the same way when we stopped for gas or to eat at the drive-ins. I realized he had to be killed. My father's motel looked like my only chance. So I talked Bart into staying there with me overnight. He had no idea who the place belonged to. I didn't know what I was going to do. I only knew it bad to be something drastic. Once I was back with Angel in the desert, that was the end of me. Even if he didn't kill me, it meant I'd have to go on living with him. Anything was better than that. So I wrote a note to Donny in the bathroom, and dropped it out the window. He was always crazy about me."

Her mouth had grown softer. She looked remarkably young and virginal. The faint blue hollows under her eyes were dewy. "Donny shot Bart with Bart's own gun. He had more nerve than I had. I lost my nerve when I went back into the room this morning. I didn't know about the blood in the bathroom. It was the last straw."

She was wrong. Something crashed in the kitchen. A cool draft swept the living room. A gun spoke twice, out of sight. Donny fell backward through the doorway, a piece of brownish paper clutched in his hand. Blood gleamed on his shoulder like a red badge.

I stepped behind the cot and pulled the girl down to the floor with me. Gino came through the door, his two-colored sports shoe stepping on Donny's laboring chest. I shot the gun out of his hand. He floundered back against the wall, clutching at his wrist.

I sighted carefully for my second shot, until the black bar of his eyebrows was steady in the sights of the .38. The hole it made was invisible. Gino fell loosely forward, prone on the floor beside the man he had killed.

Ella Salanda ran across the room. She knelt, and cradled Donny's head in her lap.

Incredibly, he spoke, in a loud sighing voice: "You won't go away again, Ella? I did what you told me. You promised."

"Sure I promised. I won't leave you, Donny. Crazy man. Crazy fool."

"You like me better than you used to? Now?"

"I like you, Donny. You're the most man there is."

She held the poor insignificant head in her hands. He sighed, and his life came out bright-colored at the mouth. It was Donny who went away.

His hand relaxed, and I read the lipstick note she had written him on a piece of porous tissue:

Donny: This man will kill me unless you kill him first. His gun will be in his clothes on the chair beside the bed. Come in and get it at midnight and shoot to kill. Good luck. I'll stay and be your girl if you do this, just like you always wished. Love. Ella.

I looked at the pair on the floor. She was rocking his lifeless head against her breast. Beside them, Gino looked very small and lonely, a dummy leaking darkness from his brow.

Donny had his wish and I had mine. I wondered what Ella's was.

The President's Half Disme

Ellery Queen

When the Ellerys Queen sent me this beauty, I could only say, "What a sheer delight!" Let us celebrate Queen's fortieth anniversary with this sample of the master's touch.

THOSE FEW CURIOUS men who have chosen to turn off the humdrum highway to hunt for their pleasure along the back trails expect—indeed, they look confidently forward to—many strange encounters; and it is the dull stalk which does not turn up at least a hippogriff. But it remained for Ellery Queen to experience the ultimate excitement. On one of his prowls he collided with a President of the United States.

This would have been joy enough if it had occurred as you might imagine: by chance, on a dark night, in some back street of Washington, D.C., with Secret Service men closing in on the delighted Mr. Queen to question his motives by way of his pockets while a large black bulletproof limousine rushed up to spirit the President away. But mere imagination fails in this instance. What is required is the power of fancy, for the truth is fantastic. Ellery's encounter with the President of the United States took place, not on a dark night, but in the unromantic light of several days (although the night played its role, too). Nor was it by chance: the meeting was arranged by a farmer's daughter. And it was not in Washington, D.C., for this President presided over the affairs of the nation from a different city altogether. Not that the meeting took place in that city, either; it did not take place in a city at all, but on a farm some miles south of Philadelphia. Oddest of all, there was no limousine to spirit the Chief Executive away, for while the President was a man of great wealth, he was still too poor to possess an automobile and, what is more, not all the resources of his Government—indeed, not all the riches of the world— could have provided one for him.

There are even more curious facets to this jewel of paradox. This was an encounter in the purest sense, and yet, physically, it did not occur at all. The President in question was dead. And while there are those who would not blink at a rubbing of shoulders or a clasping of hands even though one of the parties was in his grave, and to such persons the thought might occur that the meeting took place on a psychic plane—alas, Ellery Queen is not of their company. He does not believe in ghosts, consequently he never encounters them. So he did not collide with the President's shade, either.

And yet their meeting was as palpable as, say, the meeting between two chess masters, one in London and the other in New York, who never leave their respective armchairs and still play a game to a decision. It is even more wonderful than that, for while the chess players merely annihilate space, Ellery and the father of his country annihilated time—a century and a half of it.

In fine, this is the story of how Ellery Queen matched wits with George Washington.

THOSE WHO ARE finicky about their fashions complain that the arms of coincidence are too long; but in this case the Designer might say that He cut to measure. Or, to put it another way, an event often brews its own mood. Whatever the cause, the fact is The Adventure of the President's Half Disme, which was to concern itself with the events surrounding President Washington's fifty-ninth birthday, actually first engrossed Ellery on February the nineteenth and culminated three days later.

Ellery was in his study that morning, wrestling with several reluctant victims of violence, none of them quite flesh and blood, since his novel was still in the planning stage. So he was annoyed when Nikki came in with a card.

"James Ezekiel Patch," growled the great man; he was never in his best humor during the planning stage. "I don't know any James Ezekiel Patch, Nikki. Toss the fellow out and get back to transcribing those notes on Possible Motives—"

"Why, Ellery," said Nikki. "This isn't like you at all."

"What isn't like me?"

"To renege on an appointment."

"Appointment? Does this Patch character claim—?"

"He doesn't merely claim it. He proves it."

"Someone's balmy," snarled Mr. Queen; and he strode into the living room to contend with James Ezekiel Patch. This, he perceived as soon as James Ezekiel Patch rose from the Queen fireside chair, was likely to be a heroic project. Mr. Patch, notwithstanding his mild, even studious, eyes, seemed to rise indefinitely; he was a large, a very large, man.

"Now what's all this, what's all this?" demanded Ellery fiercely; for after all Nikki was there.

"That's what I'd like to know," said the large man amiably. "What did you want with me, Mr. Queen?"

"What did I want with you! What did you want with me?"

"I find this very strange, Mr. Queen."

"Now see here, Mr. Patch, I happen to be extremely busy this morning—"

"So am I." Mr. Patch's large thick neck was reddening, and his tone was no longer amiable. Ellery took a cautious step backward as his visitor lumbered forward to thrust a slip of yellow paper under his nose. "Did you send me this wire, or didn't you?"

Ellery considered it tactically expedient to take the telegram, although for strategic reasons he did so with a bellicose scowl.

IMPERATIVE YOU CALL AT MY HOME TOMORROW
FEBRUARY NINETEEN PROMPTLY TEN A.M. SIGNED
ELLERY QUEEN

"Well, sir?" thundered Mr. Patch. "Do you have something on Washington for me, or don't you?"

"Washington?" said Ellery absently, studying the telegram.

"*George* Washington, Mr. Queen! I'm Patch the antiquarian. I *collect* Washington. I'm an *authority* on Washington. I have a large fortune, and I spend it all on Washington! I'd never have wasted my time this morning if your name hadn't been signed to this wire! This is my busiest week of the year. I have engagements to speak on Washington—"

"Desist, Mr. Patch," said Ellery. "This is either a practical joke, or—"

"The Baroness Tchek," announced Nikki clearly. "With another telegram." And then she added: "And Professor John Cecil Shaw, ditto."

THE THREE TELEGRAMS WERE IDENTICAL.

"Of course I didn't send them," said Ellery thoughtfully, regarding his three visitors. Baroness Tchek was a short powerful woman, resembling a dumpling with gray hair; an angry dumpling. Professor Shaw was lank and long-jawed, wearing a sack suit which hung in some places and failed in its purpose by inches at the extremities. Along with Mr. Patch, they constituted as deliciously queer a trio as had ever congregated in the Queen apartment. Their host suddenly determined not to let go of them. "On the other hand, someone obviously did, using my name..."

"Then there's nothing more to be said," snapped the Baroness, snapping her bag for emphasis.

"I should think there's a great deal more to be said," began Professor Shaw in a troubled way. 'Wasting people's time this way—"

"It's not going to waste any more of *my* time," growled the large Mr. Patch. "Washington's Birthday only three days off—!"

"Exactly," smiled Ellery. "Won't you sit down? There's more in this than meets the eye... Baroness Tchek, if I'm not mistaken, you're the one who brought that fabulous collection of rare coins into the

United States just before Hitler invaded Czechoslovakia? You're in the rare coin business in New York now?"

"Unfortunately," said the Baroness coldly, "one must eat."

"And you, sir? I seem to know you."

"Rare books," said the Professor in the same troubled way.

"Of course. John Cecil Shaw, the rare book collector. We've met at Mim's and other places. I abandon my first theory. There's a pattern here, distinctly unhumorous. An antiquarian, a coin dealer, and a collector of rare books—Nikki? Whom have you out there this time?"

"If this one collects anything," muttered Nikki into her employer's ear, "I'll bet it has two legs and hair on its chest. A darned pretty girl—"

"Named Martha Clarke," said a cool voice; and Ellery turned to find himself regarding one of the most satisfying sights in the world.

"Ah. I take it, Miss Clarke, you also received one of these wires signed with my name?"

"Oh, no," said the pretty girl. "I'm the one who sent them."

THERE WAS something about the comely Miss Clarke which inspired, if not confidence, at least an openness of mind. Perhaps it was the self-possessed manner in which she sat all of them, including Ellery, down in Ellery's living room while she waited on the hearth rug, like a conductor on the podium, for them to settle in their chairs. And it was the measure of Miss Clarke's assurance that none of them was indignant, only curious.

"I'll make it snappy," said Martha Clarke briskly. "I did what I did the way I did it because, first, I had to make sure I could see Mr. Patch, Baroness Tchek, and Professor Shaw today. Second, because I may need a detective before I'm through... Third," she added, almost absently, "because I'm pretty desperate.

"My name is Martha Clarke. My father Tobias is a farmer. Our farm lies just south of Philadelphia, it was built by a Clarke in 1761, and it's been in our family ever since. I won't go gooey on you. We're broke, and there's a mortgage. Unless Papa and I can raise six thousand dollars in the next couple of weeks, we lose the old homestead."

Professor Shaw looked vague. But the Baroness said: "Deplorable, Miss Clarke. Now if I'm to run my auction this afternoon—"

And James Ezekiel Patch grumbled: "If it's money you want, young woman—"

"Certainly it's money I want. But I have something to sell."

"Ah!" said the Baroness.

"Oh?" said the Professor.

"Hm," said the antiquarian.

Mr. Queen said nothing, and Miss Porter zealously chewed the end of her pencil.

"The other day, while I was cleaning out the attic, I found an old book."

"Well, now," said Professor Shaw indulgently. "An old book, eh?"

"It's called *The Diary of Simeon Clarke*. Simeon Clarke was Papa's great-great-great-something or other. His *Diary* was privately printed in 1792 in Philadelphia, Professor, by a second cousin of his, Jonathan, who was in the printing business there."

"Jonathan Clarke. *The Diary of Simeon Clarke*," mumbled the cadaverous book collector. "I don't believe I know either, Miss Clarke. Have you...?"

Martha Clarke carefully unclasped a large Manila envelope and drew forth a single yellowed sheet of badly printed paper. "The title page was loose, so I brought it along."

Professor Shaw silently examined Miss Clarke's exhibit, and Ellery got up to squint at it.

"Of course," said the Professor after a long scrutiny, in which he held the sheet up to the light, peered apparently at individual characters, and performed other mysterious rites, "mere age doesn't connote rarity, nor does rarity of itself constitute value. And while this page looks genuine for the purported period, and is rare enough to be unknown to me, still..."

"Suppose I told you," said Miss Martha Clarke, "that the chief purpose of the Diary—which I have at home—is to tell the story of how George Washington visited Simeon Clarke's farm in the winter of 1791—"

"Clarke's farm? 1791?" exclaimed James Ezekiel Patch. "Preposterous. There's no record of—"

"And of what George Washington buried there," the farmer's daughter concluded.

BY EXECUTIVE ORDER, the Queen telephone was taken off its hook, the door was bolted, the shades were drawn, and the long interrogation began. By the middle of the afternoon, the unknown chapter in the life of the Father of His Country was fairly sketched.

Early on an icy gray February morning in 1791, Farmer Clarke had looked up from the fence he was mending to observe a splendid cortège galloping down on him from the direction of the City of Philadelphia. Outriders thundered in the van, followed by a considerable company of gentlemen on horseback and several great coaches-and-six driven by liveried Negroes.

To Simeon Clarke's astonishment, the entire equipage stopped before his farmhouse. He began to run. He could hear the creak of springs and the snorting of sleek and sweating horses. Gentlemen and lackeys were leaping to the frozen ground, and by the time Simeon had reached the farmhouse, all were elbowing about the first coach, a magnificent affair bearing a coat of arms.

Craning, the farmer saw within the coach a very large, great-nosed gentleman clad in a black velvet suit and a black cloak faced with gold; there was a cocked hat on his wigged head and a great sword in a white leather scabbard at his side. This personage was on one knee, leaning with an expression of considerable anxiety over a chubby lady of middle age, swathed in furs, who was half-sitting, half-lying on the upholstered seat, her eyes closed and her cheeks waxen under the rouge. Another gentleman, soberly attired, was stooping over the lady, his fingers on one pale wrist.

"I fear," he was saying with great gravity to the kneeling man, "that it would be imprudent to proceed another yard in this weather, Your Excellency. Lady Washington requires physicking and a warm bed immediately."

Lady Washington! Then the large, richly dressed gentleman was the President! Simeon Clarke pushed excitedly through the throng.

"Your Mightiness! Sir!" he cried. "I am Simeon Clarke. This is my farm. We have warm beds, Sarah and I!"

The President considered Simeon briefly. "I thank you, Farmer Clarke. No, no, Dr. Craik. I shall assist Lady Washington myself."

And George Washington carried Martha Washington into the little Pennsylvania farmhouse of Simeon and Sarah Clarke. An aide informed the Clarkes that President Washington had been on his way to Virginia to celebrate his fifty-ninth birthday in the privacy of Mount Vernon.

Instead, he passed his birthday on the Clarke farm, for the physician insisted that the President's lady could not be moved, even back to the nearby Capital, without risking complications. On His Excellency's order, the entire incident was kept secret. "It would give needless alarm to the people," he said. But he did not leave Martha's bedside for three days and three nights. Presumably during those seventy-two hours, while his lady recovered from her indisposition, the President devoted some thought to his hosts, for on the fourth morning he sent black Christopher, his body servant, to summon the Clarkes.

They found George Washington by the kitchen fire, shaven and powdered and in immaculate dress, his stem features composed. "I am told, Farmer Clarke, that you and your good wife refuse reimbursement for the livestock you have slaughtered in the accommodation of our large company."

"You're my President, Sir," said Simeon. "I wouldn't take money."

"We—we wouldn't take money, Your Worship," stammered Sarah.

"Nevertheless, Lady Washington and I would acknowledge your hospitality in some kind. If you give me leave, I shall plant with my own hands a grove of oak saplings behind your house. And beneath one of the saplings I propose to bury two of my personal possessions." Washington's eyes twinkled ever so slightly. "It is my birthday —I feel a venturesome spirit. Come, Farmer Clarke and Mistress Clarke, would you like that?"

"What—what were they?" choked James Ezekiel Patch, the Washington collector. He was pale.

Martha Clarke replied: "The sword at Washington's side, in its white leather scabbard, and a silver coin the President carried in a secret pocket."

"Silver *coin?*" breathed Baroness Tchek, the rare coin dealer. "What kind of coin, Miss Clarke?"

"The *Diary* calls it 'a half disme,' with an *s*," replied Martha Clarke, frowning. "I guess that's the way they spelled 'dime' in those days. The book's full of queer spellings."

"A United States of America half disme?" asked the Baroness in a very odd way.

"That's what it says, Baroness."

"And this was in 1791?"

"Yes."

The Baroness snorted, beginning to rise. "I thought your story was too impossibly romantic, young woman. The United States Mint didn't begin to strike off half dismes until 1792!"

"Half dismes or any other U.S. coinage, I believe," said Ellery. "How come, Miss Clarke?"

"It was an experimental coin," said Miss Clarke coolly. 'The *Diary* isn't clear as to whether it was the Mint which struck it off, or some private agency—maybe Washington himself didn't tell Simeon—but the President did say to Simeon that the half disme in his pocket had been coined from silver he himself had furnished and had been presented to him as a keepsake."

"There's a half disme with a story like that behind it in the possession of The American Numismatic Society," muttered the Baroness, "but it's definitely called one of the earliest coins struck off by the Mint It's possible, I suppose, that in 1791, the preceding year, some specimen coins may have been struck off—"

"Possible my foot," said Miss Clarke. "It's so. The *Diary* says so. I imagine President Washington was pretty interested in the coins to be issued by the new country he was head of."

"Miss Clarke, I—I want that half disme. I mean—I'd like to buy it from you," said the Baroness.

"And I," said Mr. Patch carefully, "would like to ah...purchase Washington's sword."

'The *Diary*," moaned Professor Shaw, "I'll buy *The Diary of Simeon Clarke* from you, Miss Clarke!"

"I'll be happy to sell it to you, Professor Shaw—as I said, I found it in the attic and I have it locked up in a highboy in the parlor at home. But as for the other two, things..." Martha Clarke paused, and Ellery looked delighted. He thought he knew what was coming. "I'll sell you the sword, Mr. Patch, and you the half disme, Baroness Tchek, provided—" and now Miss Clarke turned her clear eyes on Ellery, "—provided you, Mr. Queen, will be kind enough to find them."

AND THERE WAS the farmhouse in the frosty Pennsylvania morning, set in the barren winter acres, and looking as bleak as only a little Revolutionary house with a mortgage on its head can look in the month of February.

"There's an apple orchard over there," said Nikki as they got out of Ellery's car, "But where's the grove of oaks? I don't see any!" And then she added, sweetly: "Do you, Ellery?"

Ellery's lips tightened. They tightened further when his solo on the front-door knocker brought no response.

"Let's go around," he said briefly; and Nikki preceded him with cheerful step.

Behind the house there was a barn; and beyond the barn there was comfort, at least for Ellery. For beyond the barn there were twelve ugly holes in the earth, and beside each hole lay either a freshly felled oak tree and its stump, or an ancient stump by itself, freshly uprooted. On one of the stumps sat an old man in earth-stained blue jeans, smoking a corncob pugnaciously.

"Tobias Clarke?" asked Ellery.

"Yump."

"I'm Ellery Queen. This is Miss Porter. Your daughter visited me in New York yesterday—"

"Know all about it."

"May I ask where Martha is?"

"Station. Meetin' them there other folks." Tobias Clarke spat and looked away—at the holes. "Don't know what ye're all comin' down here for. Wasn't nothin' under them oaks. Dug 'em all up t'other day. Trees that were standin' and the stumps of the ones that'd fallen years back. Look at them holes. Hired hand and me dug down most to China. Washin'ton's Grove, always been called. Now look at it. Fire-wood—for someone else, I guess." There was iron bitterness in his tone. "We're losin' this farm, Mister, unless..." And Tobias Clarke stopped. "Well maybe we won't," he said. "There's always that there book Martha found."

"Professor Shaw, the rare book collector, offered your daughter two thousand dollars for it if he's satisfied with it, Mr. Clarke," said Nikki.

"So, she told me last night when she got back from New York," said Tobias Clarke. "Two thousand—and we need six." He grinned, and he spat again.

"Well," said Nikki sadly to Ellery, "that's that." She hoped he would immediately get into the car and drive back to New York —immediately.

But Ellery showed no disposition to be sensible. "Perhaps, Mr. Clark, some trees died in the course of time and just disappeared, stumps, roots, and all. Martha—" *Martha!* "—said the *Diary* doesn't mention the exact number Washington planted here."

"Look at them holes. Twelve of 'em, ain't there? In a triangle. Man plants trees in a triangle, he plants trees in a triangle. Ye don't see no place between holes big enough for another tree, do ye? Anyways, there was the same distance between all the trees. No, sir, Mister, twelve was all there was ever; and I looked under all twelve."

"What's the extra tree doing in the center of the triangle? You haven't uprooted that one, Mr. Clarke."

Tobias Clarke spat once more. "Don't know much about trees, do ye? That's a cherry saplin' I set in myself six years ago. Ain't got nothin' to do with George Washington."

Nikki tittered.

"If you'd sift the earth in those holes—"

"I sifted it, Look, Mister, either somebody dug that stuff up a hundred years ago, or the whole yarn's a Saturday night whopper. Which it most likely is. There's Martha now with them other folks." And Tobias Clarke added, spitting for the fourth time, "Don't let me be keepin' ye."

"IT REVEALS WASHINGTON RATHER ER...OUT of character," said James Ezekiel Patch that evening.

They were sitting about the fire in the parlor, as heavy with gloom as with Miss Clarke's dinner; and that, at least in Miss Porter's view, was heavy indeed. Baroness Tchek wore the expression of one who is trapped in a cave; there was no further train until morning, and she had not yet resigned herself to a night in a farmhouse bed. The better part of the day had been spent poring over *The Diary of Simeon Clarke,* searching for a clue to the buried Washingtonia. But there was no clue; the pertinent passage referred merely to "*a Triangle of Oake Trees behinde the red Barn which His Excellency the President did plant with his own Hands, as he had promis'd me, and then did burie his Sworde and the Half Disme for his Pleasure in a Case of copper beneathe one of the Oakes, the which, he said (the Case), bad been fashion'd by Mr. Revere of Boston who is experimenting with this Mettle in his Furnasses.*"

"How out of character, Mr. Patch?" asked Ellery. He bad been staring into the fire for a long time, scarcely listening.

"Washington wasn't given to romanticism," said the large man dryly. "No folderol about him. I don't know of anything in his life which prepares us for such a yarn as this. I'm beginning to think—"

"But Professor Shaw himself says the *Diary* is no forgery!" cried Martha Clarke.

"Oh, the book's authentic enough." Professor Shaw seemed unhappy. "But it may simply be a literary hoax, Miss Clarke. The woods are full of them. I'm afraid that unless the story is confirmed by the discovery of that copper case with its contents..."

"Oh, dear," said Nikki impulsively; and for a moment she was sorry for Martha Clarke, she really was.

But Ellery said: "I believe it. Pennsylvania farmers in 1791 weren't given to literary hoaxes, Professor Shaw. As for Washington, Mr. Patch—no man can be so rigidly consistent. And with his wife just recovering from an illness—on his own birthday..." And Ellery fell silent again.

Almost immediately he leaped from his chair. "Mr. Clarke!"

Tobias stirred from his dark corner. "What?"

"Did you ever hear your father, or grandfather—anyone in your family—talk of *another barn behind the house?*"

Martha stared at him. Then she cried: "Papa, that's it! It was a different barn, in a different place, and the original Washington's Grove was cut down, or died—"

"Nope," said Tobias Clarke. "Never was but this one barn. Still got some of its original timbers. Ye can see the date burned into the crosstree—1761."

NIKKI WAS UP EARLY. A steady *hack-hack-hack* borne on the frosty air woke her. She peered out of her back window, the coverlet up to her nose, to see Mr. Ellery Queen against the dawn, like a pioneer, wielding an ax powerfully.

Nikki dressed quickly, shivering, flung her mink-dyed muskrat over her shoulders, and ran downstairs, out of the house, and around it past the barn.

"Ellery! What do you think you're doing? It's practically the middle of the night!"

"Chopping," said Ellery, chopping.

"There's *mountains* of firewood stacked against the barn," said Nikki. "Really, Ellery, I think this is carrying a flirtation too far." Ellery did not reply. "And anyway, there's something—something gruesome and indecent about chopping up trees George Washington planted. It's vandalism."

"Just a thought," panted Ellery, pausing for a moment. "A hundred and fifty-odd years is a long time, Nikki. Lots of queer things could happen, even to a tree, in that time. For instance—"

"The copper case," breathed Nikki, visibly. "The roots grew *around* it. It's *in* one of these stumps!"

"Now you're functioning," said Ellery, and he raised the ax again.

He was still at it two hours later, when Martha Clarke announced breakfast.

AT 11:30 A.M., Nikki returned from driving the Professor, the Baroness, and James Ezekiel Patch to the railroad station. She found Mr. Queen seated before the fire in the kitchen in his undershirt, while Martha Clarke caressed his naked right arm.

"Oh!" said Nikki faintly. "I *beg* your pardon."

"Where you going, Nikki?" said Ellery irritably. "Come in. Martha's rubbing liniment into my biceps."

"He's not very accustomed to chopping wood, is he?" asked Martha Clarke in a cheerful voice.

"Reduced those foul 'oakes' to splinters," groaned Ellery. "Martha, ouch!"

"I should think you'd be satisfied *now,*" said Nikki coldly. "I suggest we imitate Patch, Shaw, and the Baroness, Ellery—there's a 3:05. We can't impose on Miss Clarke's hospitality forever."

To Nikki's horror, Martha Clarke chose this moment to burst into tears.

"Martha!"

Nikki felt like leaping upon her and shaking the cool look back into her perfidious eyes.

"Here—here, now, Martha."

That's right, thought Nikki contemptuously. *Embrace her in front of me!* "It's those three rats. Running out that way! Don't worry—I'll find that sword and half disme for you yet."

"You'll never find them," sobbed Martha, wetting Ellery's undershirt. "Because they're not here. They *never* were here. When you s-stop to think of it...*burying* that coin, his sword...if the story were true, he'd have given them to Simeon and Sarah..."

"Not necessarily, not necessarily," said Ellery with a hateful haste. "The old boy had a sense of history, Martha. They all did in those days. They knew they were men of destiny, and that the eyes of posterity were upon them. Burying 'em is *just* what Washington would have done!"

"Do you really th—think so?"

Oh...pfui.

"But even if he did bury them," Martha sniffled, "it doesn't stand to reason Simeon and Sarah would have let them *stay* buried. They'd have dug that copper box up like rabbits the minute G-George turned his back."

"Two simple countryfolk?" cried Ellery. "Salt of the earth? The new American earth? Disregard the wishes of His Mightiness, George Washington, First President of the United States? Are you out of your mind? And anyway, what would Simeon do with a dress-sword?"

Beat it into a plowshare, thought Nikki spitefully, *that's what he'd do.*

"And that half disme. How much could it have been worth in 1791? Martha, they're here under your farm somewhere. You wait and see—"

"I wish I could b-believe it...Ellery."

"Shucks, child. Now stop crying—"

From the door, Miss Porter said stiffly: "You might put your shirt back on, Superman, before you catch pneumonia."

MR. QUEEN PROWLED about the Clarke acres for the remainder of that day, his nose at a low altitude. He spent some time in the barn. He devoted at least twenty minutes to each of the twelve holes in the earth. He reinspected the oaken wreckage of his axwork, like a pale-ontologist examining an ancient petrifaction for the impression of a dinosaur foot. He measured off the distance between the holes; and, for a moment, a faint tremor of emotion shook him. George Washington had been a surveyor in his youth; here was evidence that his passion for exactitude had not wearied with the years. As far as Ellery could make out, the twelve oaks had been set into the earth at exactly equal distances, in an equilateral triangle.

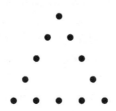

It was at this point that Ellery had seated himself upon the seat of a cultivator behind the barn, wondering at his suddenly accelerated circulation. Little memories were knocking at the door. And as he opened to admit them, it was as if he were admitting a personality. It was, of course, at this time that the sense of personal conflict first obtruded. He had merely to shut his eyes in order to materialize a tall, large-featured man carefully pacing off the distances between twelve points—pacing them off in a sort of objective challenge to the unborn future. George Washington...

The man Washington had from the beginning possessed an affinity for numbers. It had remained with him all his life. To count things, not so much for the sake of the things, perhaps, as for the counting, had been of the utmost importance to him. As a boy in Mr. Williams's school in Westmoreland, he excelled in arithmetic. Long division, subtraction, weights and measures—to calculate cords of wood and pecks of peas, pints and gallons and avoirdupois—young George delighted in these as other boys delighted in horseplay. As a man, he merely directed his passion into the channel of his possessions. Through his possessions he apparently satisfied his curious need for enumeration. He was not content simply to keep accounts of the acreage he owned, its yield, his slaves, his pounds and pence. Ellery recalled the extraordinary case of Washington and the seed. He once calculated the number of seeds in a pound troy weight of red clover. Not appeased by the statistics on red clover, Washington then went to work on a pound of timothy seed. His conclusions were: 71,000 and 298,000. His appetite unsatisfied, he thereupon fell upon the problem of New River grass. Here he tackled a calculation worthy of his prowess: his mathematical labors produced the great, pacifying figure of 844,800.

This man was so obsessed with numbers, Ellery thought, staring at the ruins of Washington's Grove, *that he counted the windows in each house of his Mount Vernon estate and the number of "Paynes" in each window of each house, and then triumphantly recorded the exact number of each in his own handwriting.*

It was like a hunger, requiring periodic appeasement. In 1747, as a boy of fifteen, George Washington drew "A Plan of Major Law: Washingtons Turnip Field as Survey'd by me." In 1786, at the age of fifty-four,

General Washington, the most famous man in the world, occupied himself with determining the exact elevation of his piazza above the Potomac's high water mark. No doubt he experienced a warmer satisfaction thereafter for knowing that when he sat upon his piazza looking down upon the river he was exactly 124 feet 10½ inches above it.

And in 1791, as President of the United States, Ellery mused, *he was striding about right here, setting saplings into the ground, twelve of them in an equilateral triangle, and beneath one of them he buried a copper case containing his sword and the half disme coined from his own silver. Beneath one of them...* But it was not beneath one of them. Or had it been? And had long ago been dug up by a Clarke? But the story had apparently died with Simeon and Sarah. On the other hand...

Ellery found himself irrationally reluctant to conclude the obvious. George Washington's lifelong absorption with figures kept intruding. Twelve trees, equidistant, in an equilateral triangle.

"What is it?" he kept asking himself, almost angrily. "Why isn't it satisfying me?"

And then, in the gathering dusk, a very odd explanation insinuated itself. *Because it wouldn't have satisfied him!*

That's silly, Ellery said to himself abruptly. *It has all the earmarks of a satisfying experience. There is no more satisfying figure in all geometry than an equilateral triangle. It is closed, symmetrical, definite, a whole and balanced and finished thing.*

But it wouldn't have satisfied George Washington...for all its symmetry and perfection.

Then perhaps there is a symmetry and perfection beyond the cold beauty of figures?

At this point, Ellery began to question his own postulates...lost in the dark and to his time...

THEY FOUND HIM AT TEN-THIRTY, crouched on the cultivator seat, numb and staring.

He permitted himself to be led into the house, he suffered Nikki to subject him to the indignity of having his shoes and socks stripped off and his frozen feet rubbed to life, he ate Martha Clarke's dinner—all with a detachment and indifference which alarmed the girls and even made old Tobias look uneasy.

"If it's going to have this effect on him—" began Martha, and then she said: "Ellery, give it up. Forget it." But she had to shake him before he heard her.

He shook his head. "They're there."

"*Where?*" cried the girls simultaneously.

"In Washington's Grove."

"Ye found 'em?" croaked Tobias Clarke, half-rising.

"No."

The Clarkes and Nikki exchanged glances.

"Then how can you be so certain they're buried there, Ellery?" asked Nikki gently.

Ellery looked bewildered. "Darned if I know *how* I know," he said, and he even laughed a little. "Maybe George Washington told me." Then he stopped laughing and went into the fire-lit parlor and—pointedly—slid the doors shut.

AT TEN MINUTES PAST MIDNIGHT, Martha Clarke gave up the contest.

"Isn't he *ever* going to come out of there?" she said, yawning.

"You never can tell what Ellery will do," replied Nikki.

"Well, I can't keep my eyes open another minute."

"Funny," said Nikki. "I'm not the least bit sleepy."

"You city girls."

"You country girls."

They laughed. Then they stopped laughing, and for a moment there was no sound in the kitchen but the patient sentry walk of the grandfather clock and the snores of Tobias assaulting the ceiling from above.

"Well," said Martha. Then she said: "I just *can't*. Are you staying up, Nikki?"

"For a little while. You go to bed, Martha."

"Yes. Well. Good night."

"Good night, Martha."

At the door Martha turned suddenly: "Did he say *George Washington told him?*"

"Yes."

Martha went rather quickly up the stairs.

Nikki waited fifteen minutes. Then she tiptoed to the foot of the stairs and listened. She heard Tobias snuffling and snorting as he turned over in his bed, and an uneasy moan from the direction of Martha's bedroom, as if she were dreaming an unwholesome dream. Nikki set her jaw grimly and went to the parlor doors and slid them open.

Ellery was on his knees before the fire. His elbows were resting on the floor. His face was propped in his hands. In this attitude his posterior was considerably higher than his head.

"Ellery!"

"Huh?"

"Ellery, what on earth—?"

"Nikki. I thought you'd gone to bed long ago." In the firelight his face was haggard.

"But what have you been *doing!* You look exhausted!"

"I am. I've been wrestling with a man who could bend a horseshoe with his naked hands. A very strong man. In more ways than one."

"What are you talking about? Who?"

"George Washington. Go to bed, Nikki."

"George...Washington?"

"Go to bed."

"...*Wrestling* with him?"

"Trying to break through his defenses. Get into his mind. It's not an easy mind to get into. He's been dead such a long time—that makes the difference. The dead are stubborn, Nikki. Aren't you going to bed?"

Nikki backed out shivering. The house *was* icy.

I⊤ WAS EVEN icier when an inhuman bellow accompanied by a thunder that shook the Revolutionary walls of her bedroom brought Nikki out of bed with a yelping leap.

But it was only Ellery.

He was somewhere up the hall, in the first glacial light of dawn, hammering on Martha Clarke's door.

"Martha. *Martha!* Wake up, damn you, and tell me where I can find a book in this damned house! A biography of Washington—a history of the United States—an almanac...*anything!*"

THE PARLOR FIRE had long since given up the ghost. Nikki and Martha in wrappers, and Tobias Clarke in an ancient bathrobe over his marbled long underwear, stood around shivering and bewildered as a disheveled, daemonic Ellery leafed eagerly through a 1921 edition of *The Farmer's Fact Book and Complete Compendium.*

"Here it is!" The words shot out of his mouth like bullets, leaving puffs of smoke.

"What is it, Ellery?"

"What on earth are you looking for?"

"He's loony, I tell ye!"

Ellery turned with a look of ineffable peace, closing the book.

"That's it," he said. "That's it."

"What's it?"

"Vermont. The State of Vermont."

"Vermont...?"

"*Vermont?*"

"Vermont. What in the crawlin' creeper's Vermont got to do with—?"

"Vermont," said Ellery with a tired smile, "did not enter the Union until March fourth, 1791. So that proves it, don't you see?"

"Proves *what?*" shrieked Nikki.

"Where George Washington buried his sword and half disme."

"BECAUSE," said Ellery in the rapidly lightening dawn behind the barn, "Vermont was the fourteenth State to do so. The *fourteenth*. Tobias, would you get me an ax, please?"

"An ax," mumbled Tobias. He shuffled away, shaking his head.

"Come on, Ellery, I'm d-dying of c-cold!" chattered Nikki, dancing up and down before the cultivator.

"Ellery," said Martha Clarke piteously, "I don't understand any of this."

"It's very simple, Martha—oh, thank you, Tobias—as simple," said Ellery, "as simple arithmetic. Numbers, my dears—numbers tell this remarkable story. Numbers and their influence on our first President who was, above all things, a number-man. That was my key. I merely had to discover the lock to fit it into. Vermont was the lock. And the door's open."

Nikki seated herself on the cultivator. You had to give Ellery his head in a situation like this; you couldn't drive him for beans. *Well,* she thought grudgingly, *seeing how pale and how tired-looking he was after a night's wrestling with George Washington, he's earned it.*

"The number was wrong," said Ellery solemnly, leaning on Tobias's ax. "Twelve trees. Washington apparently planted twelve trees—Simeon Clarke's *Diary* never did mention the number twelve, but the evidence seemed unquestionable—there were twelve oaks in an equilateral triangle, each one an equal distance from its neighbor.

"And yet . . . I felt that *twelve* oaks couldn't be, perfect as the triangle was. Not if they were planted by George Washington. Not on February the twenty-second, New Style, in the year of our Lord 1791.

"Because on February the twenty-second, 1791—in fact, until March the fourth, when Vermont entered the Union to swell its original number by one—there was *another* number in the United States so important, so revered, so much a part of the common speech and the common living—and dying—that it was more than a number; it was a solemn and sacred thing; almost not a number at all. It overshadowed other numbers like the still-unborn Paul Bunyan. It was memorialized on the new American flag in the number of its stars and the number of its stripes. It was a number of which George Washington was the standard-bearer!—the head and only recently the strong right arm of the new Republic which had been born out of the blood and muscle of its integers. It was a number which was in the hearts and minds and mouths of all Americans.

"No. If George Washington, who was not merely the living symbol of all this, but carried with him that extraordinary compulsion toward numbers which characterized his whole temperament besides, had wished to plant a number of oak trees to commemorate a birthday visit in the year 1791...he would have, he could have, selected only one number out of all the mathematical trillions at his command—the *number thirteen.*"

The sun was looking over the edge of Pennsylvania at Washington's Grove.

"George Washington planted thirteen trees here that day, and under one of them he buried Paul Revere's copper case. Twelve of the trees he arranged in an equilateral triangle, and we know that the historic treasure was not under any of the twelve. Therefore be must have buried the case under the thirteenth—a thirteenth oak sapling which grew to oakhood and, some time during the past century and a half, withered and died and vanished, vanished so utterly that it left no trace, not even its roots.

"Where would Washington have planted that thirteenth oak? Because beneath the spot where it once stood—there lies the copper case containing his sword and the first coin to be struck off in the new United States."

And Ellery glanced tenderly at the cherry sapling which Tobias Clarke had set into the earth in the middle of Washington's Grove six years before.

"Washington the surveyor, the geometer, the man whose mind cried out for integral symmetries? Obviously, in only one place: *In the center of the triangle.* Any other place would be unthinkable."

And Ellery hefted Tobias's ax and strode toward the six-year-old tree. He raised the ax.

But suddenly he lowered it, and turned, and said in a rather startled way: "See here! Isn't today...?"

"Washington's Birthday," said Nikki.

Ellery grinned, and began to chop down the cherry tree.

Amateur Standing

Suzanne Blanc

This exercise in the niceties of deft plotting has never before been published. It's one that's a pleasure to introduce.

EVERY WEEKDAY MORNING for twenty-odd years, Francis Whitcomb had climbed out of bed at exactly seven o'clock. On winter mornings like this he would close the windows, light the gas wall heater, pick up his clothes, and pad away to the kitchen to dress. Although he was always very careful to avoid awakening Emma, sometimes, before he could steal through the bedroom door, her huge body would stir ominously. Slowly the tangled nest of her iron-gray hair would rise above the covers, then her pale, flabby face would emerge. She would glare at him with sleep-glazed, reptilian eyes and call him an "awkward, bumbling fool."

At such moments, Francis found his wife monstrously ugly. Corseted and groomed, Emma was considered a handsome woman, but Francis was never able to forget how she looked in the harsh light of morning.

This morning he had quietly crawled out of bed, closed the windows and opened the petcock on the heater—all precisely as usual. But here his long-established routine varied. Instead of lighting the gas, he let it hiss unimpeded into the room, swiftly gathered up his clothes and, barely glancing at Emma, shut her into the death chamber behind him.

Fortunately for Francis, he was blissfully unaware of the dangerous properties of his murder weapon. In the kitchen, without even considering the possibilities of explosion, he plugged in the coffee pot and toaster. As he shaved at the cracked mirror over the sink he pictured the deadly fumes filling the bedroom, contained by the walls, the windows, the door. He imagined it rising like water, covering first the floor, lapping against the underside of the bed, creeping up over the mattress, seeping in under the blankets with Emma. Since the gas company is reluctant to issue such statistics, he had no idea how long it would take for the fumes to kill her. In three hours, maybe four, certainly by noon at the latest, Emma would be dead.

At seven forty-five, carrying the lunch sack Emma had prepared the night before, Francis hurried along the chill, bright street to the trolley stop. The brown paper sack was one of the many small, humiliating economies Emma forced on him, and generally Francis was uncomfortably aware of the status token in his hand. However, since this was the last lunch sack he would ever have to carry, its burden became a pleasant reminder. He smiled benignly at Mary Anderson as she ran past him on the way to school, tipped his hat to her mother who was sweeping off the front porch. At the corner he followed a friendly knot of people into the streetcar, exchanged a few pleasantries with the conductor, and took his customary seat next to the window. It could not have been a more ordinary way in which to start a new life.

Hiding behind the daily paper, Francis was secure in the knowledge that nothing in his appearance or habits betrayed him. To everyone on the car he was the same, inoffensive, sandy-haired man who always boarded at Thirty-first, sat in the same seat and meekly got off in front of Grayson's Lumber and Hardware. It was sufficient for him to know that this was only protective coloration. Inside, he was a David who had struck a deadly blow against Goliath.

Unable to concentrate on his paper, Francis watched the streets click monotonously past, wondering who would notify him that Emma was gone. His boss, Mr. Grayson? Dr. Johnson? No, probably

Joe Pollock. Joe was desk sergeant now down at the station, "Lucky" Joe who had married Mabel Richards. Francis remembered how jealous he had been of the policeman when they were both courting Emma. Yes, it would probably be Joe who would have to tell him that Emma was dead.

Sad-faced, solemn, he would come into Grayson's. "Francis," he would say in a somber tone. "I'm afraid I have some bad news for you."

"Bad news?" Francis would ask, portraying just a hint of apprehension.

"You better sit down, Francis. Prepare yourself for a shock."

"What's happened? Nothing's happened to Emma!"

The policeman would blow his red trumpet of a nose. "She's dead, Francis. There's been an accident."

"That's not possible! She was asleep when I left."

"She died in her sleep, Francis, from gas fumes. The heater was on, the flame must have gone out."

Francis would bury his face in his hands then. "It's my fault, all my fault! The regulator hasn't been working right. I kept putting off having it fixed."

"Don't blame yourself, Francis. These things happen."

He could feel Joe Pollock's hand press his shoulder, looked up startled from his daydream to find that it was not Joe at all, but the conductor. "Your stop, Mr. Whitcomb."

The trolley stopped directly in front of Grayson's. "You don't need a car," Emma always said. "It's a foolish waste of money." Well, by next week he would be able to have a car, waste money as foolishly as he pleased.

He walked into the store, nodded stiffly at Miss Adams, who was already working over the accounts, and went into the back room to put on his gray work jacket. Generally he thought of Miss Adams with mild disapproval. She emitted a constant mingled aroma of perfume and gin that was associated in Francis' mind with dark, dimly lit bars and swarthy, hot-eyed men. But, unexpectedly, he noticed that Miss Adams had a vivid charm, hair that shone orange under the artificial light, a white, flashing smile.

He thought, *I wonder what it would be like to spend an evening with her—later, of course,* he amended cautiously. *After a suitable period of mourning for Emma.*

They would go to one of those bars and he would talk to her about his wife. "A wonderful person," he would say. "You remember her, Miss Adams, a large woman, but beautiful in her own way."

"What about me, Mr. Whitcomb?" Miss Adams would pout. "They tell me I'm not so bad."

"You're not bad at all, Miss Adams," Francis would agree. "Not bad at all."

He stole a surreptitious glance in the bookkeeper's direction, saw only the orange crest of her hair bent over the ledger and, musing pleasantly, picked up his backlog of hardware orders. He was hard at work when Mr. Grayson swept pompously through to his private domain.

THE TEMPO of the morning slowly accelerated. The telephone rang, customers came in. Every time he would hear the bell or see the door open, Francis would wonder whether this was it, whether this time it would be someone with the news about Emma.

By nine-thirty, he was beginning to grow a little apprehensive. What if Emma were still lying there when he returned home? He had hoped never to see her again, not even to open the coffin.

Shortly after ten o'clock, a call did come for him. With his heart thumping against the cage of his ribs, he finished waiting on a customer before picking up the receiver.

"Whitcomb speaking."

And then the shock came. It was Emma's voice at the other end of the line. "Francis, I've been trying to get you for hours. That phone's been busy. What in the world do you people do down there?" She paused as if expecting an explanation, then continued angrily. "Did you light the gas before you left this morning?"

Francis' heart was clogging his throat. He managed, "Of course, my dear."

"Then that heater's acting up again. How many times do I have to tell you about it? I woke up and found that flame out."

"Well, it was a good thing you did wake up," Francis said weakly, beads of sweat bubbling up on his forehead.

"On any other day I wouldn't have. But the garbage men made so much racket I couldn't sleep. I've got half a mind to complain to the mayor." Momentarily distracted, she reverted to the main theme. "You call Mr. Slavin at the gas company right now. Have him send someone out. A situation like that is dangerous. Why, I might have been killed!"

"Yes, my dear, you might have," Francis mumbled.

"What did you say?"

"I said I'd call Slavin."

He hung up, wiped the film of sweat from his face and, with robot response, dialed the gas company. Whatever temptation there might have been to delay was erased by the thought that Emma would be waiting when he got home. She was alive, very much alive—as dominant and terrifying and penurious as ever. The muscles of his stomach cramped in disappointment.

"What's the matter, Mr. Whitcomb?" he heard Miss Adams say. "You look sick."

"I am. The flame on the gas heater went out, and my wife almost suffocated."

"All's well that ends well, I always say, Mr. Whitcomb," Miss Adams contributed pertly. "Good thing she noticed it in time. Of course, I wouldn't have gas in my house. Too dangerous."

It was because he had heard the same comment so often, because periodically the paper carried stories of houses exploding or people suffocating that Francis Whitcomb had decided to gas his way to freedom. From the very beginning, when he first started to think of murdering Emma, he had known that her death would have to be an accident.

But in spite of the ease with which such matters are arranged in fiction, he had discovered that, in real life, murder is not so simple. They owned no car with which he could tamper, and send Emma speeding to her death. There were no stairs in the house down which she could be pushed to a broken neck. And, if there had been stairs, she would probably have picked herself up at the bottom and come after him with a meat cleaver. Emma was invincible, indestructible. Even his flawless scheme with the gas had failed.

He returned to work, his mind and stomach churning in futile rebellion. The day that had started with such bright hopes settled in one of despair.

AT NOON, he sat in the back room on a sawhorse, surrounded by bins of nails and bolts, and opened his lunch.

"Deviled eggs again," he thought morosely, peeking between the two slices of tasteless bread.

It was always deviled egg sandwiches. Emma lacked imagination. That was another of the many things he disliked about her, that and her gluttony and her angry voice and her continuous penny-pinching.

Perhaps because he was so depressed, the sandwich tasted worse than usual. He managed to swallow only a few bites before his throat and stomach rebelled. Throwing the rest into the incinerator, he wandered out into the lumber yard.

There the clean, crisp smell of freshly sawed wood momentarily revived him. The knot in his stomach loosened. Everywhere around him was the potential for committing a perfect murder. For instance the brakes on one of the big trucks could fail...or an imperfectly stacked pile of lumber could come crashing down...or the safety guard on the giant saw could come loose. Perfect, no doubt, for killing one of the men who worked in the yard, useless as a method for killing Emma. And bloody, too. At the thought of blood, Francis' stomach started to churn more violently than ever.

Probably it was the combination of frustration and the images of gore that made him feel so squeamish. After he returned to work, he kept thinking that the waves of nausea and the pains in his stomach would pass, but they grew steadily more acute. By mid-afternoon, he was so desperately ill that he was forced to lie down.

In all the years he had been at Grayson's he had never been so desperately ill, and everyone was concerned. Miss Adams clucked over him compassionately. Mr. Grayson insisted on sending him home in a taxi.

"I've called Dr. Johnson for you, Francis," he said. "He'll be over as soon as he can get away."

On the way home Francis watched the taxi meter, fearfully anticipating the tirade that would greet him at this unusual expense. He must have looked worse than he felt, for Emma said nothing. She didn't even complain about the cost when the doctor came. But there was a definite limit to her forbearance.

After poking and thumping and questioning Francis, Dr. Johnson said, "If he's not better tomorrow, we'll have to put him in the hospital."

And that was when Emma exploded. "We can't afford hospitals, doctor," she snapped. "What do you think we are, millionaires?"

It's just like her, Francis thought, to begrudge him medical care and he reconciled himself to dying right there on the couch. He was reckoning without Dr. Johnson, however.

The doctor was diplomatically firm. "There are some things we have to afford, Mrs. Whitcomb. If Francis doesn't feel better by morning, we'd better find out what's wrong."

Emma sounded suddenly worried. "You mean it really could be serious, doctor? What do you think is the matter?"

Dr. Johnson shrugged. "It's hard to say without testing. It may be nothing worse than nervous indigestion, or a mild form of food poisoning."

Emma and the doctor murmured together for a long time at the front door, but Francis made no effort to hear them. Something the doctor had said kept revolving on the turntable of his mind. Poison. The unpleasant taste of the deviled egg sandwich returned. He remembered stories he had read of bodies disinterred decades after a murder in which traces of arsenic were found. There was a sack of weed-killer in the shed, and poison would be so easy.

He could mix the weed-killer in with the sugar or that chocolate syrup Emma poured over everything. Poisoning would be a form of poetic justice in which his wife's gluttony and penny-pinching would kill her. If she were dying, Emma would never spend the money on a hospital.

Francis' hopes soared towards freedom. He would have that date with Miss Adams after all. At the rebirth of hope the knot in his stomach dissolved, the nausea receded.

He smiled serenely, listening to Emma slam the door after Doctor Johnson and thump away to the kitchen. He heard her opening the refrigerator door, imagined her taking out the brown can of chocolate syrup. Now she was rinsing out the glass.

BUT IT WAS NOT a glass that Emma Whitcomb was rinsing. She was washing away the remnants of the deviled egg spread she had prepared for Francis' lunch. There was some left that she had intended to use tomorrow. With that doctor snooping around, however, it was too dangerous. With hospitals and tests, using poison was no longer possible. She would have to find some other way to get rid of that worm she had married, something foolproof, like the gas that had seeped from the defective heater.

"That's it," she mumbled optimistically. "I'll arrange an accident!"

And, humming cheerfully to herself, Emma Whitcomb put on the kettle for a soothing cup of tea.

The Peppermint-Striped Goodbye

Ron Goulart

Parody is the sincerest form of flattery so, you Ross Macdonalds, Ray Chandlers, et al., feel praised. You're being imitated, and by one who can express himself superbly.

Chapter 1

THE DRIVE-IN, all harsh glass and stiff redwood and brittle aluminum and sharp No. 7 nails, stood on the oceanside of the bright road like some undecided suicide. My carhop had a look of frozen hopefulness and the flawed walk of a windup doll with a faulty gudgeon pin. Shifting in the seat of my late model car, I eased the barrel of my stiff black .38 Police Special so that it stopped cutting off the circulation in my left leg.

"Where's the town of San Mineo?" I asked the girl, my voice an echo of all the lost hopes of all of us.

"Back that way about twenty miles," she said.

I'd thought so. Sometimes the intricate labyrinth that is Southern California gets one up on me. But there is, as my once-wife used to point out, an intense, harsh, sun-dried stubbornness about Ross Pewter. She often talked like that.

It was stubborn of me to drive my late model car, gunning it too much on the sharp death-edged curves of the road that wound by the sea, twenty miles in the wrong direction. I was thirty-six now, and sometimes the harsh sun-dried motor trips through the fever-heat madness that is Southern California made me feel that time's winged chariot was behind me. Other times it was a lettuce truck. Nobody passed Ross Pewter on the road.

"Do you wish to see a menu?" the carhop asked. Her voice had the ring of too much laughter deferred in it.

"No," I told her. I backed out of the place, afraid of the already ghost-town look of it, and cannoned back toward San Mineo and my client.

"Pewter," I said aloud as my late model car flashed like a dazed locust down the mirage of the state highway, "Pewter, some of these encounters you get into in the pursuit of a case seem to be without meaning."

I would have answered myself that life itself is at times, most times, meaningless. But a highway patrol cycle, its motor like the throaty cough of an old man who has come to Los Angeles from Ohio and found that his Social Security checks are being sent still to his Ohio address, started up behind me. The pursuit began, and I had to ride the car hard to elude it.

Chapter 2

The pillars that held up the porch of the big house reminded me of the detail of the capital and entablature of the Ionic temple at Fortuna Virilis at Rome. The entablature, cornice, and architrave were encrusted with carved ornament, a motif of formalized acanthus leaf enriching the design. and the scrolls terminated in rosettes.

I almost wished this were the house I was going to visit.

Sighing, and dislodging the barrel of my pistol from a tender part of my thigh, I crossed the rich moneyed street and approached the home of old Tro Bultitude.

Decay seemed to drift all around, carried like pollen on the hot red wind of this late Southern California afternoon. Even the pilasters, the balustrades, and the cornices of the sprawling Bultitude mansion seemed decayed. It sat like the waiting wedding cake in that book by Charles Dickens.

The thought of it all filled me with sadness, and the actual pollen in the air started my hay fever going again. The butler was a heavy-set man, all thick hair and musty black clothes, and there was about him the faint smell of Saturday matinees in small Midwestern movie theaters now renovated and made into supermarkets and coin laundries.

"Blow off, Jack," he said.

"The name is Pewter," I said. "Tell your boss I'm here to see him."

"Scram, Jacko. We got illness in the family. All the Colonel's unmarried daughters are down with nymphomania."

I didn't speak. I just showed him the barrel of my .38.

"What's that hanging on the end of it?" he asked.

I looked. "Some elastic from my shorts, it seems. Want to make a quip about it?"

"I'll quip you," said the butler, snarling. "You remind me of all the lonely self-abusing one-suited bill collectors that haunted the time-troubled corridors of my long-ago youth."

"I'll do the metaphors around here," I said and went for him. I got two nice chops at his jaw, and he tumbled back like a condemned building that has just been hit by a runaway truck.

"Let's not waste any more time," called an old lifeworn voice from inside.

I vaulted the fallen butler and found myself not in a hallway, but at once in a giant white-walled room. As I looked on, steam began to come from jets low in the wall.

"The name is Pewter," I said to the crumbled old man who sat in a sun chair, wrapped in a towel as white as the flash of a .38 like mine. "You've got a problem?"

"Vachel Geesewand said you'd cleared up that business in Santa Monica," said Bultitude.

"I cleared up the whole damn town before I quit."

"Good. My problem," said the old man, "is simply this. About twenty-two years ago in Connecticut—the name of the town doesn't matter—a young man named Earl K. M. Hoseblender was riding a bicycle down East Thirty-fourth Street, heading for a hardware store."

"Go on," I said, interested now.

"My mind wanders," he admitted. "That isn't the right problem. That one the police will handle. What I want you to do is find my daughter, Alicia."

"I can do that."

"Alicia is a strange girl," said the old man. "For a long time she wore a false beard and hung out with the surfers at Zuma Beach. They drove around in an old ice-cream wagon they'd painted with peppermint stripes."

"Red and white stripes?"

"You've guessed it," said Tro Bultitude. "Then, about a year ago, there was an accident."

"What kind of an accident?"

"Alicia never told me. I do know that the bell fell off the ice-cream wagon, she's talked about that often. And a boy named Kip may have broken his left ankle. It was all a year ago, a long time ago for a twenty-year-old like Alicia.

"You see, Mr. Pewter, Alicia has not had an untroubled childhood. When she was four, my first wife—the former Hazel Wadlow Whitney—fell unaccountably from the top of a Christmas tree and succumbed. Alicia was the only witness." He sighed a dry dead sigh, like leaves being swept up by a slipshod gardener. "At fourteen she was unavoidably involved in a bank robbery in Connecticut. The town will be nameless."

"Is it the same town Hoseblender was riding his bicycle in?"

"No," he admitted. "It's a different nameless town."

"Do you have any pictures of your daughter?"

"Yes, but you'll have to be careful who you show them to, since they're pornographic. Another unfortunate moment in the poor child's past."

"When'd she leave?"

"The day after my fourth wife—the former Hazel Wadlow Whitney—fell off the cupola."

"I thought Hazel Wadlow Whitney was your first wife?"

"This is a different Hazel Wadlow Whitney. I have a tendency to marry women with that name. It has upset Alicia more than once. When she was fifteen, she ran away to Topeka, Kansas, and was later arrested for trying to break the Menninger Brothers' windows."

"Any idea where she might be?"

"You might look for that candy-striped ice-cream wagon."

I scowled at his finished old lusterless eyes. "You're keeping something back from me."

"Very well," he said, making a feminine gesture. "She is not alone. There is a strong possibility she may be with her half-brother. You see, fifteen years ago I discovered a foundling on my doorstep. He was nearly five at the time and quite bright. The note pinned to him explained that he had an IQ of 185."

"How does that make him a half-brother to Alicia?"

"I can't tell you that."

"A hundred dollars a day and expenses is my fee," I told him.

"Dawes will give you an envelope full of money, Mr. Pewter. If you'll excuse me, I have to take a steam bath. I suffer from a malignant disease, and steam seems to be good for me."

The room, now that I noticed it, was as foggy as the 2900 block on Jackson Street in San Francisco. I said goodbye, and went out to find the butler and my money.

Chapter 3

Something old Bultitude had said gave me a hunch, and I took a jet to Connecticut as soon as I left him.

The night seems timeless when you are hurtling through it at a fast clip—like a marble in some pinball machine in a grease-and-chili-smelling place on some hot, dry side street on the underbelly of Southern California. We all of us drag the past with us like one of those big silver trailers that clog the L.A. highways. Looking, all of us, for a place to pull off the road and park the damn thing, but we never do it.

Spent time is somewhat like the bird in that poem by Coleridge, and we carry it around our neck like a gift necktie that we have to wear to please the giver, who gave it to us like somebody passing out the second-rate wine now that the guests, who sit around like numbed patients in some sort of cosmic dentist's waiting room, are too unsober to know or care.

I suppose you've felt like that when you're flying, too.

Chapter 4

The cops beat me up in Connecticut. They always do. But I found out what I wanted. By noon, on a hot, dry, sticky-ninety and-climbing day, I was back at the drive-in I'd gone to by mistake.

The kitchen was like all the meals they made you eat as a lonely child. It smelled of oatmeal and fried foods and stale chocolate cake.

"You," I said to the fry cook.

He was a pale youth of about twenty. His face had the worn look of one who has lost two falls out of three—lost too many battles with the dark side of himself.

"Don't bug me now, mister," he said. "I've got to fry three orders of oatmeal."

I picked a soft spot in his belly and gave him a stiff-fingered jab there. He fell over onto the stale chocolate cake, making the silent falling sound that a giant tree does when it topples alone in a distant wood.

"I know you're Albert B. Bultitude," I told the kid, jerking him to his feet. "Yesterday when I came in here I saw the overcoat."

"You weren't in this kitchen yesterday, mister."

"Don't mix me up while I'm trying to explain this case," I said. "They told me some things in Connecticut."

"Sure, they're a knowledgeable bunch in Connecticut. You take Westport, for instance, they have a great many gifted people there."

"Forget that," I told him. "I know who your mother is."

His eyes flickered like a cigarette lighter about to run out of fluid. "How did you guess?"

"She let the towel slip when she was in the steam bath and I figured it out."

"Well, you're right. Our mistake was keeping the past festering too long."

"It wasn't Hazel Wadlow Whitney who fell from the cupola, it was Tro Bultitude, pushed by you. I thought Dawes was too tough. He's really your Uncle Brewster from Maine. Still the whole business about the silverware doesn't make sense to me."

"I never heard of any silverware."

"Good. Then I'll leave that part out."

"I guess you know about Alicia, too."

"There is no Alicia," I said. "There never was. Alicia is really Tony, your other half-brother. He drove the car that time in Connecticut. The accident with the ice-cream wagon made him walk funny, and then he decided to try the Alicia bit."

"It's odd how the past catches up with us," said Albert.

"The only thing is," I said, watching the oatmeal burn away to ashes, "I still don't see why your mother hired me at all. She's accomplished only the arrest of her son for the murder of her husband."

"Mother's been rather dotty since she fell off the Christmas tree that time."

I needed a lungful of fresh air. "Let's go, Albert I know some cops in L.A. who aren't corrupt, and I'm turning you over to them."

Outside Albert stared at the bright, intense blue of the ocean. He hesitated for a long second, and then waved boyishly at the mindless timeless water.

"Goodbye," he called. "I don't think I'll be seeing the ocean again for a while."

He was right.

Marmalade Wine

Joan Aiken

How should one advertise it? Marmalade Wine, for that Taste of Terror?

"Paradise," Blacker said to himself, moving forward into the wood. "Paradise. Fairyland."

He was a man given to exaggeration; poetic license he called it, and his friends called it "Blacker's little flights of fancy," or something less polite, but on this occasion he spoke nothing but the truth.

The wood stood silent about him, tall, golden, with afternoon sunlight slanting through the half-unfurled leaves of early summer. Underfoot, anemones palely carpeted the ground. A cuckoo called.

"Paradise," Blacker repeated, closed the gate behind him, and strode down the overgrown path, looking for a spot in which to eat his ham sandwich. Hazel bushes thickened at either side until the circular blue eye of the gateway by which he had come in dwindled to a pinpoint and vanished. The taller trees over-topping the hazels were not yet in full leaf and gave little cover; it was very hot in the wood and very still.

Suddenly Blacker stopped short with an exclamation of surprise and regret: lying among the dog's-mercury by the path was the body of a cock-pheasant in the full splendor of its spring plumage. Blacker turned the bird over with the townsman's pity and curiosity at such evidence of nature's unkindness; the feathers, purple-bronze, green, and gold, were smooth under his hand as a girl's hair.

"Poor thing," he said aloud, "what can have happened to it?"

He walked on, wondering if he could turn the incident to account. "Threnody for a Pheasant in May." Too precious? Too sentimental? Perhaps a weekly would take it. He began choosing rhymes, staring at his feet as he walked, abandoning his conscious rapture at the beauty around him.

> *Stricken to death...and something...leafy ride,*
> *Before his...something...fully flaunt his pride.*

Or would a shorter line be better, something utterly simple and heartfelt, limpid tears of grief like spring rain dripping off the petals of a flower?

It was odd, Blacker thought, increasing his pace, how difficult he found writing nature poetry; nature was beautiful, maybe, but it was not stimulating. And it was nature poetry that *Field and Garden* wanted. Still, that pheasant ought to be worth five guineas. *Tread lightly past, Where he lies still, And something last...*

Damn! In his absorption he had nearly trodden on *another* pheasant. What was happening to the birds? Blacker, who objected to occurrences with no visible explanation, walked on, frowning.

The path bore downhill to the right, and leaving the hazel coppice, crossed a tiny valley. Below him, Blacker was surprised to see a small, secretive flint cottage, surrounded on three sides by trees. In front of it was a patch of turf. A deck chair stood there, and a man was peacefully stretched out in it, enjoying the afternoon sun.

Blacker's first impulse was to turn back; he felt as if he had walked into somebody's garden, and was filled with mild irritation at the unexpectedness of the encounter; *there ought to have been some warning signs, dash it all.* The wood had seemed as deserted as Eden itself. But his turning round would have an appearance of guilt and furtiveness; on second thought, he decided to go boldly past the cottage. After all, there was no fence, and the path was not marked private in any way; he had a perfect right to be there.

"Good afternoon," said the man pleasantly as Blacker approached. "Remarkably fine weather, is it not?"

"I do hope I'm not trespassing."

Studying the man, Blacker revised his first guess. This was no gamekeeper; there was distinction in every line of the thin, sculptured face. What most attracted Blacker's attention were the hands, holding a small gilt coffee-cup; they were as white, frail, and attenuated as the pale roots of water-plants.

"Not at all," the man said cordially. "In fact, you arrive at a most opportune moment; you are very welcome. I was just wishing for a little company. Delightful as I find this sylvan retreat, it becomes, all of a sudden, a little *dull,* a little *banal.* I do trust that you have time to sit down and share my after lunch coffee and liqueur."

As he spoke, he reached behind him and brought out a second deck chair from the cottage porch.

"Why, thank you; I should be delighted," said Blacker, wondering if he had the strength of character to take out the ham sandwich and eat it in front of this patrician hermit.

Before he made up his mind, the man had gone into the house and returned with another gilt cup full of black, fragrant coffee, hot as Tartarus, which he handed to Blacker. He carried also a tiny glass, and into this, from a blackcurrant-cordial bottle, he carefully poured a clear, colorless liquor.

Blacker sniffed his glassful with caution, mistrusting the bottle and its evidence of home brewing, but the scent, aromatic and powerful, was similar to that of curaçao, and the liquid moved in its glass with an oily smoothness. It certainly was not cow slip wine.

"Well," said his host, reseating himself and gesturing slightly with his glass, "how do you do?" He sipped delicately.

"Cheers," said Blacker, and added, "My name's Roger Blacker." It sounded a little lame.

The liqueur was not curaçao, but akin to it, and quite remarkably potent; Blacker, who was very hungry, felt the fumes rise up inside his head as if an orange tree had taken root there and was putting out leaves and golden glowing fruit.

"Sir Francis Deeking," the other man said, and then Blacker

understood why his hands had seemed so spectacular, so porten-
tously out of the common.

"The surgeon? But surely you don't live down here?"

Deeking waved a hand deprecatingly. "A weekend retreat. A
hermitage, to which I can retire from the strain of my calling."

"It certainly is very remote," Blacker remarked. "It must be five
miles from the nearest road."

"Six. And you, my dear Mr. Blacker, what is your profession?"

"Oh, a writer," said Blacker modestly. The drink was having its
usual effect on him; he managed to convey not that he was a jour-
nalist on a twopenny daily with literary yearnings, but that he was a
philosopher and essayist of rare quality, a sort of second Bacon. All
the time he spoke, while drawn out most flatteringly by the questions
of Sir Francis, he was recalling journalistic scraps of information
about his host: the operation on the Indian Prince; the Cabinet
Minister's appendix; the amputation performed on that unfortunate
ballerina who had both feet crushed in a railway accident; the major
operation which had proved so miraculously successful on the American heiress.

"You must feel like a god," he said suddenly, noticing with
surprise that his glass was empty. Sir Francis waved the remark aside.

"We all have our godlike attributes," he said, leaning forward.
"Now you, Mr Blacker, a writer, a creative artist—do you not know a
power akin to godhead when you transfer your thought to paper?"

"Well, not exactly then," said Blacker, feeling the liqueur moving
inside his head in golden and russet-colored clouds. "Not *so* much
then, but I do have one unusual power, a power not shared by many
people, of foretelling the future. For instance, as I was coming
through the wood, I *knew* this house would be here. I knew I should
find you sitting in front of it. I can look at the list of runners in a race,
and the name of the winner fairly leaps out at me from the page, as if
it was printed in golden ink. Forthcoming events—air disasters, train
crashes—I always sense in advance. I begin to have a terrible feeling
of impending doom, as if my brain was a volcano just on the point of
eruption."

What was that other item of news about Sir Francis Deeking, he wondered, a recent report, a tiny paragraph that had caught his eye in *The Times?* He could not recall it.

"*Really?*" Sir Francis was looking at him with the keenest interest; his eyes, hooded and fanatical under their heavy lids, held brilliant points of light. "I have always longed to know somebody with such a power. It must be a terrifying responsibility."

"Oh, it is," Blacker said. He contrived to look bowed under the weight of supernatural cares; noticed that his glass was full again, and drained it. "Of course, I don't use the faculty for my own ends; something fundamental in me rises up to prevent that. It's as basic, you know, as the instinct forbidding cannibalism or incest—"

"Quite, quite," Sir Francis agreed. "But for another person, you would be able to give warnings, advise profitable courses of action—? My dear fellow, your glass is empty. Allow me."

"This is marvelous stuff," Blacker said hazily. "It's like a wreath of orange blossom." He gestured with his finger.

"I distill it myself; from marmalade. But do go on with what you were saying. Could you, for instance, tell me the winner of this afternoon's Manchester Plate?"

"Bow Bells," Blacker said unhesitatingly. It was the only name he could remember.

"You interest me enormously. And the result of today's Aldwych by-election? Do you know that?"

"Unwin, the Liberal, will get in by a majority of two hundred and eighty-two. He won't take his seat, though. He'll be killed at seven this evening in a lift accident at his hotel." Blacker was well away by now.

"Will he, indeed?" Sir Francis appeared delighted. "A pestilent fellow. I have sat on several boards with him. Do continue."

Blacker required little encouragement He told the story of the financier whom he had warned in time of the oil company crash; the dream about the famous violinist which had resulted in the man's cancelling his passage on the ill-fated *Orion;* and the tragic tale of the bullfighter who had ignored his warning.

"But I'm talking too much about myself," he said at length, partly because he noticed an ominous clogging of his tongue, a refusal of his thoughts to marshal themselves. He cast about for an impersonal topic, something simple.

"The pheasants," he said. "What's happened to the pheasants? Cut down in their prime. It—it's terrible. I found four in the wood up there, four or five."

"Really?" Sir Francis seemed callously uninterested in the fate of the pheasants. "It's the chemical sprays they use on the crops, I understand. Bound to upset the ecology; they never work out the probable results beforehand. Now if *you* were in charge, my dear Mr. Blacker—but forgive me, it is a hot afternoon, and you must be tired and footsore if you have walked from Witherstow this morning—let me suggest that you have a short sleep..."

His voice seemed to come from farther and farther away; a network of sun-colored leaves laced themselves in front of Blacker's eyes. Gratefully he leaned back and stretched out his aching feet.

Some time after this Blacker roused a little—or was it only a dream?—to see Sir Francis standing by him, rubbing his hands, with a face of jubilation.

"My dear fellow, my dear Mr Blacker, what a *lusus naturae* you are. I can never be sufficiently grateful that you came my way. Bow Bells walked home—positively *ambled*. I have been listening to the commentary. What a misfortune that I had no time to place money on the horse—but never mind, never mind, that can be remedied another time.

"It is unkind of me to disturb your well-earned rest, though; drink this last thimbleful and finish your nap while the sun is on the wood."

As Blacker's head sank back against the deck chair again, Sir Francis leaned forward and gently took the glass from his hand.

Sweet river of dreams, thought Blacker, *fancy the horse actually winning. I wish I'd had a fiver on it myself; I could do with a new pair of shoes. I should have undone these before I dozed off, they're too tight or something. I must wake up soon, ought to be on my way in half an hour or so...*

WHEN BLACKER FINALLY WOKE, he found that he was lying on a narrow bed, indoors, covered with a couple of blankets. His head ached and throbbed with a shattering intensity, and it took a few minutes for his vision to clear; then he saw that the was in a small white cell-like room which contained nothing but the bed he was on and a chair. It was very nearly dark.

He tried to struggle up, but a strange numbness and heaviness had invaded the lower part of his body, and after hoisting himself on to his elbow he felt so sick that he abandoned the effort and lay down again.

That stuff must have the effect of a knockout drop, he thought ruefully; *what a fool I was to drink it. I'll have to apologize to Sir Francis. What time can it be?*

Brisk light footsteps approached the door, and Sir Francis came in. He was carrying a portable radio which he placed on the window sill.

"Ah, my dear Blacker, I see you have come round. Allow me to offer you a drink."

He raised Blacker skillfully, and gave him a drink of water from a cup with a rim and a spout.

"Now let me settle you down again. Excellent. We shall soon have you—well, not on your feet, but sitting up and taking nourishment." He laughed a little. "You can have some beef tea presently."

"I am so sorry," Blacker said. "I really need not trespass on your hospitality any longer. I shall be quite all right in a minute."

"No trespass, my dear friend. You are not at all in the way. I hope that you will be here for a long and pleasant stay. These surroundings, so restful, so conducive to a writer's inspiration—what could be more suitable for you? You need not think that I shall disturb you. I am in London all week, but shall keep you company at weekends—pray, pray don't think that you will be a nuisance or *de trop*. On the contrary, I am hoping that you can do me the kindness of giving me the Stock Exchange prices in advance, which will amply compensate for any small trouble I have taken. No, no, you must feel quite at home—please consider, indeed, that this *is* your home."

Stock Exchange prices? It took Blacker a moment to remember, then he thought, *Oh lord, my tongue has played me false as usual.* He tried to recall what stupidities he had been guilty of.

"Those stories," he said lamely, "they were all a bit exaggerated, you know. About my foretelling the future. I can't really. That horse's winning was a pure coincidence, I'm afraid."

"Modesty, modesty." Sir Francis was smiling, but he had gone rather pale, and Blacker noticed a beading of sweat along his cheekbones. "I am sure you will be invaluable. Since my retirement, I find it absolutely necessary to augment my income by judicious investment."

All of a sudden Blacker remembered the gist of that small paragraph in *The Times. Nervous breakdown. Complete rest. Retirement.*

"I—I really must go now," he said uneasily, trying to push himself upright. "I meant to be back in town by seven."

"Oh, but Mr. Blacker, that is quite out of the question. Indeed, so as to preclude any such action, I have amputated your feet. But you need not worry; I know you will be very happy here. And I feel certain that you are wrong to doubt your own powers. Let us listen to the nine o'clock news in order to be quite satisfied that the detestable Unwin did fall down the hotel lift shaft."

He walked over to the portable radio and switched it on.

Counter Intelligence

Robert L. Fish

When you finish this story and stop to consider what it was about, you realize what a masterful job of storytelling has taken place. Here you can appreciate the art of the artist.

I HAVE LONG since ceased to be amazed at bumping into Kek Huuygens anywhere in the world, or in any condition of financial peak or depression. He is a charming fellow, brilliant and persuasive, who buys his share of the drinks when his pocketbook permits—and with the added attraction that he does not use his considerable talents at deception against his close friends. I have often wondered just how far Kek Huuygens might have gone in life had a policy of strict moral turpitude been one of his inviolate precepts.

This time, I ran into him in Paris. My newspaper had transferred me back there after an absence of almost eight years, and this particular day, I was walking morosely back from the office to my hotel, reflecting unhappily on the changes that had taken place in the city since I was last there. I was edging past a crowded sidewalk cafe when an arm reached out to detain me. I turned and found myself staring into Kek Huuygens' smiling eyes.

"Have a seat," he said calmly, almost as if it had been but hours since we had met instead of at least three years—and that time across an ocean. He raised a beckoning arm for the waiter, his eyes never leaving my face. "The last time I saw you, I was unfortunate enough to have to ask you to buy me a drink. Allow me to repay you."

"Kek Huuygens!" I exclaimed delightedly, and dropped into a chair at his side. Besides being excellent company, Huuygens has always been good for copy, and one of the changes in Paris that had discouraged me was the very lack of copy; French man, in my absence, had seemingly become civilized. My eyebrows raised as my glance flickered over the figure across from me. The excellent cut of his obviously expensive suit, the jaunty angle of his Homburg, the trim insolence of his mustache, not to mention the freshness of his boutonniere at that late hour of the afternoon, all were in sharp contrast to his appearance the last time I had seen him in New York.

His eyes followed my inspection with sardonic amusement. "What will you have to drink?"

"A brandy," I said, grinning at him. I allowed my grin to fade into a rather doubtful grimace; one thing I thought I had learned about Huuygens was how to jar a story out of him. I ran my eye over him again. "Illegality seems to be more profitable than when last we met."

He placed my order with the waiter who had finally appeared, and then returned his attention to me. "On the contrary," he said with a faint smile. "I finally took the advice of all my well-meaning friends and discovered, to my complete astonishment, that the rewards of being on the side of the law can be far greater than I had ever anticipated."

"Oh?" I tried not to sound skeptical.

His eyes twinkled at my poor attempt at deception. "I shall not keep it a secret from you," he said dryly. "I am forced, however, to ask you to keep what I am about to tell you a secret from everyone else."

I stared at him. "But why?" I asked unhappily.

"In the interests of that law and order you are always extolling," he replied even more dryly. We waited in silence while the waiter placed my brandy before me; he slipped the saucer onto Huuygens' pile and disappeared. Kek's eyes were steady upon my face. I shrugged, raised my glass in a small gesture of defeat, and sipped. Huuygens nodded, satisfied with my implied promise, and leaned back.

Now that I realize the benefits that can derive from honesty (Huuygens said, smiling in my direction), I shall have to review America again in a different light. However, just after I last saw you, I had not as yet been converted, and since it becomes increasingly embarrassing to sponge on friends, I managed to return to France, where I have a cousin I actually enjoy sponging on. Immediately following the war, he and I were sort of partners in black market foodstuffs, but we split up when I realized that the man was completely dishonest. Besides, in those days, they were beginning to impose the death penalty for this particular naughtiness, and there are limits to the extent I will indulge in gambling—especially with my life.

In any event, there must have been something about foodstuffs that attracted my cousin, because when I got back to Paris, I found he had turned to legality with a vengeance, and was the owner of a chain of what have become known throughout the world as supermarkets. I personally cannot understand the success of these sterile, automated dispensers of comestibles, all so daintily packaged in transparent plastic—especially in France, since it is obviously impossible to haggle with a price stamped in purple ink on the bottom of a tin. However, there it is; the fact was that my cousin was rolling in money. And while he was far from pleased to add me to his *ménage*, even temporarily, there was very little he could do about it. Normally, I hate to stoop to threatening a man with his past, but in his case, it took no great appeasement of my conscience.

For a while, I thought his wife would prove an even greater obstacle. She was built like a corseted Brahma bull, with a trailing mustache, an eye like a laser beam, and a voice that made me think of nothing so much as a shovel being dragged across rough concrete. However, he apparently explained to her the alternatives to my presence, and after that, she was actually quite innocuous.

Do not think that I was pleased myself to be in this position of practically begging, but there was nothing else I could do. Even the most modest of schemes requires capital, and I was broke. And while I could bring myself to accept—and even insist upon—my cousin's hospitality, I could not use my knowledge of his past to extract money from him. It would have been against my principles. However, the situation wasn't all bad; my cousin had a fine cook, a nubile and willing housemaid, an extensive library and an excellent cellar, so I found myself settling in quite comfortably, and actually even in danger of vegetating.

One evening, however, my cousin returned home in a preoccupied mood. Throughout dinner, a time he usually spent in alternately stuffing himself and listing his assets, he sat quiet and scowling at his plate, nor did he touch his dessert. Something was obviously wrong, and on the offhand chance that it might involve me or my sinecure in his home, I nailed him immediately after dinner in the library.

"Stavros," I said—you must understand that while both of us were Poles, and I had long since adopted the fiction of being Dutch, my cousin, for reasons I cannot attempt to explain, preferred the pretense of a Greek background. Maybe it was useful in his business. But I digress. In any event, I said, "Stavros, something is bothering you. Can I be of any assistance to you?"

He began to wave his hand in a fashion to indicate denial, and then he suddenly paused and stared at me thoughtfully through narrowed eyes. "Do you know," he said slowly, "possibly you can. Certainly if there is some scheme here, some attempt to be over-clever, you would be the ideal one to ferret it out."

"Scheme?" I asked, and poured myself a generous brandy. I sat down opposite him. "What are you talking about?"

He hesitated as if reluctant to take me into his confidence, but then the weight of his problem overcame his irresolution.

He leaned forward. "Do you know anything about supermarkets?"

My eyebrows raised. I was about to give him the same opinions I have just voiced to you, but then I realized it would serve no purpose. "No," I said simply. "I know that people serve themselves from shelves and pass before a clerk who sums up their purchases. They pay and take the stuff with them. That's all I do know."

He nodded. "And that's all you should know. Or anyone should know. But somebody appears to know something else." He paused a moment and then leaned forward again. "Kek, in the supermarket business, we are used to pilfering—small items that women put into their purses, or tuck into a baby carriage beneath the blankets; things that children steal and sometimes eat right in the store, or hide in their boots—"

"Horrible!" I murmured.

"Yes," he agreed. "But—and this is the important thing—we can calculate to the merest fraction of a percent the exact amount we will lose through this thievery. It is done scientifically, on computers, based on multiple experiences and probability curves, and these calculations are never wrong." He sighed helplessly. "I mean, they were never wrong before. But now—my God!"

"Tell me," I suggested.

"Yes," he said more calmly. "Well, in our largest store, the percentages have gone absolutely berserk! Stealing on a scale that is impossible! And the frightening thing is that we don't know how it is done!" He pounded one fist against his forehead in desperation. "I have received the report from the detective agency today. I have had detectives pose as customers, as cashiers, as clerks unloading cartons or stamping prices on tins. I have had the store watched, day and night, both from the outside and the inside, week after week—and yet, it continues. I have done everything possible, and now, I am about to go out of my mind. If somebody has discovered a method of pilfering that our system cannot cope with..." He shrugged fatalistically and shivered.

He did not have to spell it out for me. I reached for the bottle of brandy, nodding sympathetically. "And how does your system work?"

He got to his feet and began to pace back and forth across the thick rug of the library. It was evident that the subject was close to his heart, and had he been delineating success rather than failure, his attitude could only have been described as enthusiastic.

"This store has eight check-out counters," he said. "At each is stationed a clerk who punches the keys of the cash register for each purchase. These figures are reproduced on a continuous tape within the register, and no one has access to this record except the head auditor in the main office. The manager of the store removes it..." He saw my eyes light up, and shook his head. "No. The manager removes a small box that contains the tape, but he cannot open this box. He sends the boxes in daily, together with the cash he has collected, and they always balance."

He paused and then raised a finger in a slight gesture, as if equating one thing with another. "At the same time, we have our constant inventory controls of the stocks, and these are also in the hands of people not connected with the individual store, and people of utmost confidence. And we also employ an outside firm of auditors to spot-check these stocks from time to time. Of late, I have had them checking daily." He raised his two hands, palms upwards. "A comparison of the register tapes and the inventory records indicates the unseen losses which, as I say, are completely calculable. At least, in every store in the chain except this one."

"But, surely," I said. "A dishonest clerk…"

He shook his head. "We follow the established procedures of the American supermarkets, and to steal from a supermarket on a large scale is far from being as simple as it may appear to you at first. Believe me."

Knowing him, I believed him. "What can I do to help you?"

He frowned. "I honestly don't know. But someone has apparently discovered a means of pilfering, of swindling us, that we cannot resolve. And since your experience—" He paused and then raised one hand apologetically. "I would not consider asking your help just in return for your—your—" He wanted to say "sponging" but couldn't bring himself to it; he was never the bravest of men, "Your presence as a guest in my house…" It was weak, and he knew it. His voice firmed, but with bitterness behind it. "If you can discover what is going on and put a stop to it, there will be a reward."

"How great a reward?" I asked quietly. The thing was beginning to intrigue me.

He bit his lip. "One-five-ten thousand francs!" he said.

"They *have* been doing a job on you, haven't they?" I said gently.

"Yes," he replied simply. "They certainly have."

"Tomorrow, then, I shall be a customer in that store," I said, and reached over for the bottle of brandy. I admit there was a bit of bravado in my tone, but he said nothing.

And so we left it at that…

KEK HUUYGENS PAUSED in his tale and peered at me across the table. "Speaking of brandy," he said politely, "your glass is empty." He raised a manicured hand for the waiter. "As I recall, on our last visit, I was placed in your debt to the amount of two drinks."

I stared at him. I was still irritated at having been sworn to secrecy. "If we are all now to be firmly committed to a policy of honesty," I said a bit shortly, "it was actually three."

He smiled at me with evident enjoyment of my position. "Then it shall be three. I trust you."

The waiter came and replenished our glasses. Kek Huuygens sipped his drink and then leaned back again, remembering.

THE FOLLOWING day was a Saturday (Huuygens continued evenly), with weather pleasant enough to allow me to walk, which, considering my financial situation, was just as well. I had offered to do the shopping for the cook in order to appear at the market in the proper guise of a customer, but it seems that owners of supermarkets do not buy at retail. However, I am sure that had she accepted, the funds she would have doled out would have been calculated to a sou to accord with the list she would have furnished. I'm afraid my status in that household was no great secret.

My cousin was then living—and still lives, as a matter of fact—in the Avenue Michelet in St. Ouen, and since the store in question was located in Clichy, the walk really wasn't too bad. As I strolled along, I put my mind to work on various means of swindling a supermarket, based on the system of security I had had outlined to me the evening before. But I soon abandoned this exercise. To hear my cousin describe it, all standard methods had been thoroughly investigated, and I knew him well enough to know that the scheme would have to be incredibly simple to have escaped his detection.

I am quite serious. I was sure that under the weight of that study, any complicated scheme would have been bound to be discovered; and besides, I have always preferred simple schemes myself. They are the only ones with any chance of success. So I gave up all thought of the matter until I could see the arena of battle in person, and just walked along enjoying the lovely weather.

When I first set eyes on the supermarket, my first thought was that I had taken a wrong tum somewhere and had ended up at the aerodrome of Bourget, because the place looked like nothing so much as a hangar set in the middle of a huge concrete apron. That, of course, was the car park. I had seen similar installations in the States, but I had had no idea that my cousin's wealth extended to properties of such dimension. For a moment, I felt a twinge of sympathy for the person or persons who were draining a portion of that wealth away, but then I thought of the reward, as well as of my need for it. With a shrug, I pushed through the swinging doors that led to the interior.

I had never been in a supermarket on a Saturday before, and at first, I thought I had inadvertently stumbled onto a riot of some proportion, or possibly a student demonstration, because the place was jammed with noisy people, all apparently going in different directions; but after a moment, I could see that there was a bit of organization to the confusion, and I took a shopping cart and pushed into the melee. I shall never understand why, with so many fine American customs and inventions to choose from, Europeans always seem to select the very worst ones to copy, such as supermarkets, television, or—but again, I digress.

The aisles of the store had arrows mounted above them in a futile effort to get traffic to flow along a rational pattern, but naturally, nobody was paying the slightest attention to them. I managed, by using my shopping cart as a battering ram, to cover about one-third of the store, but I then abandoned it in favor of doing a solo. This involved quite a bit of side-stepping and agile pirouetting, but it did allow a more rapid coverage of the area. Any fears I had had about appearing out of place as a non-shopper were forsaken at once. In that mob, I could have been nude or playing the bagpipe, and still have remained entirely unnoticed for a week.

I took the store, section by section, paying particular heed at first to those clerks who dispensed such non-packaged items as meat and vegetables. I was pleased to note that, despite the regimentation of such modern mechanical means of distribution, fruits were still being mauled, pinched, and squeezed in time-honored fashion; but no world-shaking ideas sprang from this observation. I paused to watch young lads hastily piling tins in mounds to replace the attritional inroads of the thundering herd, but other than a forced admiration for their acrobatic skills, nothing came of this. I studied the entrances, the exits, the freezers, the shelves, the windows, even—to give you some idea of the bankruptcy of my thoughts—the fans set high in the arched roof above.

Eventually, I worked my way to the front of the store and the check-out counters. There was a long line of impatient consumers before each one, and so great was the crowd that even the manager had been pressed into service, and was standing over his register at the end of the line, sweating away like the hired help, pounding on the keys. The other check-out clerks were no less busy, but at least they were more attractive. And I do mean attractive—if that is not too light a word for girls that are beautiful. There were three redheads, two brunettes, and three blondes; and whoever handled the personnel hiring for my cousin's chain of supermarkets deserved a merit badge for good taste.

I stood with my back against a precarious mountain of soap boxes and watched their dainty hands fly over the register keys, watched them bend down to pack their sales into paper sacks, noting particularly the gaping of their blouses as they performed these necessary chores. It added nothing toward the solution of my problem, of course, but at least it was a pleasant respite in a day that was beginning to promise nothing but failure. And suddenly remembering that fact brought my mind back to business, and once again, I started back through the aisles.

Well, to make a long story short, I spent another fruitless two hours wandering through that hungry crowd, and for all the good it did, I might just as well have stayed home with the housemaid. I saw, of course, all the obvious possibilities, such as backing a truck up to the rear door and simply carting away a load of things, but I was sure that these had been thoroughly checked. And so, with one last adoring look at the beautiful girls at the check-out counters, I finally gave up and headed back toward my cousin's home.

I walked slowly, reviewing everything I had seen on my tour of the huge premises, but other than the beauty of the girls, I could think of nothing even worth recalling. As a rule, I do not mind failure; in my life, it has occurred rather frequently and I have learned to be philosophical about it I did, of course, mind the loss of the ten-thousand-franc reward, but since I saw no way of earning it, I put that thought aside as well, and allowed my memory to drift back to the girls at the check-out counters.

And then, all at once, I saw the entire scheme.

OF COURSE! Simple—as I knew it would have to be—and beautiful—as all truly great schemes are! It came to me so complete, it struck me so sharply, that I stopped dead in my tracks, and a lady behind me, pushing a pram, bumped into me; but after my ordeal with shopping carts that morning, I barely noticed it. She pushed past me, muttering darkly, but I paid no attention. My mind was racing, for immediately upon comprehending the scheme, I had also seen a way to improve upon it—or at least, to improve upon it as far as I, personally, was concerned. I must have stood in that spot for at least ten minutes, reviewing the entire thing in my mind, before I turned about and started back to the supermarket.

The line at the manager's counter was, as were all the others, quite long, but I placed myself at its end and waited patiently, eyeing the girls at the other counters appreciatively until my turn came.

When at last I faced the manager, he looked up with a frown when he noted that I had no merchandise with me. *"Monsieur,"* I said, "If I could speak with you a moment..."

He glared at me impatiently. "Solicitations are not allowed, and if you are selling anything, we do no purchasing here," he said brusquely. "All that is handled at the central office. And now, if you will pardon me..."

I bent over and whispered something in his ear. His hand, which had already been reaching for a package from the next customer, froze. His eyes widened, then closed for several moments, then reopened. For a period of at least ten seconds, he said nothing; he merely stared at me with horror. And then, as I knew he would, he pushed down a small gate that directed the customers to go to a different line and led me into his office.

Our conversation was short, but quite pointed. When I walked out, I left behind me a disappointed man, it is true—but also a greatly relieved man. In a way, I felt sorry for him, because he had invented a truly great scheme, but unfortunately, in this life, one must always look out for oneself, and the failure of his plan was definitely necessary to the success of my own.

WELL, as you can well believe, I returned to my cousin's home at a much more spritely pace, let myself in and went directly to the library.

As usual, on a Saturday afternoon, Stavros was seated at his desk going over his personal accounts. At my entrance, he looked up, and at the expression on my face—for I am no great dissembler—he jumped excitedly to his feet and hurried in my direction.

"Kek! You have discovered it!" he exclaimed. His tone was a neat blend of hope and disbelief.

"I have," I said, as modestly as I could under the circumstances, and proceeded to pour myself a drink.

"Wonderful! Marvelous!" He was almost beside himself with joy. "One morning in the supermarket and you find what a dozen detectives were unable to locate in four months. Fantastic! And when I think of what they cost me..." He swallowed the balance of this thought as being economically unsuitable for expression. He stared at me almost proudly. "How did they work it?"

I did my best to look shocked. "That was not our bargain," I said reprovingly. "I agreed—in return for ten thousand francs—to discover the scheme and put a stop to it. That was all you asked of me. I did not agree to disclose it."

His face fell. "So!" he said heavily. "You did not really discover it! I should have known better! You are merely attempting—"

I held up my hand. "As a guest in your house," I said, "permit me to prevent you from insulting me. I said I discovered the means by which you have systematically been swindled, and I have." I walked over and seated myself on the corner of his desk, taking, of course, my drink with me.

"Tell me," I said, "how long will it take you and your auditors to determine that I am telling the truth? How long will it take your financial experts to discover that the losses have stopped?"

He frowned at me in great indecision. My cousin, despite his many good qualities, such as an unerring palate for brandy and a sharp eye for presentable housemaids, suffers from a suspicious nature. "I will have a good indication within a week," he said slowly. "And in two weeks I can be absolutely certain."

"Good!" I said heartily. "Then, giving you two weeks to acquire your absolute certainty, I shall expect your check for ten thousand francs. Fortunately," I added aloofly, "I prevented you from saying anything that would require—in addition to the money—an apology." And I started to rise.

"Wait!" he said. He shook his head and began to pace back and forth. It was evident that he did not like the situation. He swallowed once or twice and finally came out with what was on his mind. "Why?" he enquired plaintively. "Why won't you tell me the scheme?"

"I'll tell you in two weeks," I said.

"You'll tell me the scheme in two weeks?" he asked. Hope had returned to his voice.

"No," I said politely. "In two weeks, I'll tell you why I *won't* tell you."

And with that I downed my drink and started for the door. It had occurred to me that I had missed lunch, and besides, on a Saturday afternoon, I had become accustomed to a nap. I could almost feel his eyes burning through my back as I turned the handle of the door.

KEK HUUYGENS PAUSED and smiled at me. "Of course," he said apologetically, "now that I've explained everything, you can see the wonderful scheme, and my subsequent plan, so you can now understand why I was forced to ask for your promise of secrecy..."

"I see nothing of the sort!" I'm afraid my voice rose a bit. "I do *not* see the scheme, nor do I see your plan, nor do I understand the need for my silence! As a matter of fact—"

He held up a hand to stop the flow of my language and looked at me almost with pity. "Well," he said, "have another brandy and you soon will." He called over the waiter, and then looked at me again and shrugged for my stupidity. "Prosit," he said, holding up his glass.

WELL (HUUYGENS CONTINUED, finally putting his glass to one side), the two weeks passed. Far too slowly for my liking, but pass they did. Each evening, Stavros would return from his office and I could tell from the look in his eyes that the figures were bearing out my promise that the losses would stop. But being the stubborn man he is, he could not bring himself to admit that I was shortly due for a check. Once or twice, I could have sworn that he was on the verge of claiming that the losses had *not* stopped, but despite his cupidity, he was not downright stupid, and something must have told him this would not have worked for an instant.

In any event, two weeks from that Saturday, I went into the library and pulled a chair up to face him across his desk. "Well?" I asked quietly.

He sighed. 'The losses have stopped," he admitted, albeit with hesitancy. "I shall draw you a check in the amount agreed upon." He stared at me. "And in return, you will tell me why you will *not* tell me..." He could not go on; it was evident that he was under a certain amount of stress.

"Certainly," I said equably. "I will not describe the scheme to you because I have discovered—and stopped—a nefarious means of dishonesty which, were it ever bruited about, could lead to similar attempts by others in supermarkets. In your own chain of supermarkets, to be exact. Attempts, I might mention, that I guarantee would be equally successful. At great cost to you. And since you are no fool..."

Stavros stared at me with growing knowledge of what I was saying. "I am the worst kind of fool," he said at last, bitterly. "I should have known better than to say one word to you about this. You, of all people!" He shoved the papers on the desk away from him with an angry motion, as if they somehow represented the dishonesty he was always so ardently combatting. His eyes came up. "What do you have in mind?"

'Well," I said in a reasonable tone of voice, "I thought that ten thousand francs a week would be ample payment for seeing that the scheme is not repeated in any of the other stores." I held up my hand. "This would be in addition to the reward which I have already earned."

He clenched his teeth and glared at me. "This is blackmail!" he said tightly. "This is a crime!"

"A crime?" I asked innocently. "To prevent stealing? To see that you are not bankrupt through pilfering? Any other action on my part, it seems to me, could only be interpreted as being dishonest. And, to be frank, would lead you into disaster in short order." I looked at him evenly across the desk. "Well?"

One thing about Stavros is that he knows when he is beaten. I could almost hear the wheels click in his head as he calculated my demands against his losses should they spread to the other stores.

"I assume," he said in a voice drained of emotion, "that with this income, you will be able to move from my home into a place of your own?"

"I have spent the last two weeks locating a suitable apartment," I assured him. "With this income, I can swing it."

"Then allow me to help you by according with your wishes," he said politely. "Of course, you know that I shall have to continue spending money on detectives."

"I imagined you would," I said coldly, and got to my feet. "Otherwise, my demands would have been much higher."

And that's how we left it.

KEK HUUYGENS GRINNED at me across the table. "And so I live a comfortable life," he said. His hand gestured idly, including his wardrobe and the sidewalk cafe in general. "And shall continue to—at least, until my cousin figures out how he was being swindled.

Which is almost impossible, since it has been stopped and the evidence removed from the area of his investigation."

"But I still don't understand it," I said in irritation. "How did the scheme work? What did you whisper into the ear of the manager of that store?"

"Have another brandy," he said, and waited once again until we were served. I could barely contain my impatience, but Huuygens, in one of his moods, is not to be rushed.

When our glasses were again full, he viewed me in quite another manner—seriously this time—and then nodded as if he had come to an important decision.

"I can trust you," he said at last. "And it is too good a story to remain untold, although only by me—" his finger came up, "—and not by you. What I said to the manager of the store was this: *'You are the ninth counter.'*"

I had started to raise my glass to my mouth, but paused and set it down untouched. I opened my mouth to say something, and then closed it again as his words came through to me in all their meaning. Kek nodded, happy that I had at last seen the light

"Yes," he said quietly. "Stavros had told me there were eight check-out counters. And there were eight girls checking out goods at these counters. But the manager had added a ninth counter which he handled himself. And which was completely beyond the control of my cousin's vaunted auditors." He grinned at me. "Beautiful, isn't it?"

"It is," I admitted. "Truly beautiful."

He raised his glass. "To beautiful schemes," he said. And then added quietly, a glint in his eye, "And if I buy the next one, you will then owe me two."

The Man Who Played Too Well

Don Von Elsner

Nobody, but nobody writes detective stories like Don Von Elsner. And no other detective but his Jake Winkman gets write-ups in Oswald Jacoby's bridge columns. But no one else in fiction and very few in real life play bridge the way Jake Winkman does. If you don't believe it, read on.

BRIDGE PRO Jake Winkman stood at the window of the luxurious suite where Edna Mayberry Mallory had installed him in her imposing Tudor mansion. He fingered his black tie and frowned.

There was nothing wrong with the view. It commanded a sweep of broad marble terrace and a trellised rose garden with curvaceous and inviting pathways that sloped down to the lake, where gentle swells, gray-blue in the twilight, were breaking considerably against a carefully manicured beach. It always seemed a little unreal to him that the rich could contrive to have problems.

Jeanne, the Countess d'Allerez, and Prince Sergio Polensky emerged from the garden to ascend the broad marble steps of the terrace. The Prince had his arm around her and was whispering something, doubtless tender and exotically accented, into her delicate ear. Slim and seductive, the Countess was wearing a gown that featured provocatively little above the waist but billowed enticingly below. It fit perfectly, Jake decided, into the theme of his well-chosen surroundings, but did nothing to erase his frown.

A weekend of bridge and swimming in the rarified atmosphere of conservative Lake Forest was all very well, and he had been a guest here before. The stakes would be as unrealistically high as Monopoly money; and his losses, in the improbable event that he suffered any, would be graciously absorbed by his hostess, while his winnings would be strictly between him and Internal Revenue. Not that winning would necessarily be easy. The rich, he knew, were often surprisingly adept at the game, some of them possessing an almost uncanny sense of values, while others exhibited a well-calculated dash and flair. None of them, with only a paltry few thousand at stake, was ever intimidated from backing his judgment. And he would be playing with the nobility, no less. But this time it had to be different.

He had known it the moment he had answered the phone in his Hollywood apartment that morning and heard Edna's voice. "Wink, I know it's unpardonably short notice, but could you possibly catch a plane...this morning...yes, for the weekend...you see, my sister, Jeanne, is here...and a Prince Polensky...and Fred is away...Argentina, I think...I can't promise you anything exciting...but...I'd appreciate your coming, Wink..."

He had shrugged. What do you say to a woman whom you once called at three o'clock in the morning—a black and desperate morning—and asked for a million dollars—pledging what ever was left of a shopworn soul as security—and what if that woman had calmly said, "Of course, Wink...cash, I suppose...oh, dear, would eight o'clock be soon enough?" The fact that Edna Mallory was the world's ninth richest woman—or was it eighth?—was really beside the point. It was also beside the point that, as it turned out, he hadn't needed the million after all.

In the limousine from O'Hare, Edna had been her usual bland and unruffled self. Her foster sister, Jeanne, had arrived from Paris for an indefinite visit two weeks before. Instead of being pale and depressed as an aftermath of her divorce from the Count, however, she had appeared little short of radiant. True, the Count had kept her money and left her virtually penniless, but then he really needed it more because, after all, he was keeping three separate ménages in different parts of Spain. And there hadn't been any children, at least not Jeanne's.

Jeanne's radiance, it seemed, stemmed from not merely one new interest, but two. One was bridge.

Jake listened resignedly. "And the other was the Prince, whom she lost little time in importing."

Edna's tone and expression remained unchanged. "Exactly. He has an even more impressive title than the Count, of course, but I think the real attraction comes from his being, of all things, a bridge expert. Jeanne asked if she might invite him, and of course I agreed.

"Oh, dear," Edna said. "Did I give a wrong impression? Forgive me. He is personable, extremely attentive, and a very fine bridge player indeed. Of course, Fred..."

When Fred Mallory, third, the utilities baron, had taken Edna Mayberry's hand—and her distillery millions—it had been more like a merger than a marriage. Jake wondered whether they'd had to get approval from the Justice Department.

"Spare me," he said. "I can read Fred's meter without a flashlight. But what's this about Jeanne being broke? If she's your sister, she must have got a vat full of dough—more than one lousy Count could siphon off."

"Oh, my. I do make things so difficult, don't I? You see, Jeanne was the daughter of my father's second wife. He provided quite generously for her—a million, I think—but the bulk of the estate came to me."

They were entering the hallowed confines of the world's richest community, stately trees framing an array of impressive estates. Even the air, Jake fancied, smelled different—like freshly minted money. "So she's holding her silver spoon under the spigot for another droplet or two?"

"In a way, I suppose." Edna wafted her handkerchief. She always gave the impression of being overly warm, but Jake had yet to see her really sweat. "You see, after the divorce, Fred helped me set up a trust fund for her with an ample income, but we didn't feel—Fred didn't feel..."

"Like kicking in with the candle-power to light up three more *ménages* in Spain?" He paused. "Edna, did Fred ask you to call me in —like the adjustment department—to win back the money he blew playing against Jeanne and the Prince, and before he throws the master switch?"

"Of course not, Wink. It's true, we did lose a little—about thirty-five thousand, I think. But then, Fred and I always play wretchedly together. Besides, I take care of all expenses connected with bridge."

They had turned through an imposing gateway and were cruising along a curving driveway through what appeared to be a public park —minus the public. "I gather that Jeanne and the Prince like to play set. Who made up the fourth after Fred pulled the pin?"

"Our neighbor, Randy Maxwell. You know Randy. We played the last four nights. We lost—altogether, I think—about twenty five thousand. Not over thirty."

Randy Maxwell was an electronics engineer who had snowballed a few patents and a gift for finance into a mountain of gold. A widower in his early fifties, Randy now piddled around the house in a three-million-dollar workshop and read books on philosophy. But Jake knew him for a keen and competent bridge player.

Fred Mallory was something else; a strict hatchet man at the bridge table, but the hatchet only worked one way—North and South. Yet each, playing with Edna, had lost about the same amount. *The Prince,* he decided, *must be a hell of a bridge player.*

He put a firm but tender hand on Edna's arm as the car drew up to the front door. "Edna, did you call me from California just to check on whether your game was slipping?" He did not mention that he had canceled a lecture and run out on two new clients in order to come.

She was looking straight ahead. "I realize it was selfish of me, Wink. I—just wanted to make sure. You're the only one..."

He looked at her, this middle-aged, bovine-faced woman with her potato-sack shape, and wondered whether any passion could transcend the fondness and admiration he felt toward her. She could have bought and refurbished a destroyer for a private yacht and filled it with the sycophants of her choice, people who would toady and grovel twenty-four hours a day to assure her that she was both beautiful and brilliant, or even—God forbid—sexy. Instead she chose to spend a fortune traveling month after month to major bridge tournaments, subjecting herself to the rigors of the pasteboard jungle and the grueling discipline of crossing swords with the sharpest wits in the kingdom of competitive sports. She paid the price in blood and guts and paid it like a lady because, deep down, it was more important to her to be a "do-er" than a mere "be-er."

With the footman holding the door and staring stonily, he leaned over and kissed her...

AT DINNER, the Prince orchestrated the table talk like a maestro, remarking on how he had followed Winkman's exploits for years, both at and away from the bridge table, and scattering the names of European bridge luminaries like a flower girl as he tripped from chalet to chateau with a sprinkling of discreetly spiced anecdotes.

Clearly outgunned, Jake took a leaf from Edna's book and went along quietly. The famous Winkman wit, he knew, was chiefly notable for its backfires, and he sensed an undercurrent that was already combustible enough. He patted Edna's plump knee under the table to express solidarity among the minority, and they repaired to the card room for liqueurs.

After two hours, Jake was convinced that Edna was not fighting a slump, and the idea that her game might have slipped he had considered ridiculous from the first, She had been his client for more than a dozen years—second oldest to Doc McCreedy—and her game was still growing, maturing, becoming stronger both technically and tactically. *But had she thought so?* With Edna you could never tell. They had won two small rubbers and lost a larger, slowly played one, and her errors, judged analytically, were minimal. She went down on a small slam that could have been made, but Jake, following the fall of the cards, endorsed her misguess.

"Oh, dear," Edna said. "I was afraid I should have taken a different view. I just can't seem to bring home the close ones."

"Pretty hard," Jake shrugged. "So far the defense around here has operated like its legs were crossed and wired."

It was true. From the moment the cards were dealt, the Prince had put away his cultured pearls of patter and begun to play with an almost mechanized concentration. Moreover, his game was strictly engineered for high-stake rubber bridge, a style often difficult for the matchpoint tournament-oriented player to adjust to. His bidding was both daring and disruptive, pushing distributional hands unconscionably; while on defense he keyed solely upon defeating the contract. In high-class tournament competition his style would have earned a reputation for unreliable and erratic bidding, imprecise defense, and fetched him below average results. But he had coached the Countess well, and they made a formidable combination where the payoff was in big swings. Nevertheless, when the session ended, Jake and Edna had a small but tidy plus.

"Oh, dear," Edna said, meticulously dating the score sheet and passing it to the Prince and Jeanne for their initials. "It was such a pleasant session, wasn't it? I'm sure we all thoroughly enjoyed it."

The Countess, relieved of her quiet intentness, yawned prettily and stretched. The moment was perilous, but her bodice held together. There was a faintly calculating glint in her eye as she stood up and tucked her arm under Jake's.

"I'm only sorry," she said, "I didn't take Edna up on those lessons from you long ago." She squeezed his arm and emphasized it with a little pressure from her thigh as they moved toward the stairs. Her manner was obvious enough even to put a crack in the Prince's faultless façade, particularly when she stood aside and insisted that the Prince and Edna precede them up the stairs.

Jake, whose reputation with the fair sex was considered by many to exceed even his prowess at the bridge table, recognized that he was being operated upon, but was unclear as to just how extensive a program the Countess might have in mind. He returned the pressure to let her know the game was on, and prepared to await developments, the Prince's darkly clouded face notwithstanding. He didn't think he'd overdone it, but the Countess lost her balance slightly, causing him to glance down. Stepping from tread to tread revealed her slippers beneath her floor-length gown. To his surprise, they were neither needle-heeled nor next-to-nothing sandals, but quite substantial affairs with sensible Cuban heels.

She covered the moment with a gay little laugh. "I'm afraid my balance is a trifle off, Jake. Fallen arches. My doctor in Paris has me taking special exercises and even insists on my wearing clumsy shoes. Swimming tomorrow? Elevenish?"

"That should do it," Jake said, eyes narrowed thoughtfully. "I ought to be braced for you in a bikini by then."

THE NEXT DAY, however, brought one of those quick changes in weather for which the Windy City and its suburbs are noted. Thunderstorms and a stiff breeze and angry white-capped rollers invaded the beach, and Winkman passed the morning losing a few dollars to Polensky at billiards.

Jeanne appeared for lunch wearing an avocado sweater, cerise stretch pants, and dark green boots, while Edna wore a hand-crafted holomu that looked like a hand-me-down from the washer-woman. Jake could feel the impact like a *thud* in the brisket, but Edna seemed unaware of the beating she was taking on the fashion front. Luncheon over, they turned as one to the card room.

During the first rubber, while Jake was continuing his appraisal of the Prince's game, Edna pulled to a five club contract—when three no trump was cold.

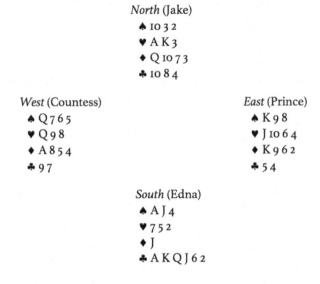

North (Jake)
♠ 10 3 2
♥ A K 3
♦ Q 10 7 3
♣ 10 8 4

West (Countess)
♠ Q 7 6 5
♥ Q 9 8
♦ A 8 5 4
♣ 9 7

East (Prince)
♠ K 9 8
♥ J 10 6 4
♦ K 9 6 2
♣ 5 4

South (Edna)
♠ A J 4
♥ 7 5 2
♦ J
♣ A K Q J 6 2

Jeanne led the spade five, with Edna capturing the king with the ace to lead the ace and a small club to dummy's ten. She then made the only play which would give her a chance for the contract—a small diamond—and one that would have prevailed far more often than not. The Prince took his time and then produced the killing play —up with the king. When Edna later tried a ruffing finesse with the diamond queen to dispose of her losing heart, Jeanne produced the diamond ace for a one trick set.

"I'm terribly sorry, Wink. I shouldn't have pulled."

He shrugged. "Polensky just pulled another devastator on you. We still get the hundred honors."

The Prince's eyes flashed. "Thank you, but it was elementary. If Mrs. Mallory had the ace of diamonds, the hand was cold. I had nothing to lose."

Jake let it pass. The world was full of bad analyses, including, sadly, many of his own. But switch the singleton jack of diamonds for the singleton ace, and give Jeanne the spade jack for the seven, and the Prince's play would have looked pretty silly.

But there was no denying the effectiveness of his dashing style. He and Jeanne hit a small slam that was cold but hard to reach, and followed it up with a grand slam that was tighter than an actor's girdle. But it wiped out Winkman's winnings and put the icing on the session. They abandoned the table for cocktails, and then went upstairs to change for dinner.

THE EVENING SESSION got underway with Jeanne, ravishing in another floor-length creation, producing an unexpected defense.

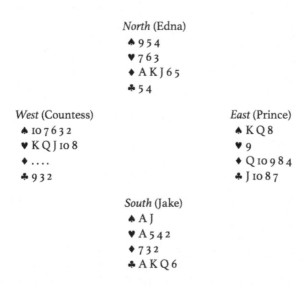

North (Edna)
♠ 9 5 4
♥ 7 6 3
♦ A K J 6 5
♣ 5 4

West (Countess)
♠ 10 7 6 3 2
♥ K Q J 10 8
♦ . . . .
♣ 9 3 2

East (Prince)
♠ K Q 8
♥ 9
♦ Q 10 9 8 4
♣ J 10 8 7

South (Jake)
♠ A J
♥ A 5 4 2
♦ 7 3 2
♣ A K Q 6

Jake opened with a club, over which Jeanne bid a Michaels two clubs, showing a weakish hand length in the majors. Edna called two diamonds, and Jake reached for three no trump, promptly doubled by the Prince.

Jeanne led the heart king, which held, and continued with the queen, taken by Jake, the Prince discarding the diamond four. This play virtually marked Polensky with five diamonds, and Jake's lead to the diamond king confirmed the situation when Jeanne showed out. Jake then cashed three rounds of clubs, and when Jeanne followed to all of them, be had a pretty solid inferential count on both defenders' hands—West 5-5-0-3, East 3-1-5-4. He judged further that the Prince might well have a spade trick, as well as minor suit stoppers, for his double. If so, the forceps were in position for a suicide squeeze, and he threw Jeanne in with a heart. She promptly cashed another heart, the Prince discarding first the spade eight and then the diamond nine, to bring about this position:

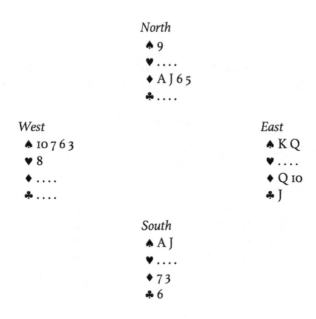

North
♠ 9
♥ . . . .
♦ A J 6 5
♣ . . . .

West
♠ 10 7 6 3
♥ 8
♦ . . . .
♣ . . . .

East
♠ K Q
♥ . . . .
♦ Q 10
♣ J

South
♠ A J
♥ . . . .
♦ 7 3
♣ 6

If Jeanne now cashed her last heart—as Jake confidently expected —the Prince would be ground in the teeth of a progressive squeeze. But after looking long and wistfully at her good heart, the Countess reluctantly led a spade, and there was no way to keep Polensky from taking two tricks.

The Prince dabbed a handkerchief to his forehead. "Pretty play, *petite.*"

"I've had it done to me before," Jake sighed. "By someone like Sheinwold and Kaplan. But one of you is better looking, and the other makes it literally royal."

Jeanne laughed gaily, but as one close contract after an other fell to a withering defense, and as she and the Prince piled up the score, she finally turned to Edna. "I'm really sorry, dear sister. I know how you must feel—when you take your game so seriously."

"On the contrary," Edna responded easily. "I can't remember when I've enjoyed myself so much. Wink has proved a marvelous catalyst. Your and the Prince's game has grown so much stronger since he came. It's become almost exquisitely relentless." She sighed and waved her handkerchief. "I do hope I'm learning something."

The Prince was nimble. "Mrs. Mallory is too modest much. Your game superb is. We have been very lucky. It is of a certainty that about our cards complain we cannot."

Jake bit down on his tongue. This savored of the patronizing pap used to console pigeons in a high-stake game where they did not belong. He had spotted far too many flaws in the Prince's game to warrant any such condescension toward Edna. "Is it possible but," he asked dryly, "to deal while one the manure spreads? I have the feeling that our luck about may later turn."

And turn it did, but only for the worse. It seemed as if the Prince, resenting Jake's drollery, had determined to turn it on in earnest. The cards cooperated, and Jake and Edna took a merciless flogging. But Jake, as with almost everything else, had a technique for dealing with such situations. Having ruthlessly exorcised all superstition, he knew that judgment could be a chemical fugitive, and that once depression replaces perception at the bridge table, the victim will be contributing far more to his beating than the opponents. His answer was to forget the score, wipe out all previous hands, and to concentrate on each new hand as a fresh and isolated problem. And shuffle the hell out of the cards. He did not say it was easy, and he was grateful that Edna had learned the lesson well.

Her stability in the face of repeated debacles allowed him to keep his analytical searchlight cool and probing.

North (Prince)
♠ A Q 7 3
♥ K 8 4
♦ 10 7 2
♣ 10 9 7

West (Edna)
♠ J 9 8 4
♥ 10 7 6 3 2
♦ A 3
♣ 6 5

East (Jake)
♠ 10 6
♥ A 9
♦ K J 9 8 4
♣ J 4 3 2

South (Jeanne)
♠ K 5 2
♥ Q J 5
♦ Q 6 5
♣ A K Q 8

Against Jeanne's three no trump, Edna opened the heart trey. Jake was up with the ace and switched to the diamond jack, with Jeanne making a well-guessed duck. He continued the diamond nine, Edna taking her ace and exiting with the heart deuce. This was technically correct but strategically dubious, since it gave declarer too good a count on the hand. For Edna was now marked with five hearts and two diamonds. Her black cards, as well as her partner's, would almost surely break 4-2 or 3-3. If the latter, declarer had the rest; if the former, and Edna held four spades, the contract was a latch.

Jeanne won in her hand and rapidly played the spade king, followed by the ace and king of clubs, playing dummy's seven and nine. Eyes bland, Jake now inwardly relaxed. The hand could still be made, of course, by cashing dummy's top spades, and leading a fourth spade to squeeze Winkman on Edna's forced heart return. But a player who would fail to unblock the club ten-nine for a simple proved finesse was not about to find the more intricate and unnecessary play. She didn't, and struggled to a one-trick set. Cashing dummy's top spades would have ruled out Edna's holding a third club.

The Prince was gentle. "So fast, *cherie,* you play. Two different ways but you could have made the hand. Unblock the clubs, or save the heart entry your hand to."

Jake said nothing, but he noted the Prince underbid the next hand the Countess played, settling for a comfortable four hearts when six was there for the price of a little skillful manipulation. But the Prince, too, was having his problems.

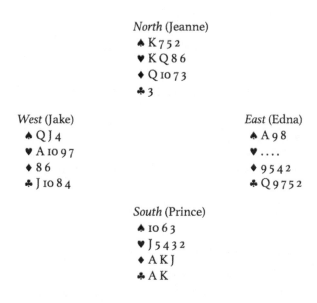

North (Jeanne)
♠ K 7 5 2
♥ K Q 8 6
♦ Q 10 7 3
♣ 3

West (Jake)
♠ Q J 4
♥ A 10 9 7
♦ 8 6
♣ J 10 8 4

East (Edna)
♠ A 9 8
♥ . . . .
♦ 9 5 4 2
♣ Q 9 7 5 2

South (Prince)
♠ 10 6 3
♥ J 5 4 3 2
♦ A K J
♣ A K

Against four hearts, Jake led the spade queen, ducked in dummy by the Prince, Edna following with the nine. Since this marked declarer with the spade ten, Jake switched to the jack of clubs. Polensky won and immediately shot a low heart toward the board, Jake calmly playing the seven. When Edna showed out, the jig was up and another ice-cold contract went down the drain. Even one of Jake's beginner clients would have been sitting on toothmarks for a month, had he made such an error.

"Tough luck, partner," Jeanne consoled, thus marking herself as either a diplomat or a dolt. "All four trumps in one hand..."

But the Prince, enjoying belated hindsight, knew better. Had all four trumps been in the East hand, nothing could prevent the loss of two trump tricks. Therefore, it could cost nothing to insure against their all being in the *West* hand by simply leading the jack.

It was food for thought. Were the opponents exhausted from wielding the lash, or grown careless with a surfeit of loot? Winkman did not think so. Rather it seemed that the Prince was smoldering over Jeanne's continued rapid but ragged dummy play. If so, it must really have been bugging him, because on the last deal he gave an almost shocking exhibition of ineptness.

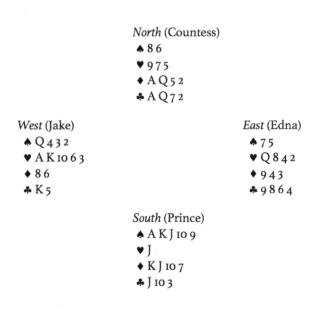

North (Countess)
♠ 8 6
♥ 9 7 5
♦ A Q 5 2
♣ A Q 7 2

West (Jake)
♠ Q 4 3 2
♥ A K 10 6 3
♦ 8 6
♣ K 5

East (Edna)
♠ 7 5
♥ Q 8 4 2
♦ 9 4 3
♣ 9 8 6 4

South (Prince)
♠ A K J 10 9
♥ J
♦ K J 10 7
♣ J 10 3

Against four spades, Jake led the heart king, Edna playing the eight. He continued with the ace, Polensky trumping. The Prince now carefully laid down the spade king and then entered dummy with a diamond to take a spade finesse on the way back. This sequence was like something from the fortieth of a cent game in the back room at the Y.W. Jake accepted the trick and played a third heart to Edna's queen. The Prince, down to two trumps, was now in trouble. He frowned and discarded a club, but this feeble maneuver was much too little and too late. Edna stoically produced a fourth heart and another cast-iron contract bit the dust.

As the cards lay, almost any line of play would have worked—except the one chosen by the Prince. Many rubber bridge players would simply cash the ace-king of spades, abandoning trumps if the queen failed to appear, and run the diamonds, conceding two trump tricks but bringing the hand home on the club finesse. Others might have tested the club finesse first, and then "adjusted" their view of how to play the trumps, according to whether the club play won or lost. A slightly more elegant line would be to enter dummy at trick three for an immediate trump finesse—a line that could prevail with the trump queen four deep in the East and the club king off-side—and would leave the spade eight to cover the fourth heart if it lost, and again reduce the hand to the club finesse. It was all very perplexing.

Nevertheless, the session broke up with Jake and Edna minus $38,000, give or take a few hundred.

JAKE SLEPT LATE. The sun was high when, clad in swim trunks and white terrycloth robe, he descended to the terrace, where a sumptuous buffet brunch awaited him.

The Countess was breath-catching in a turquoise bikini with a transparent cover-up that achieved the near-ultimate in futility. The Prince was sartorially resplendent in a tailored robe of bronze and purple with a coat of arms over the left breast. As be turned to accompany Jeanne down to the sand, Jake half-expected to see *POLENSKY* stenciled across the back. He even sported custom-built beach sandals.

When they were out of earshot, Edna turned to Jake. "Oh, dear," she said. "I know my game is plodding and uninspired, Wink. But I feel so outclassed. And Jeanne is little more than a beginner. Perhaps I should start all over. What do you think?"

He dispatched the last of his eggs Benedict and poured himself another cup of coffee. He was deft enough at tampering with the truth, but, with Edna, there was hardly ever any need. Inside her doughy exterior, she had a lovely core of toughness that he had seen often bent, but never broken. But he could sense that she was uniquely vulnerable now, and that the breaking point was perilously close. Was that why, without quite knowing it herself, she had sent for him? He mentally riffled through his file of clichés, but after a dozen years of coaching her under the stress of tournament pressure, there was very little he had left to say.

He put down his coffee cup. "Your game is not the greatest, Edna. Maybe someday it will be. But it has integrity, and it's always around the target." He paused, groping. "Bridge and golf are very similar disciplines." Edna in her culottes would never make the cover of *Vogue,* but she was a steady and competent performer on the links. "Horton Smith was a great golfer in the Hagen era, and, like most pros, a deadly putter. The press, always seeking the sensational, gave rise to the belief that Smith won tournaments because he knocked the ball in the cup from anywhere on the green. Once asked the secret of great putting, he gave a simple, unsensational answer. 'The guy who sinks the most putts,' he said, 'is the guy who's closest to the pin.' Remember that, Edna."

Jake strolled down to the beach and caught the Prince emerging from the surf. Polensky made a business of arranging his beach towel, but there was a moment when he stood barefoot, erect, and quite close. Jake slid his eyes to the horizon and back to make sure. The Prince's eyes were a good two inches below his own.

"Where's the beautiful Countess?" he asked.

"Along the bitch she swims, and then back walks to exercise her feet," the Prince volunteered, quickly dropping onto his towel.

Jeanne appeared around an abutment that shielded the private beach and walked toward them along the hard-surfaced shore just above the wave-line. "Hi, champ!" she called to Winkman, accentuating the sway of her hips a trifle. "Say," she added, coming closer, "you look like an Olympics champion instead of a bridge expert."

"But which Olympics?" Jake sighed. "Anyway, it's an illusion. We have so many in our culture, don't we?"

She laughed. "Is this a new game? Find the hidden stiletto in that remark?"

He shrugged. "My stilettos are never too hard to find, Countess. Just check the nearest bull's-eye."

He left her biting a pensive lip and walked out into the surf. As a Midwestern boy, he knew the coldness of the water in the Great Lakes, but years of sheltered living around tepid pools had softened him unmercifully. He had to clench his teeth to keep going, and total immersion rivaled the ecstasy of crawling into a casket of ice. But after a dozen strokes or so, he began actually to enjoy it. It was so brutally elemental, it gave one a sense of conquest to survive. He turned and began to sidestroke his way along parallel to the beach. It was in such repetitive and mechanical activities that be often did his best thinking.

Cheating, of course, was always a thing to be considered. But to attempt to cheat against him would have required a rather massive ego. In his time he bad been retained by trans Atlantic cruise ships, various old line clubs, private blue book clients, and even by operators of back room cigar store games. Regardless of the site, the means were always limited, and be could almost check them off in his sleep. The adept dealer, the marked cards, the cold deck, the sloppy shuffler, the one-at-a time-card-picker-upper. Then there were the tired old mechanical props that every bridge pro knows by heart. The tinted glasses, the hearing aid, contact lenses, the motorized wheelchair, the electronic cane, the peephole, the colleague with the binoculars, the hole in the ceiling, the taps from the floor below. Moreover, he was certain that Edna, in her bland and simplistic way, bad managed to inform her guests of Winkman's familiarity with this sordid side of card life. It all made for a nice problem. Keeping the solution equally genteel might not be so easy. But he thought again of that sweat-racked night, when, with no other place to turn and with a man's life in the balance, he had turned to Edna...

He was becoming numb. He had heard that people had frozen to death that way, in a sort of tranquil euphoria, and switched to a vigorous overhand stroke, heading directly for the beach. He came ashore at a private beach two estates to the north of the Mallorys'. It was deserted and be was plodding along, heading back, when a cheery voice called to him.

Jake recognized it at once as coming from Randy Maxwell. He turned to see the financier beckoning to him. Maxwell was attired in disreputable shorts and a stained T-shirt, and was standing at the entrance to what appeared to be a well-tended jungle. Jake joined him and saw that the trees concealed a squat functional building of concrete and hollow tile.

"My hobby shop," Randy explained. "Since the word 'work' is vulgarly *de trop* around here, I had to draw it up as a 'summer house' to get a building permit—and then hide it."

Inside, even Jake's unsophisticated eye could detect a few hundred thousand dollars' worth of electronic toys. "What do you do in here?" he asked. "Besides compute relative strength indices on the Dow Jones averages."

Randy laughed. "Believe it or not, I've got a computer that does just that. Mainly, I piddle. What I'm really trying to do, I suppose, is recapture what I had in my garage down on South Sangamon Street twenty-five years ago. I used to piddle with impractical, noncommercial things, and one year I made twelve million. Now, of course, such things are done in what is called a laboratory, and it's considered unseemly for me to be caught in one. I pay young squirts fabulous salaries to do what I'd cheerfully do for nothing." He pointed to the array of equipment. "But it isn't the same. I just don't get the ideas any more."

"Even the Greeks didn't have a word for it," Jake said. "Slip me another Polaroid, and I'll sit down and weep with you, Alexander."

Maxwell shook his head. "It would spoil you, Jake. I wouldn't want to be a party to that. Integrity is fine, but it's twice as fine when it costs till it hurts." He turned cheerful again. "Here." He handed Jake two plastic boxes about the size of matchboxes. "Let's try something."

"Behind you and to your left," Randy went on, "there's a cabinet with a shelf full of large capacitors."

"What's a capacitor?"

"A radio-electronic device. There are also some small condensers."

"Same question."

"Same answer. I am going to tell you how many of each. Listen closely."

Suddenly Jake became aware of a soundless tingling in his left hand and recognized a series of six impulses. Then came a series of shorter or lighter impulses. "Six capacitors and ten condensers," he said. "The last time I was in your house you had a bottle of Scotch that talked in a whiskey tenor. I liked that trick better."

"Me, too," Randy said. "But we have to be practical."

"Indeed. And what will this thing do? Communicate with your refrigerator to give you different colored ice cubes?"

"It is one of the world's great myths, Jake, that real progress comes from creating to fill a need. Such efforts are always stodgy and pedestrian. Create first; find the need later. Check that cabinet."

Jake checked and found the six capacitors and ten condensers.

"Now move a number of condensers down to the next shelf and tell me how many by pressing down with your right thumb."

Jake moved three, and pressed down on the black box in his right hand three times.

"Three," Randy said. "Isn't that nice? No wires, no sound." A phone rang. "Damn," he said, putting it down. "Another directors' meeting. Got to run. Stop over for a drink before you leave, Jake."

Jake resumed his stroll along the beach, coming presently to the abutment where he had first spotted Jeanne. He found himself almost treading on her small but well-formed footprints.

Edna's beach was deserted, and he gathered up his robe and headed directly for his shower. Coming out, he began carefully to pack. He worked at remaining cool and dispassionate, sipping rye and water because it seemed to him to have a clean taste. Sometimes he even brushed his teeth with it. But the sour nausea was not in his mouth or stomach. He took a deep breath, followed the broad upstairs hall to the south wing, and tapped on Jeanne's door.

The Countess was reclining on a love seat in canary yellow lounging pajamas and looked almost feverishly fetching. She sat up and gave him a warm smile. "Let me fix you a drink. What a pleasant surprise. But this is hardly the hour for a seduction, is it?"

Jake sat down across from her and accepted the drink. "I wouldn't know. I haven't gotten around to punching a time card on it."

She laughed. "You're such a devastating rebuker, Wink. Do you really enjoy cutting people up, or is it just a pose?"

"In this case, neither," Jake said. "It's a job. Something like swabbing down the head—somebody has to do it. It'll help if we omit the head-shrinker jargon about sibling hostilities. You and Edna were raised as sisters, but you have everything, and she's a dowdy frump. You glitter and sparkle and have royal consorts, and all she can do is blink her bovine eyes. Of course, it's unbelievably cruel that she should have the money instead of you. But I don't think money is the whole story, Jeanne. You could marry a bundle. It's got to be something else. Edna's got something that infuriates you. It completely distorts your perspective. You've spent years pirouetting around her, mercilessly tossing your darts, artfully searching out her most vulnerable parts. You do it with your clothes, your style, your men—you'd even toss in an affair with me, once you sensed it would wound her. But Edna won't show hurt. That's an aristocracy that you just can't comprehend. Over the years, you've hit her with every thing in your sick arsenal. But she won't show hurt. She just chews her cud and endures it. But suppose you could humiliate her at bridge? She couldn't pretend to ignore that, could she? And with me as her partner? The skin should really be thin and tender there, shouldn't it? But your vaulting fury overreached itself."

The Countess's face was a white mask. "Indeed? In what way?"

"You got carried away by the caprice of a few cards. You wanted the ecstasy of plunging the knife yourself. You played the dummy too fast for little Sergie to clue you. Not that he's the greatest..."

Her face was suddenly mottled with rage. "Why, you—you point-count gigolo. You cheap pasteboard mercenary. Don't you dare speak to me that way. Don't tell me you're really fond of the old sow! How much is she paying you? Tell me that!" She was standing over him, her bodice heaving.

Jake sipped his drink. "Edna would never pay me for a favor, Jeanne. Besides, anything I could do for her was paid for long, long ago—and not with money." He looked out the window. "I'm a cream-puff as well as a dreamer, Jeanne. I can't protect Edna from all the hurts in the world, much as I might like to, but I can protect her from a pair of filthy frauds—and will."

She turned suddenly calculating. "Oh, come now. Let's not make wildly slanderous statements. Besides, Sergio—"

Jake sighed. "Sergio said we can always buy him. But you see, Countess, Sergie is sadly two inches shorter on the beach than in the drawing room."

Her eyes narrowed. "So he wears elevator shoes. What has a little male vanity got to do with anything?"

"About the same amount," Jake said, "as phony fallen arches. Half-firm sand takes a fairly revealing footprint. You may be fallen, Countess, but the problem is not in your arches."

"Just what are you getting at?"

"Many things. None of them pretty. I suspect that against Fred and Randy all you really needed was the receiver, which you could hide in your hair, and, consequently, there was no mention of your bad arches and clumsy shoes. But when I came into the act, you had to go on two-way communication. That's why you wanted me beside you and Edna ahead of you when you went up the stairs. Is that enough? I'll deal with Sergie later."

She gave him a venomous glare. "That does it! The only thing you'll deal with later is my attorney." She grasped the top of her pajamas, ready to rip. "If you're not out of here in five seconds with your lips sealed, I'm going to scream rape!"

But Jake wasn't there to protest. "Excuse me for being rude to the crude," he said, from the region of her closet. "A topless bridge player should make a peek worth even more than two finesses. But I'm after even bigger skin game."

He returned with an armload of her shoes. Whether it was this or his remark that inhibited her, she did not scream. Several of them, he noted, were made by a custom cobbler in Florence, and had one feature in common—a nice substantial heel. A little toying revealed the clever way in which they could be detached, and the equally deft manner in which they bad been hollowed. Quite enough to conceal a little black box—one in each heel.

He sighed. The rich often spoke in parables. Randy Maxwell would never dream of accusing one of Edna's guests of rooking him out of thirty grand. But he'd spend a week figuring out how it was done, drop suave and subtle suggestions to Edna about importing Jake Winkman, and then contrive to get Jake to do the dirty work. But the really important task remained.

The Countess, watching him, had difficulty lighting a cigarette. She blew out a cloud of smoke. "Okay. Now what?"

"I go through the rest of your shoes and search the room until I find the transmitter and receiver—or you hand them to me."

She dug them out from behind the cushions of the love seat and handed them to him, a look of actual triumph suddenly lighting her eyes, "There. Now call Edna and explain to her how her little sister and ward abused her hospitality and cheated her. Go on. Maybe she'll prefer charges, and we can make an international thing out of it."

He smiled ruefully. "No wonder you're such a lousy bridge player. Listen to me, Jeanne. I don't think you're all that bad, or all that stupid. Besides, I need your help. Edna wouldn't prefer charges. She'd probably apologize for inspiring your perfidy. But she'd be hurt, and we don't really want that, do we?"

She gawked. "Are you kidding? *I* should cooperate with you to spare that cretin's feelings! Just how will you manage that?"

"By cutting out your heart, if I have to," Jake said. "We're going downstairs in a few minutes for a session of bridge—and just in case there's more of these around—you'll be wearing bedroom slippers."

She sat forward in rigid disbelief. "So you can cut Serg and me to pieces just to plaster up Edna's ego? And take back our hard-earned money? Do you realize how much time and effort we— Try to make me!"

"If you insist." He moved to the door. "I'll let pride put a pitchfork to your derrière. You see, Jeanne, Sergie is not a bridge expert."

"Not a bridge expert!" She actually goggled. "What do you mean? Why everyone—even Edna—has complimented him on his game. At Nice and Cannes he was always a big winner."

Jake shook his head. "He played too well," he said, "on defense. When he was practically looking at all four hands. Bridge doesn't work that way. There are a hundred fine dummy players for every topflight defensive player, He is a middling fair casino-style player— what we call a palooka-killer. Since you asked for it, brace yourself: Sergie is a con man. He promoted you for the sole purpose of getting into this house and out again—with a bundle. By involving you, he provided himself with complete immunity even if he was caught. If I know the type—and believe me I do—I'll bet he brought his mistress along when he followed you over here. He's got her stashed at some downtown hotel. Hasn't he made a quick trip or two to see his 'consulate'?"

A flash of terror mixed with betrayal lit up her eyes. "That's a lie! Serge is madly in love with me. We're going to be married. It was only because of his love for me that we needed—"

"Another fifty thousand shares of RCA. Face it, Jeanne. After our afternoon session, Serge will check with you during the dinner break. Don't tell him I've drawn his fangs. Simply say that you consider yourself a better bridge player than Edna and that, since his is better than mine, why not enjoy the added sport of beating us fair and square? If you really have a sophisticated sense of humor, you'll enjoy the look that comes into his eye. But within an hour after the evening session starts, little Sergie is going to get an urgent call. His Upper Slobovian uncle, the grand duke, is dying in Zurich. Surely he's told you about the grand duke…"

Her mouth was like a thin fresh scar. "You are the most despicable, cynical, skeptical rat-fink I've encountered. Get out!"

THE AFTERNOON SESSION was a subdued affair, with both the Countess and the Prince playing with a withdrawn, almost desperate intentness. Edna, appearing not to notice, was nonetheless impelled to flow copious coats of lacquer to preserve a patina of social grace. The cards ran flat and indecisive, but Jake drove them, scoring game after game with the aid of a little inept defense. Three times he pushed to the five level in quest of dubious slams, but each time, failing to hold the critical controls, Edna correctly signed him off. He was almost equally relentless in presenting Edna with tough, brutally stretched contracts, but she bagged far more than her share with beautifully judged dummy play.

"Oh, dear," she observed, as the session broke up. "I seem to be so lucky today." Her eyes met Jake's blandly. "You played magnificently, Wink. It's such a pleasure, isn't it? Thank you. Shall we resume about eight? I must tell Hanson."

She presented the score to Jeanne and the Prince. They were down $27,000.

EDNA'S PERFORMANCE AT DINNER, Jake decided, deserved at the very least an Academy Award. She was serenely solicitous, fumbled the table talk into channels that were as bland as an ulcer diet, and avoided any word or mannerism that might hint at a feeling of triumph. How much did she know? Or suspect? He'd be damned if he could tell. He thought of Kipling and of treating those two imposters—"triumph and disaster"—just the same.

He was seated at her right—and that was another thing. For there were two other guests tonight—Randy Maxwell and a dowager by the name of Mrs. Adrian Phelps. Like a litany, it kept bugging him. *How much did Edna know?* He put down his coffee cup, picked up her chubby hand and kissed it... No one seemed to take the slightest notice, least of all Edna.

THE EVENING SESSION was scarcely under way before Jake and Edna smoothly assumed a comfortable margin. Maxwell and Mrs. Phelps were playing a quiet game of Persian rummy at a nearby table. The Prince made one of his dashing bids, ran into a rock-crusher in Jake's hand, and got pulverized. Randy and Mrs. Phelps came over to observe the carnage. It was almost a relief when Hanson appeared to inform the Prince of an urgent phone call. He excused himself to take it in the library. When he returned, his face was clouded.

"I am prostrated," he announced. "An unpardonable turn of events. I must at once leave. It concerns a matter about which I cannot speak." He bowed deeply and headed rapidly for the stairs. The Countess looked as if she had been drugged, but Jake noted a tiny ember smoldering in her eye.

The whole tempo went into a new gear. Many things happened fast, but there was an almost stage-like coordination about them, so that they seemed to take place with slow-motion definition. Edna withdrew to a nearby escritoire and carefully wrote a check. The Prince's bag appeared almost as if by magic in the front hall, followed by the Prince himself. He accepted Edna's check, clicked his heels, and was gone, a waiting cab whisking him away. Mrs. Phelps was in his seat at the bridge table, calmly shuffling the cards.

Randy Maxwell lit a cigar and nudged Jake toward the library. "The call came from the Uppingham Hotel on East Delaware, but it was a little cryptic." He blew out a puff of smoke. "You did want me to tap the phone, didn't you?"

Jake shrugged. "What else, Steinmetz? It was probably better than bribing Hanson to listen in."

"Oh, much better," Randy agreed. "Some people are so devious." He took a small radio from his pocket. "I just happen to have this tuned to the cab company's frequency."

There was a squawk..."thirty-seven to dispatch...pickup at Mallory...destination Pierpont Plaza...ten-four."

Maxwell pocketed the radio and turned to Jake. "You see? Perhaps we can have that drink next time."

Jake's bags had replaced the Prince's in the hall, and a Mercedes was idling under the *porte-cochère*.

"Mrs. Mallory ordered it brought round when she saw your bags," Hanson said, "I daresay you'll leave it at the airport, sir?"

Jake nodded. "I'd rather not disturb Mrs. Mallory just now. Say goodbye for me when she's free. In fact, give her a kiss for me, Hanson."

"Only you could do that, sir. You're the only one I've ever seen—I think I may have said too much, sir."

Jeanne was in the front seat. He whipped the car out through the long curving driveway. "You're about to get your ego shattered, Countess. Are you sure you can take it?"

"Drop the Countess stuff, Wink. I'm a skurvy, rotten nothing. I need a catharsis."

"Castor oil is cheap."

"But it won't make me into an Edna?"

"Only Edna could make Edna."

She was silent for several miles. "Wink, what do you honestly think of my bridge game?"

"With or without an electronic mirror? Without, it stinks."

"I *know* it stinks. I meant do I have the latent ability?"

"Anyone has the ability; not everyone the guts."

Nothing more was said until Jake pulled into the parking lot of the Pierpont Plaza on Chicago's near-North side. She handed him a small camera. "Randy said to give you this. It has a built-in electronic flash that will take pictures in any light."

"Polensky," Jake told the desk clerk."Give me his room number and tell him Jake Winkman's on his way up."

THE PRINCE WAS COMPLETELY URBANE. So was the bleached blonde with the long cigarette holder who lounged on the divan. "It was thoughtful of you to spare Mrs. Mallory the scene," he said. "But you have had a trip for nothing." He completely ignored Jeanne. "Mrs. Mallory will not make the charge. Nor Mr. Maxwell. Nor will she stop the check." He shrugged his shoulders. "So there is to discuss really nothing."

"True," Jake admitted. He unstrapped one of the Prince's bags, sprawling the contents on the floor, and came up with a shoe. He calmly detached a heel, placed shoe and heel on an end table, and proceeded to photograph them.

The Prince suddenly changed to a tiger, showing his fangs in the form of a small automatic. "Give me that camera. I demand also payment for my ruined shoe. Then out get or I will shoot!"

Jake snapped his picture. "Sergie, you are many things, but a gunman isn't one of them. Besides, Mr. Maxwell doesn't trust me. I spotted two detectives from the Bronco squad in the lobby." He snapped a picture of the blonde. "Be a good fellow and give me the check."

The tiger turned to a fawning jackal. "But that I cannot. I have the expenses." His eyes slithered to the blonde. "Very heavy expenses. And I need money Europe to return." He spread his arms. "Let us like gentlemen the compromise make."

The blonde began to pack. It didn't take her long.

Winkman shook his head. "These pictures and a full report will go to the American Contract Bridge League and the World Bridge Federation. You'll be blown from Oslo to Oskaloosa, right down to your denture charts. You've had it, Sergie. The check."

The blonde hustled her bags to the door. "Serg, you always were a yellow fink. The man says two words and you curl up like wet spaghetti. He hasn't a thing on you that would stand up. You could sue and double your money on a settlement. Mrs. Mallory would no more let this come out in court than fly. Her own sister... The least you could do is beat this man up and throw him out. Goodbye!" She slammed the door.

The Prince was nervously lighting a cigarette. He flung it down in a sudden gesture of ultimate frustration and made a desperate lunge at Winkman. At the last second, Jake stepped aside and measured him for a Judo sweep that scythed his legs from under him and dropped him like a bag of wet cement.

He leaned down and retrieved Edna's check from the Prince's wallet. Maxwell's check was missing, but there was $20,000 in large denomination bills with the bank's paper strap still around them.

He held out his hand to Jeanne. "Give me your lighter."

White-faced, she handed it to him and he touched the flame to the check.

THREE MORE TIMES on the way to the airport, he asked to borrow her lighter.

"That—that woman," Jeanne said, as they pulled into O'Hare, "She was right, wasn't she? You just psyched him."

He looked at her and sadly shook his head. "Let's just say I seldom psych."

She sat up as if suddenly galvanized. "Good heavens! Do you actually believe that Edna might have done it? Reveal herself and the great Fred Mallory as dupes and unwitting shills—and her own sister as a crook! Do you honestly think—"

"I don't know," Jake said softly. "Edna's a quality person. I suspect she'd choose the integrity that cost her the most. I'm glad it won't be necessary. Lighter, please."

She was silent as he slid out of the car, gathered his grips, and handed her the envelope with the $20,000 for Randy Maxwell.

"Jake...wait. Why have you kept borrowing my lighter? What happened to that beautiful gold lighter Edna gave you?"

"It's in Sergie's pocket with his fingerprints all over it. I put it there when he went to answer the phone. If he'd made a fuss—as his mistress suggested—I'd have nailed him on grand larceny. And don't kid yourself that I wouldn't have pressed the charge."

She sat looking up at him for a long moment. "For a dumpy, frumpy woman like Edna?"

"No," he said. "Just for Edna."

In the rotunda, he picked up a public phone, and got Edna. "I think Jeanne is coming home," he said. He hoped he had got the right inflection on the word "home." But with Edna you could never tell.

"Thank you, Wink, we're waiting. It's been such a pleasant day, hasn't it?"

Never Hit a Lady

Fred S. Tobey

Short and neat! That is the art of the short short.

"YOU REALLY OUGHT to get married, Paul," George said. "It simply isn't right for a man of forty to be living alone."

If I hadn't known him for such a busybody, I would have thought George was joking. He thinks he can speak as he pleases to me because he's older, and was a close friend of my father's before the auto accident that killed both my parents and crippled my brother.

"Bring a woman into this house? Ridiculous!"

"Paul, you have no idea what a woman's touch could do for this place—and for you, too. You need a new incentive."

"What I need," I said, "is just to be left alone. Don't forget I took care of my brother for twenty years. I'm entitled to relax a little."

All four of us were in the accident, the whole family. I came through all right except for a concussion that made me fuzzy in the head for a year or two. Taking care of my crippled brother was a terrible chore, but I faced up to my duty. Mother always told us a gentleman never shirks his responsibilities.

"I couldn't help thinking," said George, "after your brother tumbled down the stairs in his wheelchair last year and broke his neck, that at least you would now have a chance to enjoy life a bit."

"That's exactly what I'm doing. Fixing up the house the way I want it. Have you seen the new retaining wall I'm building out back? I'll have twice as big a flower garden after that place is filled in."

I might have added that I also would be able to buy the fill without an argument, now that my brother was gone. Our parents left quite a lot of money, but it had dwindled to the point where it wasn't really enough to take care of two of us. I'm afraid that toward the end, my brother and I quarreled quite a bit about how the money was to be spent.

"Paul," said George, "I've a friend I've been wanting you to meet. Quite an attractive woman. She's pretty much alone in the world. Suppose I bring her over?"

I absolutely forbade it, but he went on trying to persuade me. "Don't get the idea that she's a fortune hunter," he said. "She's got money. Travels all the time. That would be good for you, Paul— getting out to see a little of the world."

"I like it right where I am."

But George is never content unless he is arranging someone else's life, so he brought her in spite of anything I could say, and of course I had no choice but to be polite to her. No true gentleman is ever impolite to a lady. Mother always told us that.

The entire evening was a nightmare. Cynthia mistook my politeness for genuine cordiality. I caught her looking around the living room as if she were thinking of how to rearrange the furniture.

When George stopped in to see me the next day, he was jubilant. "Cynthia liked you."

"Did she indeed? Well, I'm afraid it wasn't mutual."

"Oh, come on, Paul," he said. "Admit that she's an attractive woman. You'd make a handsome couple."

"She's a determined woman who would run every minute of my life."

"Maybe that's what you need," he said. The fool!

"Just leave me alone, George. Please don't bring her here again."

A FEW DAYS LATER, however, when I was in the backyard working on my new wall, I heard his voice and turned to see him approaching—with Cynthia striding vigorously along beside him. Of course I had to play the host and make them welcome despite my true feelings.

"What are you going to do about that cavity under the big boulder?" George asked.

"The wall will cover it."

"You ought to fill it with something," said George.

Cynthia leaned over to peer into the opening. Suddenly, I thought how perfectly that big-boned, muscular frame would fill the cavity, if I could just bring myself to push her into it! I saw myself bashing Cynthia over the head with a rock, rolling her into the opening and saying to George, "There! You wanted it filled, didn't you?"

But quite apart from the foolishness of doing such a thing in front of a witness, I would have been utterly incapable of striking Cynthia, despite the repugnance I felt for her at that moment. No true gentleman ever raises his hand against a lady. If Mother said that to us once, she said it a hundred times.

YOU CAN IMAGINE how delighted I was when George called to say that he was going away for a month on a business trip. "Call up Cynthia and take her out," he said, "I think she's becoming quite fond of you, Paul."

I most certainly would *not* call Cynthia, and of course it was unthinkable that she would call on me without her old friend George. As Mother used to say so often, a lady simply does not call unescorted on a gentleman.

MY WALL WAS COMING ALONG FAMOUSLY when, one sunny Saturday afternoon, I was surprised to hear footsteps on the gravel behind me. I swung around and was absolutely dumfounded to see Cynthia standing there, quite alone.

"Hello, Paul," she said brazenly. "You didn't call, so I stopped by to tell you I have two tickets to the show that's opening tonight at the Belmont. You'll go, won't you?"

It was less a question than a statement of the inevitable. I stood speechless, my trowel in one hand and a rock in the other, while Cynthia drew a pamphlet from her purse and began reading aloud about the show at the Belmont.

WHEN GEORGE RETURNED, he paid me a visit. "How are you and Cynthia getting along?" he asked. "I called at her apartment, but there was no answer."

"I haven't seen her," I replied. "Probably she's away on one of those trips of hers."

"Very likely," said George. "Well, I'll keep trying to reach her. I want to get you two together again as soon as she comes back."

But Cynthia did not come back. George says he always thought some day she'd find some place she liked so much that she'd just stay there, but he worries because she doesn't write, and says he misses her.

Frankly, I can't imagine why he would—a woman like that who could call on a man unescorted. She certainly was no lady.

Farewell to the Faulkners

Miriam Allen deFord

*There is an eerie quality to this tale as the characters, one by one,
disappear. But at the same time, Miriam is telling a classic detective story
and the clues are there to point a finger at the villain.*

MISS HARRIET FAULKNER never missed a Friday evening symphony
concert. Riding home now in a taxi—only her brother Philip ever
drove the roomy Faulkner car—she hummed a bit of Brahms to
herself and reflected comfortably that really her life was as satisfac-
tory a one as often falls to human lot. She had never missed love or
marriage very much—*both,* she thought, *are overrated;* her parents
had died so many years ago that now they were only a vague
memory; she bad always been reasonably well off; she had her music,
to which she was devoted; and she had dear Caroline and dear Philip.

There were things about Caroline, of course, that Harriet de-
plored; chiefly her insensitivity to music—some of the dreadful
noises that Caroline permitted to pour from the radio made her sister
dash to her own room in dismay. Caroline was so set in her ways, too
—always the same habits at the same hours, hardly ever leaving the
house, having no life or interests outside of her home and her family;
really, she was an old woman at sixty, whereas Harriet, only a year

younger, still felt quite brisk and youthful. But take it all in all, Caroline was a darling, and Harriet was very happy with her.

Philip, their junior by sixteen and seventeen years respectively, seemed more like a nephew than a brother. He had been one of those unexpected babies who sometimes arrive long after the family is considered complete. Their mother had paid for his birth with her life, and three years later their father had followed her. Caroline and Harriet had devoted their youth to raising their young brother. And they had made a good job of it, Harriet reflected.

It hadn't been easy, in the early years. Philip had been a rebellious child, resenting discipline. And as a youth he had had wild ideas. That dreadful ambition to go on the stage, for example; and that awful episode during his college days with that impossible girl, Mary Dwight, he had wanted to marry! But they had been firm, and the money was all theirs till Philip came of age, so in the end they had won. They had made Philip into a lawyer, as they had always intended to do. As for the girl—

Harriet shuddered slightly as an unwelcome memory assailed her —the only time she and Caroline had seen the person who for nearly twenty years had been known to them only as "that woman." Philip had dared to bring her home with him to meet his sisters. They had seen at once that she would never do. Tall, aggressive, brassy, with a strident voice—the last person in the world to take into their home— and of course they had never dreamt that Philip would leave the house. They had been so cool that the girl, for all her aplomb, had burst into tears, and Philip had taken her away. That night they had made him promise on their mother's Bible that he would not see her again.

And then—why *was* she thinking of all those unpleasant things? The music must have stirred her more than she realized. Then, when Philip had been admitted to the bar, at twenty-five, be had floored them with the revelation that he had broken his solemn vow and married that woman—worse, that he had bought a house—in Woodacre, fortunately, not in the city—and intended to live there with her, and his sisters could like it or lump it

Things had finally adjusted themselves, of course. Blood is thicker than water, after all. Philip kept his old room, and after a few years he spent half his time at home, leaving that creature alone in Woodacre, whether she liked it or not. Her name was never mentioned in the Faulkner house on Pacific Avenue, and of course they had never seen her again. It was a silent compromise, with Philip forgiven on strict conditions.

Except for that one lapse, he was a model brother now, and most dependable. For years they had not even had to worry about investment of their property. Philip, whose legal practice took up little of his time—he accepted nothing but civil suits and was fussy about those—managed everything for all of them.

The money, quite a sizable fortune, though nothing stupendous, had been left by their father's will to his three children equally. Until Caroline became twenty-one, a bank had been the trustee. Then Caroline had the management, with the bank's guidance, for another year; after which Harriet came into her share, and they had managed Philip's property jointly for sixteen years more. As soon as Philip had been admitted to the bar, the whole business had been put in his hands by his sisters, who were glad to be rid of the worry of it. Since bills were always paid and there was always plenty in their drawing-accounts, they had discouraged Philip from even making annual reports. What was the use, when it really belonged to all of them, and they all lived together?

Thinking idly of these matters, Harriet reached the big wooden gingerbread house on Pacific Avenue. Taxis drew up to the front door, of course; but when they used their own car, they drove it by the side-path to the rear garage, once a stable.

The house was an anomaly. Three stories, basement, and attic, with turrets and cupolas and stained-glass windows, it was in the best style of the 1880s and still stood in its own garden. The saplings dear father had planted were big shady trees now. On either side rose tall modernistic apartment houses. When the last Faulkner was gone, their house too would be torn down and another apartment house would take its place; but that would be a long time yet. Meanwhile, they were fortunate in still having their privacy. In both cases the sides of the apartment houses looking down upon them were pierced only by airshafts and narrow lead-glassed bathroom windows: they could pretend at least that they lived in their own exclusive world

The only difficulty nowadays was that servants balked at working in a house lacking so many modern improvements. But even so, they managed. They still had old William, who came daily to tend the garden and do the heavy work; and after a difficult interregnum they had Mamie back again. Mamie had come to them as cook after mother died. Then she had married. Caroline had offered to raise her pay to fantastic heights to dissuade her, but it had been useless. In the face of argument and prophecy, Mamie had insisted on abandoning them for her young policeman.

It was Harriet, worn out by an endless succession of surly and inefficient servants, who had traveled all the way to the Mission District and persuaded Mamie to come back to them. Caroline could never have accomplished it, Harriet sometimes thought smugly. When she was twenty-two, Harriet had been courted and proposed to. Her suitor had been rejected, of course; but since then Harriet had felt herself an authority on men. She had known, as Caroline would not have known, that Fred Mullins, not Mamie, was the stumbling-block. Mullins had just been promoted to the detective force, and he didn't want his wife working in another woman's kitchen. But he was a soft-hearted Irishman, and Harriet—small, fragile, and appealing for all her dignity—had won him over. Mamie could no longer "live in," naturally—she arrived at eight and left after preparing their dinner—but figuratively Harriet bore her home in triumph; and she was still with them, even though Fred Mullins by now was a full-fledged inspector on the homicide squad—indeed, a senior inspector, and very near the retirement age.

Yes, they managed very well. They never had guests, they seldom went out, and there were rooms they never went near except to dust them. Of late years Philip was there more than he had been at first. Harriet and Caroline could not imagine what he did in that ridiculous cottage in Woodacre, especially on weekends. Surely that woman's company could not be very entertaining. In college he had been something of an athlete, but though he was tall and strong still, he had never been one for hunting or fishing. Oh well, as long as he kept his two lives separate, and was there when his sisters wanted him, Harriet could not complain.

"After all—men!" she sighed philosophically as the taxi came to a stop.

She paid the driver crisply, carefully adding an exact ten percent tip, and as he drove away, reached into her handbag for the door key.

It was nearly half-past eleven, yet there were lights in the front windows, upstairs and down, as she could see well, even though the shades were drawn. Through the closed door she could hear a raucous female voice singing something horrible on Caroline's radio. What on earth had got into her sister? Usually she was sound asleep by the time Harriet came back from the symphony.

Annoyed, Harriet inserted the key. It did not turn. She took it out and tried again. On an impulse, she turned the knob. It yielded: the door was unlocked, This was really too bad of Caroline—inexcusably careless.

Crossly, Harriet marched into the living room and snapped off the radio abruptly. In the sudden silence she called: "Caroline! Where are you, Caroline?" There was no answer.

Caroline's favorite chair was drawn up to the fireplace, as usual; her interminable knitting lay on the little table beside it. A book she had been reading—Caroline could knit and read at the same time— lay face down on the seat of the chair. Harriet sniffed. Something was burning. She hurried out to the lighted kitchen. Smoke was coming from a saucepan on the stove. Hastily Harriet turned off the gas and with a holder carried the hot saucepan to the sink. It contained the scorched residue of milk—Caroline's nightly boiled milk, which she drank every evening at nine-thirty.

Alarmed now, Harriet ran upstairs to her sister's room. It too was brightly-lit. Caroline's bed was turned down; her nightgown and dressing gown lay across it, her woolly slippers at its foot. But Caroline was not there.

A thought struck Harriet. She ran back to the kitchen. Flopsy's bed was empty. Could Caroline have left the house to take Flopsy for his walk? It was Harriet's nightly task, but this evening it had been hard to find a taxi, and she had been later than usual. But would Caroline have left the radio going and the milk cooking? Anyway, there was a faint yapping outside the kitchen door. Harriet opened it

—it too was unlocked—and let in a cold and shivering poodle, quite alone.

Systematically, Harriet searched the house. Somewhere Caroline must be lying ill. But the unlocked doors? As she searched she called, but no answer came. She entered every room, opened every closet, forced herself to the attic, the basement, the garden, with a flashlight. Still no Caroline.

Panic-stricken, back in the living room, Harriet threw herself into a chair and tried to think. Had Caroline suddenly gone insane and rushed out of the house? Had robbers broken in and kidnapped her? She ran to the front door again and looked wildly up and down the street. It was after midnight by now, and neither pedestrian nor car was in sight. It was a foggy, windy night, and very dark. Harriet shuddered at the thought of running about those silent streets, not knowing where to go or what to do. For a moment she even meditated phoning the police. But that was only a sign of terror. If something dreadful had happened to one of the Faulkners, it must be kept strictly to the Faulkners. No Faulkner yet had ever provided entertainment for the public on the front page of a newspaper.

There was only one thing left to do. Thank heaven Philip had a telephone in that Godforsaken cottage of his. She hated waking him, and dreaded hearing that woman's voice—she'd always been lucky so far on the few occasions when she had had to phone Philip there instead of at the office—but the time had come when even Harriet Faulkner could no longer cope with the situation. She needed a man.

The operator rang and rang, but there was no answer. Harriet nearly collapsed: had something happened to Philip too? And then, just as she was giving up in despair, his voice sounded.

"Who is it?" he demanded. "For heaven's sake, Harriet! We were sound asleep! What's the matter?"

She was almost incoherent, but by making her stop and speak slowly in short sentences, Philip finally managed to get the story. At first he made light of it.

"Good Lord, Harriet, nothing's wrong. There's probably some simple explanation. Maybe Caroline took Flopsy out for an airing and met somebody she knew and was detained. She'll be walking in any minute. What time is it, anyway? I went to bed early."

Harriet told him the time, and explained about Flopsy.

"Well—are you sure she hasn't fainted—isn't lying under the couch or something?"

"I've been everywhere! I've looked in every corner—the garden too, and the garage. Oh, Philip, do you think I should call the police?"

Philip showed the instantaneous Faulkner reaction. "No—not yet, anyway. Wait—I tell you what, Harriet, I'll get dressed and drive down. I can make it in a little over an hour."

"I hate to have you do it, dear, but—" In spite of all her efforts, Harriet's voice quavered.

"Okay, Harriet. Hold everything. Take a drink of that sherry of yours and keep calm. I'll be there as fast as I can—and if I find Caroline sitting there safe and sound, I'll tell her plenty! Chin up, Harriet; we'll laugh about this, all three of us, in the morning."

But they didn't laugh about it in the morning. All three of them never laughed about anything again. For that was the last of Caroline Faulkner.

HARRIET WAS PROSTRATED, and glad to leave everything to Philip, who after all was a lawyer. Philip decided that this was not a matter for the police. Caroline, so far as they knew, had not been injured or killed; she had simply disappeared. Time enough for a public scandal if she should be found wandering somewhere, suffering from amnesia. The thing to do was to try to find her. He engaged a discreet agency, the Biggs Company, gave them all the data, and told them to spare no energy or cost. They worked hard and sent in a thumping bill; but after two months they had to give up the search. Some dozen wretched women, in no way resembling Caroline, had been tracked down and interviewed by Philip. Of Caroline herself there was no trace.

Time went on, and somehow Harriet and Philip adjusted themselves to existence without their sister. Old William, the handyman, had to be told, of course, and Mamie. But there were few acquaintances and no intimate family friends to worry about. Caroline had lived apart from even the small world of her sister, or the larger world of her brother. To the few casual inquiries, they answered vaguely that Caroline wasn't very well, or that she was out of town for a rest. Gradually the impression arose among the three or four persons who knew of Caroline's existence at all that she had probably lost her mind—you know how it is when those old families run to seed, my dear!—and was in a private home somewhere. Perhaps it would be more tactful not to mention her again. Nobody but Harriet and Philip really cared.

For a while, Philip spent most of his nights with Harriet in the city, presumably leaving that woman to fare for herself in Woodacre. It was Harriet who, in an effort to be fair, suggested that he resume the way of life to which he was accustomed. She herself went out more often now—to the theater and lectures and concerts and the opera—and she had not the slightest nervousness about coming home to an empty house, or spending the night alone in it. Tentatively Philip suggested a companion or secretary; but he might have known Harriet would pooh-pooh such an idea instantly. She wasn't a helpless old woman! He even broached the idea of asking the Mullinses to give up their flat and move to the big half-used house; but Harriet, as he might have expected, was horrified.

"What! A stranger—a policeman—living here, in dear father's house! Why, Philip!"

Philip made no further recommendations.

"I'm perfectly all right," she said brightly over Friday breakfast, some six months later, "run along and come home soon again."

Philip looked relieved, in spite of himself. "The place does need some work done on it," he muttered. Harriet sniffed.

Since he was forbidden to mention "that woman," he took refuge in describing the constant improvements he planned on his "estate." Recently he had had a barbed wire fence put around his twenty acres, and had posted it with signs threatening trespassers. He wanted no hikers or hunters tearing down his bushes or trampling his undergrowth.

"Lucky to have had the wire for years—couldn't get it now," he explained to Harriet.

"Silly to bother," she said ungraciously.

He smiled rather stiffly as he kissed her goodbye. He would take the car downtown and drive straight up from the office, he said. Now that gas was rationed, he used the car very little, keeping it in the garage most of the time. And with a thirty-five mile speed limit, it took longer to go and come than it used to.

But he wanted to get home before dark, to see to that fence. Harriet sniffed again.

This time it was Mamie who telephoned him, at eight o'clock on Saturday morning.

Except for changes arising from Harriet's different habits, the story was repeated. Mamie had come to work as usual to find the front door unlocked and lights on behind drawn shades in the living room and Harriet's bedroom. Harriet's reading glasses lay in the open book of Double-Crostics on which she had been working, and beside it stood a half-finished glass of sherry. Her bed also had been turned down and her night attire laid on it, but it had not been slept in. Flopsy was whining and scratching at the unlocked kitchen door.

Harriet herself was gone.

This was no case for the Biggs Company. Disliking it very much, Philip had to go to the police.

"And nobody lower than a captain would do him, the desk sergeant told me," Fred Mullins reported that night to his wife. "'Tell your captain that Mr. Philip Faulkner wishes to speak to him,' says he, high and mighty, to O'Rourke."

"Oh, well now, Fred, it's distracted the poor man is, with the queer things happening to both my poor ladies," said Mamie pacifically. "And, after all, Mr. Philip's a big lawyer, and the Faulkners is big people."

"You and your Faulkners!" grumbled Fred. "I wonder I've let my wife work in someone's kitchen so long. It was the little one got around me, that time. Don't cry now, Mamie girl—I don't blame you for feelin' bad. I'm sorry meself, and if it turns out to be a matter for the squad, I'll do everything I can to help."

"For the homicide squad! What ever do you mean, Fred? Do you think poor Miss Harriet—and maybe Miss Caroline—was murdered?"

"And if not, where are they?" asked Mullins practically.

Which was practically the same thing Captain of Detectives Joyce had been saying to Philip earlier in the day.

The captain was considerably annoyed. "If you'd come to us six months ago—"

"I know, Captain. It's what I should have done. I know it as an attorney, even though I've never had any dealing with criminal cases. But my sister—both my sisters—are very conventional in their ideas. The mere thought of the family name of our personal affairs—being made public—I guess." He laughed apologetically. "We Faulkners are rather an old-fashioned lot. Our father, you know, was a pretty prominent man; he—"

"Yes, yes, I know," said the captain brusquely. He dreaded, from sad experience, getting mixed up with any of what he called bitterly "that Pacific Heights crowd."

"For the present," he added stiffly, "it will be kept a matter for the police department only. The papers will not be given anything by us."

"Thank you, Captain. After all, since no crime had been committed—"

"We don't know whether one has or not. That's what we're going to find out. And if it has, Mr. Faulkner, I might as well tell you that it will be treated exactly as if it had happened down on Skid Road."

"Oh, certainly—certainly," said Philip quickly. "I leave the whole thing in your competent hands."

BUT FOR ALL THE department's best efforts, and willing cooperation offered by Philip, the police were as baffled as the Biggs Company had been. They interviewed Philip and Mamie exhaustively; they analyzed the sherry; they fine-toothed the premises; they took fingerprints;

they talked to everybody in both apartment houses next door. Not a single clue developed. It was simply a grotesque, bizarre happening, without explanation or meaning. Caroline and Harriet Faulkner, two commonplace elderly women, had vanished, six months apart. They were gone, and nobody could find out where or why.

For several weeks Philip spent every night in the house, with the lights on, as if to welcome either or both of his sisters if they should return. When a month passed without word of either of them, he came to a resolution.

"I'm closing up the house, Mamie," he said. "You'll be glad enough to stay at home, after all these years. William will have no trouble finding a job nowadays. I'll take Flopsy with me."

Worry had made Philip expansive. He went on, more to himself than to the old cook. "I never thought I'd give up the family home. But after what's happened—it sounds superstitious, but it's hard not to feel there's a curse on this house."

it is indeed, Mr. Philip. I feel the same way meself. What are you goin' to do—rent the house?"

Philip shuddered. "I'm going to lock it up, just as it is, furniture and all, and let it stay that way. After all, Mamie, perhaps some day this—this mystery will be solved; Miss Caroline and Miss Harriet may come home again. If not—well, after the war I suppose it will have to be torn down. It's the last one-family house in the block." He made his plans to close the house the next Wednesday.

Until then, Mamie was to come daily as usual, while Philip stayed away from his office; and after a brief trip to Woodacre, he helped her pack his personal belongings and what few things he wanted to take with him, cover the furniture, and store Caroline's and Harriet's things in the attic.

"If you could get here a little early tomorrow morning, Mamie," he suggested on Tuesday evening. "The water and gas and electricity and telephone will be turned off soon, and there will be a lot of last-minute things to do before I leave."

"Sure, I'll be here by seven, Mr. Philip. And I'll make you a grand breakfast for the last one you eat in your own home. Curse or no curse, you must be sad to be going. I'm sad meself."

Indeed, Mamie was almost in tears. It was the end of many years' faithful service.

"That's good of you, Mamie," said Philip, touched. "And when you go, take everything from the pantry home with you. All I want is the basket we packed with the wine. And, Mamie—here's a little something for all your extra work this week, and all the years you've been our mainstay here."

"Oh, Mr. Philip!" Mamie took the envelope with a shaking hand. "God bless you, Mr. Philip! And if you want me to help out any time—"

"We'll be seeing each other, Mamie, don't worry. Run along now, and I'll be looking forward to that special breakfast."

"At seven sharp I'll be here, Mr. Philip."

Mamie hurried to catch her bus and get home before Fred came off duty. Philip looked with distaste at the living room, swathed in covers and no longer habitable. They had left the dining room and kitchen for the last. He ate the cold supper Mamie had left for him, put the dishes in the kitchen for her to wash in the morning, uncovered an armchair and dragged it in from the living room, and settled down by the dining-table. The secretary he shared with two other lawyers in a suite of offices downtown had telephoned him during the afternoon, and he had some notes to make and letters to write in connection with two or three pending cases.

Though ever since Harriet had vanished he had spent all his nights alone in what he had finally called a house with a curse on it, tonight it seemed emptier and gloomier than ever. Already it possessed the uneasy silence of an empty building. It was hard to put his mind to his work.

At last he got up and went to the basket he had mentioned to Mamie. Among the bottles of sherry and port and burgundy was an unopened pint of brandy. Philip Faulkner drank very little, but tonight brandy was just what he needed.

He opened the bottle, found a glass, drank a stiff jolt, and resolutely opened his briefcase and laid out the papers he needed. Flopsy was asleep in his bed in the kitchen.

IT WAS POOR MAMIE AGAIN, hurrying in at seven, who found the doors unlocked, Flopsy in the garden, lights on in the empty living room, the dining room, and Philip's bedroom, his bed turned down and his pajamas and slippers by it, the dining-table scattered with legal papers, Philip's pen open on a half-finished note, the bottle and glass beside it—and no one in the chair. No one in the house but herself. Philip Faulkner had followed his sisters.

This time Mamie phoned her husband. And Fred, telling her to wait there till someone came, took the matter immediately to Captain Joyce.

As soon as Mamie's story had been taken down, and she had gone home, weeping, with Flopsy in her arms, the house and grounds were searched thoroughly, and Philip's office was visited. Then the investigation moved on to Woodacre. There was no longer any question of keeping the affair out of the newspapers. Three mysterious disappearances in a prominent family—no clues—police (as usual) baffled —it was a lulu of a story. In three out of the four daily papers it shared the first page with the war news. There were no pictures available of Caroline or Harriet, but one was dug up of Philip from his college annual, and another from a group at some Civilian Defense function; and the house was photographed from every angle. *"Is There a Curse on This House?"* asked *The Morning Investigator* under a view of the front door—much to the embarrassment of the residents of the exclusive apartment houses on both sides. People came to stand and gape at the Faulkner home, and paid no attention whatever to the indignant doormen who tried to shoo them away.

THE NEXT MORNING, with a deputy sheriff in tow, since this was another county, Fred Mullins cut the barbed wire and trampled through Philip's cherished underbrush to his cottage. "What kind of woman is this wife of his?" he asked Deputy Davis.

Davis shook his head.

"I've lived here, man and boy, all my life, and darned if I ever saw her. Once in a while, before he put this fence up, kids passing through would get a glimpse of a woman's figure passing the window.

He did all the shopping in the town—what he *did;* most of the stuff they used he brought from the city. When he was away, she never set foot out of the house—leastwise, if she did, nobody saw her. Wish I could have my wife trained like that!"

"He's ashamed of her, that's what I gather from what my wife's told me—things she's overheard all these years. Probably married her when she was young and pretty, and the veneer wore off. These high-up snobs, that's the way they handle things, I guess."

"Folks here always figured she was maybe kind of—funny, and he wouldn't let her go out where people'd find it out."

"Well, here's where *we* find out. There's smoke coming from that chimney."

They banged on the door. After a few moments, steps crossed the floor and the door opened.

The woman who stood there, looking with bewilderment and consternation at the two men confronting her, was tall and gaunt. Obviously she was an urban product, from her too-golden hair to inappropriate high-heeled and open-toed shoes. Everything about her which would have gone unnoticed in a darkened cocktail bar— her hair, her lipstick, her mascara, her nail polish glared grotesquely in her surroundings. The one thing she did not look like was what she was—practically a hermit in the country for a score of years.

"What is it? What do you want? Who are you?" she asked in a rapid staccato. Her voice was low and husky—again a voice for a cocktail bar, not for a cottage in the woods.

"We're the police, lady," announced Fred Mullins bluntly. She was a type he disliked at sight. "You Mrs. Faulkner? We're looking for your husband. Is he here?"

"Here? Philip? The police? What's wrong?"

"He's missin', that's what's wrong. Just like his sisters. Dead, maybe, all of 'em, for all we know."

She gave a little scream, and swayed on her high heels. The deputy sheriff pushed forward.

"We want to talk to you," he said. "Let's go in the house."

"Why, I never—" murmured the woman. But she backed into the room and Davis and Fred followed her.

"Sit down," Fred ordered. "We'll talk to you in a minute. We want to look around first."

The cottage contained only two rooms, with a kitchen alcove and a cubbyhole just big enough to hold a toilet and a shower. It needed only a glance to see that there was no one in it but the three of them.

The woman had dropped into a chair and sat there stiffly, staring at them dazedly, occasionally licking her dry, too red lips.

"Now, Mrs. Faulkner," Fred finished his brief inspection of the house and planted himself in a chair facing her. "Tell us all about it."

"I don't know what you mean," she said in that husky, rapid tone. "Where is Philip? What's happened to him?"

"That's what we want to know," said Fred grimly. "You know what happened to his sisters, don't you? Well, now it's happened to him too."

"You mean," she whispered, "that he's—disappeared?"

"They found the place yesterday, all open and lit up and just the way it was with the other two."

"Oh!"

"When did you see him last?" Davis put in.

"Not for nearly a month, except for one night last week. He said he was going to stay down there till his sister Harriet turned up or he got things settled. He—he phoned me last night, though. He said he'd be up tonight And now you've come instead."

"You were pretty sore at those sisters of his, weren't you?" growled Fred Mullins. "You must have been pretty sore at him too, by this time, keeping you hidden like this—a woman like you."

"What are you driving at?" The woman's voice grew strident. "I never left this house—ask this man, if he's from around here. Philip wouldn't let me. He wouldn't even let me answer the phone, even if he wasn't here, unless he told me when he was going to call me himself. It wasn't until last week that he left any money here for me—and that was for a special purpose. How could I have got away from here to—for anything?"

"You're talking a lot, lady. I guess you'd better come along with us."

"Oh, no!" she screamed. "Listen—I'll tell the truth! I wasn't ever going to, but if he's disappeared, then I must."

"Okay, talk. They're all dead, ain't they? Who killed them?"

Mrs. Faulkner struggled to regain her composure. "I never saw those sisters, except once, years ago, before we were married. They wouldn't let me set foot again in that old cemetery vault they called a house—all I ever saw of it was the front parlor, and darned little of that. But I know they had Philip buffaloed—plenty. The only thing he ever did in his life against their will was to marry me. Unless you count taking all their money, of course," she added calmly.

"What!"

"Oh, yes, I found that out long ago. He had charge of their property, you know. I don't understand that kind of thing, my self, but one way or another he gradually got all their stocks or securities or whatever you call it into his hands. He'd say, 'Sign this—I'm selling this to buy you something better,' and old Caroline or Harriet would sign. He paid all their bills, and he kept money in the bank for them to draw on. If either of them had ever asked for an accounting, the whole game would have been up, but he knew they never would.

"The only thing was, being so much older than he was, one of them might die any time—and then he'd be in the soup. They'd both left their money to each other, if you know what I mean, and then to him. 'After all, honey,' he used to say to me, 'it will all be mine some day—I'm just anticipating.' But of course it wouldn't have been as simple as that if one of them kicked the bucket

"So some time along last year, when his sister Caroline had a spell with her heart, and he was afraid she wasn't going to get over it, he made up his mind he didn't dare let either of them die a natural death. They had to disappear, for good, instead. Then in seven years, he figured, he could go to court and ask to have them declared legally dead, he said they call it."

"You mean to say he told you all this?" Davis demanded. "Why should he put his own safety in your hands?"

"Why, I'm his wife—I couldn't testify against him. He told me so."

"I see. And you were livin' on that money too, weren't you?" said Fred. "Well, then, what else did you find out?"

Her eyes widened in surprise. "How he killed them, of course. And how he staged the disappearances."

"And how did he kill them?" demanded Fred.

"With—with his hands," she whispered. "His hands are awful strong. They thought he was up here, but he didn't go, either time. He just drove around till dark and then drove home, around back to that garage they had. And then he went in the house, where his sister was alone—first Caroline, and then Harriet—and I guess he said something like 'I didn't go to Woodacre after all,' and then suddenly he stepped behind her and put his thumbs on her neck and strangled her. They were little, both of them, you know.

"And then," she went on, "he carried the—he carried his sister out back through the kitchen, and put her in the baggage compartment of the car, and drove up here. He'd dug a—a place out here in the woods, out where I couldn't see from the house, and covered it up with leaves and stuff so it wouldn't show, and he put her in it and put the earth back and fixed it up with plants on it so nobody could tell.

"The first time, he was out doing—that, when he heard the phone ring. He just got here in time before it stopped ringing—like I told you, he never let me answer it. I got a black eye once for just trying to.

"With Harriet, it was the next morning before your wife rang, so he had time for a good sleep first," she concluded simply.

"Well, if you knew all this, even for a month," Davis exploded, "why in the name of heaven didn't you get out from under while he was away from here? Didn't you figure *you might be next?* You couldn't testify against him, but it certainly wouldn't be healthy for him to have you around knowing all about it. Some time you might divorce him, and then where would he be? He must have been crazy in the first place to tell you, and you must have been crazy not to get out fast."

"But I wouldn't divorce him—why would I? I haven't any money of my own, and he'd never give me any alimony, would he, if I said anything against him? Besides, he's my husband—I love him."

Davis snorted and stood up.

"Well," he exclaimed, "I give up! I've heard everything now!"

"Sit down, Davis," said Fred mildly. "The lady's got more to tell us. Now, how about this disappearance of his? He staged that too, eh? What for, and where is he now?"

Mrs. Faulkner fished a pink handkerchief from some subterranean hiding place and held it to her eyes. Her voice broke.

"That's why I'm telling you," she sobbed. "He's dead. You'll never find him. He's at the bottom of the bay."

"How do you know that?"

"Because he told me. Last week, when he was up here. You say you can't understand why he told me all this. Why, mister, you've *got* to tell things! There's got to be somebody you can tell! You couldn't hold it all in—you'd go crazy. And who can you tell, if not your wife or husband?

"So he told me. And he was awful worried. He said, 'Honey, I got away with it once, but can I do it twice? It's all for you, honey,' he said, 'so we can be together always, and they can't ever bother us again, and so there won't ever be any trouble about the money my father meant for me to have anyway. In a few more years I can claim they're dead and nobody will ever know there was anything wrong about the money.' I remember every word. 'I've always hated them,' he said, 'ever since I was a kid and they bossed me and wouldn't let me go on the stage the way I wanted, and tried to take you away from me. But it was all or nothing. It was neither of them or both. And this time I had to take it to the police. I knew I'd have to, but I'm worried.

"'They took it all right,' he said, 'but that captain I talked to might be smarter than he looked. And there's a guy on the force I wish was retired from it; he knows the whole family, and I wish he didn't. He's old, and he'll be out soon, but I couldn't wait. If he gets on the case, he might smell a rat.

"'So, honey,' he said, 'let's put it this way. I think everything's going to be all right. But if anything happens that makes me think there's real danger, they'll never catch me alive. If you ever hear *I've* disappeared, you'll know what it means. I'll stage the same act I did with them, to keep the family from shame,' he said, 'but I'll go straight to the middle of the Golden Gate Bridge and jump off the way fifty people have done before me, where the current will take me out to sea, and they'll never find me. And you go East and change your name,' he said. That was when he gave me that money I said I had—enough to go East on."

"And what were you going to live on when you got there?" asked Fred curiously.

"It's obvious, isn't it?" Davis broke in angrily. "She's not telling all she knows by a long sight. He's transferred his money somewhere, and she knows where. And he's not dead, either, by my guess—he's waiting for her and she thinks she's going to go scot-free after we've dug up the place here and found the bodies—if they *are* here. Well, she's not. She's an accessory after the fact, if nothing more, and since the murders were committed in your territory, you can have her."

"No," agreed Fred quietly, "he's not dead. But she's not an accessory."

"Damn it, Mullins, I don't understand what you're talking about."

"This," said Fred. He looked thoughtfully at their witness. She was crying again, her face in her hands.

Fred leaned over, and almost gently, he handcuffed her right wrist to his left one.

She pulled away violently and yelled. Davis gaped.

"Come on, Davis," said the detective calmly. "Didn't you ever see anyone arrested for murder before?"

"Murder!" screamed Mrs. Faulkner. "Are you crazy? I never—"

"Tell me," Mullins asked, "what was your name before you were married?"

"Mary Dwight. Why—"

"And where's your marriage certificate?"

"How do I know? Somewhere."

"Maybe. I guess you're not a very good lawyer after all. Did you really think you could get away with this?"

"I'm not a lawyer at all—my husband is—was. Oh, what are you talking about? Let me go!"

"If you're Mrs. Faulkner," snapped Fred Mullins sternly, "and you've never been familiar with that house, how did you know the garage was in back, through the kitchen?"

"He told me—he—"

"And if you never saw me before, and didn't know my name, *how did you know it was my wife who telephoned when Miss Harriet disappeared?*"

"He—"

"Sure, there was a girl named Mary Dwight that Philip Faulkner went with. Maybe he married her—but if he did, I'll bet she's planted right here on this place with his sisters. My guess is he never married her."

"But *I'm*—"

"You're a good actor, Philip Faulkner: I give you that. But you're a bum lawyer, and I think you must be crazy: and crazy or not, you're a cold-blooded murderer. Better come quietly now. I'll have your own clothes sent to you in jail."

The Dead Past

Al Nussbaum

Here is a short piece with, most definitely, an artist's touch.

WHEN HE REACHED THE GRAVE, Felix Kurtz sat on a nearby headstone and swore. At eighty-five, age hadn't diminished his ability to unleash a torrent of imaginative profanity; but the cursing did nothing to steady his shaky legs, or remedy his lack of breath, and these were the cause of his anger. Only his own weaknesses could anger him more than the failings of others. His was an active and impatient mind, trapped in a body unable to meet its demands, and he didn't like reminders of the fact.

Fifty years, half a century had passed since the funeral. He hadn't set foot inside the cemetery in all that time, but he'd had no difficulty finding the weed-covered grave with its weather-stained tombstone. When a life has been made up of one huge success followed by another and another, every failure is memorable. He'd always associated Kurtzville, the company town founded by his grandfather, with that early failure, rather than the huge profits the sale of coal had brought during the two world wars. Because of this, he'd been happy when reduced profits forced him to close the mines in the late forties and move his business headquarters to Pittsburgh. Now, Kurtzville was the Pennsylvania equivalent of the western ghost towns, and he'd returned to take away one of its citizens.

Of course, he could have delegated the job of supervising the reburial to one of the many vice-presidents of his numerous corporations. Or he could have taken no action at all. The state would have moved the grave along with all the others in the path of the new highway. The illogic of his being there neither escaped him nor troubled him. It had been a long time since he had believed himself to be a rational being. He knew that emotions of one kind or another had always governed his actions and reactions. It was only later, after a decision had been made or a deed had been done, that he had devised reasons for them. In this case, he had no reasons; he simply wanted to be present.

A flatbed truck, equipped with a winch and boom, turned at the rusted cemetery gates and bumped along the gravel trail toward Kurtz. As it passed the black limousine where Kurtz's driver was waiting, the man quickly raised his window to keep out the dust and flying stones. It stopped near the grave.

Three workmen climbed down from the cab. While two of them busied themselves removing picks and shovels from a chest behind the cab, the third approached Kurtz. "Mr. Kurtz?" he said. "Which grave is it?"

Kurtz pointed to the grave as the other men approached and dropped their tools at its foot with a clatter.

The first man squatted beside the headstone and ran his fingers over the dates. "After all this time, there ain't gonna be much left."

"Yes, there will," Kurtz contradicted. "The coffin was cast iron from the foundry in town. It took six strong men to carry it."

"Anyhow, this is gonna take a while, mister. If ya wanta wait in your car, I'll call ya when we're ready to use the winch to lift it."

"Don't take all day—I'm paying you people by the hour, you know," Kurtz said, and turned toward the limousine...

FROM THE WINDOW of his office overlooking the main entrance to the mine property, Felix Kurtz saw Myron Shay adjust his cravat with nervous fingers as he stated his business to a company policeman. Explanations were unnecessary. Everyone in the company town knew about the artist who had arrived during the excitement of the last cave-in to make drawings for a Washington, D.C., newspaper. They knew too that Kurtz had hired him away from the newspaper on the pretext of having him paint a portrait of his sister Emily, thereby cunningly avoiding publicity which might have resulted in legislation to force expensive safety measures in the mines.

Minutes later a clerk, holding his green eyeshade deferentially at his side, came to say that Myron Shay was downstairs. Kurtz told him to send the man up. He was pleased by the good fortune, whatever its cause, that had brought Shay to him when he was about to send for him.

Myron Shay was approximately twenty-five, ten years younger than Felix Kurtz, and they differed greatly. Kurtz was tall, powerfully built, and favored dark suits, suitable for trips down into the mines. Shay was slightly built, given to wearing light browns and blues and the bright yellow, ivory-buttoned spats of a dandy. Kurtz combed his black mane straight back and had a large mustache whose ends were stiffly waxed, while Shay's blond hair was parted neatly in the middle, and his pink face appeared to have no need of a razor.

"I thought you were an accomplished artist," Kurtz said, seizing the initiative. "I thought you said you worked effectively in all mediums."

Shay stood in front of Kurtz's mahogany desk and shifted his weight from foot to foot. "Yes, sir—clay, stone, oils, charcoal—"

"Is it your normal practice to spend over a month on one small likeness?"

"Well, sir, I—"

"No matter, no matter." Kurtz waved him to silence with a gesture of impatience. "I do not propose to pay for your services unless they are completed satisfactorily by Friday of this week." The newspaper artist no longer represented an immediate threat to him, but Kurtz wanted him away before something happened to alter the situation.

"Oh, I wouldn't think of charging you, sir," Myron Shay said.

Kurtz frowned. "What do you mean?"

Shay moved his hands nervously, as a man will who is forced to speak when he is used to expressing himself in other ways. "Your sister and I—Emily and I are in love. We wish to marry. I—I've come to ask your blessing."

Kurtz laughed humorlessly, then stood and came around the desk. "*You* want to marry *my* sister?"

"Yes, sir. I love her and—"

"Love her? Do you think you're the first man who's pretended an interest in her simply because she's my sister? Well, let me be the first to inform you she is underage and has no funds of her own. And just because I hired you to paint her portrait, don't think I'm unaware of how plain she is."

"Sir! Emily is not unattractive, and she's a very warm and sensitive human being."

"Enough of this foolishness! My sister is not going to be tied to any second-rate opportunist. I suppose you think I'll offer you money to stay away from Emily. If you do, you're mistaken. I own this town and everything in it. Nothing happens here without my knowledge and consent."

Kurtz reached out swiftly and grasped one of the artist's wrists in each huge hand. "You're threatening something of mine, so I'll do the same for you." He raised his arms until Shay's long tapered fingers dangled limply in front of his face. "You have fifteen minutes to return to the loft you're using for a studio, pack your equipment into your automobile, and take the road out of town. If you fail to leave, I'll have these fingers smashed into sausage meat."

To emphasize his last two words, Kurtz spun the younger man around and pushed him from the room, pausing only long enough to throw open the door. White-faced, Shay walked past the whispering clerks and left the mine offices without looking back.

Kurtz motioned to a clerk and said: "Telephone Miss Kurtz. Tell her to come down here right away."

The man returned in a few minutes. "She isn't at home, Mr. Kurtz. The maid said she went to sit for her portrait."

Kurtz snatched his hat from the rack and left his office, slapping the hat against his right thigh like a riding crop. "I'll be back later," he called over his shoulder, and descended the steps two at a time. He paused at the main gate to order two company policemen to come with him, then signaled for his sedan. Kurtz climbed into the front seat with the driver, and the two company policemen sat in the rear.

When they reached the street where the artist's studio was located, Shay and Emily were pulling away from the curb in an open car. Shay looked back once, then his vehicle picked up speed.

"Catch them! Cut them off!" Kurtz shouted at his driver. The man pushed the accelerator to the floor, but the large sedan was unable to gain on the smaller automobile. The two vehicles sped along the cobblestone street, and Kurtz pounded the dashboard with his fists. "Stop them!" he shouted. "Stop them!"

The reports of two closely spaced pistol shots crashed above the roar of the racing engines. Kurtz turned in amazement to find one of his policemen leaning from the window of the sedan with his weapon in his hand. Ahead of them, the smaller car swerved once, then slowed and stopped.

Kurtz's driver skidded to a halt behind it, and all four men rushed forward. They found Myron Shay cradling Emily in his arms, while a red stain on her dress grew rapidly larger.

LATER, at the company hospital, Dr. Moreau came out of the private room and closed the door quietly behind him, his frown almost hidden on a face already deeply etched by time. Both Kurtz and Shay took steps toward him, but he fixed his bloodshot eyes on the younger man and spoke to him, ignoring Kurtz. They exchanged a few words of rapid French, then the elderly doctor patted Shay on the shoulder and Shay went to the door of the sickroom.

Kurtz moved to follow, but the doctor stepped in front of him. "How did it happen?" he asked in English.

Kurtz licked his lips. "An accident...a sad misunderstanding. Emily was running away with that—that artist! I was trying to over-take them, and one of my policemen thought a crime had been committed."

"I suppose it was young Shay who was going to have the accident —like the other young men you had beaten after they showed an interest in your sister," the doctor said dryly.

The shock was wearing off, and Kurtz didn't like underlings to talk back to him. "Look, you old drunk, don't preach to me. I hired you when no one else would." He didn't mention that he paid the doctor far less than he would have had to pay someone else. "You have only two jobs in this town—taking care of the sick and seeing to it that the dead are buried. Confine your self to your duties as doctor-mortician, nothing else."

"Yes, sir," the doctor said meekly, but his narrowed eyes glinted.

"Fine. We understand each other. Now, how come you and Shay seem so friendly? Is he a foreigner too?"

"He studied in Paris and speaks French," Moreau explained. "We met when he arrived here and found we have interests in common."

Kurtz stared at the doctor's red-veined nose. "Mutual interests? Like what—whiskey and gin?"

"Chess and conversation," the doctor said. "The French language is well suited to talk of art and literature."

Kurtz waved a finger imperiously under Moreau's nose. "How suited is your English to talk of medicine? What's my sister's condition? How soon can she leave here?"

"The bullet passed through the seat before striking her. It didn't penetrate very deeply, and no vital organ seems to have been damaged, but she lost a great deal of blood," the doctor said. "I wouldn't recommend moving her for at least a week. She must have complete rest—no excitement. Then, if there are no complications..." He held one hand out with the palm up in a noncommittal yet pointed gesture.

Kurtz paused. "All right, doctor, but I advise you to stay sober."

The doctor drew himself up stiffly. "I never drink when I have a patient."

"See that you don't," Kurtz said.

THE FOLLOWING days were unhappy ones for Felix Kurtz. It was obvious that the news of Emily's accident had spread. Everyone knew he had suffered his first failure—the artist hadn't been frightened away. Whenever Kurtz turned quickly, he caught people smiling at him, and groups of miners fell silent whenever he appeared. Kurtz had known that his employees hated him, but he was mildly surprised to find that his sister's misfortune was a source of amusement because of the embarrassment it caused him.

Kurtz didn't like being laughed at, but for the moment he was helpless to do anything about it. Emily was too sick to leave the hospital, and Myron Shay had virtually moved into the place to be near her. Kurtz was forced to postpone his efforts to break up the romance until the girl was stronger. Then he'd see how long he remained an object of ridicule. In the meantime, the looks of fear he got from the young couple during his daily visits made it possible for him to endure his humiliation. Both he and they knew their days together were numbered.

And then the unexpected happened. Ten days after the accident, Kurtz was called to the hospital. He was met by a stone-faced Dr. Moreau, who informed him Emily had died during the night. Kurtz raised the sheet and looked at the still form for a moment; then, completely without a sign of emotion, he ordered Dr. Moreau to make the funeral arrangements.

Myron Shay left town without attending the funeral; thereby proving Kurtz had been correct about him all along...

"MR. KURTZ! MR. KURTZ!" It was the chauffeur's voice, and Kurtz awoke to find him shaking his arm. "They're ready to lift the coffin."

"Don't shout, you fool. I was merely resting my eyes." He climbed stiffly from the car and joined the workmen at the open grave.

The truck was beside the hole and heavy chains had been fastened to the rusty coffin in preparation for hoisting it to the bed of the truck. Two men were set to operate the winch and boom while the other was in position to guide the coffin.

"Well, what are you waiting for? Get on with it. Time is money, you know. And be careful—that's heavy."

"Not as heavy as it was," the foreman said. "There's so much rust in the grave, there can't be more than a thin shell left."

The man waved his hand and the winch began to turn, taking up the slack in the chain. Then the dull red of the iron coffin rose into the open and swayed gently from the boom while the foreman steadied it with one outstretched arm.

Suddenly, the edge of the grave collapsed under the weight of one of the truck's rear wheels. As the wheel dropped, causing the truck to tilt, the coffin swung away, smashed into a nearby headstone, then crashed to the ground.

The men on the truck bed hung onto the winch and stared open-mouthed at the coffin. Kurtz went to it and looked down.

A two-foot section of the lid had shattered, revealing the reclining figure of a young woman, wearing the high-necked, long-sleeved fashion of half a century before. One of her ears had been damaged by a piece of the cover, and he touched it with trembling fingers.

The wax ear, like all of the dummy's other delicate features, had been formed with loving care by the sensitive hands of an artist.

The Cries of Love

Patricia Highsmith

When it comes to man's inhumanity to man, or woman's to woman,
Patricia Highsmith not only can see it, she can very hauntingly reveal it.

HATTIE PULLED the little chain of the reading lamp, drew the covers over her shoulders and lay tense, waiting for Alice's sniffs and coughs to subside.

"Alice?" she said.

No response. Yes, she was sleeping already, though she said she never closed an eye before the clock struck eleven.

Hattie eased herself to the edge of the bed and slowly put out a white-stockinged foot. She twisted round to look at Alice, of whom nothing was visible except a thin nose projecting between the ruffle of her nightcap and the sheet pulled over her mouth. She was quite still.

Hattie rose gently from the bed, her breath coming short with excitement. In the semi-darkness, she could see the two sets of false teeth in their glasses of water on the bed table. She giggled nervously.

Like a white ghost, she made her way across the room, past the Victorian settee. She stopped at the sewing table, lifted the folding top, and groped among the spools and pattern papers until she found the scissors. Then, holding them tightly, she crossed the room again.

She had left the wardrobe door slightly ajar earlier in the evening, and it swung open noiselessly. Hattie reached a trembling hand into the blackness, felt the two woolen coats, a few dresses. Finally she touched a fuzzy thing, and lifted the hanger down. The scissors slipped out of her hand. There was a clatter, followed by her half-suppressed laughter. She peeked round the wardrobe door at Alice, motionless on the bed. Alice was rather hard of hearing.

With her white toes turned up stiffly, Hattie clumped to the easy chair by the window where a bar of moonlight slanted, and sat down with the scissors and the angora sweater in her lap. In the moonlight her face gleamed, toothless and demoniacal. She examined the sweater in the manner of a person who toys with a piece of steak before deciding where to put his knife.

It was really a lovely sweater. Alice had received it the week before from her niece as a birthday present. Alice would never have indulged herself in such a luxury. She was happy as a child with the sweater, and had worn it every day over her dresses.

The scissors cut purringly up the soft wool sleeves, between the wristbands and the shoulders. She considered. There should be one more cut. The back, of course. But only about a foot long, so it wouldn't be immediately visible.

A few seconds later, she had put the scissors back into the table, hung the sweater in the wardrobe, and was lying under the covers. She heaved a tremendous sigh. She thought of the gaping sleeves, of Alice's face in the morning. The sweater was quite beyond repair, and she was immensely pleased with herself.

THEY WERE AWAKENED at eight-thirty by the hotel maid. It was a ritual that never failed: three bony raps on the door and a bawling voice with a hint of insolence: "Eight-thirty! You can get breakfast now!" Then Hattie, who always woke first, would poke Alice's shoulder.

Mechanically, they sat up on their respective sides of the bed and pulled their nightgowns over their heads, revealing clean white undergarments. They said nothing. Seven years of co-existence had pared their conversation to an economical core.

This morning, however, Hattie's mind was on the sweater. She felt self-conscious, but she could think of nothing to say or do to relieve the tension, so she spent more time than usual with her hair. She had a braid nearly two feet long that she wound around her head, and every morning she undid it for its hundred strokes. Her hair was her only vanity. Finally, she stood, shifting uneasily, pretending to be fastening the snaps on her dress.

Alice seemed to take an age at the washbasin, gargling with her solution of tepid water and salt. She held stubbornly to water and salt in the mornings, despite Hattie's tempting bottle of red mouthwash setting on the shelf.

"What are you giggling at now?" Alice turned from the basin, her face wet and smiling a little.

Hattie could say nothing, looked at the teeth in the glass on the bed table and giggled again. "Here's your teeth." She reached the glass awkwardly to Alice. "I thought you were going down to breakfast without them."

"Now when did I *ever* go off without my teeth, Hattie?"

Alice smiled to herself. *It's going to be a good day,* she thought. Mrs. Crumm and her sister were back from a weekend, and they could all play gin rummy together in the afternoon. She walked to the wardrobe in her stockinged feet.

Hattie watched as she took down the powder-blue dress, the one that went best with the beige angora sweater. She fastened all the little buttons in front. Then she took the sweater from the hanger and put one arm into a sleeve.

"Oh!" she breathed painfully. Then, like a hurt child, her eyes almost closed and her face twisted petulantly. Tears came quickly down her cheeks. "H-Hattie—"

Hattie smirked, uncomfortable yet enjoying herself thoroughly. "Well, I do know!" she exclaimed. "I wonder who could have done a trick like that!" She went to the bed and sat down, doubled up with laughter.

"Hattie, you did this," Alice declared in an unsteady voice. She clutched the sweater to her. "Hattie, you're just wicked!"

Lying across the bed, Hattie was almost hysterical. "You know I didn't now, Alice...hah-haw!... Why do you think I'd—" Her voice was choked off by incontrollable laughing.

Hattie lay there several minutes before she was calm enough to go down to breakfast. And when she left the room, Alice was sitting in the big chair by the window, sobbing, her face buried in the angora sweater.

ALICE DID NOT COME DOWN until she was called for lunch. She chatted at the table with Mrs. Crumm and her sister and took no notice of Hattie. Hattie sat opposite her, silent and restless, but not at all sorry for what she had done. She could have endured days of indifference on Alice's part without feeling the slightest remorse.

It was a beautiful day. After lunch, they went with Mrs, Crumm, her sister, and the hotel hostess, Mrs. Holland, and sat in Gramercy Park.

Alice pretended to be absorbed in her book. It was a detective story by her favorite author, borrowed from the hotel's circulating library. Mrs. Crumm and her sister did most of the talking. A weekend trip provided conversation for several afternoons, and Mrs. Crumm was able to remember every item of food she had eaten for days running.

The monotonous tones of the voices, the warmth of the sunshine, lulled Alice into half-sleep. The page was blurred to her eyes.

Earlier in the day, she had planned to adopt an attitude toward Hattie. She should be cool and aloof. It was not the first time Hattie had committed an outrage. There had been the ink spilt on her lace tablecloth months ago, the day before she was going to give it to her niece... And her missing volume of Tennyson that was bound in morocco. She was sure Hattie had it somewhere.

She decided that that evening she should calmly pack her bag, write Hattie a note, short but well-worded, and leave the hotel. She would go to another hotel in the neighborhood, let it be known through Mrs. Crumm where she was, and have the satisfaction of Hattie's coming to her and apologizing. But the fact was, she was not at all sure Hattie would come to her, and this embarrassing possibility prevented her from taking such a dangerous course. What if she had to spend the rest of her life alone? It was much easier to stay where she was, to have a pleasant game of gin rummy in the afternoons, and to take out her revenge in little ways. It was also more ladylike, she consoled herself. She did not think beyond this, of the particular times she would say or do things calculated to hurt Hattie. The opportunities would just come of themselves.

Mrs. Holland nudged her. "We're going to get some ice cream now. Then we're going to play some gin rummy."

"I was just at the most exciting part of the book." But Alice rose with the others, and was almost cheerful as they walked to the drugstore.

Alice won at gin rummy, and felt pleased with herself. Hattie, watching her uneasily all day, was much relieved when she decreed speaking terms again.

Nevertheless, the thought of the ruined sweater rankled in Alice's mind, and prodded her with a sense of injustice. Indeed, she was ashamed of herself for being able to take it as lightly as she did. It was letting Hattie walk over her. She wished she could muster a really strong hatred.

They were in their room reading at nine o'clock. Every vestige of Hattie's shyness or pretended contrition had vanished.

"Wasn't it a nice day?" Hattie ventured.

"Um-hm." Alice did not raise her head.

"Well," Hattie made the inevitable remark through the inevitable yawn, "I think I'll be going off to bed."

And a few minutes later they were both in bed, propped up by four pillows, Hattie with the newspaper and Alice with her detective story. They were silent for a while, then Hattie adjusted her pillows and lay down.

"Good night, Alice."

"Good night."

Soon Alice pulled out the light, and there was absolute silence in the room except for the soft ticking of the clock and the occasional purr of an automobile The clock on the mantel whirred and began to strike ten.

Alice lay open-eyed. All day her tears bad been restrained, and now she began to cry. But they were not the childish tears of the morning, she felt. She wiped her nose on the top of the sheet.

She raised herself on one elbow. The darkish braid of hair outlined Hattie's neck and shoulder against the white bedclothes. She felt very strong, strong enough to murder Hattie with her own hands. But the idea of murder passed from her mind as swiftly as it had entered. Her revenge had to be something that would last, that would hurt, something that Hattie must endure, and that she herself could enjoy.

Then it came to her, and she was out of bed, walking boldly to the sewing table, as Hattie had done twenty-four hours before...and she was standing by the bed, bending over Hattie, peering at her placid, sleeping face through her tears and her shortsighted eyes. Two quick strokes of the scissors would cut through the braid, right near the head. But Alice lowered the scissors just a little, to where the braid was tighter. She squeezed the scissors with both hands, made them chew on the braid, as Hattie slowly awakened with the touch of cold metal on her neck. *Whack,* and it was done.

"What is it?...What—?" Hattie said.

The braid was off, lying like a dark gray snake on the bed cover.

Alice's instant of self-defense was unnecessary, because Hattie felt the end of the braid's stump. "Alice!"

Alice stood a few feet away, staring at Hattie, who was sitting up in bed, and suddenly Alice was overcome with mirth. She tittered, and at the same time tears started in her eyes. "You did it to me!" she said. "You cut my sweater!"

Alice's instant of self-defense was unnecessary, because Hattie was absolutely crumpled and stunned. She started to get out of bed, as if to go to the mirror, but sat back again, moaning and weeping, feeling of the horrid thing at the end of her hair. Then she lay down again, still moaning into her pillow. Alice stayed up, and sat finally in the easy chair. She was full of energy, not sleepy at all. But toward dawn, when Hattie slept, Alice crept between the covers.

HATTIE DID NOT SPEAK to her in the morning, and did not look at her. Hattie put the braid away in a drawer, Then she tied a scarf around her head to go down to breakfast, and in the dining room, Hattie took another table from the one at which Alice and she usually sat. Alice saw her speaking to Mrs. Holland after breakfast.

A few minutes later, Mrs. Holland came over to Alice, who was reading in a corner of the lounge.

"I think," Mrs. Holland said gently, "that you and your friend might be happier if you had separate rooms for a while, don't you?"

This took Alice by surprise, though at the same time she had been expecting something worse. Her prepared statement about the spilt ink, the missing Tennyson, and the ruined angora subsided in her, and she said quite briskly, "I do indeed, Mrs. Holland. I'm agreeable to anything Hattie wishes."

Alice offered to move out, but it was Hattie who did. She moved to a smaller room three doors down on the same floor.

That night, Alice could not sleep. It was not that she thought about Hattie particularly, or that she felt in the least sorry for what she had done—she decidedly didn't—but that things, the room, the darkness, even the clock's ticking, were so different because she was alone. A couple of times during the night, she heard a footstep outside the door, and thought it might be Hattie coming back, but it was only people visiting the W.C. at the end of the hall. It occurred to Alice that she could knock on Hattie's door and apologize but, she asked herself, *why should I?*

IN THE MORNING, Alice could tell from Hattie's appearance that she hadn't slept either. Again, they did not speak or look at each other all day, and during the gin rummy and tea at four, they managed to take different tables.

Alice slept very badly that night also, and blamed it on the lamb stew at dinner, which she was having trouble digesting. Hattie would have the same trouble, perhaps, as her digestion was, if anything, worse.

THREE MORE DAYS and night passed, and the ravages of Hattie's and Alice's sleepless nights became apparent on their faces. Mrs. Holland noticed, and offered Alice some sedatives, which she politely declined. Alice had her pride, she wasn't going to show anyone she was disturbed by Hattie's absence, and besides, she thought it was weak and self-indulgent to yield to sleeping pills—though perhaps Hattie would.

ON THE FIFTH DAY, at three in the afternoon, Hattie knocked on Alice's door. Her head was still swathed in a scarf, one of three that Hattie possessed, and this was one Alice had given her last Christmas.

"Alice, I want to say I'm sorry, if *you're* sorry," Hattie said, her lips twisting and pursing as she fought to keep back the tears.

This was or should have been a moment of triumph for Alice. It was, mainly, she felt, though something—she was not sure what—tarnished it a little, made it not quite pure victory. "I am sorry about your braid, if you're sorry about my sweater," she replied.

"I am," said Hattie.

"And about the ink stain on my tablecloth and...where is my volume of Alfred Lord Tennyson's poems?"

"I have not got it," Hattie said, still tremulous with tears.

"You haven't *got* it?"

"No," Hattie declared positively.

And in a flash, Alice knew what had really happened: Hattie had at some point, in some place, destroyed it, so it was in a way true now that she hadn't "got" it. Alice knew, too, that she must not stick over this, that she ought to forgive and forget it, though neither emotionally nor intellectually did she come to this decision: she simply knew it, and behaved accordingly, saying, "Very well, Hattie. You may move back, if you wish."

Hattie then moved back, though at the card game at four-thirty they still sat at separate tables.

Hattie, having swallowed the biggest lump of pride she had ever swallowed in knocking on Alice's door and saying she was sorry, slept very much better back in the old arrangement, but suffered a lurking sense of unfairness. After all, a book of poems and a sweater could be replaced, but could her hair? Alice had got back at her all right, and then some. The score was not quite even.

After a few days, Hattie and Alice were back to normal, saying little to each other, but outwardly being congenial, taking meals and playing cards at the same table. Mrs. Holland seemed pleased.

It crossed Alice's mind to buy Hattie some expensive hair tonic she saw in a Madison Avenue window one day while on an outing with Mrs. Holland and the group. But Alice didn't. Neither did she buy a "special treatment" for hair which she saw advertised in the back of a magazine, guaranteed to make the hair grow thicker and faster, but Alice read every word of the advertisements.

Meanwhile, Hattie struggled in silence with her stump of braid, brushed her hair faithfully as usual, but only when Alice was having her bath or was out of the room, so Alice would not see it. Nothing in Alice's possession now seemed important enough for Hattie's vengeance. But Christmas was coming soon. Hattie determined to wait patiently and see what Alice got then.

Something Evil in the House

Celia Fremlin

Should this story be called "Gothica Moderne"? The house is small and very un-Gothic, but what difference does it make when the evil is there?

LOOKING BACK, I find it very hard to say just when it was that I first began to feel anxious about my niece, Linda. No, anxious is not quite the right word, for of course I have been anxious about her many times during the ten years she has been in my care. You see, she has never been a robust girl, and when she first came to live with me, a nervous, delicate child of twelve, she seemed so frail that I really wondered sometimes if she would survive to grow up.

However, I am happy to say that she grew stronger as the years passed, and I flatter myself that by gentle, common sense handling and abundant affection, I have turned her into as strong and healthy a young woman as she could ever have hoped to be. Stronger, I am sure (though perhaps I shouldn't say this), than she would have been if my poor sister Angela had lived to bring her up.

No, it was not anxiety about Linda's health that has troubled me during the past weeks; nor was it simply a natural anxiety about the wisdom of her engagement to John Barrow. He seemed a pleasant enough young man, with his freckled, snub-nosed face and ginger hair. Though I have to admit I didn't really take to him myself—he made me uneasy in some way I can't describe. But I would not dream of allowing any prejudice of mine to stand in the way of the young couple—there is nothing I detest more than this sort of interference by the older generation.

All the same, I must face the fact that it was only after I heard of their engagement that I began to experience any qualms about Linda —those first tremors of a fear that was to grow and grow until it became an icy terror that never left me, day or night.

I think it was in September that I first became aware of my uneasiness—a gusty September evening with autumn in the wind, in the trees, everywhere. I was cycling up the long gentle hill from the village after a particularly wearisome and inconclusive committee meeting of the Women's Institute. I was tired, so tired that before I reached the turning into our lane, I found myself getting off my bicycle to push it up the remainder of the slope—a thing I have never done before.

For in spite of my fifty-four years I am a strong woman, and a busy one. I cycle everywhere, in all weathers, and it is rare indeed for me to feel tired. Certainly the gentle incline between the village and our house had never troubled me before. But tonight, somehow, the bicycle might have been made of lead—I felt as if I had cycled fifteen miles instead of the bare one and a half from the village; and when I turned into the dripping lane, and the evening became almost night under the overhanging trees, I became aware not only of tiredness, but of an indefinable foreboding. The dampness and the autumn dusk seemed to have crept into my very soul, bringing their darkness with them.

Well, I am not a fanciful woman. I soon pulled myself together when I reached home, switched on the lights, and made myself a cup of tea. Strong and sweet it was, the way I always like it. Linda often laughs at me about my tea—she likes hers so thin and weak that I sometimes wonder why she bothers to pour the water into the teapot at all, instead of straight from the kettle to her cup!

So there I sat, the comfortable old kitchen chair drawn up to the glowing stove, and I waited for the warmth and the sweet tea to work their familiar magic. But somehow, this evening, they failed. Perhaps I was really *too* tired; or perhaps it was the annoyance of noticing from the kitchen clock that it was already after eight. As I have told you, I am a busy woman, and to find that the tiresome meeting must have taken a good two hours longer than usual was provoking, especially as I had planned to spend a long evening working on the Girls' Brigade accounts.

Whatever it may have been, somehow I couldn't relax. The stove crackled merrily, the tea was delicious, yet I sat, still tense and uneasy, as if waiting for something.

And then, somehow, I must have gone to sleep, quite suddenly, because the next thing I knew I was dreaming. Quite a simple, ordinary sort of dream it will seem to you—nothing alarming, nothing even unusual in it, and yet you will have to take my word for it that it had all the quality of a nightmare.

I dreamed that I was watching Linda at work in the new house. I should explain that for the past few months Linda has not been living here with me, but in lodgings in the little town where she works, about six miles from here. It is easier for her to get to and from her office, and also it means that she and John can spend their evenings working at the new house they have been lucky enough to get in the Estate on the outskirts of the town. The house is not quite finished yet, and they are doing all the decorating themselves—I believe John is putting up shelves and cupboards and all kinds of clever fittings. I am telling you this so that you will see that there was nothing intrinsically nightmarish about the setting of my dream—on the contrary, the little place must have been full of happiness and bustling activity —the most unlikely background for a nightmare that you could possibly imagine.

Well, in my dream I was there with them. Not with them in any active sense, you understand, but hovering in that disembodied way one does in dreams—an observer, not an actor on the scene. Somewhere near the top of the stairs I seemed to be, and looking down I could see Linda through the door of one of the empty little rooms. It was late afternoon in my dream, and the pale rainy light gleamed on her flaxen-pale hair, making it look almost metallic—a sort of shining gray. She had her back to me, and she seemed absorbed in painting the far wall of the room—I heard that suck-sucking noise of the paint brush with extraordinary vividness.

And as I watched her, I began to feel afraid. She looked so tiny and thin, and unprotected; her fair, childlike head seemed poised so precariously on her white neck—even her absorption in the painting seemed in my dream to add somehow to her peril. I opened my mouth to warn her—to warn her of I know not what—but I could make no sound, as is the way of dreams. It was then that the whole thing slipped into a nightmare.

I tried to scream, to run, I struggled in vain to wake up—and as the nightmare mounted I became aware of footsteps, coming nearer and nearer through the empty house.

"It's only John!" I told myself in the dream, but even as the words formed in my brain, I knew that I had touched the very core of my terror. This man whose every glance and movement had always filled me with uneasiness—already the light from some upstairs room was casting his shadow, huge and hideous, across the landing—

I struggled like a thing demented to break the paralysis of nightmare. And then, somehow, I was running, running, running...

I woke up sick and shaking, the sweat pouring down my face. For a moment, I thought a great hammering on the door had awakened me, but then I realized that it was only the beating of my heart, thundering and pounding so that it seemed to shake the room.

Well, I have told you before that I am a strong woman, not given to nerves and fancies. Linda is the one who suffers from that sort of thing, not me. Time and again in her childhood I had to go to her in the night and soothe her back to sleep again after some wild dream. But for *me*, a grown woman, who never in her life has feared anyone or run away from anything—for *me* to wake up weak and shaking like a baby from some childish nightmare! I shook it off angrily, got out of my chair and fetched my papers, and as far as I can remember, worked on the Girls' Brigade accounts far into the night.

I THOUGHT NO MORE about it until, perhaps a week later, the same thing happened again. The same sort of rainy evening, the same coming home unusually tired—and then the same dream. Well, not quite the same. This time Linda wasn't painting; she was on hands and knees, staining the floor or something of the sort. And there were no footsteps. This time nothing happened at all; only there was a sense of evil, of brooding hatred, which seemed to fill the little house. Somehow I felt it to be focused on the little figure kneeling in its gaily patterned work apron. The hatred seemed to thicken round her—I could feel giant waves of it converging on her, mounting silently, silkily, till they hung poised above her head in ghastly, silent strength. Again I tried to scream a warning; again no sound came; and again I woke, weak and trembling, in my chair.

This time I was really worried. The tie between Linda and me is very close—closer, I think, than the tie between Linda and her mother could ever have been. Common sense sort of person though I am, I could not help wondering whether these dreams were not some kind of warning. Should I call her, and ask if everything was all right?

I scolded myself for the very idea! I mustn't give way to such foolish, hysterical fancies—I have always prided myself on letting Linda lead her own life, and not smothering her with possessive anxiety, as her mother would have surely done.

Stop! I mustn't keep speaking of Linda's mother like this—of Angela, my own sister. Angela has been dead many years now, and whatever wrong I may have suffered from her once has all been forgotten and forgiven years ago—I am not a woman to harbor grievances. But, of course, all this business of Linda's approaching marriage was bound to bring it back to me in a way. I couldn't help remembering that I, too, was once preparing a little house for my marriage, that Richard had once looked into my eyes as John now looks into Linda's.

Well, I suppose most old maids have some ancient, and usually boring, love story hidden somewhere in their pasts, and I don't think mine will interest you much—it doesn't even interest me after all these years, so I will tell it as briefly as I can.

When I fell in love with Richard, I was already twenty-eight, tall and angular, and a schoolteacher in the bargain. So it seemed to me a miracle that he, so handsome, so gay and charming, should love me in return, and ask me to marry him. Our only difficulty was that my parents were both dead, and I was the sole support of my younger sister, Angela, We talked it over and decided to wait a year, until Angela had left school and could support herself.

But at the end of the year it appeared that Angela had set her heart on a musical career. Tearfully she begged me to see her through her first two years at college, after that, she was sure she could fend for herself.

Well, Richard was difficult this time, and I suppose one can hardly blame him. He accused me of caring more for my sister than for him, of making myself a doormat, and much else that I forget. But at last it was agreed to wait the two years, and meantime to work and save for a home together.

And work and save we did. By the end of the two years we had bought a little house, and we spent our evenings decorating and putting finishing touches to it, just as Linda and John are doing now.

Then came another blow. Angela failed her exams. Again I was caught up in the old conflict; Richard angry and obstinate, Angela tearful and beseeching me to give her one more chance, for only six months this time. Once again I agreed, stipulating that this time would really be the last. To my surprise, after his first outburst, Richard became quite reasonable about it; and soon after that he was sent away on a series of business trips, so that we saw much less of each other.

Then, one afternoon at the end of May, not long before the six months were up, something happened. I was sitting on the lawn correcting papers when Angela came out of the house and walked slowly toward me. I remember noticing how sweetly pretty she looked with her flaxen hair and big blue eyes—just like Linda's now. The spring sunshine seemed to light up the delicacy of her too-pale skin, making it seem rare and lovely. She sat down on the grass beside me without speaking, and something in her silence made me lay down my pen.

"What is it, Angela?" I said. "Is anything the matter?"

She looked up at me then, her blue eyes full of childish defiance, and a sort of pride.

"Yes," she said. "I'm going to have a baby." She paused, looking me full in the face. "Richard's baby."

I didn't say anything. I don't even remember feeling anything.

Even then, I suppose, I was a strong-minded person who did not allow her feelings to run away with her. Angela was still talking.

"And it's no use blaming *us,* Madge," she was saying. "What do you expect, after you've kept him dangling all these years?" I remember the papers in front of me, dazzling-white in the May sunshine. One of the children had written "Nappoleon"—like that, with two p's—over and over again in her theme. There must have been half a dozen of them just on the one page. I felt I would go mad if I had to go on looking at them, so I took my pen and crossed them out, one after another, in red ink. Even to *this* day, I have a foolish feeling that I would go mad if I ever saw "Nappoleon" spelled like that again.

I felt as if a long time had passed, and Angela must have got up and gone away ages ago; but no, there she was, still talking.

'Well, *you* may not care, Madge," she was saying. "I don't suppose you'd stop correcting your old papers if the world blew up. But what about *me?* What am I to *do?*"

"Do?" I said gently. "Why, Richard must marry you, of course. I'll talk to him myself."

Well, they were married, and Linda was born, a delicate, sickly little thing, weighing barely five pounds. Angela, too, was poorly. She had been terribly nervous and ill during her pregnancy and took a long time to recover; and it was tacitly agreed that there should be no more children. A pity, because I knew Richard would have liked a large family. Strange how I, a strong, healthy woman who could have raised half a dozen children without turning a hair, should have been denied the chance, while poor sickly Angela...

Ah, well, that is life. And I suppose my maternal feelings were largely satisfied by caring for delicate little Linda—it seemed only natural that when first her father and then Angela died, the little orphan should come and live with me. And indeed I loved her dearly. She was my poor sister's child as well as Richard's, and my only fear has been that I may love her too deeply, too possessively, and so cramp her freedom.

Perhaps this fear is unfounded. Anyway, it was this that prevented me from lifting the telephone receiver then and there on that rainy September night, dialing her number, and asking if all was well. If I had done so, would it have made any difference in what followed? Could I have checked the march of tragedy, then and there, when I woke from that second dream?

I didn't know. I still don't know. All I know is that as I sat there in the silent room, listening to the rain beating against my windows out of the night, my fears somehow became clearer came into focus, as it were. I knew now, with absolute certainty, that what I feared had something to do with Linda's forthcoming marriage, her marriage to John Barlow.

But what could it be? What *could* I be afraid of? He was such a pleasant, ordinary young man, from a respected local family; he had a good job; he loved Linda deeply. Well, he seemed to. And yet, as I thought about it, as I remembered the uneasiness I always felt in his presence, it occurred to me that this uneasiness—this anxiety for Linda's safety—was always at its height when he made some gesture of affection toward her—a light caress, perhaps—a quick, intimate glance across a crowded room...

Common sense. Common sense has been my ally throughout life, and I called in its aid now.

"There is nothing wrong!" I said aloud. "There is nothing wrong with this young man!"

And then I went to bed.

It must have been nearly three weeks later when I had the dream again. I had seen Linda in the meantime, and she seemed as well and happy as I have ever known her. The only cloud on her horizon was that for the next fortnight John would be working late, and so they wouldn't be able to spend the evenings painting and carpentering together in the new house.

"But I'll go on by myself, Auntie," she assured me. "I want to start on the woodwork in that front room tonight. Pale green, we thought, to go with the pale yellow..." She chattered on, happily and gaily, seeming to make nonsense of my fears.

"It sounds lovely, dear," I said. "Don't knock yourself out, though, working too hard."

For Linda *does* get tired easily. In spite of the thirty years difference in our ages, I can always outpace her on our long rambles over the hill, and arrive home fresh and vigorous while she is sometimes quite white with exhaustion.

"No, Auntie, don't worry," she said, standing on tiptoe to kiss me —she is such a little thing; "I won't get tired. I'm so happy I don't think I'll ever get tired again!"

Reassuring enough, you'd have thought. And yet, somehow, it didn't reassure me. Her very happiness—even the irrelevant fact that John would be working late—seemed somehow to add to the intangible peril I could feel gathering round her.

AND THREE NIGHTS LATER, I dreamed the dream again.

This time she was alone in the little house. I don't know how I knew it with such certainty in the dream, but I did—her aloneness seemed to fill the unfurnished rooms with echoes. She seemed nervous, too. She was no longer painting with the absorbed concentration of my previous dreams, but jerkily, uncertainly. She kept starting, turning round, listening; and I, hovering somewhere on the stairs as before, seemed to be listening too.

Listening for what? For the fear which I knew was creeping like fog into the little house? Or for something more? "It's a dream!" I tried to scream, with soundless lips. "Don't be afraid, Linda, it's only a dream! I've had it before, I'll wake up soon! It's all right, I'm waking right now, I can hear the banging—"

I started awake in my chair, bolt upright, deafened by the now familiar thumping of my heart.

But was it my heart? Could that imperious knocking, which shook the house, be merely my heart? The knocking became interspersed with a frantic ringing of the bell. This was no dream.

I staggered to my feet and somehow got down the passage to the front door and flung it open. There in the rainy night was Linda, wild and white and disheveled, flinging herself into my arms.

"Oh, Auntie, Auntie, I thought you were out—asleep—I couldn't make you hear—I rang and rang..."

I soothed her as best I could. I took her into the kitchen and made her a cup of the weak, thin tea she loves, and heard her story.

And after all it wasn't much of a story. Just that she had gone to the new house as usual after work, and had settled down to painting the front room. For a while, she said, she had worked quite happily, and then suddenly she had heard a sound—a shuffling sound—so faint that she might almost have imagined it.

"And that was all, really, Auntie," she said, looking up at me, shamefaced. "But somehow it frightened me so. I ought to have gone and looked round the house, but I didn't dare. I tried to go on working, but from then on there was such an awful feeling—I can't describe it—as if there was something evil in the house, something close behind me, waiting to get its hands round my throat. Oh, Auntie, I know it sounds silly. It's the kind of thing I used to dream when I was a little girl. Do you remember?"

Indeed I did remember. I took her on my lap and soothed her now just as I had done then, when she was a little sobbing girl awake and frightened in the depth of the night.

And then I told her she must go home.

"Auntie!" she protested. "But Auntie, can't I stay here with you for the night? That's why I came. I *must* stay!"

But I was adamant. I can't tell you why, but some instinct warned me that, come what may, she must not stay here tonight. Whatever fear or danger might be elsewhere, they could never be as great as they would be here, in this house, tonight.

So I made her go home, to her lodgings in the town. I couldn't explain it to her, or even to myself. In vain, she protested that the last bus had gone, that her old room here was ready for her. But I was inflexible.

I rang up a taxi, and as it disappeared with her round the corner of the lane, casting a weird radiance behind it, I heaved a great sigh of relief, as if a great task had been accomplished—as if I had just dragged her to shore out of a dark and stormy sea.

THE NEXT MORNING, I found that my instinct had not been without foundation. There *had* been danger lurking round my house the night before. For when I went to get my bicycle to go and help about the Mothers' Outing, I found it in its usual place in the shed, but the tires and mudguard were spattered with a kind of thick yellow clay. There is no clay like that anywhere between here and the village. Where could it have come from? Who had been riding my bicycle through unfamiliar mud in the rain and wind last night? Who had put it back silently in the shed, and as silently gone away?

As I stood there, bewildered and shaken, the telephone rang indoors. It was Linda, and she sounded tense, distraught.

"Auntie, will you do something for me? Will you come with me to the house tonight and stay there while I do the painting and—sort of keep watch for me? I expect you'll think it's silly, but I *know* there was somebody there last night—and I'm frightened. Will you come, Auntie?"

There could be only one answer. I got through my day's work as fast as I could, and by six o'clock I was waiting for Linda on the steps of her office. As we hurried through the darkening streets, Linda was apologetic.

"I know it's awfully silly, Auntie, but John's still working late, and he doesn't even know if he'll finish in time to come and fetch me. I feel scared there without him. And the upstairs lights won't go on again—John hasn't had time to see the electrician about it yet—and it's so dark and lonely. Do you think someone really *was* there last night, Auntie?"

I didn't tell her about the mud on my bicycle. There seemed no point in alarming her further. Besides, what was there to tell? There was no reason to suppose it had any connection.

"Watch out, Auntie, it's terribly muddy along this bit where the builders have been."

I stared down at the thick yellow clay already clinging heavily to my shoes; and straight in front of us, among a cluster of partially finished red-brick houses, stood Linda's future home. It stared at us with its little empty windows out of the October dusk. A light breeze rose, but stirred nothing in that wilderness of mud, raw brickwork, and scaffolding. Linda and I hesitated, looked at each other.

"Come on," I said, and a minute later we were in the empty house.

We arranged that she should settle down to her painting in the downstairs front room just as if she were alone, and I was to sit on the stairs, near the top, where I could command a view of both upstairs and down. If anyone should come in, by either the front or back door, I should see them before they could reach Linda.

I was very quiet as I sat there in the darkness. The light streamed out of the downstairs room where Linda was working, and I could see her through the open door, with her back to me, just as she had been in my dream. How like poor Angela she was, with her pale hair and her white, fragile neck! She was working steadily now, absorbed, confident—reassured, I suppose, by my presence in the house.

As I sat there, I could feel the stair behind me pressing a little into my spine—a strangely familiar pressure. My whole pose indeed seemed familiar—every muscle seemed to fall into place, as if by long practice, as I sat there, half leaning against the banisters, staring down into the glare of light.

And then, suddenly, I knew. I knew who had cycled in black hatred through the rainy darkness and the yellow mud. I knew who had waited here, night after night, watching Linda as a cat watches a mouse. I knew what horror was closing in even now on this poor fragile child, on this sickly, puny brat who had kept *my* lovely, sturdy children from coming into the world—the sons and daughters *I* could have given Richard, tall and strong—the children he should have had—the children *I* could have borne him.

I was creeping downstairs now, on tiptoe, in my stockinged feet, with a light, almost prancing movement, yet silent as a shadow. I could see my hands clutching in front of me like a lobster's claws, itching for the feel of her white neck.

At the foot of the stairs now—at the door of the room—and still she worked on, her back to me, oblivious.

I tried to cry out, to warn her. "She's coming, Linda!" I tried to scream: "I can see her hands clawing behind you!" But no sound came from my drawn-back lips, no sound from my swift light feet.

Then, just as in my dream, there were footsteps through the house, quick and loud, a man's footsteps, hurrying, running, rushing—rushing to save Linda, to save us both.

The Tilt of Death

Rod Amateau and David Davis

Here is a wildly imaginative tale which is just plain fun. And half the fun is in the way it's told.

I ALWAYS HAD a yen to be a fisherman. I don't mean just fishing in a quiet pond on Sunday afternoons. I mean an Ernest Hemingway-Crunch and Des kind of fishing. I mean big-game fishing with a fighting-chair and outriggers and a flying bridge and me the skipper with a full charter and an icebox stacked with *cerveza*.

Everyone has some sort of dream, but never really expects it to happen, and it never does. Mine happened—all the way.

Here I am, six weeks short of my fortieth birthday, owner and skipper of the *Pescadora*, thirty-eight feet of twin-dieseled fishing fool. I say, without fear of contradiction, that my boat is the sweetest running charter out of Boca Negra, Chile, where the summers are winters and the winters are summers, and it doesn't mean a damn because the marlin can't read a calendar and they're hitting all the time.

That's how it is now.

Let me tell you how it was: lousy.

I was a salesman for the Sequoia Life and Casualty and lived a commuter's life, nine to six Monday through Friday, fifty weeks a year selling life insurance. Every day I made a half-a-hundred phone calls. Sequoia provided me with Diners, Carte Blanche, American Express. Every day I had rich, boozy lunches with different "prospects." Every morning, it was the 8:05 into Penn Station and the 6:12 home to Mineola, New York, every night.

Saturday was family day. Family: Jimmie eight, Jennifer six, Nancy thirty-one, Hey-Dog four, Chevrolet two, Mortgage thirty.

What with the crabgrass, stopped-up toilets, car wash, supermarket, kiddie-matinees, my Saturday was one big cliché. The only thing I looked forward to was my every-other-weekly haircut. I got to sit down for a half hour and skim through girlie magazines. What a great barber! He used a vibrator.

Five o'clock: I'd had my second martini and was changing clothes to go to somebody's house for booze and barbecue.

Midnight: home, a little oiled but functioning. I'd pay off the babysitter, drink a club soda, lock the doors, brush my teeth, slap a little cologne on my face, and va-va-va-voom into the bedroom. Too late! My wife was asleep.

One time I reversed the procedure. I maneuvered it so Nancy paid the babysitter, locked up. I even passed up the club soda and, believe me, I could have used it. Into the bathroom, teeth brushed, cologne on the face, under the covers, waiting for my wife, grinning in the dark with anticipation. Too late! *I* fell asleep.

Sunday morning? Maybe, if the kids didn't wake up before we did —only they always did because they didn't go to those Saturday night barbecues. What a pity, because I really loved my wife. What a woman!

Wife, mother, homemaker extraordinaire; attractive, cheerful, understanding, practical; very, very practical, she balanced our bank statement every month, never dented the Chevy fenders, bought two for twenty-five instead of one at thirteen. Kept canned water in the cellar in case of a red alert. For the children's sake, we always traveled on separate airplanes. She even balanced our budget so tight I could buy $150,000 worth of life insurance. In case of something tragic, she and the kids would be provided for. I couldn't argue with that; I sold the stuff myself.

Sundays, I usually tried to get in some fishing, but practical Nancy pointed out that my Sunday fishing excursions on Sheepshead Bay cost me $8.00 per mackerel. I pointed out that it was a sport—good for the kids.

Once, I even took them along, but Jimmie got a fishhook through his thumb and Jennifer threw up into the live-bait tank. The rest of the anglers on this half-day boat were pretty sore. The boat made a U-turn and headed home. What with the $7.50 for Jimmie's tetanus shot and the $35.00 to replace the dead bait, Nancy dry-docked any future fishing.

Then came the event that changed my life. I went for my annual medical checkup to our family doctor, Jerome Hale, M.D. Jerry and I had roomed together in college. He was the best man at my wedding, delivered both my kids.

This day my best friend had the worst news to give me. My electrocardiogram said tilt! Sadly, gravely, Jerry told me I had a severe coronary malfunction: something to do with the valves and blood and surrounding muscle tissue and I had approximately three months to live. Like I said, the worst kind of news. I was in shock.

Jerry was marvelous. He canceled his appointments for the rest of that day and put me through the tests again and again. Same results. I remember being deeply appreciative of the way Jerry handled the whole horrifying thing.

We took a long walk by the ocean. We talked a little about life and a lot about death. Jerry got pretty misty, and I ended by cheering him up.

I went home and broke the tragic news to my wife. She went to pieces, got hysterical. The kids were sent to sleep over at a neighbor's. She took two tranquilizers, and then we sat down and went over the whole picture together.

Thank God for the insurance policy. She and the kids would never be public charges. Now her being practical really paid off. She took a pencil and paper and figured out that she could cut down expenses all around, sell the house, and get an apartment. That way, the $150,000 policy would see both kids through college.

Then she asked me how I was going to spend my time—the short time I had left. I was stumped. I hadn't thought about it. I'd never died before. Anyway, I couldn't care less. I said I'd probably spend my time winding things up at the office.

Nancy said to hell with the office. What had the office ever done for me, except overwork my heart? I couldn't argue with her there. She put her arms around me and said—I'll remember these words as long as I live—"Why don't you go fishing?" Pause. "I said, *fishing.*"

I must have looked pretty surprised.

"Pete, I'm not talking about a half-day boat out of Sheepshead Bay or even Montauk Point. I mean fishing like you've always wanted to do. The Caribbean, the Mediterranean—anywhere! Go. Enjoy yourself. Have a ball. You owe it to yourself."

By this time I'd figured it was the tranquilizer talking and not her. I was wrong. She meant every word.

"Of course I'd love to have you here with me," Nancy wept, "especially these last weeks together, but I'm not going to be selfish. I've been selfish about you too long."

She felt pretty guilty depriving me of fishing all these years. She wanted me to enjoy my last few months.

Her plan was: buy the best fishing tackle; fly first-class to where the fishing was best, anywhere in the world; live it up, suites in the finest hotels.

"Go," she said. "Take a leave of absence from Sequoia. Eat, drink, fish and be merry."

I couldn't believe it. An excursion like that could cost a fortune. Who could afford that kind of money? Then she told me who could afford that kind of money—Sequoia Life and Casualty, the company I diligently worked for.

I had Diners, Carte Blanche, American Express, a whole wallet full of credit cards thoughtfully provided by Sequoia Life. Nancy pointed out that I could sign my way onto every airline, every hotel, every restaurant, every men's shop on earth. I could even charter a boat and crew. I could even add on lavish tips. I could even—"Just a minute! What happens when the bills start coming in?"

"From overseas? It'll take two, three months for the bills to get back to the office. By then—" She didn't finish. She didn't have to. I knew what she meant.

"They'll collect from you," I said.

"They can't. When you leave it'll look like you deserted me and the children. You were obviously under great emotional stress, not responsible for your actions. After all, it's not like you're an embezzler, and I can't see Sequoia Life taking revenge on a bereaved widow and two small children."

"Gee, I don't know, Nancy. I don't think—"

"Pete. What have you got to lose?"

She had me there. That's a practical woman. She even thought of placing an inconspicuous, but completely legal, disclaimer in the *Daily Law Journal*—"Not responsible for debts other than my own, Mrs. Nancy Ingersoll"—and that's just the way it all worked out.

The first thing I charged on Diners was a genuine yachting cap from Abercrombie & Fitch with gold braid so thick I could have gotten saluted by Admiral Rickover. I've always liked yachting caps.

In rapid succession I discovered I also always liked matched saddle-leather luggage from Mark Cross; a complete deep sea fishing outfit from Hammacher-Schlemmer; silk suits tailored by Dunhill; a Patek Phillipe chronograph from Cartier's.

I divided the above charges as equitably as possible between Diners and American Express. Realizing I'd neglected Carte Blanche, I made up for it by charging them for my first class Mexicana Airlines ticket to Acapulco—one way, of course.

Boy, what I'd been missing all my life! I fell into that South of the Border groove like I'd been born to it. Everybody gets sick when they go to Mexico. Not me; I'd never felt better. I checked into the Las Brisas Hotel—my own bungalow, my own private swimming pool, and completely stocked bar for $140 a day. I chartered a boat and put it on my hotel tab. What the hell!

Eighty minutes out, I hooked into my first marlin. I'd read all about big-game fishing, but I never dreamed it was this exciting. It was! It was a great fight, and I won. Afterward, I started thinking that it must must have been a big strain on my heart, but what with all the cheering and congratulations from the skipper and the deckhands, I forgot all about it.

That fish weighed out to 160 kilos. That's 320 pounds! That night, I phoned Nancy at home in the States (on my hotel tab). I told her about the marlin. She told me about the kids. I told her about my suite at the Las Brisas. She told me about the toilet stopping up again. I told her what was happening in Acapulco, she told me what was happening in Mineola. She told me how much she missed me, and I was about to tell her how much I missed her when my other phone started ringing. I threw her a long-distance kiss.

The other phone? My dance teacher, Miss Rivera. She was in the lobby, on her way up.

Miss Rivera was sensational. Her dancing was good, too. She discovered I had natural rhythm, so I went ahead and took the whole course. Why not? I added it to my hotel tab. Cha-Cha, Pachanga, Mambo, Tango, Merengue, Rumba, but I stayed away from the Watusi. I didn't want to overtax my heart

No se puede imaginar vd, que fácil es apprender hablar y comunicarse uno en Espanol en Acapulco.

English translation: They got Berlitz here, too (Carte Blanche).

Every day in Acapulco was *magnifico*. Fishing, swimming, dancing, drinking, and every night I phoned my wife.

The weeks went by *muy rapidamente*, and every other night I phoned my wife.

I don't know what it was with this Mexican climate, but if I drank this much back in Mineola I'd have a hangover all the time. Here, I drank and danced the night away, grabbed a couple hours of sleep and bounced out of bed to go fishing. Too, no matter how busy I was, I found time to phone my wife at least once a week.

They told me there was some great fishing in Brazil. I flew down. I caught some sailfish, loved Rio. My Brazilian dancing teacher, Miss Santos, discovered I had natural rhythm. The boys in the band gave my Bossa Nova a standing ovation. Of course, my having bought them all a round of drinks didn't hurt any, but as our Latin-American neighbors so aptly put it: *"Póngalo en la cuenta, por favor."* ("Please put it on the bill.")

Costa Rica was wonderful, but none of their fishing boats were air-conditioned. I went on to Jamaica. I flew to Montego Bay and checked in at the Round Hill. The Royal Suite compared favorably with the El Presidente Suite in Rio.

I learned to hunt manta ray with a pneumatic harpoon while drinking rum grogs.

The food at the Round Hill was fabulous: French Turtle Soup, Caribbean Red Snapper, Austrian Boar Gami, Neapolitan ice cream, and Irish Coffee, all paid for by American Express. Miss Tizanne, my Jamaican dancing teacher, discovered I had natural rhythm. We went to the Ocean Cove and limbo danced to the steel band till 4 a.m.

That night I had my first attack! I awoke in a cold sweat, gasping for breath, jabbing pains shooting through the left side of my chest This is it!

With effort, I phoned the hotel doctor, who came immediately and examined me.

"Heart attack?" I asked.

"Heartburn," he answered. "Careful with the rich food."

He gave me a tablespoon of medicine and a bill for $25. I took the medicine and put his bill on my hotel tab.

I made a mental note to find out if there's a hotel priest. In case of real emergency, I can put my funeral on the hotel tab. I heard there was a big school of tuna boiling off Costa Gorda in Southern Portugal, I packed my matched luggage, signed my hotel tab and flew to Lisbon.

The following morning, I was tied into a king-size bluefin who had made up his mind that he wasn't going to wind up in a can. Bad heart or no bad heart, I fought him for three and a half hours and when we docked and weighed him in, I found I had me a record; biggest tuna ever landed in Costa Gorda.

The town went wild. That night the drinks were on me and Diners. A great party! I took over the ballroom of the Vasco da Gama Hotel and hired a band.

I was so happy I put a phone call through to my wife, to tell her about my conquest—but there was no answer. I guess she was staying over at her mother's.

Miss Freitas, my Portuguese dancing teacher, discovered I had natural rhythm, and we Sambaed into the night.

I guess Portuguese brandy is a lot stronger than ours, because next thing I knew we all stripped to the waist, Indian wrestling—the boys against the girls. Now that's the honest truth. We were Indian wrestling—but it must have looked pretty peculiar to Jerry Hale when he walked in; Jerry Hale, my doctor, my buddy, all the way from Mineola, Long Island.

"Jerry! What the hell are you doing here?"

We went outside in the dawn, where we could talk. He was mortified, embarrassed, apologetic. He told me, with great difficulty, that the chances of an electrocardiograph machine malfunctioning are a million to one.

I was that one.

The electrical cathodes had become magnetized, and had misinterpreted my cardiac impulses. In short, there was a short! My heart was perfect! I would live to be a senior citizen.

Blood drained from my head. My knees got rubbery. I knew Jerry was right because if ever I was going to get a heart attack, this was the time. It passed, and in its place? Instant sobriety!

I seized Jerry by the throat. "You quack! I'll report you to the A.M.A.! Why didn't you let me die!"

Jerry was stunned. He hadn't counted on this kind of reaction. I told him everything. I told him that I must have signed close to $20,000 in charges on my credit cards. $20,000? 40! 60! 70! With the tips? 100! 100,000!

I'd signed close to $100,000, so safe in the knowledge I was dying, and wouldn't have to pay. Now I would live. My lord! Who'd pay those bills? Me!

Jerry's face hardened. He was shocked, unsympathetic. How could I have done such a stupid, dishonest thing?

I told him it was *his* fault. I told him Nancy and I had worked out the plan because of his inaccurate prognosis! We blamed and cross-blamed and cross-cross-blamed under the warm rays of Portugal's morning sun.

Jerry lit his pipe, thought deeply. "Pete," he said. "there's only one thing to do. Turn yourself in. I'll stand behind you every inch of the way. I'll explain, as your doctor, that you were emotionally unbalanced, and not responsible for your actions. They'll understand."

"Horse-puckey!" I said. "A hundred thousand dollars' worth of high-life? Not them! Diners Club will serve me my last meal. American Express will crucify me to a plastic cross, and Carte Blanche will do unspeakable things to me in French. And how about my career,

Sequoia Life and Casualty, when they see those bills? For me, they'll reopen Alcatraz. And Nancy—what about my poor wife?"

I began to sob. I hadn't cried like this since Tom Mix died. No! Never! I couldn't go back. I was in too deep. I threw myself on the mercy of my buddy, my doctor.

"Help me, Jerry! Help me!" Tears rolled down my cheeks.

"I don't know. I just don't know. The only reason I'd even consider helping is that I feel pretty lousy about this. It's as much my fault as yours." He put his arm around me. "I don't know. I guess we can find a way if we both look real hard."

"Yeah. Let's look real hard, Jerry."

"I've got a glimmer of a notion, but I don't know if you're prepared to make such a gigantic sacrifice."

"What? What sacrifice?"

"Nancy and the kids are prepared for your death—emotionally, spiritually, and financially, so..." Jerry shook his head. "No, it's too big a sacrifice."

I waited hopefully while he lit his pipe again.

"It's simply this: if you were to die, your problem would be nonexistent."

I thought it over. "You're right, Jerry. It *is* too big a sacrifice."

He hadn't meant *really* die. Just make it *seem* as if I'd died. Like this: "From all outward appearances, you have your anticipated heart attack and die. I witness the death and, as your doctor, sign your death certificate. The body is sealed in a coffin and shipped home for interment. Nancy and the kids collect your life insurance. As for all your debts—well, they can't collect from a corpse." He stopped to relight his pipe. "Exactly whose corpse are we talking about?"

"Not yours," Jerry said.

"Are we talking about murder?"

"Of course not. Every public morgue has a percentage of un-claimed, unidentified bodies. We find one, claim it, identify it as you. Then we ship it home."

"What happens when Nancy opens the coffin? Won't she sort of expect it to be everloving me?"

"Nancy," Jerry said, "will not open the coffin. I'll see to that. I'll prevail upon her to remember you as you were—alive!"

"What about me? What happens to me? I won't be able to see my wife and kids."

Jerry fooled with his pipe. "Remember, I spoke of sacrifice? This is what I meant."

"*Never* to see Nancy and the kids again?"

"It doesn't have to be 'never'. At the end of seven years you can come back. Statute of limitations."

"*Seven* years?"

"It's either that, or seven years in jail for fraud and grand theft."

Some choice! Well, I knew the kids would get along okay without me; after all, they hadn't seen much of me lately, anyway—but what about Nancy? Poor thing, if she found out I was alive somewhere, she'd drop everything and rush to join me. I guess our marriage was always a little one-sided. She was always crazy about me but, for her sake, better a dead husband than a live convict.

Some choice! No choice! I had to carry out Jerry's plan.

It wasn't as easy as Jerry had said, either. You just don't come across unclaimed, unidentified bodies in Southern Portugal. We looked in every morgue from Annuncio to Zapatas. No luck. All the stiffs were spoken for.

"Telephone books! Why don't we load a coffin with telephone books?"

Jerry quashed that idea. We couldn't take the risk of the U. S. Customs opening the box. Somewhere there had to be a corpus delicti without a toe tag—and there was, in a small village called Santo Tomas. The morgue attendant said he had died of an apparent heart attack, was about forty, five feet eleven, one hundred and seventy-five pounds. My measurements exactly!

Down the long corridor we went, into the icebox and opening the huge grisly file drawer. Jerry stepped forward, pulled back the sheet. The morgue attendant was correct. He was the right model, but the wrong shade. A Negro!

Jerry was beautiful. "That's the man," he said. "That's my patient, Mr. Peter Ingersoll of Mineola, Long Island."

Jerry spent the rest of the day in meetings with the District Medical Officer, the local undertaker and the Prefect of Police. There were endless official forms to be filled out, signed and notarized.

"Jerry," I managed to whisper, "now you've *got* to make sure Nancy doesn't open that coffin."

It was spooky, being present at the signing of my own death certificate, but I could still smile.

That evening, back at the Vasco da Gama Hotel in Costa Gorda I checked out, signing my hotel bill for the last time with the name "Peter Ingersoll."

Then and there, in the main lobby, with plenty of witnesses, I suffered my fatal heart attack, as per Jerry's instructions. I was very convincing. I should have gotten the Academy Award. Jerry identified himself as my physician and, supposedly, whisked me away to the hospital.

The next day, everyone at the Vasco da Gama was saddened to learn that I had never reached the hospital. I'd breathed my last in a little town called Santo Tomas.

Exit Peter Ingersoll. Enter Man Without A Country—The Flying Dutchman—The Wandering Presbyterian.

THE ONE WORD that best describes Jerry is "neat." His office was always orderly, his bachelor apartment immaculate, his car gleamed of buffed wax. It came as no surprise to me that he had arranged everything so perfectly.

First, I had a new name: Fred C. Dobbs. Also, I had an impossible-to-tell-from-the-real-thing New Zealand passport with my occupation listed as sheep rancher. I got my head shaved and concentrated very hard on growing a mustache. My real passport, my wallet, credit cards and personal belongings were packaged and attached to the outside of the coffin. The coffin was consigned to the Hermanos Rubeira Mortuary in Lisbon, awaiting the first boat to New York.

Jerry and I caught a train to Lisbon and taxied to the airport. He bought me a one-way ticket to Tel Aviv.

"Believe me, Pete, nobody will be looking for you there." He gave me all the cash he had in his pockets.

Loudspeaker: "El Al Airlines, Flight Eighteen, now boarding from West Concourse."

At this point, Jerry held out his hand, but it turned into a hug. I'm not ashamed to say it—we both had tears in our eyes.

Jerry turned and hurried away without looking back.

It was only then, as I walked down the long causeway toward Customs, that the pressure was over. For the first time, I realized what tremendous risks Jerry was taking in my behalf. He was putting his entire professional career on the line, just to right a wrong that a machine had made.

At Customs, everything was in order—except: "*Senhor* Dobbs, your immunization record, *por favor*."

"My what?" It was a big except.

"The medical certificate of vaccination for smallpox. Also, your injections for yellow fever and typhoid. I must stamp them, or you cannot enter Israel,.

"I don't think I have one."

The Customs Officer laughed. "Of course you have one, *Senhor*. You had to have a certificate to enter Portugal."

My newly shaven head broke into a sweat. He was right. Of course I had a medical certificate—only it was attached to my old passport, which, in turn, was attached to "my" new coffin. I opened my mouth to gasp for air and heard myself say, "How silly of me. I must have left it in my hotel. I'll take the shots in Tel Aviv."

"Impossible, *Senhor* Dobbs. You may not board the airplane without it."

I didn't want to press it. I was afraid of attracting attention. I was in a box—and I don't mean the one at Hermanos Rubeira Mortuary. If I went to the Ministry of Health and claimed that I'd lost my certificate, they would check the record and discover that no Fred C. Dobbs, sheep rancher from New Zealand, had ever entered Portugal. I needed a doctor to provide me—

Doctor? Dr. Jerry Hale, M.D.!

I remembered Jerry lighting his pipe with matches that said "Hotel Nacional." I booked a reservation on the next flight to Tel Aviv, then grabbed a taxi into Lisbon.

THE HOTEL NACIONAL had the kind of lobby you usually see in Alfred Hitchcock pictures; a lot of marble, some potted palms, overhead revolving fans and a lot of foreign types. I asked the desk clerk if a Dr. Hale was registered. He was. My hunch had been right.

"Would you ring his room, please?"

"Dr. Hale is out."

I must have beaten him here from the airport.

"Perhaps, *Senhor*, you wish to speak with Mrs. Hale."

Mrs. Hale? Obviously, they had two Hales registered. Jerry was a bachelor.

"I'm looking for Dr. Jerome Hale."

"Exactly, *Senhor*," the room clerk said. "Dr. Jerome Hale is out. As I said, Mrs. Hale is upstairs."

"Thank you, I'll wait."

I bought a Portuguese newspaper. It didn't matter. I wasn't going to read it, anyway. What I really wanted to do was sit down, hide behind the newspaper and think this over. *It can't be his mother. She died during the Eisenhower administration. His nurse, maybe. Susy Rambeau? Naah! Broad-beamed with varicose veins and support hose. Naah! Local talent? Could be. But when did he find the time? He made time. Made time. Son of a gun! That Jerry must be a bigger swinger than I gave him credit for. Look at that crossword puzzle—in Portuguese, yet. Can't be any tougher than the one in the Sunday* Times.

Jerry entered the lobby from the street entrance. I could see what had delayed him. He was carrying a pair of stuffed toy ducks and an orchid corsage. Whoever he had stashed upstairs, in the room, was getting the baby-doll treatment. That son of a gun!

I was about to get out of my chair and flag Jerry down when I heard the desk clerk's voice.

"Good afternoon, Mrs. Hale."

I turned to see a lady emerging from the elevator. Son of a gun! Son of a gun, nothing!

Mrs. Hale turned out to be my wife!

Nancy flew into Jerry's arms and gave him the kind of kiss she hadn't given me in years.

"Daddy Jerry! Daddy Jerry!" My kids! Racing out of the elevator to hug Jerry. Daddy Jerry?

Pooned and harpooned!

He gave the toy ducks to the kids. They got busy with them right away. The corsage was for Nancy. I kept the newspaper up in front of my purple face and listened.

"Where is he?" Nancy asked.

"On a plane to Israel. I saw it take off myself."

"Was he suspicious?"

"Are you kidding? He practically kissed my ring."

She threw her head back and laughed, exposing a whole top row of pearly white caps that had cost me plenty.

"Love me, Nancy?"

"Haven't I always?"

Right about then I should have leaped up, pried them apart and yelled: "Get your lips off my wife!" Then I should have slapped her across the face and punched Jerry in the nose. But then, there's a lot of things I should have done. Like? Like consult another doctor when Jerry told me I was dying; like ask myself how come Nancy was so anxious for me to go off alone and have a good time, all of a sudden; like wondering why Nancy went to Jerry instead of a gynecologist for her female problems; like ask myself what kind of doctor prescribes fake corpses, phony passports, and one-way tickets to Israel; like ask myself why she was so anxious for me to carry $150,000 worth of life insurance; like look closer at my little boy, Jimmy, whose eyes were blue like Jerry's instead of brown like mine.

Instead, I sat watching my best friend making out with my wife while she laughed at me through teeth I'd paid for—and I still hadn't gotten my shots for Israel.

As if this weren't enough, my own kid—well, at least her eyes are brown—little Jennifer, was about to discover me. She'd wound up her toy duck and the damned thing quacked its way right to my feet and stopped. I bent down and picked it up, handed it to her. She looked right at me and said, "Thank you, Mister."

My own kid! *He's* "Daddy Jerry" and *I'm* "Mister"! The kid hadn't recognized me with the shaved head and the mustache. Off they all went to a festive dinner, while I sat in the lobby of a Portuguese hotel, holding a newspaper I couldn't read, a wanted criminal, without money, job, hair, or future.

Some people are good sports...I mean, if they lose, they shrug it off and try harder the next time. I'm not one of those people. I've always been a sore loser, and at that moment I was sore. I was sore as hell!

I put down the newspaper, went out of the Nacional and walked miles—just walked. At dusk, I found myself seated on a park bench on Plaza del Palacio. In the street, a truck backfired loudly, sending hundreds of pigeons winging skyward in fright They wheeled and glided and circled, soared and dipped directly over my head. I looked up at them and yelled, "Go ahead! Why not? Everybody else has!"

Then, I walked some more and ended up at the airlines ticket office. I canceled my flight because I still hadn't gotten my shots. Guess what was right next door to the airplane office? The Hermanos Rubeira Mortuary. That's where "my body" was awaiting transfer to the U.S.A.

On an impulse I can't explain, I went inside. I wanted to see the man who was taking my "place." Why? To feel superior, I guess; comforted, maybe. He was the only man I knew who was worse off than me.

Inside, I passed myself off as a friend of the deceased Mr. Ingersoll. One of the Rubeira brothers ushered me into a small back room. There he was—the "Unknown Negro"—wearing my best suit, face set into a smile.

I was probably wrong. He was better off than I was. At least, he would get a decent funeral.

In the adjoining room, which was larger and fancier, a small group of Americans were commiserating with each other over the casket of a Colonel R. K. Durham. He'd been a mighty tobacco tycoon from Charleston, South Carolina. His wife, his lawyer, his two sons and their wives, the American Consul and his wife, were all gathered lachrymosely. He'd died while on a European vacation, and his body was being shipped home for an elaborate funeral.

He hadn't been one of your phony Southern Colonels. He was a real one—with a commission in the Minutemen. He would be buried with full military honors in the Durham family's mausoleum in the cemetery of the Sons of the Confederacy. The sealed caskets of "Pete Ingersoll" and Colonel Durham would share an icebox on the boat trip home. This would be the closest the Colonel had ever come to integration.

An attendant entered and told me that everyone would have to leave, because both coffins were to be inspected by Portuguese Customs so that they could be sealed and put on board ship in the morning. He left me one last moment alone with "Pete."

I don't remember just how the idea came to me. One moment my head was empty and the next, there it was—detailed, devilish, and delicious—the perfect revenge on that quack Jerry Hale and my dear wife.

Up on the ceiling was a skylight. Nimbly, I jumped up on the coffin, reached up to the skylight, and unlatched the catch. First step!

I taxied to the Hotel Nacional to finesse my way into finding out what room Jerry was registered in. In the lobby, I picked up the house phone. "Dr. Hale, please. Room 308."

"*Senhor, el doctor* Hale is in 517. I'll ring him for you."

The operator rang. No answer. Good. I hung up, went to the stairway and puffed up five flights. I couldn't take a chance on the elevator operator remembering my shaved head.

Fifth floor, I walked down the corridor. Chambermaids were turning down the beds for the night. From one of the doorknobs I swiped a celluloid *DO NOT DISTURB* sign. At Room 517, I knocked, to make certain no one was in. No one was. I checked the hall, both ways, then inserted the celluloid card between the door jamb and the latch. It clicked. The door swung open. I affixed the card to the outside knob, entered the room and closed the door behind me.

The room had the scent of Nancy's perfume, but that only spurred me on. I knew what I was after and went right for it. In Jerry's medical bag he carried a leather card case with his professional calling cards. There were a couple of dozen. Carefully, I pulled out two. They would never be missed. Printed cards, they were—with name, address and office phone. If he ever got his hands on my insurance money, he'd have his cards engraved.

I closed the bag, shut the closet door, threw a baleful glance at the bed, and slipped out of the room. In the corridor, I was about to return the *DO NOT DISTURB* sign from where it came, but obviously I was too late!

A chambermaid had passkeyed her way in to turn down the bed and, judging from the angry voices and hastily donned bathrobes, she had found an embarrassed couple in it. I put the sign on another door, hurried down the stairs to the lobby and out into the street. End Step Two.

From a hardware store, I bought a crowbar, a hammer, a pair of garden gloves, a flashlight and a small strip of felt. From a shoe store, I bought canvas sneakers; from a men's store, a hat. I was pretty tired of people staring at my shaved head.

Later, I sat in a cafe across from the Hermanos Rubeira Mortuary and waited for the Portuguese Customs officials to leave. They did, after a good deal of handshaking all around. A quarter of an hour later, all the Hermanos had locked up and gone.

I went around to the alley, slipped on my gloves and tennis shoes. I used a pair of discarded crates to hoist myself up on the roof. I made it to the skylight. It was just as I left it—unlatched.

I opened it and lowered myself into the small room. I landed on top of "Pete Ingersoll's" sealed casket.

I went right to work. With the crowbar, I pried open the lid of Colonel Durham's coffin. I did the same to "Pete Ingersoll's."

Then I switched bodies. The unknown Negro would be shipped to South Carolina to lie in state with the Sons of the Confederacy; Colonel R. K. Durham, to Mineola, Long Island. Reverently, I reclasped each corpse's bands in prayerful position and placed one of Dr. Jerry Hale's calling cards between the thumb and index finger of each of the deceased.

The felt strip muffled the blows of the hammer as I put the nails back into the coffin lids, sealing them.

It had all worked beautifully. I'd had plenty of time and no kibitzers. I'd enjoyed every moment, anticipating the results.

I hoisted myself up, through the skylight, onto the roof and down into the alley. End Step Three.

THE NEXT DAY, I was deep in the shadowed background of Pier 26, mingling with the crowd of bon voyagers who'd come down to see the departure of the S.S. *Santa Maria*. Destination: U.S.A.

I saw both coffins delivered dockside and winched aboard, all superintended by the dedicated Hermanos Rubeira. I saw the Colonel's wife and family, clad in mourning, grieving up a storm.

If they'd only known who was in that casket, they'd really have had something to cry about.

I pulled my hat brim down over my eyes when I spotted Jerry, Nancy, and the kids. They weren't in mourning. They were in love. She held on to him like Cher hangs on to Sonny. Everybody went up the gangplank. There was confetti and music and a lot of thrown kisses and finally the S.S. *Santa Maria* slid away from the dock

Up on deck, I saw the Colonel's family. They were still weeping away. On the fantail, I saw Jerry and Nancy. With their arms around each other and the wind blowing and the happy smiles, they looked like a travel poster.

I turned on my heel and walked away, whistling.

That same morning, I got my shots from a doctor who was used to asking no questions. He was a veterinarian. For fifty dollars I got smallpox, typhoid, yellow fever, and distemper.

By two that afternoon I turned in my El Al ticket for a one way to Valparaiso, Chile. I'd heard the fishing in Chile was great.

Besides, the only fish you get in Israel is smoked.

FROM HOMETOWN NEWSPAPERS and shortwave news broadcasts, I pieced together the events that occurred back in the States. In rapid events:

The coffins were delivered to their proper destinations. At the cemetery of the Sons of the Confederacy, the Colonel's coffin was laid in state. The town flags flew at half-mast. The tobacco factories were closed for the day, so the workers could attend the Colonel's funeral. The Drum and Bugle Corps were in dress uniforms. Confederate flags were displayed everywhere.

As the band played "Dixie" in funeral tempo, the Minutemen Drill Team fired a volley in salute.

Then, the coffin was opened for everyone to file by and pay their last respects...

The hysteria and confusion finally subsided, and was replaced by indignation. The cooler heads sought to fix the blame for this—the grisliest, sickest joke of the century.

It was then they found, clutched in the hand of the smiling Negro, Dr. Jerry Hale's calling card.

At Mineola's Haven-of-Rest Cemetery, there was no turnout to speak of for "my" funeral. The neighbors didn't show up because there was a big barbecue at Larry Heath's. None of my bosses at Sequoia Life and Casualty showed, either. They were in mourning over all my credit card bills that were starting to come in. So, there were just Nancy, Jerry, the kids, Nancy's mother and a minister provided by the undertakers.

As they were lowering "my" casket into the grave and the minister was doing the ashes-to-ashes stuff, Haven-of-Rest was suddenly filled with people.

There were a dozen policemen, a bunch of red-faced angry-talking people with Southern accents, Colonel Durham's entire next-of-kin, and two field representatives from the N.A.A.C.P. All of them were pretty mad, and all of them were looking for Dr. Jerry Hale.

The County Coroner asked Jerry just who was in the coffin. Jerry replied that it was Pete Ingersoll. He had witnessed the death and signed the death certificate himself, and so there was no need to open the coffin.

"The hell there isn't," said the Coroner. "Open it up, boys. Open it wide."

They did.

I wish I could have seen the expression on Jerry's face when he saw the Colonel stretched out, big smile on his face, with Jerry's calling card clutched in his fingers.

Afterward, the Colonel's body was taken South and finally buried in the Cemetery of the Sons of the Confederacy. The flags and bugles and the band playing "Dixie" and the Minutemen and all—but it just wasn't the same. The heart had gone out of the whole business by now, what with the extensive autopsy they'd performed on the Colonel to find out whether he'd died of natural causes.

As for Jerry and Nancy, they had to answer everybody's questions:

District Attorney: What happened to Ingersoll?

Police: When did you last see the Colonel alive?

Medical Examiner: Doctor Hale, does the word "malpractice'" mean anything to you?

Sequoia Life: You expect us to pay you $150,000 without proof of your husband's death?!

District Attorney: What happened to Ingersoll?

N.A.A.C.P.: What is your purpose for this die-in?

American Express, Carte Banche, Diners Club: You expect us to believe that?

Police: What happened to Ingersoll? What was he to you?

C.I.A.: Are you aware, Dr. Hale, that the Negro you planted in the Colonel's coffin was Chief of our African Bureau?

Jimmy: Mommy, what did Daddy Jerry do to Daddy Pete?

Long Distance Operator: Missus, if there was a Peter Ingersoll here in Tel Aviv, would I keep it from you? *Shalom.*

WHOEVER SAID crime doesn't pay was all wrong. With the healthy outdoor life I lead, not to mention no aggravation or high-pressure living, I'm good for another thirty years. By that time I'll be too dead to care. Anyway, if I were to die today, I've got no complaints. I've lived. The three months I spent dying was the greatest time of my life.

The Moon of Montezuma

Cornell Woolrich

This is a rare piece, and a beautiful one. It is long, but it weaves a spell.
Surely no one but Woolrich could create such mood.

THE HIRED car was very old. The girl in it was very young. They were
both American. Which was strange here in this far-off place, this
other world, as remote from things American as anywhere could be.

The car was a vintage model, made by some concern whose very
name has been forgotten by now; a relic of the teens or early twenties,
built high and squared-off at the top, like a box on wheels.

It crawled precariously to the top of the long, winding, sharply
ascending rutted road—wheezing, gasping, threatening to slip backward at any moment, but never doing so; miraculously managing to
inch on up.

It stopped at last, opposite what seemed to be a blank, biscuit-
colored wall. This had a thick door set into it, but no other openings.
A skimpy tendril or two of bougainvillea, burningly mauve, crept
downward over its top here and there. There were cracks in the wall,
and an occasional place where the plaster facing had fallen off to
reveal the adobe underpart.

The girl peered out from the car. Her hair was blonde, her skin
fair. She looked unreal in these surroundings of violent color;

somehow completely out of key with them. She was extremely tired-looking; there were shadows under her blue eyes. She was holding a very young baby wrapped into a little cone-shaped bundle in a blanket A baby not more than a few weeks old. And beside the collar of her coat a rosebud was pinned. Scarcely opened, yet dying already. Red as a glowing coal. Or a drop of blood.

She looked at the driver, then back to the blank wall again. "Is this where?"

He shrugged. He didn't understand her language. He said something to her. A great deal of something.

She shook her head bewilderedly. His language was as mysterious to her. She consulted the piece of paper she was holding in her hand, then looked again at the place where they'd stopped. "But there's no house here. There's just a wall."

He flicked the little pennant on his meter so that it sprang upright. Underneath it said "7.50." She could read that, at least. He opened the creaking door, to show her what he meant.

"Pay me, *Señorita*. I have to go all the way back to the town."

She got out reluctantly, a forlorn, lost figure. "Wait here," she said. "Wait for me until I find out."

He understood the sense of her faltering gesture. He shook his head firmly. He became very voluble. He had to go back to where he belonged, he had no business being all the way out here. It would be dark soon. His was the only auto in the whole town.

She paid him, guessing at the unfamiliar money she still didn't understand. When he stopped nodding, she stopped giving it to him. There was very little left—a paper bill or two, a handful of coins. She reached in and dragged out a bulky bag and stood that on the ground beside her. Then she turned around and looked at the inscrutable wall.

The car turned creakily and went down the long, rutted road, back into the little town below.

She was left there, with child, with baggage, with a scrap of paper in her hand. She went over to the door in the wall, looked about for something to ring. There was a short length of rope hanging there against the side of the door. She tugged at it and a bell, the kind with hanging clapper, jangled loosely.

The child opened its eyes momentarily, then closed them again. Blue eyes, like hers.

The door opened, narrowly but with surprising quickness. An old woman stood looking at her. Glittering black eyes, gnarled face the color of tobacco, blue *reboso* coifed about her head to hide every vestige of hair, one end of the scarf looped rearward over her throat. There was something malignant in the idol-like face, something almost Aztec.

"*Señorita* wishes?" she breathed suspiciously.

"Can you read?" The girl showed her the scrap of paper. That talisman that had brought her so far.

The old woman touched her eyes, shook her head. She couldn't read.

"But isn't this—isn't this—" Her tired tongue stumbled over the unfamiliar words. "*Caminode...*"

The old woman pointed vaguely in dismissal. "Go, ask them in the town, they can answer your questions there." She tried to close the heavy door again.

The girl planted her foot against it, held it open. "Let me in. I was told to come here. This is the place I was told to come. I'm tired, and I have no place to go." For a moment her face was wreathed in lines of weeping, then she curbed them. "Let me come in and rest a minute until I can find out. I've come such a long way. All night long, that terrible train from Mexico City, and before that the long trip down from the border..." She pushed the door now with her free hand as well as her foot.

"I beg you, *Señorita*," the old woman said with sullen gravity, "do not enter here now. Do not force your way in here. There has been a death in this house."

"*¿Qué pasa?*" a younger, higher voice suddenly said from somewhere unseen behind her.

The crone stopped her clawing, turned her head. Suddenly she had whisked from sight as though jerked on a wire, and a young girl had taken her place in the door opening.

The same age as the intruder, perhaps even a trifle younger. Jet-black hair parted arrow-straight along the center of her head. Her skin the color of old ivory. The same glittering black eyes as the old one, but larger, younger. Even more liquid, as though they had recently been shedding tears. There was the same cruelty implicit in them too, but not yet as apparent. There was about her whole beauty, and she was beautiful, a tinge of cruelty, of barbarism. That same mask-like Aztec cast of expression, of age-old racial inheritance.

"¿Si?"

"Can you understand me?" the girl pleaded, hoping against hope for a moment.

There was a flash of perfect white teeth, but the black hair moved negatively. "The *señorita* is lost, perhaps?"

Somehow, the American sensed the meaning of the words. "This is where they told me to come. I inquired in Mexico City. The American consul. They even told me how to get here, what trains. I wrote him, and I never heard. I've been writing him and writing him, and I never heard. But this must be the place. This is where I've been writing, *Camino de las Rosas*..." A dry sob escaped with the last.

The liquid black eyes had narrowed momentarily. "The *señorita* looks for who?"

"Bill. Bill Taylor." She tried to turn it into Spanish, with the pitiful resources at her command. "*Señor* Taylor. *Señor* Bill Taylor. Look, I'll show you his picture." She fumbled in her handbag, drew out a small snapshot, handed it to the waiting girl. It was a picture of herself and a young man. "Him. I'm looking for him. Now do you understand?"

For a moment, there seemed to have been a sharp intake of breath, but it might have been an illusion. The dark-haired girl smiled ruefully. Then she shook her bead.

"Don't you know him? Isn't he here? Isn't this his house?" She pointed to the wall alongside her. "But it must be. Then whose house is it?"

The dark-haired girl pointed to herself, then to the old woman hovering and hissing surreptitiously in the background. "*Casa de nosotros*. The house of Chata and her mother. Nobody else."

"Then he isn't here?" The American leaned her back for a moment hopelessly against the wall, turning the other way, to face out from it. She let her head roll a little to one side. "What am I going to do? Where is he, what became of him? I haven't even enough money to go back. I have nowhere to go. They warned me back home not to come down here alone like this, looking for him—oh, I should have listened!"

The black eyes were speculatively narrow again, had been for some time. She pointed to the snapshot. "Hermano? He is the brother of the *señorita*, or—?"

The blonde stranger touched her own ring finger. This time the sob came first. "He's my husband! I had to pawn my wedding ring to help pay my way here. I've got to find him! He was going to send for me later—and then he never did."

The black eyes had flicked downward to the child, almost unnoticeably, then up again. Once more she pointed to the snapshot.

The blonde nodded. "It's his. Ours. I don't think he even knows about it. I wrote him, and I never heard back..."

The other's head turned sharply aside for a moment, conferring with the old woman. In profile, her cameo-like beauty was woven more expressive. So was the razor-sharpness of its latent cruelty.

Abruptly, she reached out with both hands. "*Entra. Entra.* Come in. Rest. Refresh yourself." The door was suddenly open at full width, revealing a patio in the center of which was a profusion of white roses. The bushes were not many, perhaps six all told, but they were all in full bloom, weighted down with their masses of flowers. They were arranged in a hollow square. Around the outside ran a border of red-tiled flooring. In the center there was a deep gaping hole—a well, either being dug or being repaired. It was lined with a casing of shoring planks that protruded above its lip. A litter of construction tools lay around, lending a transient ugliness to the otherwise beautiful little enclosure: a wheelbarrow, several buckets, a mixing trough, a sack of cement, shovels and picks, and an undulating mound of misplaced earth brought up out of the cavity.

There was no one working at it now, it was too late in the day. Silence hung heavily. In the background was the house proper, its rooms ranged single file around three sides of the enclosure, each one characteristically opening onto it with its own individual doorway. The old houses of Moorish Africa, of which this was a lineal

descendant, had been like that: blind to the street, windowless, clois-
tered, each living its life about its own inner, secretive courtyard.
Twice transplanted; first to Spain, then to the newer Spain across the
waters.

Now that entry had at last been granted, the blonde girl was
momentarily hesitant about entering. "But if—but if this isn't his
house, what good is it to come in?"

The insistent hands of the other reached her, drew her, gently but
firmly, across the threshold. In the background, the old woman still
looked on with a secretive malignancy that might have been due
solely to the wizened lines in her face.

"*Pase, pase,*" the dark-haired girl was coaxing her. Step in.
"*Descansa.*" Rest. She snapped her fingers with sudden, concealed
authority behind her own back, and the old woman, seeming to
understand the esoteric signal, sidled around to the side of them and
out to the road for a moment, looked quickly up the road, then
quickly down, picked up the bag standing there and drew it inside
with her, leaning totteringly against its weight.

SUDDENLY THE THICK wall-door had closed behind her and the
blonde wayfarer was in, whether she wanted to be or not. The
silence, the remoteness, was as if a thick, smothering velvet curtain
had fallen all at once. Although the road had been empty, the diffuse,
imponderable noises of the world had been out there somehow.
Although this patio courtyard was unroofed and open to the same
evening sky, and only a thick wall separated it from the outside, there
was a stillness, a hush, as though it were a thousand miles away, or
deep down within the earth.

They led her, one on each side of her—the girl with the slightest
of forward-guiding hands just above her waist, the old woman still
struggling with the bag—along the red-tiled walk skirting the roses,
in under the overhanging portico of the house proper, and in through
one of the doorways. It had no door as such; only a curtain of
wooden-beaded strings was its sole provision for privacy and isola-
tion. These clicked and hissed when they were stirred.

Within were cool plaster walls painted a pastel color halfway up, allowed to remain undyed the rest of the way; an equally cool tiled flooring; an iron bedstead; an ebony chair or two, stiff, tortuously hand-carved, with rush bottomed seats and backs. A serape of burning emerald and orange stripes, placed on the floor alongside the bed, served as a rug. A smaller one, of sapphire and cerise bands, affixed to the wall, served as the only decoration.

They sat her down in one of the chairs, the baby still in her arms. Chata, after a moment's hesitancy, summoned up a sort of defiant boldness, reached out and deliberately removed the small traveling hat from her head without asking permission. Her expressive eyes widened for a moment, then narrowed again, as they took in the exotic blonde hair in all its unhampered abundance.

Her eyes now went to the child, but more as an afterthought than as if that were her primary interest, and she leaned forward and admired and played with him a little, as women do with a child, any women, of any race. Dabbing her finger at his chin, at his button of a nose, taking one of his little hands momentarily in hers, then relinquishing it again. There was something a trifle mechanical about her playing; there was no real feeling for the child at all.

She said something to the old woman, and the latter came back after a short interval with milk in an earthenware bowl. "He'll have to drink it with a nipple," the young mother said. "He's too tiny." She handed him for a moment to Chata to hold for her, fumbled with her bag, opened it and got out his feeding bottle. She poured some of the milk into that, then recapped it and took him up to feed him.

She had caught a curious look on Chata's face in the moment or two she was holding him. As though she were studying the child closely; but not with melting fondness, with a completely detached, almost cold curiosity.

They remained looking on for a few moments; then they slipped out and left her, the old woman first, Chata a moment later, with a few murmured words and a half-gesture toward the mouth, that she sensed as meaning she was to come and have something to eat with them when she was ready.

She fed him first, and then she turned back the covers and laid him down on the bed. She found two large-size safety pins in her bag and pinned the covers down tight on either side of him, so that he could not roll off and fall down. His eyes were already closed again, one tiny fist bent backward toward his head. She kissed him softly, with a smothered sob—that was for the failure of the long pilgrimage that had brought her all this way—then tiptoed out.

There was an aromatic odor of spicy cooking hovering disembodiedly about the patio, but just where it was originating from she couldn't determine. Of the surrounding six doorways, three were pitch-black. From one there was a dim, smoldering red glow peering. From another a paler, yellow light was cast subduedly. She mistakenly went toward this.

It was two doors down from the one from which she had just emerged. If they were together in there, they must be talking in whispers. She couldn't hear a sound, not even the faintest murmur.

It had grown darker now; it was full night already, with the swiftness of the mountainous latitudes. The square of sky over the patio was soft and dark as indigo velour, with magnificent stars like many-legged silver spiders festooned on its underside. Below them, the white roses gleamed phosphorescently in the starlight, with a magnesium-like glow. There was a tiny splash from the depths of the well as a pebble or grain of dislodged earth fell in.

She made her way toward the yellow-ombre doorway. Her attention had been on other things: the starlight, the sheen of the roses; and she turned the doorway and entered the room too quickly, without stopping outside to look in first. She was already well over the threshold and in before she stopped short, frozen there, with a stilled intake of fright and an instinctive clutching of both hands toward her throat.

The light came from two pairs of tapers. Between them rested a small bier that was perhaps only a trestled plank shrouded with a cloth. One pair stood at the head of it, one pair at the foot.

On the bier lay a dead child. An infant, perhaps days younger than her own. In fine white robes. Gardenias and white rosebuds disposed about it in impromptu arrangement, to form a little nest or bower. On the wall was a religious image; under it in a red glass cup burned a holy light.

The child lay there so still, as if waiting to be picked up and taken into its mother's arms. Its tiny hands were folded on its breast.

She drew a step closer, staring. A step closer, a step closer. Its hair was blond; fair, golden blond.

There was horror lurking in this somewhere. She was suddenly terribly frightened. She took another step, and then another. She wasn't moving her feet, something was drawing them.

She was beside it now. The sickening, cloying odor of the gardenias was swirling about her head like a tide. The infant's little eyes had been closed. She reached down gently, lifted an eyelid, then snatched her hand away. The baby's eyes had been blue.

Horror might have found her then, but it was given no time. She whirled suddenly, not in fright so much as mechanistic nervousness, and Chata was standing motionless in full center of the doorway, looking in at her.

THE BLACK HEAD gave a toss of arrogance. "My child, yes. My little son." And in the flowery language that can express itself as English never can, without the risk of being ridiculous: "The son of my heart." For a moment her face crumbled and a gust of violent emotion swept across it, instantly was gone again.

But it hadn't been grief, it had been almost maniacal rage. The rage of the savage who resents a loss, does not know how to accept it.

"I'm sorry, I didn't know—I didn't mean to come in here—"

"Come, there is some food for you," Chata cut her short curtly. She turned on her heel and went down the shadowy arcade toward the other lighted doorway, the more distant one her self-invited guest should have sought out in the first place.

The American went more slowly, turning in the murky afterglow beyond the threshold to look lingeringly back inside again: *I will not think of this for a while. Later, I know, I must, but not now. That in this house where he said he lived there is a child lying dead whose hair is golden, whose eyes were blue.*

Chata had reappeared in the designated doorway through which she wanted her to follow, to mark it out for her, to hasten her coming. The American advanced toward it, and went in in turn.

They squatted on the floor to eat, as the Japanese do. The old woman palmed it, and Chata palmed it in turn, to have her do likewise, and to show her where.

She sank awkwardly down as they were, feeling her legs to be too long, but managing somehow to dispose of them with a fanned-out effect to the side. An earthenware bowl of rice and red beans was set down before her.

She felt a little faint for a moment, for the need of food, as the aroma reached her, heavy and succulent. She wanted to crouch down over it, and up-end the entire bowl against her face, to get its entire contents in all at one time.

The old woman handed her a tortilla, a round flat cake, paper-thin, of pestled maize, limp as a wet rag. She held it in her own hand helplessly, did not know what to do with it They had no eating utensils.

The old woman took it back from her, deftly rolled it into a hollowed tube, returned it. She did with it as she saw them doing with theirs; held the bowl up closer to her mouth and scooped up the food in it by means of the tortilla.

The food was unaccustomedly piquant; it prickled, baffled the tastebuds of her tongue. A freakish thought from nowhere suddenly flitted through her mind: *I should be careful. If they wanted to poison me...* And then: *But why should they want to harm me? I've done them no harm; my being here certainly does them no harm.*

And because it held no solid substance, the thought misted away again.

She was so exhausted, her eyes were already drooping closed before the meal was finished. She recovered with a start, and they had both been watching her fixedly. She could tell that by the way fluidity of motion set in again, as happens when people try to cover up the rigid intentness that has just preceded it. Each motion only started as she resumed her observation of it.

"*Tienes sueño,*" Chata murmured. "*¿Quieres acostarte?*" And she motioned toward the doorway without looking at it herself.

Somehow, the American understood the intention of the words

by the fact of the gesture, and the fact that Chata had not risen from the floor herself, but remained squatting. She was not being told to leave the house, she was being told that she might remain within the house and go and lie down with her child if she needed to.

She stumbled to her feet awkwardly, almost threatened to topple for a moment with fatigue. Then steadied herself.

"*Gracia.*" She faltered. "*Gracia, mucho.*" Two pitiful words.

They did not look at her. They were looking down at the emptied food bowls before them. They did not turn their eyes toward her as when somebody is departing from your presence. They kept them on the ground before them as if holding them leashed, waiting for the departure to have been completed.

She draggingly made the turn of the doorway and left them behind her.

The patio seemed to have brightened while she'd been away. It was bleached an almost dazzling white now, with the shadows of the roses and their leaves an equally intense black. Like splotches and drippings of ink beneath each separate component one. Or like a lace mantilla flung open upon a snowdrift.

A raging, glowering full moon had come up, was peering down over the side of the sky-well above the patio.

That was the last thing she saw as she leaned for a moment, inert with fatigue, against the doorway of the room in which her child lay. Then she dragged herself in to topple headlong upon the bed and, already fast asleep, to circle her child with one protective arm, moving as if of its own instinct.

Not the meek, the pallid, gentle moon of home. This was the savage moon that had shone down on Montezuma and Cuauhtemoc, and came back looking for them now. The primitive moon that had once looked down on terraced heathen cities and human sacrifices. The moon of Anahuac.

Now the moon of the Aztecs is at the zenith, and all the world lies still. Full and white, the white of bones, the white of a skull; blistering the center of the sky-well with its throbbing, not touching it on any side. Now the patio is a piebald place of black and white, burning in the downward-teeming light. Not a leaf moves, not a petal falls, in this fierce amalgam.

Now the lurid glow from within the *brazero* had dimmed, and is just a threaded crimson outline against contrasting surfaces, skipping the space in between. It traces, like a fine wire, two figures coifed with *rebosos*. One against the wall, inanimate, like one of the mummies of her race that used to be sat upright in the rock catacombs. Eyes alone move quick above the mouth-shrouded *reboso*.

The other teetering slightly to and fro. Ever so slightly, in time to a whispering. A whispering that is like a steady sighing in the night; a whispering that does not come through the muffling *rebosos*.

The whispering stops. She raises something. A small stone.

A whetstone. She spits. She returns it to the floor again. The whispering begins once more. The whispering that is not of the voice, but of a hungry panting in the night. A hissing thirst. The roses sleep pale upon the blackness of a dream. The haunted moon looks down, lonely for Montezuma and his nation, seeking across the land.

The whispering stops now. The shrouded figure in the center of the room holds out something toward the one propped passive against the wall. Something slim, sharp, grip foremost. The wire-outline from the *brazero*-mouth finds it for a moment, runs around it like a current, flashes into a momentary highlight, a burnished blur, then runs off it again and leaves it to the darkness.

The other takes it. Her hands go up briefly. The *reboso* falls away from her head, her shoulders. Two long plaits of dark glossy hair hang down revealed against the copper satin that is now her upper body. Her mouth opens slightly. She places the sharp thing crosswise to it. Her teeth fasten on it. Her hand leaves it there, rigid, immovable.

Her hands execute a swift circling about her head. The two long plaits whip from sight, like snakes scampering to safety amidst rocks. She twines them, tucks them up.

She rises slowly with the grace of unhurried flexibility, back continuing to the wall. She girds her skirt up high about her thighs and interlaces it between, so that it holds itself there. Unclothed now, save for a broad swathing about the waist and hips, knife in mouth, she begins to move. Sideward toward the entrance, like a ruddy flame coursing along the wall, with no trace behind it.

Nothing is said. There is nothing to be said.

NOTHING WAS SAID BEFORE. Nothing needed to be said. Dark eyes understood dark eyes. Dark thoughts met dark thoughts and understood, without the need of a word.

Nothing will be said after it is over. Never, not in a thousand days from now, not in a thousand months. Never again. The old gods never had a commandment not to kill. That was another God in another land. The gods of Anahuac demanded the taking of human life, that was their nature. And who should know better than the gods what its real value is, for it is they who give it in the first place.

The flame is at the doorway now, first erect, then writhing, the way a flame does. Then the figure goes down on hands and knees, low, crouching, for craft, for stealth, for the approach to kill. The big cats in the mountains do it this way, belly-flat, and the tribe of Montezuma did it this way too, half a thousand years ago. And the blood remembers what the heart has never learned. The approach to kill.

On hands and knees the figure comes pacing along beside the wall that flanks the patio, lithe, sinuous, knife in mouth perpendicular to its course. In moonlight and out of it, as each successive archway of the portico circles high above it, comes down to join its support, and is gone again to the rear. The moon is a caress on supple skin. The moon of Anahuac understands, the moon is in league, the moon will not betray.

Slowly along the portico creeps the death-approach, now borax-white in archway-hemisphere, now clay-blue in slanted support-ephemera. The knife-blade winks, like a little haze puff of white dust, then the shadow hides it again.

The roses dream, the well lies hushed, not a straggling grain topples into it to mar it. No sound, no sound at all. Along the wall crawls life, bringing an end to life.

Past the opening where the death-tapers burn all night. She

doesn't even turn her head as she passes. What is dead is gone. What is dead does not matter any more. There were no souls in Anahuac, just bodies that come to stir, then stop and stir no longer.

What is dead does not matter any more. The love of a man, that is what matters to a woman. If she has not his child, she cannot hold his love. If she loses his child, then she must get another.

And now the other entrance is coming nearer as the wraith-like figure creeps on. Like smoke, like mist, Bickering along at the base of a wall. It seems to move of its own accord, sidling along the wall as if it were a black slab or panel traveling on hidden wheels or pulleys at the end of a draw cord. Coming nearer all the time, black, coffin-shaped, against the bluish-pale wall Growing taller, growing wider, growing greater.

AND THEN A SOUND, a small night sound, a futile, helpless sound—a child whimpers slightly in its sleep.

But instantly the figure stops, crouched. Is as still as if it had never moved a moment ago, would never move again. Not a further ripple, not a fluctuation, not a belated muscular contraction, not even the pulsing of breath. As the mountain lioness would stop as it stalked an alerted kill.

The child whimpers troubledly again. It is having a dream perhaps. Something, someone, stirs. Not the child. A heavier, a larger body than the child. There is a faint rustling, as when someone turns against overlying covers.

Then the sibilance of a soothing, bated voice, making a hushing sound. *"Sh-h-h. Sh-h-h."* Vibrant with a light motion. The motion of rocking interfolded arms.

A drowsy murmur of words, almost inchoate. "Sleep, darling. We'll find your daddy soon."

The moon glares down patiently, remorselessly, waiting. The moon will wait. The night will wait.

Seconds of time pass. Breathing sounds from within the doorway on the stillness now, in soft, slow, rhythmic waves. With little ripples in the space between each wave. Breathing of a mother, and elfin echo of her arm-cradled child. The shadow moves along the wall.

The open doorway, from within, would be a sheet of silver or of mercury, thin but glowing, if any eye were open there upon it. Then suddenly, down low at its base, comes motion, comes intrusion. A creeping, curved thing circles the stone wall-breadth, loses itself again in the darkness on the near side. Now once again the opening is an unmarred sheet of silver, fuming, sheeny.

Not even a shadow glides along the floor now, for there is no longer light to shape one. Nothing. Only death moving in invisibility.

The unseen current of the breathing still rides upon the darkness, to and fro, to and fro; lightly upon the surface of the darkness, like an evanescent pool of water stirring this way and that way.

Then suddenly it plunges deep, as if an unexpected vent, an outlet, had been driven through for it, gurgling, swirling, hollowing and sinking in timbre. A deep, spiraling breath that is the end of all breaths. No more than that. Then evaporation, the silence of death, in an arid, a denuded place.

The breathing of the child peers through again in a moment, now that its overshadowing counterpoint has been erased. It is taken up by other arms. Held pressed to another breast.

In the room of the smoldering *brazero* the other figure waits; patient, head inclined, *roboso*-coifed. The soft pad of bare feet comes along the patio tiles outside, exultant-quick. No need to crawl now. There are no longer other ears to overhear. Bare feet, proud and graceful; coolly firm, like bare feet wading through the moon-milk.

She comes in triumphant, erect and willowy, holding something in her arms, close to her breast. What a woman is supposed to hold. What a woman is born to hold.

She sinks down there on her knees before the other, the other who once held her thus in turn. She turns her head slightly in indication, holds it bent awkwardly askance, for her hands are not free. The old woman's hands go to her coil-wound hair, trace to the back of her head, draw out the knife for her.

Before her on the floor stands an earthenware bowl holding water. The knife splashes into it. The old woman begins to scrub and knead its blade dexterously between her fingers.

The younger one, sitting at ease now upon the backs of her heels, frees one hand, takes up the palm leaf, fans the *brazero* to a renewed glow. Scarlet comes back into the room, then vermilion. Even light orange, in splashes here and there upon their bodies and their faces.

She speaks, staring with copper-plated mask into the orange maw of the *brazero*. "My man has a son again. I have his son again. I will not lose my man now."

She places the baby's head to her breast, the new-made mother, and begins to suckle him.

"You have done well, my daughter. You have done as a woman should." Thus a mother's approbation to her daughter, in olden Anahuac.

THE MOON OF MONTEZUMA, well-content, is on the wane now, slanting downward on the opposite side of the patio. Such sights as these it once knew well in Anahuac; now its hungering loneliness has been in a measure assuaged, for it has glimpsed them once again.

The moon has gone now; it is the darkness before dawn. Soon the sun will come, the cosmic male-force. The time of women is rapidly ending, the time of men will be at hand.

They are both in the room with the trestle bier and the flowers and the gold-tongued papers. The little wax doll is a naked wax doll now, its wrappings taken from it, cast aside. Lumpy, foreshortened, like a squat clay image fashioned by the soft-slapping hands of some awkward, unpracticed potter.

The old woman is holding a charcoal sack, black-smudged, tautly wide at its mouth. She brings it up just under the bier, holds it steady, in the way of a catch-all.

Chata's hands reach out, scoop, roll something toward her.

The bier is empty and the charcoal sack has swelled full at the bottom.

The old woman quickly folds it over and winds it about itself. She passes it to Chata. Deft swirling and tightening of Chata's *reboso* about her own figure, and it has gone, and Chata's arms with it, hidden within.

The old woman takes apart the bier. Takes down the two pitiful planks from the trestles that supported them. A gardenia petal or two slides down them to the floor.

"Go far," she counsels knowingly.

"I will go far up the mountain, where it is bare. Where the buzzards can see it easily from overhead. By the time the sun goes down, it will be gone. Small bones like this they will even carry up with them and scatter."

The old woman pinches one taper-wick and it goes out. She moves on toward another and pinches that.

Darkness blots the room. In the air a faint trace of gardenias remains. How long does the scent of gardenias last? How long does life last? And when each has gone, where is it each has gone?

They move across the moonless patio now, one back of the other. The wooden door in the street wall jars and creaks back aslant. The old woman sidles forth. Chata waits. The old woman reinserts herself. Her finger flicks permissive safety toward the aperture.

The girl slips out, just an Indian girl enswathed, a lump under her *reboso*, the margin of it drawn up over her mouth against the unhealthful night air.

It is daybreak now. Clay-blue and dove-gray, rapidly paling with white. The old woman is sitting crouched upon her haunches, in patient immobility, just within the door.

She must have heard an almost wraith-like footfall that no other ears could have caught. She rose suddenly. She waited a bated moment, inclined toward the door, then she unfastened and swung open the door.

Chata slipped in on the instant, *reboso* flat against her now. No more lump saddling her hip.

The old woman closed the door, went after her to the deeper recesses of the patio. "You went far?"

Chata unhooded her *reboso* from bead and shoulders with that negligent racial grace she was never without. "I went far. I went up where it is bare rock. Where no weed grows that will hide it from the sailing wings in the sky. They will see it. Already they were coming from afar as I looked back from below. By sundown it will be gone."

The old woman nodded. "You have done well, my daughter," she praised her dignifiedly.

Beside the well in the patio there was something lying now. Another mound beside the mound of disinterred earth. And alongside it, parallel to one side of the well, a deep narrow trough lay dug, almost looking like a grave.

The rose bushes had all been pulled out and lay there expiring on their sides now, roots striking skyward like frozen snakes.

"They were in the way," the old woman grunted, "I had to. I deepened it below where they left it when they were here last. The new earth I took out is apart, over there, in that smaller pile by itself. So we will know it from the earth they took out when they were last here. See, it is darker and fresher."

"He liked them," Chata said. "He will ask why it is, when he comes back."

"Tell him the men did it, Fulgencio and his helper."

"But if he asks them, when he goes to pay them for the work, they will say they did not, they left them in."

"Then we will plant them in again, lightly at the top, before they come back to resume their work. I will cut off their roots short, so that it can be done."

"They will die that way."

The old woman nodded craftily. "But only after a while. He will see them still in place, though dead. Then we will say it was the work of the men that did it. Then Fulgencio and his helper will not be able to say they did not do it. For they were alive when the work began, and they will be dead when it was done."

CHATA DID NOT HAVE to ask her to help. With one accord, with no further words between them, they went to the mound beside the mound of earth. The mound that was not earth. The mound that was concealing rags and bundled charcoal sacking. One went to one end, one to the other. Chata pried into the rags for a moment, made an opening, peered into it. It centered on a red rosebud, withered and falling apart, but still affixed by a pin to the dark-blue cloth of a coat

"She wore a rose upon her coat," she hissed vengefully. "I saw it when she came in last night. She must have brought it with her from Tapatzingo, for there are none of that color growing here. He must have liked to see them on her." She swerved her head and spat into the trough alongside. "It is dead now," she said exultingly.

"As she is," glowered the old woman, tight-lipped. "Let it go with her, for the worms to see."

They both scissored their arms, and the one mound over turned and dropped, was engulfed by the other. Then Chata took up the shovel the workmen had left, and began lessening the second mound, the mound that was of earth. She knew just what they did and how they went about it, she had watched them for so many days now. The old woman, spreading her *reboso* flat upon the ground nearby, busied herself palming and urging the newer fill over onto it, the fill that she herself had taken out to make more depth.

When it was filled, she tied the corners into a bundle and carried it from sight. She came back with the *reboso* empty and began over again. After the second time, the pile of new fill was gone.

Chata had disappeared from the thighs down, was moving about as in a grave, trampling, flattening, with downbeating of her feet.

IN MIDMORNING, when Fulgencio and his nephew came, languid, to their slow-moving work, the white roses were all luxuriating around the well again, with a slender stick lurking here and there to prop them. Everything was as it had been. If the pile of disinterred earth they had left was a little lower, or if the depression waiting to take it back was a little shallower, who could tell? Who measured such things?

The old woman brought out a jug of *pulque* to them, so that they might refresh themselves. Their eyes were red when they left at sundown, and their breaths and their sweat were sour. But it had made their work go quicker, with snatches of song, and with laughter, and with stumblings of foot. And it had made the earth they shoveled back, the hollow they filled, the tiles they cemented back atop, the roses they brushed against and bent, all dance and blur in fumes of *maguey*.

But the task was completed, and when the door was closed upon their swaying, drooping-lidded forms, they needed to come back no more.

SEVEN TIMES THE SUN RISES, seven times it falls. Then fourteen. Then, perhaps, twenty-one. Who knows, who counts it? Hasn't it risen a thousand years in Anahuac, to fall again, to rise again?

Then one day, in its declining hours, there is a heavy knocking of men's hands on the outside of the wooden door in the street wall. The hands of men who have a right to enter, who may not be refused; their knocking tells that.

They know it for what it is at first sound, Chata and the old woman. They have known it was coming. There is another law in Anahuac now than the old one.

Eyes meet eyes. The trace of a nod is exchanged. A nod that confirms. That is all. No fear, no sudden startlement. No fear, because no sense of guilt. The old law did not depend on signs of fear, proofs and evidences, witnesses. The old law was wise, the new law is a fool.

The old woman struggles to her feet, pads forth across the patio toward the street-door, resounding now like a drum. Chata remains as she was, dexterously plaiting withes into a basket, golden-haired child on its back on the sun-cozened ground beside her, little legs fumbling in air.

The old woman comes back with two of mixed blood. Anahuac is in their faces, but so is the other race, with its quick mobility of feature that tells every thought. One in uniform of those who enforce the law, one in attire such as Chata's own man wears when he has returned from his prospecting trips in the distant mountains and walks the streets of the town with her on Sunday, or takes his ease without her in the *cantina* with the men of the other women.

They come and stand over her, where she squats at her work, look down on her. Their shadows shade her, blot out the sun in the corner of the patio in which she is, are like thick blue stripes blanketing her and the child from some intangible serape.

Slowly her eyes go upward to them, liquid, dark, grave, respectful but not afraid, as a woman's do to strange men who come where she has a right to be.

"Stand. We are of the police. From Tapatzingo, on the other side of the mountain. We are here to speak to you."

She puts her basket-weaving aside and rises, graceful, unfrightened.

"And you are?" the one who speaks for the two of them, the one without uniform, goes on.

"Chata."

"Any last name?"

"We use no second name among us." That is the other race, two names for every one person.

"And the old one?"

"Mother of Chata."

"And who is the man here?"

"In the mountains. That way, far that way. He goes to look for silver. He works it when he finds it. He has been long gone, but he will come soon now, the time is drawing near."

"Now listen. A woman entered here, some time three weeks ago. A woman with a child. A *norteña*, a *gringa*, understand? One of those from up there. She has not been seen again. She did not go back to where she came from. To the great City of Mexico. In the City of Mexico, the consul of her country has asked the police to find out where she is. The police of the City of Mexico have asked us to learn what became of her."

Both heads shake. "No. No woman entered here."

He turns to the one in uniform. "Bring him in."

The hired-car driver shuffles forward, escorted by the uniform.

Chata looks at him gravely, no more. Gravely but untroubledly.

"This man says he brought her here. She got out. He went back without her."

Both heads nod now. The young one that their eyes are on, the old one disregarded in the background.

"There was a knock upon our door, one such day, many days ago. A woman with a child stood there, from another place. She spoke, and we could not understand her speech. She showed us a paper, but we cannot read writing. We closed the door. She did not knock again."

He turns on the hired-car driver. "Did you see them admit her?"

"No, *Señor*," the latter falters, too frightened to tell any thing but the truth. "I only let her out somewhere along here. I did not wait to see where she went. It was late, and I wanted to get back to my woman. I had driven her all the way from Tapatzingo, where the train stops."

"Then you did not see her come in here?"

"I did not see her go in anywhere. I turned around and went the other way, and it was getting dark."

"This child here, does it look like the one she had with her?"

"I could not see it, she held it to her."

"This is the child of my man," Chata says with sultry dignity. "He has yellow hair like this. Tell, then."

"Her man is *gringo*, everyone has seen him. She had a *gringo* child a while ago, everyone knows that," the man stammers unhappily.

"Then you, perhaps, know more about where she went than these two do! You did bring her out this way! Take him outside and hold him. At least I'll have something to report on."

The policeman drags him out again, pleading and whining. "No, *Señor*, no! I do not know—I drove back without her! For the love of God, *Señor*, the love of God!"

He turns to Chata. "Show me this house. I want to see it."

She shows it to him, room by room. Rooms that know nothing can tell nothing. Then back to the patio again. The other one is waiting for him there, alone now.

"And this *pozo*? It seems cleaner, newer, this tiling, than elsewhere around it." He taps his foot on it.

"It kept falling in, around the sides. Cement was put around them to hold the dirt back."

"Who had it done?"

"It was the order of my man, before he left. It made our water bad. He told two men to do it for him while he was away."

"And who carried it out?"

"Fulgencio and his nephew, in the town. They did not come right away, and they took long, but finally they finished."

He jotted the name. "We will ask."

She nodded acquiescently. "They will tell."

He takes his foot off it at last, moves away. He seems to be finished, he seems to be about to go. Then suddenly, curtly, "Come." And he flexed his finger for her benefit.

For the first time her face shows something. The skin draws back rearward of her eyes, pulling them oblique.

"Where?" she whispers.

"To the town. To Tapatzingo. To the headquarters."

She shakes her head repeatedly, mutely appalled. Creeps backward a step with each shake. Yet even now it is less than outright fear; it is more an unreasoning obstinacy. An awe in the face of something one is too simple to understand. The cringing of a wide-eyed child.

"Nothing will happen to you," he says impatiently. "You won't be held. Just to sign a paper. A statement for you to put your name to."

Her back has come to rest against one of the archway supports now. She can retreat no further. She cowers against it, then sinks down, then turns and clasps her arms about it, holding onto it in desperate appeal.

"I cannot write. I do not know how to make those marks." He is standing over her now, trying to reason with her.

"*Valgame dios! What a criatura!*"

She transfers her embrace suddenly from the inanimate pilaster to his legs, winding her arms about them in supplication.

"No, *patrón*, no! Don't take me to Tapatzingo! They'll keep me there. I know how they treat our kind. I'll never get back again."

Her eyes plead upward at him, dark pools of mournfulness.

He looks more closely at her, as if seeming to see her face for the first time. Or at least as if seeming to see it as a woman's face and not just that of a witness.

"And you like this gringo you house with?" he remarks at a tangent. "Why did you not go with one of your own?"

"One goes with the man who chooses one."

"Women are thus," he admits patronizingly. *Asi son las mujeres.*

She releases his pinioned legs, but still crouches at his feet, looking questioningly upward.

He is still studying her face. "He could have done worse." He reaches down and wags her chin a little with two pinched fingers.

She rises, slowly turns away from him. She does not smile. Her coquetry is more basic than the shallow superficiality of a smile. More gripping in its pull. It is in the slow, enfolding way she draws her *reboso* tight about her and hugs it to her shoulders and her waist. It is in the very way she walks. It is in the coalescing of the sunlit dust-motes all about her in the air as she passes, forming almost a haze, a passional halo.

In fact, she gives him not another look. Yet every step of the way she pulls his eyes with her. And as she passes where a flowering plant stands in a green glazed mould, she tears one of the flowers off. She doesn't drop it, just carries it along with her in her hand.

She approaches one of the room-openings, and still without turning, still without looking back, goes within.

He stands there staring at the empty doorway.

The old woman squats down by the child, takes it up, and lowers her head as if attentively waiting.

He looks at the policeman, and the policeman at him, and everything that was unspoken until now is spoken in that look between them.

"Wait for me outside the house. I'll be out later."

The policeman goes outside and closes the wall-door after him.

LATER SHE COMES out of the room by herself, ahead of the man. She rejoins the old woman and child, and squats down by them on her knees and heels. The old woman passes the child into her arms. She rocks it lullingly, looks down at it protectively, touches a speck from its brow with one finger. She is placid, self-assured.

Then the man comes out again. He is tracing one side of his mustache with the edge of one finger.

He comes and stops, standing over her, as he did when he and the other one first came in here.

He smiles a little, very sparingly, with only the corner of his mouth. Half-indulgently, half-contemptuously.

He speaks. But to whom? Scarcely to her, for his eyes go up over her, stare thoughtfully over her head; and the police man isn't present to be addressed. To his own sense of duty, perhaps, reassuring it. "Well—you don't need to come in, then, most likely. You've told me all you can. No need to question you further. I can attend to the paper myself. And we always have the driver, anyway, if they want to go ahead with it."

He turns on his heel. His long shadow undulates off her. *"Adios, india,"* he flings carelessly at her over his shoulder, from the wall-door.

"Adios, patrón," she murmurs obsequiously.

The old woman goes over to the door in his wake, to make sure it is shut fast from the inside. Comes back, sinks down again.

Nothing is said.

IN THE PURPLE bloodshed of a sunset afterglow, the tired horse brings its tired rider to a halt before the biscuit-colored wall with the bougainvillea unravelling along it Having ridden the day, having ridden the night, and many days and many nights, the ride is at last done.

For a moment they stand there, both motionless, horse with its neck slanted to ground, rider with his head dropped almost to saddle-grip. He has been riding asleep for the past hour or so. But riding true, for the horse knows the way.

Then the man stirs, raises his head, slings his leg off, comes to the ground. Face mahogany from the high sierra sun, golden glisten filming its lower part, like dust of that other metal, the one even more precious than that he seeks and lives by. Dust-paled shirt opened to the navel. Service automatic of another country, of another army, that both once were his, bedded at his flank. Bulging saddlebags upon the burro tethered behind, of ore, of precious crushed rock, to be taken to the assay office down at Tapatzingo. Blue eyes that have forgotten all their ties, and thus will stay young as they are now forever. Bill Taylor's home. Bill Taylor, once of Iowa, once of Colorado.

Home? What is home? Home is where a house is that you come back to when the rainy season is about to begin, to wait until the next dry season comes around. Home is where your woman is, that you come back to in the intervals between a greater love—the only real love—the lust for riches buried in the earth, that are your own if you can find them.

Perhaps you do not call it home, even to yourself. Perhaps you call them "my house," "my woman." What if there was another "my house," "my woman," before this one? It makes no difference. This woman is enough for now.

Perhaps the guns sounded too loud at Anzio or at Omaha Beach, at Guadalcanal or at Okinawa. Perhaps when they stilled again, some kind of strength had been blasted from you that other men still have. And then again perhaps it was some kind of weakness that other men still have. What is strength, what is weakness, what is loyalty, what is perfidy?

The guns taught only one thing, but they taught it well: of what consequence is life? Of what consequence is a man? And, therefore, of what consequence if he tramples love in one place and goes to find it in the next? The little moment that he has, let him be at peace, far from the guns and all that remind him of them.

So the man who once was Bill Taylor has come back to his house, in the dusk, in the mountains, in Anahuac.

He doesn't have to knock, the soft hoof-plod of his horse has long ago been heard, has sent its long-awaited message. Of what use is a house to a man if he must knock before he enters? The door swings wide, as it never does and never will to anyone but him. Flitting of a figure, firefly-quick, and Chata is entwined about him.

He goes in, faltering a little from long weariness, from long disuse of his legs, she welded to his side, half-supporting, already resting, restoring him, as is a woman's reason for being.

The door closes behind them. She palms him to wait, then whisks away.

He stands there, looking about.

She comes back, holding something bebundled in her arms.

"What happened to the roses?" be asks dimly.

She does not answer. She is holding something up toward him, white teeth proudly displayed in her face. The one moment in a woman's whole life. The moment of fulfillment.

"Your son," she breathes dutifully.

Who can think of roses when he has a son?

TWO OF THE tiles that Fulgencio had laid began to part. Slowly. So slowly who could say they had not always been that way? And yet they had not. Since they could not part horizontally because of the other tiles all around them, their parting was vertical, they began to slant upward, out of true.

At last, the strain became too great. They had no resiliency by which to slant along the one side, remain flat along the other. They cracked along the line of greatest strain, and then they crumbled there, disintegrated into a mosaic. And then the smaller, lighter pieces were disturbed still more, and finally lay about like scattered pebbles, out of their original bed.

And then it began to grow. The new rosebush.

There had been rosebushes there before. Why should there not be one there now again?

IT WAS FULL-GROWN NOW, the new rosebush. And he had gone and come again, Bill Taylor; and gone, and come again. Then suddenly, in the time for roses to bloom, it burst into flower. Like a splattering of blood, drenching that one particular part of the patio. Every rose as red as the heart.

He smiled with pleasant surprise when he first saw it, and he said how beautiful it was. He called to her and made her come out there where he was and stand beside him and take the sight in.

"Look. Look what we have now. I always liked them better than the white ones."

"I already saw them," she said sullenly. "You are only seeing them now for the first time, but I saw them many days ago, coming through little by little."

And she tried to move away, but he held her there by the shoulder, in command. "Take good care of it now. Water it. Treat it well."

In a few days he noticed that the sun was scorching it, that the leaves were burning here and there.

He called her out there, and his face was dark. His voice was harsh and curt, as when you speak to a disobedient dog. "Didn't I tell you to look after this rosebush? Why haven't you? Water it now! Water it well!"

She obeyed him. She had to. But as she moved about it, tending to it, on her face, turned from him, there was the ancient hatred of woman for woman, when there is but one man between the two of them.

She watered it the next day, and the next. It throve, it flourished, jeering at her with liquid diamonds dangling from each leaf, and pearls of moisture rolling lazily about the crevices of its tight-packed satin petals. And when his eyes were not upon her, and she struck at it viciously with her hand, it bit back at her, and tore a drop of blood from her palm.

Of what use to move around the ground on two firm feet, to be warm, to be flesh, if his eyes scarce rested on you any more? Or if they did, no longer saw you as they once had, but went right through you as if you were not there?

Of what use to have buried her in the ground if he stayed now always closer to her than to you, moving his chair now by her out there in the sun? If he put his face down close to her and inhaled the memory of her and the essence of her soul? She filled the patio with her sad perfume, and even in the very act of breathing in itself, he drew something of her into himself, and they became one.

She held sibilant conference with the old woman beside the

brazero in the evening as they prepared his meal. "It is she. She has come back again. He puts his face down close, down close to her many red mouths, and she whispers to him. She tries to tell him that she lies there, she tries to tell him that his son was given him by her and not by me."

The old woman nodded sagely. These things are so. "Then you must do again as you did once before. There is no other way."

"He will be angered as the thunder rolling in a mountain gorge."

"Better a blow from a man's hand than to lose him to another woman."

AGAIN THE NIGHT of a full moon, again she crept forth, hands to ground, as she had once before. This time from his very side, from his very bed. Again a knife between her teeth blazed intermittently in the moonlight. But this time she didn't creep sideward along the portico, from room-entry to room-entry; this time she paced her way straight outward into mid-patio. And this time her *reboso* was twined tight about her, not cast off; for the victim had no ears with which to hear her should the garment impede or betray; and the victim had no feet on which to start up and run away.

Slowly she toiled and undulated under the enormous spotlight of the moon. Nearer, nearer. Until the shadows of the little leaves made black freckles on her back.

Nearer, nearer. To kill a second time the same rival.

Nearer, nearer. To where the rosebush lay floating on layers of moon-smoke.

THEY FOUND her the next morning, he and the old woman. They found the mute evidences of the struggle there had been; like a contest between two active agencies, between two opposing wills. A struggle in the silent moonlight

There was a place where the tiled surfacing, the cement shoring, faultily applied by the pulque-drugged Fulgencio and his nephew, had given way and dislodged itself over the lip of the well and down into it, as had been its wont before the repairs were applied. Too much weight incautiously brought too near the edge, in some terrible, oblivious throe of fury or of self-preservation.

Over this ravage the rosebush, stricken, gashed along its stem, stretched taut, bent like a bow; at one end its manifold roots still clinging tenaciously to the soil, like countless crooked grasping fingers; at the other its flowered head, captive but unsubdued, dipping downward into the mouth of the well.

And from its thorns, caught fast in a confusion hopeless of extrication, it supported two opposite ends of the *reboso*, whipped and wound and spiraled together into one, from some aimless swaying and counter-swaying weight at the other end.

A weight that had stopped swaying long before the moon waned; that hung straight and limp now, hugging the wall of the well. Head sharply askew, as if listening to the mocking voice whispering through from the soil alongside, where the roots of the rose bush found their source.

No water had touched her. She had not died the death of water. She had died the death that comes without a sound, the death that is like the snapping of a twig, of a broken neck.

THEY LIFTED HER UP. They laid her tenderly there upon the ground

She did not move. The rosebush did; it slowly righted to upward. Leaving upon the ground a profusion of petals, like drops of blood shed in combat.

The rosebush lived, but she was dead.

Now he sits there in the sun, by the rosebush; the world forgotten, other places that once were home, other times, other loves, forgotten. It is good to sit there in the sun, your son playing at your feet. This is a better love, this is the only lasting love. For a woman dies when you do, but a son lives on. He is you and you are he, and thus you do not die at all.

And when his eyes close in the sun and he dozes, as a man does when his youth is running out, perhaps now and then a petal will fall upon his head or upon his shoulder from some near-curving branch, and lie there still. Light as a caress. Light as a kiss unseen from someone who loves you and watches over you.

The old woman squats at hand, watchful over the child. The old woman has remained, ignored. Like a dog, like a stone. Unspeaking and unspoken to.

Her eyes reveal nothing. Her lips say nothing. They will never say anything, for thus it is in Anahuac.

But the heart knows. The skies that look forever down on Anahuac know. The moon that shone on Montezuma once; it knows.

Presents
MWA Classics

Afterword

We at Mystery Writers of America hope you enjoyed this collection of stories from our great writers. *Merchants of Menace*, edited by Hillary Waugh, is the latest in a series of classic crime collections in our new program, Mystery Writers of America Classics.

Since 1945, MWA has been America's premiere organization for professional mystery writers, a group dedicated to learning from each other, helping new members, and sharing our successes and good times. One way we celebrate our talent is through the production of original, themed anthologies, published more or less yearly since 1946, in which one remarkable writer invites others to his or her collection.

Read more about our anthology program, both the new ones and classic re-issues, on our web page: https://mysterywriters.org.

And watch for future editions of Mystery Writers of America Classics. To receive notifications, please subscribe here: http://mysterywriters.org/mwa-anthologies/classics-newsletter/.

Made in the USA
Monee, IL
18 September 2020